Yama reached for a small pouch hanging from her belt and tipped the contents into my cupped hand. I looked down and saw a captive star, a shimmering golden stone whose core held countless sparks of rainbow fire.

"This has been my secret," Yama said. "I have been keeping it from you and for you, waiting for the right moment to give it back. Guard it, Himiko. It is proof that you are chosen to be the spirits' own, but only if you choose to consent."

I gazed into the stone's cold golden fire and felt a wondrous warmth envelop me. I made my choice.

Also by Esther Friesner

SPIRIT'S PRINCESS

ESTHER FRIESNER

BLUEFIRE

Text copyright © 2012 by Esther Friesner
Cover art copyright © 2012 by Larry Rostant

Visit us on the Web! randomhouse.com/teens

Educators and librarians, for a variety of teaching tools, visit us at
RHTeachersLibrarians.com

The Library of Congress has cataloged the hardcover edition
of this work as follows:
Friesner, Esther M.
Spirit's princess / Esther Friesner. — 1st ed.
p. cm.
Summary: In ancient Japan, Himiko, the privileged daughter of her clan's leader, fights the constraints and expectations imposed on young women and finds her own path, which includes secret shaman lessons.
ISBN 978-0-375-86907-5 (trade) — ISBN 978-0-375-87314-0 (pbk.) —
ISBN 978-0-375-89990-4 (ebook)
[1. Sex role—Fiction. 2. Shamans—Fiction. 3. Magic—Fiction.
4. Spirits—Fiction. 5. Japan—History—To 645—Fiction.] I. Title.
PZ7.F91662Srp 2012 [Fic]—dc22 2011010468

Printed in the United States of America
10 9 8 7 6 5 4 3 2 1
First Bluefire Edition 2013

For the land and people of Japan—
wishing you tranquility, harmony,
and good fortune

Contents

SPIRIT'S
PRINCESS

PART I
CRADLE

1
THE PINE TREE'S SHADOW

In the moonless, starless time before dawn, I crept out of my family's house to climb the ancient pine tree that towered above our village. I was only seven years old, and still scared of the dark, but I made myself leave the warm safety of our home for the vast, terrible world outside. In my mind, I had no other choice. I had made a promise to myself and to the spirits, placing my life, my fate, my future in their hands. I was sure that to turn back was to die.

Rags of mist drifted along the ground like ghosts, and the sky was a dim, threatening presence arching over the shadowed land. Springtime had come, but nighttime still held the lingering chill of winter. Every second step I took seemed to bring with it a heart-stopping noise or the swift passage of some imaginary monster, its fangs and claws a flicker of cold light whisking past the corner of my eye. I wanted to abandon my purpose at least a hundred times before I even reached the roots of the colossal tree, but whenever the urge to flee seized me, I whispered, "I can do this. I *have* to do this!" and forced myself to recall the reason I'd first decided to conquer the looming pine.

From the depths of my fear, I summoned up a vision of my big brother Aki. I had many brothers living then, three older than me, two still infants. The older ones were my mother's, the babies were the sons of Yukari and Emi, Father's junior wives, but Aki was my favorite. Even though seven years separated us, he always made time to play with me, and to tell me wonderful stories about the wild places beyond our village fields.

He knew those outlying lands well. At fourteen, Aki was counted as a man among our people, face honorably marked with his first protective tattoo, free to roam wherever he liked. How I longed for that freedom!

Freedom wasn't the only part of his life that I coveted. Even if he hadn't been respected as our clan chief's oldest son, he still would have been honored and valued as a gifted hunter. His keen eye and shrewd skill as a tracker of game filled many bellies. The tender meat of the rabbits, deer, and red-faced pheasants that he caught added savor to our rice. I envied him for the way that everyone praised him when he returned from yet another successful venture into the mountains, but not as much as I envied him for how proud Mama looked when she heard our kin cheering his name. Even Father's stern face would soften into one of his rare smiles when Aki came home. I think I envied him for that most of all.

I wanted the cheers, the admiring looks, and Father's

smile. If the only way to earn those things was to become a great hunter like my oldest brother, that was the path I'd take too, and I was sure there was only one way for me to do it: Aki would have to teach me. But . . . would he agree?

Foolishly, I thought I knew the answer before I even spoke one word about it to him. My dreams of the future were never small. I imagined learning so much of the hunter's art, and so well, that I outpaced him, leaving him in my shadow. I saw myself hauling home impossible amounts of game, stealing away all the praise and admiration that had once been his. Surely Aki would see the same inevitable future and refuse to teach me the hunter's way, to protect his own place in our clan! I had everything all figured out, start to finish, and none of it real.

What childish imaginings. But I *was* a child. I loved my brother, and feared he would stop loving me if I asked him to help fulfill my dream. And so I kept my ambitions to myself, holding back my request until frustration finally got the better of me. Had it been only yesterday that I'd found the boldness to speak? As our family sat cross-legged together on the high wooden platform just outside our door, watching the day begin to fade into evening, I took a deep breath, flung myself onto Aki's back, and draped my arms around his neck, crying, "Big Brother, I want to be like you! Teach me how to hunt, pleeeeeease? I'll do a good job, but don't worry, I promise I won't be *too* much better than you." I kissed his cheeks and his ears a dozen times, a ploy that had always worked before whenever I asked him for anything.

Not this time.

I'd prayed that he would say yes. I'd feared that he would roar an angry refusal. I'd never expected to drown in the waves of laughter that followed my impassioned plea.

Everyone laughed—everyone but Father. He looked grim and disapproving, but the rest of my family rocked with glee over what I'd just said. Father's two junior wives nearly choked on such violent storms of giggles that it woke the sleeping babies in their laps. My twelve-year-old brother, Shoichi, fell over backward whooping, his hands slapping the floor. Ten-year-old Masa curled himself up like a round, solid bale of rice and shook with so much mirth that he nearly rolled off the platform. My face went hot with embarrassment. Even Aki was laughing! It didn't matter that his laughter was soft and kind, it still cut me to the bone. I pushed away from him, threw my head back, and yowled.

One moment I was weeping loudly enough to scare the birds from every tree around, and the next I was in Aki's lap. My eyes were too filled with tears for me to see how he managed to sweep me into a comforting hug so quickly. "Don't cry, little Himiko," he said in a soothing voice. "Please don't cry. I'm sorry; we're all sorry. We didn't mean to make fun of you."

"Speak for yourself," Shoichi put in, and laughed louder, until his voice broke into hiccups.

"Aha, you see what happens to anyone who teases our little sister?" Aki said, grinning and bouncing me on his knee. "The spirits take a terrible vengeance! Beg her forgiveness, Shoichi, and maybe they'll show you mercy."

"Not—*hic!*—not if my li—*hic!*—life depended on it,"

Shoichi said sullenly before pinching his nose shut and holding his breath.

"I wish the spirits *would* punish you!" I shouted, squirming out of Aki's lap and scrambling to my feet. "*All* of you! All I said was—"

I didn't get the chance to repeat my demand to become a hunter. Father leaped up and grabbed me by the back of my tunic, holding me as if I were a badly behaved puppy. Eyes hard and narrow, he glowered at me like some midnight demon. "*Never* say such things again." His voice growled low and threatening. "They listen, even to fools like you. They watch and wait for the chance to strike us down."

He pointed at his junior wives and their infants, but I lacked the courage to look at them directly. A bad taste filled my mouth. Some would say that Yukari and Emi were living proof that Father was right to believe in the maliciousness of the spirits. It was no secret that my sweet-natured stepmothers already had lost a child in infancy each, two years after I was born, and their new babies were sickly. Though no one in our family or our clan said anything about it, it was feared that the little ones would not be with us long.

"Every curse—even yours—can be their gateway," Father said. I writhed under his words and stole a fleeting glance at my stepmothers. Would they blame me when their arms were empty again? I couldn't bear such a thought.

"And *you*, Aki!" Now Father's wrath turned on my beloved brother. "The girl is a fool, but she's hardly old enough to know up from down. *You* are a man! You should know better than to speak of their powers so lightly."

Aki knelt low, hands folded, forehead touching the platform. His voice trembled when he spoke: "I'm sorry, Father. I was rash and stupid. I accept any penalty you name for my thoughtlessness."

"No!" I cried in desperation. "Don't do anything to Aki! It's all my fault, but I didn't mean it! I *don't* wish the spirits would punish anyone! I'm sorry, I'm so sorry, I take it back. If they want to hurt anyone, let it be me, only me!" I squirmed violently, trying to escape Father's grasp so that I too could bow before him to prove my sincerity.

His grip on my tunic remained unbreakable. "Worse and worse stupidity." He shook his head and looked as if he'd bitten into a bitter root. "If you can't be wise, try being quiet!" He dropped me and strode into the house, leaving a heavy silence behind him.

Father was gone from sight, but his hard words and the look of disgust that had twisted his face lingered over me like the ghosts of the newly dead. A knot of pain seized my chest, an ache so awful that I thought I would die. I huddled on the platform, wrapped my arms around my legs, and hugged myself small, burying my face against my knees. I was too upset to cry, and no one in our family—not even Mama—dared to offer me a comforting touch or word. They were always frightened of displeasing Father. Even when he wasn't present, his will commanded us. His temper was a fact of life, like the sunrise or the wind that rippled through the green rice, and it dominated our existence.

With my eyes hidden, I didn't see Mama stand up, but I felt the wooden planks of the platform shift slightly and heard her murmur, "We should all go inside. It's time to sleep." The platform vibrated with everyone's footsteps, re-treating into the house, and then I heard Mama speak softly again, from just a little farther off, saying, "Come to bed soon, Himiko, dear. But come quietly." She left me outside, alone.

I hunched my shoulders and pressed my face against my knees even harder. I wanted to bury myself in darkness. Embarrassment and shame burned my heart. I struggled to muffle my dry, rasping sobs, so afraid that Father would hear me and that I'd be in deeper trouble than before.

"Hush, Himiko. It's all right, little one." Aki's soothing voice was a cool, whispering breeze in my ear. I felt the welcome weight of his hand patting my back. I wasn't alone after all.

"No, it's not all right," I said, refusing to look up. "He hates me. Father hates me."

"Of course not. What an idea!" Aki tried to take my hands, but I linked my fingers together in an even tighter grip on my legs, locking myself away from him. "Himiko, look at me. What are you hiding from? From me? Are you angry at me? Is it because I laughed at you? That was wrong, and then I made it worse for you with Father. What am I going to do if my favorite sister won't forgive me?"

I shook my head just a little. "I'm your *only* sister."

"Did you say something? I can't hear you." Aki tickled my ribs lightly. "Such a funny girl! You talk to your knees and you think Father hates you and you won't even look at the brother who loves you best." He sighed deeply. "How can I go on living under the same roof if you turn away from me? I'll have to go away, far into the mountains, and live with the wolves and the bears until I die. Good-bye, Himiko." I heard him get up and begin to walk off.

"Aki, don't go! I forgive you!" I was on my feet as fast as thought and leaped onto his back so suddenly that I nearly knocked the two of us off the platform. He staggered sideways, fighting to keep us from a bad fall, and managed to veer away from the edge. I squeaked with fear and held on to him tightly, my arms crossed around his neck, until his outstretched hands thudded against the side of our house and we were safe. Then I let go and slid off. He looked down at me, his face damp with sweat, but he was smiling.

"Maybe you don't need me to teach you how to hunt, Little Sister," he said lightly. "A bow and arrows would be wasted on you. You could simply jump on top of your prey and choke it to death!"

"Did I choke you, Big Brother?" I asked, genuinely alarmed.

He chuckled and squatted beside me. "You *tried*. And you almost succeeded. I don't know whether to be proud of you or afraid."

"I didn't mean to hurt you," I said plaintively. "And I didn't really want the spirits to hurt anyone. Father's right: I was stupid."

"You were angry. *I* was the stupid one, for laughing. I was sure you were only joking about wanting to learn how to hunt. I laughed at your joke, not at you."

"Why did you think I was joking?" I was genuinely puzzled.

"What else could I think? I told myself, 'Surely someone as smart as my sister knows that it's only *boys* who become hunters, not pretty little girls!' I'll bet none of your playmates ever had such a thought, did they?" He tugged a lock of my hair gently. "Now, let's go inside before—"

"Why not?"

My question took Aki by surprise. "Why not what?"

"You said girls don't become hunters. Why not?"

"Well . . . well, because that's how it is. It's not possible. Girls can't do the same things that boys do. Boys are stronger, that's all: strong enough to string a bow, to bend it, to throw a spear, and to carry home the prey."

"*I'm* strong." It was getting darker, and Mama was waiting for us to come to bed, but I wasn't going to let this question go.

"Strong for a girl, not strong enough for a hunter."

"*You* weren't always so strong." The more I argued with Aki, the more determined I became to make him see things my way. "You changed; *I'll* change!"

"But, Himiko—"

"I bet you weren't, when you were my age." I wouldn't let him speak. I was swept away by the force of my own words, all my recent sorrows forgotten. "Shoichi and Masa are nearly as old as you, and they aren't strong at all, but I've still seen you teaching them how to use the bow! Masa's clumsy—he drops the arrow five times for every once that he manages to shoot it—and Shoichi's arms are so skinny, he can hardly bend the bow. Why do you give them the chance to learn and not me? Let me try!"

"Little Sister, I'm not going to let you touch any of my weapons. It's too dangerous. You'll hurt yourself."

"It's just as dangerous for Masa and Shoichi."

"Masa and Shoichi will be men someday, and men have to deal with danger." Aki's smile was gone. "Women don't have to face wild beasts in the forests. Women don't have to go to war."

War. It was a word I didn't know, not then. I opened my mouth to ask Aki what it meant, but before I could, a hand fell on my shoulder from behind and Mama's hushed, intense voice sounded in my ear: "What are you still doing out here, making all this noise? I told you it's time for bed. Your father is ready to come out here after you himself!"

Neither Aki nor I wanted to face Father's temper a second time that night. We bowed our heads, making soft, hasty apologies, but before we hurried into the house, I managed to whisper, "Aki, if I *show* you I can do better than our brothers, will you give me a chance?"

"Himiko, not *now*," he muttered. "I told you—"

"No weapons. I promise." I grabbed his hand and squeezed it.

"All right, all right, have it your way. Now *shhh*!" The darkness of our house swallowed us, and we stole to our bedroll by the pale light of the moon.

I didn't go to sleep right away; I couldn't. My mind was whirling with plans. Aki's words echoed in my head—*"Have it your way"*—and though he'd said that solely to hush me, I seized it as proof that we'd made a bargain. I would show him I could do something that our brothers couldn't do—maybe even something that lay beyond Aki's own skills!—and he would *have* to teach me to become a hunter like him.

Something my brothers couldn't do, yet something that I could . . . What might that be? I couldn't close my eyes until I found the answer. I fought off sleep, considered and discarded dozens of ideas, groaned inwardly when plan after plan shattered, and finally, just as I was ready to give in to exhaustion, a vision came. The moonlight spilling over our threshold painted a thin pattern of shadows across the floor, a pattern that my sleep-heavy eyelids blurred into a familiar shape: the great pine tree, the one that our shaman called Grandfather, the tree that gave our clan its name and made us the Matsu, the people of the pine.

I smiled, closed my eyes, and went to sleep happy. I had my plan.

I knew what I was going to do, but not *when* I was going to do it. My dreams were filled with images of the ancient pine tree's branches in all weathers, all seasons, all times of the day and night. *Choose, Himiko! I am waiting for you.* The tree's voice rustled through my mind, heavy with the sound of creaking branches. *Choose, and come to me! Choose your time, your path, your fate, your future. Choose!*

I woke up suddenly, that voice still soft in my ears. It seemed so real! I'd never experienced such a thing before. There had been other dreams where I found myself in the rice fields or at the edge of the forest, or beside a swiftly flowing river, hearing the voices of the spirits who dwelled in the ripening grain, the birds, the beasts, the water, even the brooding stones. My drowsing mind pictured them as men and women who wore some aspect of the thing they inhabited. The pheasant spirit was cloaked in trailing feathers, and his face was stained bright red. The water spirits danced in robes that were tied with reeds, sparkled with sunlight, and frothed lightly around their feet. Towering above them all was our clan's protective power, the spirit of the pine tree, an ancient man with the benevolent, wrinkled face of a beloved grandfather and gnarled hands that looked strong enough to hold all of the Matsu clan safe.

The spirits had spoken to me many times while I slept. This was the first time a spirit's voice had followed me out of my dreams, into the waking world. I was deeply frightened. I wanted to wake Mama and have her hold me.

Shivering, I crossed my arms over my chest and hugged myself until my racing heart grew calm again. "No," I told myself, whispering so softly that my words were only the movement of my lips. "This is not how a hunter acts. Aki says that the woods are full of strange noises, but he goes on. So will I."

I glanced at the doorway and saw that it was still well before daylight. The sight of the darkened world outside chilled my bones. "It doesn't matter," I murmured. "The darkness doesn't matter; it *can't* matter if I'm going to succeed."

I closed my eyes and hugged myself even tighter, and with the clear, silent voice of my heart, I cried out into the realm of dreams and spirits: *Hear me, Grandfather Pine! I've made my choice: I'm coming. I promise that I'll climb your branches so high that only the wind will reach me. Spirits of the night, hear me too! I'm going to walk through your darkness all by myself, but I won't be afraid. I'll show you how brave I can be, as brave as Aki! And when he keeps his part of our bargain and teaches me to be a great hunter, O spirits, I promise that I'll always share what I catch with you.*

I opened my eyes slowly. I knew that I'd taken a decisive

step. I had given my word to the spirits, promised them gifts that I would never be able to give them unless I climbed the pine, won Aki's help, and seized the future I wanted. There was no going back from such a pact.

Like a wisp of smoke, I moved noiselessly, rising from my bedroll, slipping my tunic on over my head, tying the sash securely, and stealing outside. Our house was set high on stout wooden pillars, like the houses of all the nobles in our clan. We had to use a ladder to reach the ground from the platform outside our doorway. Its wavy steps were carved from a single log so that it looked like a gently tumbling hillside stream. Someone hauled it up every evening, to keep our home safe from any night-roaming dangers, beast or human. I'd never had to move it myself, and had no idea how heavy it might be. I'd never find the strength to maneuver it into place soundlessly and knew I'd have to drop from the platform to the ground, a daunting thought. My earliest memories were of Mama shrieking in terror whenever I crept too close to the edge: *"Himiko, no! Get away from there! You'll kill yourself if you fall!"*

Oh, what relief I felt when I saw that the ladder was still in place! It must have been Aki's task to pull it onto the platform, but Father's anger, my tears, and all the rest of what had happened that evening had distracted him. As my bare feet felt their way down the wooden steps, I thought I heard the voices of the spirits whispering: *See, Himiko! Here is our gift to you, proof that if you keep your word to us, you are fated to succeed.*

My joy over such good luck was like a bolt of lightning, a flare of brightness in the night that vanished the instant my feet touched the earth. Then a fresh pang of fear rushed up my spine. Our lives were filled with spirits, but they didn't all belong to the world of the living. There were also the spirits of the dead.

When I was alone in the night, all the dreadful stories that I'd heard the grown-ups tell about those angry ghosts came rushing over me like a stream in flood. They haunted the dark times, the dark places, and they envied us because we weren't bound to the same grim, lightless world that held them. Their envy could sharpen to rage at any moment, then blaze up into devastating vengeance. If they couldn't return to the light, they would drag the living into the darkness. If a hunter lingered too long in the woods after nightfall, the dead would send wolves to destroy him. If a woman was too pretty, too happy, they would wait until she was leaning over a river to admire her reflection; then they'd reach out of the shadowy waters and pull her down. And if a child strayed too far from home—

All at once I wanted nothing more than to race back up the ladder and into the house, to burrow close to my mother's side for protection and comfort. I imagined the ghosts of our clanfolk watching me, their cold fingers reaching out, their mouths gaping wide. I could hardly breathe.

"I don't want to do this," I whispered. Tears stung my eyes and trickled down my cheeks. "I want to go home." Somewhere an owl called from the treetops, and I jumped, startled. I knew that sound, but in my terror it was no longer the familiar cry of a night bird, but the voice of the wandering dead. "Oh, I want to go *home.*"

A wind sprang up, a strong gust that carried the pungent, cleansing smell of pine needles. I was suddenly wrapped in a comforting embrace of scent that worked its own strange magic. Though I heard nothing but the wind, I thought it carried the voice of the pine tree spirit, ancient and mighty: *Is this how a huntress faces the dark, Himiko? Is this how you honor your choice and keep your promise?*

I inhaled deeply, drawing the pine tree's power into myself. Then I clenched my fists and ran.

I had never run so fast in my life. I didn't stop running until I had my arms around Grandfather Pine's trunk, my face pressed against his black bark. Looking up, I saw the first branch I would need to grasp in order to begin my climb. It was just out of reach, even when I stood on my toes. I squatted like a frog, then leaped as high as I could, stretching out my arms the way I did when I wanted Aki to let me ride on his shoulders. My try fell short. My fingertips barely brushed the bottom of the branch before I tumbled back on my rump onto the thick layer of dead needles at the foot of the tree.

A fresh breeze rustled the pine tree's branches, and my ears heard the sound of the great spirit's laughter: *Ah, Himiko, is that the best you can do? Look at you! Are you truly trying to climb me, or are you only going to whimper and hope I'll bend down my branches, just to please you? Little beetle, rolling on your back, waving your legs in the air, did you really think you could conquer me? Never mind your foolish dreams and your silly promise. We make no bargains with beetles! Go home and hunt the grains of rice that fall from your mother's cooking pot. You will never—*

I will! Don't laugh at me! I couldn't risk shouting aloud, for fear of discovery, but my defiant thoughts were fierce and furious. *I'll show you that I will!*

Scowling, I retied my sash to make my tunic even shorter, freeing my legs. Then I crouched again and sprang, flinging myself at the tree with all my might! I was no frog, no beetle, but a squirrel, lithe and clever. I leaped forward and up, up, *up,* and though my hands still couldn't quite reach the lowest branch, my feet found a lucky toehold on the trunk. One kick, and my hands were holding the branch. Grinning, I pulled myself up to mount it. *Who's a beetle now?* I thought, triumphant.

After that, my ascent was long and tiring, but simple. Once off the ground, I found that the old tree's branches grew strong and close together. I dug my small fingers into limb after limb, my brow furrowed in concentration as I pulled myself higher and higher. I scraped my palms on the rough bark, my face gathered more than a few scratches from passing twigs, my arms and legs began to tire and ache, but as long as my endurance held out, there was nothing to keep me from reaching the topmost branches.

At last, I reached a place where the old pine tree's branches grew thin and began to snap off in my hands. I had climbed as high as it was safe to go. I straddled the sturdiest branch I could find and rested my back against the venerable tree, savoring victory. I was weary and sweaty, my tunic was stained and in tatters, my legs were bruised and scraped, my hands were tingling, but I had won. Now all I needed was for Aki to see me and confirm my accomplishment.

I wasn't afraid to be alone at the top of the pine. While

I'd been making my way up through those dark branches, daylight had returned to the world. The sun goddess was already sweeping away the mists of night with the sleeves of her golden gown. When I looked down from my perch, all I could see through the lower branches were a few small glimpses of the distant ground, but when I turned my eyes to the brightening sky, looking out and around me—ah!

There were the rooftops of our village—the nobles' houses like our own, tall and stately on their pillars; the homes of the common people, trim thatched roofs sheltering snug pit dwellings dug deep into the earth; the raised storehouses where we kept the heavy jars of rice after harvest time; the watchtower where the village men took turns as lookouts in the daytime hours; the wooden palisade and wide ditch that protected our settlement. Beyond our village in one direction were the cultivated fields and the shimmering water of the rice paddies; in another were the wild lands where Aki hunted game. I could see them more clearly with every passing moment as the sun goddess's smile banished the last wandering ghosts. How beautiful those thickly forested mountains were, clothed in a pattern of countless shades of green!

I glanced at my own clothing and frowned. Even if it hadn't been torn and dirty, my little cotton tunic was a dull thing, the faded tan of aged wood. Not a single splash of brighter color adorned it. Even the sash was plain. How badly I wanted to reach out and capture the rich, brilliant hues of the distant mountains, the trees, the flowers, and wrap them all around me! And there, in the distance, I saw a mountain so magnificent that it seemed to stand alone. I knew it well, having seen it many times before, when clear days let it stand revealed, but from my perch I could see it as never before. Its solitary snow-topped peak crowned graceful slopes that seemed to have captured the color of a cloudless morning sky. What wouldn't I have given to possess a shaman's magical power and steal just a touch of that brilliant blue?

I leaned my head against the old tree's trunk and whispered, "One day I'll have a dress that holds the sky. I will, Grandfather; you'll see." If I closed my eyes, I could picture it, a marvelous garment made out of clouds and wind, the shades of sunrise trailing from the sleeves, the softer tints of sunset dancing around the hem.

Wait until Aki sees me up here! I thought, smiling. *He'll be so proud of me.* I could almost hear him bragging about my feat to all the other men: *My little sister Himiko is as brave as any of us. I say we take her with us wherever we go, even when it's time to go hunting in the mountains.*

My happy daydreams didn't last. The longer I sat there, the more impatient I became. *What's keeping him? Is he so lazy? Is he going to sleep forever?* An empty stomach added to my irritation. I refused to wait for Aki any longer. If my brother wasn't going to come out of the house and acknowledge my great deed, I'd *bring* him out!

"Aki! Aki, come and see! Look at what I've done! *Aki!*"

I shouted as loudly as I could, calling my brother's name until my throat felt raw. Why didn't he come? Was he so deeply asleep, or had I climbed *too* high, so high that the wind stole my voice and swept it off into the clouds? *Maybe I should climb down, just a little,* I thought, and was about to do it when I heard the welcome sound of someone running toward the tree from the direction of our house. The branches below me hid the person from sight, but I knew who it was. Aki *had* heard me! I leaned forward on my branch, ready to enjoy my brother's praise.

"Himiko! Oh gods, how did you manage to get up there? Himiko, hold on, don't move! Someone—anyone—hurry, run, bring help! Himiko, *don't move,* do you hear me?" My mother's voice sounded loud and harsh as a crow's cry. I heard her trampling the earth as she dashed back and forth futilely, as if she were a dog tied to the old tree's trunk. Her cries rose to shrieks: "Someone come! Someone please *help me!*"

Other voices answered hers from our clan's many houses, high and low: "What's going on?" "We're coming!" "What's the matter?" From where I sat, I could see many people come rushing from their doorways.

Mama greeted them with fresh cries of distress: "It's Himiko! She's up *there*! Save her! Save my baby!"

"Baby"? I thought indignantly. *I'm no baby! She's making a big fuss over nothing.* I made a disgusted face. Even with the whole clan coming, Mama still kept calling for help again and again, until her words turned into sobs.

"Mama, don't cry!" I called. I grabbed a thin branch to steady myself as I leaned even farther forward, trying to catch sight of her face. "I'm all right. I climbed up here by myself, and I can—"

The branch snapped off in my hand, my balance deserted me, and I pitched headfirst into thin air.

I couldn't even find the breath to scream as I crashed

through the web of twigs and frail branches below. Green needles clawed my face as I plummeted. The wind of my fall filled my ears with my mother's voice shrieking my name.

A sharp blow knocked the breath out of my body, and a harsh shock brought my fall to an abrupt end. A hard line of pain radiated across my back, another under my knees. My head dangled backward over emptiness. I'd fallen, but I hadn't dropped the fatal distance all the way to the ground. Dizzy, aching, sick to my stomach, I slowly realized how close I'd come to disaster. My small hands met the rough, familiar bark of the pine tree.

I sat up slowly and saw what had stopped my fall and saved my life: two thick branches grew in graceful, uplifting curves like a pair of welcoming arms. The shock of what had happened to me ebbed as I caught my breath and felt a spiderweb of aches begin to spin itself over my body. I hurt in so many places that I couldn't begin to tell which were slight and which severe. Cradled in Grandfather Pine's embrace, I flung my arms around his trunk, leaned my head against his bark, and began to cry. I was still weeping, my cheeks sticky with streaks of resin, when one of my clansmen climbed up to bring me the rest of the way down.

He set me on my feet in front of Mama, but before she could take me into her arms, I felt a searing pain in my right leg, and it collapsed under me. I sprawled at Mama's feet, wailing. It wasn't just the agony of my shattered bone that made me yowl, but the fearful certainty I felt about *why* this had happened. All of Father's warnings about the maliciousness of the spirits crowded into my mind. Because I'd fallen, I'd failed to make Aki see me as worthy to become a hunter. Because of that, I would never be able to bring the spirits the offerings of game I'd promised them.

Because I'd broken my promise to the spirits, the spirits had broken me.

2
WHAT THE SPIRITS DESIRE

There was a great flurry of activity as I was carried into our house, stripped of my torn, filthy clothes, and washed with great care and tenderness by Mama and my stepmothers. They took turns scolding me for what I'd done, exclaiming in alarm over my injuries, drying my tears as I sobbed over how badly my leg was hurting, and assuring me over and over again that there was nothing to worry about and that I'd soon be better. It all made my head spin so much that I stopped listening to them altogether.

One of our clanfolk fetched the shaman, a thin-faced old woman named Yama. At that age, I was still a little afraid of her, with her wild, tangled hair, like a midnight sky streaked with lightning, and the array of clattering beads and bones she wore looped around her neck and dangling from the sash of her white dress. She swept down upon me and set a cup of warm, bitter liquid to my lips. I was so startled that I swallowed the whole thing in one gulp. Almost at once the pain knifing through me grew dull enough for me to bear without tears. Even when she smiled at me and touched my broken leg so gently that I felt only the faintest twinge, I found myself staring at her, speechless with awe, my thumb in my mouth as though I were an infant seeing a monster.

Yama applied a salve of honey and crushed herbs to my leg, then wrapped it securely with strips of cloth. She told me that I was a very lucky little girl to have broken only my shin and not my neck, and instructed Mama to keep me completely still until the stars said it was all right for me to move again. At her orders, my bedroll was moved into the snuggest corner of our house, out of the way when Mama, Yukari, and Emi were busy with their chores, far from all of the family comings and goings. I might as well have been a broken pot, useless and shoved aside until someone remembered to repair it or throw it away.

As soon as Mama had me settled according to Yama's directions, my three older brothers came to see me, kneeling in a row beside my bedroll. Mama tried shooing them away so that I could lie undisturbed, but they persisted. I heard Aki murmur to her, "I think Masa and Shoichi are scared by what happened. They won't believe Himiko's all right until they talk to her. And I—I can hardly believe we didn't lose her. I *need* to sit with her for just a little while. Please, Mother? *Please.*" His words persuaded her and she gave in.

Shoichi and Masa gaped at my bundled-up leg and had

a hundred questions for me about how it had felt to fall so far.

"Did you think you were going to die?" Masa asked eagerly. He was a boy who loved to hear tales where the hero's life was always dangling one breath away from catastrophe. Now that he saw I'd survived it, my morning's taste of disaster was just another adventure story to him.

Shoichi punched him lightly in the arm. "Don't be stupid. Of course not! It happened so fast, she didn't have *time* to think."

Undaunted, Masa pressed on: "Well, then, what did you think when you were climbing the pine tree? Were you scared? Did you wonder what would happen if you lost your grip? Didn't you get tired? How long did it take you to—?"

"That's enough, Masa," Aki said. "If you have to bother our little sister with questions, better ask her what you can do to make her comfortable, or if there's anything she wants to eat or drink."

"Oh." Masa was crestfallen. "I—I'll do that later. Now I have to—" He got up and scurried out of the house. Shoichi went through the motions of asking if I wanted anything, but the moment I shook my head just the slightest bit, he was gone too.

Aki clicked his tongue. "They're such children. I think they're afraid that if they do anything for you, their friends will make fun of them for being your slaves."

"Slaves?" I'd never heard that word before, not even sarcastically, the way Aki had just pronounced it.

"When two clans fight, that's a war, and sometimes the

one that wins takes people who belong to the one that lost. Those people have to spend the rest of their lives working for the clan that captured them, and so do their children, forever."

"Really?" My eyes grew large as an owl's. "Can't they ever go home?"

Aki shook his head. "Not unless their clan grows strong enough to fight again. Then their warriors might attack the clan that took them away. But I've never heard of it happening."

"Why not?"

My brother looked at me with a melancholy smile. "Because when there's a war between two clans, the one that wins makes sure that all of the enemy warriors are dead."

"I don't understand," I said. "Wouldn't their clan spirit save them?"

"Not if the other clan's guardian is stronger than theirs."

"That's silly. Why would a clan choose a weak spirit to guard them?"

Aki shrugged. "I don't think we *choose* our guardians. We've always been the Matsu clan, and we've always been protected by the pine tree spirit that gives us our name. No one can remember a time when this wasn't so."

His reasoning didn't satisfy me. In seven years of life, there had already been too many times when the best answer a grown-up could give me was *Because that's the way it's always been!* That was *not* a good enough answer for anything, as far as I was concerned.

"But what if our guardian's weak and we don't know

it? What will happen when another clan comes to fight us, and to make us be their slaves? What if the pine tree spirit isn't strong enough to save us?" I saw a future full of ghastly possibilities, and my voice began to rise in panic. "What if we should have had a better guardian and we don't find out until it's too late?"

"Little Sister, the pine tree spirit is strong enough to—"

"He wasn't even strong enough to carry *me*!"

Aki brushed my hair away from my face. "Don't worry about such things, Himiko. You didn't fall out of the pine tree because our clan guardian dropped you. It was an accident, that's all. But when his branches broke your fall and saved your life—! Well, I'd say that proves the pine tree spirit is strong enough to look after us all."

I gave Aki a searching stare. What was he trying to make me believe? He made it sound as if the spirits came and went like clouds, following the sun. When something good happened, they were there. When something bad happened, they were far away.

Were they really anywhere at all?

But I heard them speak! I told myself. *I did! I— Did I?*

A whisper of doubt hissed through my mind like a serpent. I remembered what Mama said whenever I woke up crying because our house was full of monsters: *"Hush, Himiko, it wasn't real. You imagined it all. It was just a dream. There are no monsters here."*

I'd only imagined the monsters. Had I also only imagined the spirits? I didn't know what to think, and it scared me. Aki saw my troubled look and jumped to the wrong conclusion about what was upsetting me. "Don't fret, Little

Sister; we're safe. No one has made war against the Matsu clan for many years, not since long before you were born. The gods are protecting us." He stood up slowly. "I have work to do, but I'll be back as soon as I can. Yukari and Emi had to go down to the rice fields, but Mother's just outside on the porch, taking care of the babies. You're not alone, so don't be afraid."

"I'm not afraid," I told him.

"Of course not." He chuckled. "After what you did this morning, you could face down an *oni*. A fine sight you'd be, wearing that mountain ogre's skin for a cape!"

I wasn't in the mood for Aki's teasing. There was something serious on my mind. I stretched out my hand to him. He dropped to one knee and took it. "Aki, did you see me in the pine tree?" I asked in a small, shaky voice. "Did you see how high I climbed?"

He hesitated, then shook his head reluctantly. I think he knew how important his answer was to me, but he wouldn't lie. "You were already being carried down when I came out of the house. I was there when you touched the ground and—" He made a sympathetic face, remembering my pain. "Why did you do it, Himiko? What possessed you to try such a dangerous thing?"

I stared at him in shocked silence. Didn't he *know*? Had he forgotten what he'd said to me last night? All I'd tried, all I'd risked, all the pain and shame of my failure had been done to convince him that I was just as worthy as Masa and Shoichi. And he didn't remember anything about it. It had all been for nothing.

I still loved my brother Aki with all my heart, but it

wasn't the same. He had never truly believed in me, and that changed everything.

"All right," he said at last. "You don't have to talk about it if you don't want to. The important thing is, you're alive, and you're never going to do something as dangerous as that again. Rest now, and try not to move too much; you'll heal faster. Don't make me wait *too* long to play games with my favorite little sister again. Get well quickly, and I'll gather some twigs and make you a toy deer—no, a whole *herd* of them!—and then the two of us can pretend to track them, and—"

I let go of his hand, closed my eyes, and turned my head away. "I don't want to be a hunter anymore," I said. "I'm tired." But the truth was, I wanted Aki to go away.

"I'm not surprised. You must have been up half the night, climbing that tree. Sleep well, little one." I heard the rustle of his clothing as he stood, then the soft creak of the floorboards under his departing footsteps. When the house was silent, I knew it was safe for me to cry.

I lay on my back, staring into the rafters. My chest felt like an empty eggshell. Tears trickled from the corners of my eyes and ran into my ears; I made no move to wipe them away. I was seven years old, but as far as I was concerned, my life was over; my dreams of becoming a great hunter were dead. In my heart, I knew that even if Aki had seen me riding the topmost branch of the ancient pine, he never would have let me share Masa and Shoichi's lessons. He loved me as dearly as I loved him and would give me anything in his power.

Anything except what I wanted most. In my lonesome

corner, I sobbed because the closest I would ever come to winning my desires was a little wooden deer.

"What's wrong, Daughter? Are you in pain?"

I gasped and opened my eyes to see Father's face looking down at me. He'd moved so quietly that I hadn't heard him come near. It was too dark to see his expression, but he sounded truly worried. He'd never spoken to me so gently or with so much concern before. In all of my memories, the only time I had any direct attention from him was when I did something wrong.

I sniffled and tried to stop my tears before replying. I was scared that I'd imagined the softness in his voice, and that any moment he'd start yelling at me for disturbing him with my crying. Worse, he'd make all of Mama, Yukari, and Emi's scoldings seem like nothing once he began berating me for having climbed the pine.

"I— No. Nothing's wrong. I'm—" I could barely hear my own words, uttered in a mouse's whisper.

A deep sigh answered me. "Good. That's good. When I saw you fall, I thought—" Another sigh. "I didn't know you were so brave, Himiko." I saw him lean forward, and for the first time, I felt his hand cradle my cheek. "You have a bold heart for such a little girl, but you *are* a girl. There will always be certain things that you can't do. You'll understand this when you grow up, but for now, just accept it. The gods have given me many sons, but only one daughter. I need you."

I didn't know what to say. Father sounded like a stranger, but a stranger who loved me. I feared that none of this was true. The spirits must be playing an evil joke on me, as further punishment for my broken promise. My *real* father was nowhere near. He was out in the fields, supervising our clanfolk as they worked at the vital task of tending the rice. What was happening now was only a dream. I took his hand and held it tightly.

He laughed, delighted. "What a mighty grip! Maybe the gods *did* give me nothing but sons. Our people need me to have strong sons, men who'll be able to lead and protect the Matsu clan, but I—I would be sad if I didn't have my little daughter."

"R-really?"

"Yes, *really.*" He bowed over me and kissed my forehead. "Remember that." Then he was gone.

My recovery took many days. To me, it seemed like a lifetime. I suppose it would have felt like forever if not for all the people around me. Mama, Yukari, and Emi took turns looking after me. Yama came frequently to see how my healing was progressing.

The village girls of my age came by and tried to cheer me. That was an awkward visit: the five of us played together from time to time, but I'd always preferred Aki's company and so never had become close friends with any of them. I felt they didn't really want to be there. As if to prove I was right, they didn't come back. I was surprised at how much that hurt.

Aki brought me the toy deer he'd promised, and even Shoichi and Masa came bearing little things to amuse me—a bunch of wildflowers, a bird's colorful feather, a handful of shining stones and a game we could play with them. Best of all, Father always found time to kneel beside my bedroll and to let me know in a dozen different ways that I was special to him.

How happy I was! Aki might never teach me to be a hunter, but now I didn't need that in order to earn Father's smiles. I treasured every one, never forgetting how rare they'd once been.

There were times during my healing that Father didn't smile. I was always afraid it was on account of something I'd done or failed to do. My anxiety must have shown on my face, because Father always noticed. "Don't look so worried, Himiko. There are some problems in the village that need my attention, but that's nothing to bother you, little butterfly."

"But I want to help you, Father," I said. "Isn't there something I can do?"

"Ah, now *this* is why I want a daughter! Yes, my dear, there is something you can do. You sing so prettily, you never fail to take my mind off my troubles."

I sang for him—just a silly song Emi taught me about a turtle who tried to eat the moon—and his smile returned. That made me happy, yet I wished he'd told me what his problems were. Maybe I could have helped him see them in a new way and fix them! I wanted to *help*, not merely divert him, but I had to be content with doing only what he asked. He loved his good little girl.

Mama noticed the change in Father and recognized that I was responsible for it. She took every chance she got to let me know how pleased with me she was. Once, while combing out my hair, she said, "When did you become a shaman, my dearest? You've worked magic on your father. I don't know how you do it, but may the gods bless you for lightening his heart."

"I didn't do anything," I replied. I wanted to sound modest—Father often remarked that a woman who held her nose too high soon got it covered with mud—but secretly I basked in Mama's praise.

"Tsk. You did, and I'm glad of it. He's a good man, with many burdens. That's what makes him harsh and snappish sometimes. When he was a boy, in the days when Lady Tsuki ruled our clan, he didn't have an easy life, like you do. We've been friends since he and I were infants, so I know just how hard it is for him to be happy."

"He's happy when I sing for him," I volunteered.

"I know that too; I have eyes and ears, don't I?" She gave me a fond look.

"Isn't there anything else I can do, Mama?"

She used the comb deftly, to secure my hair into a series of loops, like hers. "You're a smart girl, Himiko—when you're not climbing trees like a lizard that's lost its mind. Use *your* eyes and ears. They'll give you your answer."

I heeded Mama's advice and began to watch Father very closely. I paid attention to the things that cheered him most. My songs, Aki's success in the hunt, Masa and Shoichi's slow progress in learning how to use weapons—all these had the power to smooth the hard lines from his face; but the thing that seemed to bring him the greatest joy was when Mama, Yukari, and Emi would dance.

They didn't do it often—there was usually too much work to be done in the house and in the fields—but when they did, it was wonderful. There were times, like after the harvest season, when everyone in the village danced to celebrate having plenty to eat for the winter ahead. Men would play flutes and drums, and Yama, Father, and the rest of the noble families would bring out the hill-shaped sacred bronze bells and strike them with artfully carved sticks or bones, an offering of music to thank the gods. None of this was half as special as when Father's three wives danced for us alone.

We never knew when they might decide to do it. It usually happened after the day's work was done. One of them would begin to hum a tune, and the others would join in, swaying in time to the melody. Then they'd begin to clap in time. As soon as the rest of us heard that, we joined in. We knew what would follow! Emi was always the first to stop humming and start singing as she began the steps of the dance. Mama and Yukari wouldn't wait long after that. Soon the three of them were moving in a circle, their feet tracing a simple pattern that went forward and back, forward and back, like a honeybee sipping from a flower, hovering away, and returning to sip again. Sometimes they didn't step daintily, but stamped the ground, or the floorboards of our house, or the high platform outside our door. Their arms moved side to side with the languid grace of willow branches, and no matter how long they chose to dance, it was never long enough for us. When they were done, Father always wore his warmest smile.

I wanted to be the one to bring that smile of peace and contentment to his face. As soon as my leg healed, I would dance for him.

My decision made me even more impatient to get well.

I begged Mama to go ask our shaman for any charms or potions she could use to speed my recovery. I awaited her return eagerly, and as soon as I heard her feet on the ladder, I called out, "What did Lady Yama give you, Mama? How fast will it work? Is it medicine? What does it taste like? Oh, never mind, I don't care, I'll take it!"

Mama knelt by my bedside. Her hands were empty. "Lady Yama didn't give me any medicine for you, little one," she said.

"What, then? A charm? Magic?"

She laughed. "You act as if you believe a shaman's magic is something an ordinary person could carry home, like a borrowed basket!"

"Well, then, is *she* coming here to cast the spell that will heal me faster?" I demanded.

"She's not coming, and she didn't send you anything but *this* message." Mama made a long face, the corners of her mouth turning down sharply. She scowled so that deep lines furrowed the space between her eyebrows, turning her face into a crone's mask, and when she spoke, it was in our shaman's gruff voice: "'Tell your little one that I'll use my magic to speed things along, but first she must use magic of her own and turn herself into an old woman like me. Then she'll see how much faster the days run by!'" I could almost hear Yama's hoarse laughter echoing through my mother's imitation.

"So . . . nothing," I said sadly.

Mama stroked my brow. "I'm sorry, little one. I know it's not the answer you wanted. I hoped that at least I could cheer you by the way I told it. I suppose I'm not very good at pretending to be someone I'm not, but I *did* want to amuse you."

"Oh, you were very good at acting like Lady Yama!" I was quick to say. "You looked and sounded just like her!"

"Hmph. I hope I don't look *exactly* like her. Not yet, at any rate," Mama replied with a sniff. But she was smiling.

I swallowed my disappointment and made the best of things. My body was confined to bed, but my mind was free. I passed the time imagining the dance I'd perform for Father the very instant Yama came to remove my bandages. I created countless dances in my head, stealing the movements of birds, clouds, flowers, reeds, a rushing brook, the iridescent wings of a dragonfly. When the shaman arrived to free me, I'd be ready.

On an early summer's day, Yama climbed our ladder and made the house ring with her powerful voice: "Where's that lazy child that everyone complains about so much? Who does she think she is, one of those twittering princesses from the lands beyond the sunset? A Matsu chieftain's daughter must be made of stronger stuff. All day long she does nothing but lie in bed and make her poor family bring her whatever she wants! Ah, those days are over. I won't stand for it anymore. It's time for you to get up, Himiko! What do you say to that?"

"Good!" I shouted so loudly that Mama's face flushed. She was afraid that Yama would mistake my eagerness for insolence. Shamans knew the secrets of healing, how to read the weather signs, and the lore of plants and animals,

but their greatest power was the ability to speak to the dead as easily as to the living, and to reach the ears of the gods themselves.

"Lady Yama, please forgive my stupid daughter," Mama said, kneeling before the old woman, her forehead touching the floor. "She meant no disrespect."

Yama snorted so emphatically that it rattled the beads around her neck. "You needn't tell *me*. Don't I know her ways? I've had my eye on her since the day she was born. That was a day none of us can forget! I'm glad she's making such a racket. It means she's strong. Now fetch a stool. She'll need to sit on it so I can unbind her leg."

I began to fidget even before Mama brought the stool and helped me onto it. She had to hold me by the shoulders to keep me from wriggling myself right off the seat. I could hardly wait to be released from all the days of my captivity. I wished Father were there, but he'd gone off into the mountains with the boys and some of the other village men, on the trail of wild pigs.

It doesn't matter, I thought, grinning. *He'll see me dance soon enough. For now, I'll show Mama.* Why was Yama taking such a long time to remove the bandages? I had to hold my tongue or I'd start telling her to hurry, hurry, *hurry,* and Mama wouldn't like that at all.

"There. All done." Yama sat back on her heels and looked at my leg narrowly. "Hmm. That was not a good break, but it's healed well enough for—"

"Mama, look at me! Look what I can do!" I squirmed free from Mama's grasp and jumped to my feet, already singing and clapping my hands, ready to show her my surprise.

I was the one surprised. I clapped my hands only once before I found myself toppling sideways as my newly freed leg crumpled under me. Mama screamed, but I was too startled to draw a breath. I hit the floor and lay there, staring at the cracks between the boards, stunned and bewildered. What had happened? Had my leg broken again? Did the spirits hate me *that* much for not having kept my promise?

"Little girl, what were you thinking?" Yama's bony hands hooked themselves under my armpits and hoisted me back onto the stool. "You haven't used your legs for almost an entire season. They need to *remember* how to carry you. Give them time."

Head bowed, I took a long look at my unbandaged leg. If I'd done that first, I never would have tried to stand, let alone dance. It was all wrinkled, pale as the belly of a fish, and so scrawny that it made my kneecap look like a blown-up deer's bladder. My body had betrayed and humiliated me. I was too miserable to utter a word.

Mama had other plans. "What's the matter with you, Himiko? Thank Lady Yama for all she's done for you," she said crisply. When I mumbled a reply, she made me repeat it properly.

Our shaman was amused. "There, there, child, you go ahead and sulk. It's all right if you want to blame me for your troubles. Easier than blaming yourself, even if that's who deserves it. I didn't force you up that tree *or* shove you out of it. I just picked up the pieces and stuck them back together the best I could." She rose from the floor and swept out of our house, her dry laughter crackling through the air.

The hunting party was gone for three days. I was able to stand up and hobble around the house with Mama's help by the time they returned. Father was overjoyed to see me walking again. "I'm going to give the spirits *double* the thanksgiving offering they're due—for our success in the hunt and for your recovery," he declared, hugging me.

"And I'll add to it," Aki said.

"So will we!" Masa and Shoichi were beaming. They'd managed to make their first kills, even if all they'd brought down were some scrawny old birds. When our family ate their meat that night, it was like wood shavings in our mouths no matter how long Emi stewed it.

"They'd better not offer any of *this* to the spirits," Aki whispered to me.

I didn't feel like sharing in the joke. Why thank the spirits at all? I saw them as the ones to blame for my injury. Being confined to my bed had given me a lot of time to think about what had put me there. Perhaps I'd only imagined their voices that night, but it still hurt to remember how they'd taunted me, and that hurt pushed aside all memories of the encouraging words they'd also spoken. The pine tree had saved me from falling to my death, but I believed I wouldn't have fallen at all if he hadn't snapped the branch I was holding. I had called him Grandfather and thanked him with all my heart; it hadn't been enough.

Why does Father say he'll make a thanksgiving offering to the spirits when he knows it's really a bribe? I thought. *They don't want our thanks; they want our gifts, and if they aren't satisfied, they'll hurt us. Sometimes they'll hurt us anyway, no matter how much we give them. They'll do it just because they* can. *It's not fair. The spirits—*

And then I realized something about all the forces in my life that were bigger and stronger than I, the gods and the goddesses and all the lesser spirits of this world, the powerful beings who saw me as an insect if they noticed me at all: *they want our gifts, but the gift they want the most is fear!* It was a bitter revelation, so bitter that I didn't want to think about it further. I was sure it was one of the great secrets that the grown-ups knew, and now, so did I.

Summer drifted to a close. Every day, I grew a little stronger. I hadn't given up the idea of dancing for Father, and so I concentrated my whole attention on regaining the use of my legs. Nothing else in our village, our clan, or our household existed for me, unless it led me to walk, to run, and finally, to dance.

Whenever he could, Aki carried me down our ladder and let me walk around the village, leaning on him. It was a grand moment when I was able to take my first unassisted steps, even though my mended leg had a jerky, awkward gait.

"Never mind, Little Sister," Aki said, patting my shoulder. "Enough practice and that will change. The important thing is, you're walking on your own again. Wait until the rest of the family sees you!"

There wasn't much chance of that, not on a day when most of the village folk, including our family, would be in the fields. The sun goddess stood at the midpoint of the sky, the time to leave work for a while. Aki had chosen to use his rest time to come back to the house and help me, but the others would be dozing under the trees that grew near the rice paddies, far out of earshot no matter how loudly I called. I frowned. *Someone* should see what I'd done!

Then I remembered: *Emi's in the house! She didn't go to the fields today; she stayed home with the babies.* I didn't give a second thought to how odd that was. The women always brought their infants with them when they went to work in the paddies. They'd take turns, one or two at a time, looking after all the children. Why had Emi remained behind? I shrugged away the question. Grown-ups did all sorts of strange things. Besides, it had nothing to do with me.

"Emi!" I lifted my head, cupped my hands around my mouth, and shouted her name. "Emi! Come out, Emi! I need you!"

"Himiko, no." Aki's hand closed on my arm. His joyful look was gone. "Don't bother her now."

I was alarmed by the sudden change in him. "I only want her to see what I—"

"Let her alone. Besides, you'll—you'll wake the babies with all your shouting."

"But I won't," I protested. "They sleep through anything. They're *always* sleeping, especially Emi's son. She has to wake him up to eat, and he still falls asleep in the middle of it."

"Himiko—"

I didn't catch the note of warning in my brother's voice, or hear the creak of floorboards from the house platform. "I wonder when they'll start doing something besides eating and sleeping," I went on. "They both used to cry a lot, but they don't anymore. Does that mean they're going to start talking soon? Cousin Kura's baby was born around the same time as they were, and he's talking *and* walking! Remember the fuss everyone made?"

"Himiko, be *quiet*." Aki's sharp answer shocked me worse than a slap across the face. No one had spoken so harshly to me since before my tumble from the pine. How awful to hear Father's old, stern voice come out of Aki's mouth. "Stop chattering before—"

"It's all right, Aki." Emi's haggard face looked down at us over the edge of the platform. "I'll be right there."

She descended the ladder slowly. I watched, lost and confused, as she and Aki gazed at one another for half a dozen heartbeats without speaking.

He broke the unnerving silence. "Is he—?" She nodded. When he tried to put his arms around her, she held him away.

"Don't. I can't bear it. Not yet."

"Shall I get the others?" Aki lowered his eyes. I wanted to ask, *What are you talking about? Why do you both look so sad? You're scaring me!* But something kept me from opening my lips.

Emi shook her head. "Tell them later. There's no need for them to come back now. What for?"

"Then shall I fetch Lady Yama?"

"Yes." Her voice broke, and she began to cry.

That was when I knew that what we had all feared for so long had finally happened: my baby brother, Emi's son, was dead.

We buried him in an earthenware pot in the place

where we Matsu always gave our kin to the underworld. Yama performed all the rituals she knew to make his passage from life to death an easy one. I remember how she danced with two sacred bronze mirrors, catching the sunlight and making it leap back and forth above her head like a captive star. She sang and chanted and called out to the spirits in a dozen different ways, imploring them to come near, to guide my baby brother gently into the darkness, to have pity on our family.

I didn't hear a single answer. I didn't feel anything come near us except our sorrow.

We set aside our ordinary clothes and wore garments made of hemp. At the end of the period of mourning, Yama helped us purify ourselves with water, with evergreen branches, with salt, and by striking deep, resounding tones from the bronze bell she used to call out to the gods. When we put on our ordinary clothes again, I noticed that Emi was wearing a new dress. I asked her what she'd done with her other one. It hadn't been *that* old.

"I wrapped *him* in it," she said dully. "I didn't want him to think I'd sent him away alone. Maybe this way, his spirit will be comforted, and he'll remember me."

That was a dreadful time. Just before the harvest, Yukari's little one followed his half brother into the sunless lands. As we left the burial place, Emi put her arm around Yukari's shoulders and said, "I'm so sorry, dear one. It's my boy's fault that yours is gone. I did what I could and begged his spirit to depart in peace, but he was too young and fearful to make such a journey by himself."

Yukari leaned against her wearily. "Last time, it was my

little girl who left first, and yours was the one who followed. If they must leave us so young, it's better this way: at least they have each other."

A great shadow settled over our house. We no longer sang or told stories or even spoke about the day's events. After eating, we spent what was left of the evening in silence. Aki and Father would pass the time examining and repairing their tools and weapons, though I often noticed them sharpening the same blade or working on the same arrow night after night. Shoichi and Masa sat quietly, playing a game with black and white stones. I helped Mama, Yukari, and Emi clean up after our meal, then settled down to watch them make or mend our clothes. They taught me how to sew by giving me my own precious iron needle and showing me how it was done without a word being said.

Oh, I hated that horrible silence! I wanted to smash it, to clap my hands and shout and sing until it flew away and joy could return to our home. But I didn't dare; none of us dared to make a sound except for Father, who would bring an end to each evening's painful silence by standing up and announcing, "It's time to sleep."

When dawn came, Father and the boys fled our house as though it were on fire. Mama, Yukari, and Emi also looked for any excuse to go out rather than do chores inside, where two small ghosts haunted the shadows. Even away from the house, they hardly spoke to one another, and when any of our clanfolk tried to talk to them, they kept their replies to one or two words. There were times I thought that I too would die from the ache that seized my heart every time I looked into my stepmothers' eyes. I was stung by memories of my foolish words—*I wish the spirits* would *punish you! All of you!*—and the only thing that saved me from drowning in guilt was remembering how quickly I'd taken back my curse, calling on the spirits to punish only me.

I spent as much time as I could away from my family. Avoiding Father and the boys was easy, but the women were another story. Little by little, the three of them began to surround me whenever they could. Yukari brought me food before I was hungry, offering me all kinds of treats. Emi refused to let me take two steps without exclaiming that I was about to fall and grabbing my arm. Being free to walk as much as I wanted was impossible, and I had about as much chance of sprouting wings and flying as I did of trying to run. Mama combed my hair so often that my scalp stung all the time, and joined Yukari and Emi when they helped me into my clothes in the morning and out of them at bedtime. They did everything but chew my food for me. The few times that I was able to steal away from them and hide, they'd rouse the whole village until I was found again. I was ready to howl.

One morning, when the trees on the distant hillsides were gold and scarlet, Aki surprised everyone by declaring he wasn't going to go hunting with Father and his brothers. "Masa and Shoichi should have a chance to show how much progress they've made," he said. "Let them bring home the pheasants today, or whatever game the forest spirits choose to send us."

"Son, are you sure?" Mama sounded anxious. "They're still children. What if they have an accident? They need you to look after them."

"Father can do that better than I," Aki countered. "And if we don't give them room to grow up, they really will stay children forever. No, today I don't go anywhere with my brothers. Today belongs to Himiko and me!"

He had me riding his back and down the ladder before anyone could stop him. Mama, Yukari, and Emi stood at the edge of the platform, trying to drown us in an endless stream of warnings and instructions. Aki began to trot, then to run, until we left the sound of their voices far behind. As we passed the village lookout tower, he turned toward the hills and slowed his pace. "Women!" he exclaimed. "It's a good thing they don't know we're headed for the forest or they'd be flying after us."

"The forest?" I couldn't believe it. "Is that where you're taking me?"

"No, that's where I'm *leaving* you." He jounced me until I giggled. "I'll carry you there, but we're both walking back. It's the only way you're going to get home."

I hugged Aki's neck. "You're *wonderful,* Big Brother!" All my old, pure affection rushed back. "I never get to walk far on my own anymore."

"I know. I've been watching." He shifted my weight on his back. "You have to understand them, Himiko: Yukari and Emi hover over you because you're closest in age to the babies they lost. You're too young to remember, but this happened to them before. Back then, it was Masa's turn to be fussed over."

His words helped me understand. "They're acting like that because they still need to be *someone's* mother?"

Aki nodded. "Yes. And our mother is trying to wrap you

up in a cocoon because what happened to their children has her terrified. Every time I've seen her walking past the clan pine tree, she either glares at it or goes pale and breaks into a run. You're her baby, Himiko, and she can't forget how close she came to losing you that day."

"Well, I wish she *would* forget!" I cried. "I'm not *anyone's* baby—not Mama's or Yukari's or Emi's. I wish they'd all have *real* babies again, and leave me alone."

"You don't mean that, Himiko," Aki said kindly. "You'd hate it if no one paid attention to you. I've seen how you open up like a flower in the sun every time you sing for us."

I laid my cheek against my brother's back. "I wish I could sing again. It made Father happy. But no one even talks in the house anymore."

"Trust me, Little Sister, that will change. It'll take time, but I promise you, our house won't stay sad and silent forever."

"It takes too *much* time," I said petulantly. "Isn't there anything we can do to make the sadness go away sooner?"

"I wish that were possible." By now we were out of sight of the village, a little way up the nearest hill where the dark red leaves of young maple trees canopied the ground. He squatted near one tree trunk so that I'd have something to support and steady me when I got off his back. As he straightened up again, he added, "Maybe you should pray to the spirits for help."

I scowled. "*They* won't help. Father's right: all *they* want is the chance to hurt us. I'll bet it makes them laugh!"

"Himiko, you shouldn't say such things." My brother's eyes darted back and forth nervously, as though he'd heard

some unknown danger creeping closer to us through the
trees. I'd never seen him so frightened.

The gift they want the most is fear.

The spirits had already fed on our family's sorrow, and
now Mama and my stepmothers spent every day afraid that
something bad would happen to me. Those fears gave the
spirits a hateful feast, but if they thought they'd feed on
Aki's fears as well, I'd make them starve instead!

"You're right, Aki," I said quickly. "I was only joking."
I knew it was a flimsy excuse, but I couldn't think of a
better one.

"You shouldn't joke about the spirits at all." Aki gave
me a look so severe it made me cringe, but if it banished his
fright, I'd welcome it.

"I know. I'm sorry. I won't do it again." I bowed my
head as if I meant what I'd said.

A playful tug at one of my hair loops made me look up.
Aki was smiling again. "That's my good girl! Now, are you
going to show me you can walk all the way back to the village on your own?"

"No," I replied mischievously. "I'll show you I can *run.*"

3

"Go Away, Himiko!"

I thought I'd be able to run, that first day Aki took me into the forest, but my legs had other ideas. When I tried to go faster than a walk, the best I could do was a funny little hobble-hop, hobble-hop. I was so frustrated, I wanted to cry, but I was also so angry that I couldn't find the tears. Instead, I made a fist and pounded it against the nearest tree.

"Easy, Little Sister," Aki said, catching my wrist after the third blow. "You'll hurt yourself. Think how Mama and the others will react if I bring you home with a scraped, bleeding hand! They'll never let me take you out of their sight again. Then how would I be able to bring you back here?"

"Oh, Aki, *will* you?" My hand hurt badly from my fool-ish outburst of temper, but my brother's words numbed the sting.

"It's what I want more than anything." He sat down at the roots of the tree and motioned for me to join him. "Look around, Himiko," he said. "See how beautiful it is here. This is one of my favorite places."

"To hunt?"

"No, any animal who'd come this close to our village might as well just jump into the cook fire. Hunting's not the only thing that brings me to the forest. It's peaceful here, and the air tastes better."

I made a scornful sound. "Air doesn't taste like anything."

"That's what you think." He tilted his head back and gazed up through the rustling red leaves. "I disagree. This place is special. I believe that the spirits who live here are . . ." He paused, as if finding exactly the right word were the most important thing in the world. "They're *friendly*. They welcome me when I come, they steal all of the little things that bother me, and they send me home feeling happier. I'm as renewed as if I'd slept for a day and a night, with only joyful dreams." He turned his gaze to me. "That's why I wanted to bring you here, to share that with you. I want the spirits of this place to know you, to welcome you the way they welcome me, and to give you back the power to walk and run and do anything you wish."

"To dance?" I asked hopefully, and for a moment, I forgot that the spirits weren't friendly or welcoming, but greedy and spiteful. I wanted to dance more than I wanted to be right.

"Since when are you a dancer, Little Sister?" he asked kindly. "You'll have to show me."

I turned my head away, suddenly shy. "I'm not ready yet."

"Well, when you *are* ready, you'll do it. For now"—he stood up again—"why don't we walk back home before they send the whole village to fetch us?"

There was no need to ask who "they" were. I held out my hands for Aki to help me get up, but he just crossed his arms over his chest and smiled at me. "The less I do for you, the sooner you'll be doing more for yourself."

The trip back from the forest took much longer than the trip there. Aki remained firm about not helping me, except to offer his arm when we came to places on the trail where loose stones made the footing treacherous. It would have been an easy thing for him to let me ride on his back, but he never offered and I would have refused him if he had.

It was nearly dusk by the time we returned. Smoke trails marked the fires where our kinfolk were preparing the evening meal. We met no one as I came walking home, exulting over what I'd accomplished.

From a distance, I could just make out Mama's face in our doorway as she strained her work-weary eyes for any sight of our return. Aki saw her too. "Better get up again, Himiko," he said, kneeling. "If she so much as suspects how hard I made you work today—"

"I won't tell," I whispered as I got on his back. "Not as long as you take me there again tomorrow."

Aki did take me back to his special place in the forest, though not the next day or the one after that. He told me that it would look suspicious if he sidestepped his tasks too often. He was a man of the Matsu, and our chief's eldest son besides. The eyes of the village were always following him.

How could he neglect his duties without stirring up too many questions?

So I learned to be patient, waiting for the next time I could test the limits of my legs on the steep woodland paths. I didn't wait idly. My first trip home from the maple grove reminded me of how much I'd missed the freedom to go wherever I liked, with no one trying to hold me back. I kept a close eye on Mama, Emi, and Yukari, alert for any moment when all three would be so distracted by their own chores that each of them thought one of the others was minding me.

At first, I was caught more times than I managed to get away. Climbing down the ladder was the hardest part of making my escape. If I had a handful of rice for every time I was partway down and heard "Himiko! What do you think you're doing? Come back *right now*!" I could have fed our whole village for a year.

My failed flights made me more determined. I became stealthier, quieter, quicker. By the time the last autumn days waned, I found myself enjoying those solitary escapes better than the few times Aki took me back to the maple grove. What a shame that the challenge of evading Mama and the others was soon gone! It was becoming almost *too* easy for me to slip out of our house and off by myself before anyone missed me. When I came back at sunset, I got a scolding or three, and a lecture about what an ungrateful girl I was to vanish like that, leaving my whole family desperately worried about me.

My whole family? That was hardly true.

"What are you thinking, Himiko, running away every day and putting yourself into all sorts of danger!" Mama's voice was shrill as she chided me over our bamboo dinner platters. "Are you *trying* to kill me with worry?"

"Where do you go?" Yukari chimed in. "It had better not be the carp pond. You'll lean over too far and fall in, and *then* what will you have to say for yourself?"

"Blub-blub-blub," Masa whispered, and for the first time in far too many days, Father and my brothers laughed.

"It's not funny." Emi slapped her thighs. "We do everything for this child. She doesn't have to lift a finger. She's a pampered little princess, but does she appreciate it? *No!*" She slapped her thighs again.

"I know where she goes," Mama said, lifting her chin and giving me a withering look. "She scurries off to play with the other little girls."

Is that *what you think, Mama?* I forced myself not to laugh. Hadn't she been right there on the one day those girls came to visit me? Didn't she see how little we had to say to one another, or how relieved all of us were when I pretended to be tired and gave them an excuse to go? *Grown-ups never notice anything important,* I thought.

"And what's wrong with that?" Father finally intervened. "She's a child; she should play with other children."

"But *how* do those children play?" Mama countered. "How do we know those girls aren't throwing rocks, or stealing sharp things from the blacksmith's forge, or sneaking out of the village gates to hunt mushrooms in the woods, without knowing the good ones from the bad?"

Father raised one eyebrow. "Is that how *you* used to

play? All I remember is seeing you and the other girls arranging each other's hair or pretending to cook stew for your dolls. Did you wait until no one was watching before you started throwing rocks?"

His words made the boys snicker, which made Mama even angrier. "Oh, it's easy for *you* to make light of all this. You're not the one who spends half your days wondering where your daughter's gone."

Father leaned toward me and patted my shoulder. "I trust my daughter to take care of herself."

"She took *fine* care of herself when she climbed the sacred pine tree."

He ignored her sarcastic tone. "Himiko is no fool. She *learned* from her accident. Am I right, little one?" I nodded vigorously.

Mama wasn't convinced. "*What* did she learn? Not to climb trees! But that won't stop her from trying all the other ways to gamble with her life."

Father's good-natured smile vanished. He glowered at Mama so fiercely that she drew back as if he'd made a fist, even though he had never so much as raised a hand against any of us. "Woman, *listen* when I speak. You see dangers under every leaf. If Himiko listens to you, soon she'll be too terrified to leave the house! My daughter isn't a mouse that trembles in the corners; she's a princess of the Matsu, nobly born, the child of warriors! You, *all* of you"—he glared at his three wives—"will let her come and go the way she did before her fall. I trust her good sense, and I want her to be *strong,* is that understood?"

"Whatever you want, Husband." Mama's lips curled

into the strangest smile. When she replied to Father, her words were humble, but that mocking expression turned them into blades. "We all know how much you value strong women—women like Lady Tsuki."

Yukari gasped. Emi covered her mouth with her hands. Aki, Masa, Shoichi, and I exchanged puzzled looks. Why had Mama's words affected our stepmothers so? The two younger women seemed ready to run and hide.

Then I looked at Father. His face was dark with fury, his eyes slits. I could feel anger pouring off him in waves. For my brothers and me, this was a thousand times worse than any of Father's past rages because he said nothing, only let us feel the intensity of his wrath grow hotter and hotter, like a sword glowing red, then yellow, then blinding white in the blacksmith's forge. The longer he remained silent, the faster Mama's taunting smile dwindled until she looked as fearful as our stepmothers. When he stood up, she drew back swiftly, as if she believed he was about to lunge at her and strike her for the first time.

Then Father spoke, and it had the impact of a storm's first lightning strike: "Speak about her again, and you can find another house." He walked out the door, his food untouched, leaving Yukari and Emi to rush to Mama's side and hold her while she wept.

That was a dismal meal. My brothers and I were the only ones with the appetite for it. Every bite I took was tasteless until Mama wiped her eyes, sat up straight, and put on a calm expression.

"Himiko, is your food good?" she asked as if nothing

had happened. I nodded hesitantly. "Then I want to see you *enjoying* it. Don't fret about me or your father. It doesn't concern you."

"But I— If I hadn't run off so much, and made you worry—"

She waved my words away. "That's over."

"You heard your father," Emi said in her soft voice. "You are to come and go as you like. Play with the other children."

"The other girls," Yukari corrected her. "All we ask is that you don't take reckless chances. Please."

I promised them all that I'd be careful, and that I'd always come home before sunset. It was a very solemn moment until Masa ruined it by creeping up to me and whispering, "But don't forget to feed the carp. *Blub-blub-blub!*" and I pushed him over backward onto the dishes.

Father didn't come home that night, or at least not until after I'd gone to sleep. He was there the next morning when I woke up. He spoke courteously to Mama and his other wives, and they answered with respect, but without fear. The family uproar I'd caused the night before had worked a crude magic, destroying the cold, wordless days since my baby brothers' deaths and restoring the old ways. Our home was no longer silent, but it was at peace.

I got dressed as quickly as I could and ate breakfast with the rest of the family. At the end of our meal, Father told my brothers where they'd be working that day. "Masa, you like to joke about the carp pool. Let's see if you can help us tend to the fish and keep it clean for them."

"Can we catch some?" Masa asked, eyes shining.

"Soon. We'll be harvesting some for drying before long."

Shoichi made a face. "I like fresh carp better than dried."

"You'll like dried well enough, once winter comes," Father said gruffly, and herded my brothers away.

I started to help Mama, Yukari, and Emi clean up after breakfast. Before that was done, Yukari touched my sleeve, said "Run along now, Himiko," and sent me on my way with an encouraging smile.

What a sweet sensation, to be free! Free of the long silence, free of the shadows, free of the need to dodge Mama and my stepmothers just so I could have time to myself! I wanted that time very badly. Every one of my stolen moments had gone to exercising my legs, teaching them to answer my demands obediently. It hadn't been enough: I could walk more steadily, and I could climb up and down the house ladder without a misstep, but running was still beyond me.

And as for dancing—! I hadn't forgotten that dream. It would be mine, someday, but . . . when?

I'd have to work harder. Maybe it *would* help if I joined the other little girls. Before my accident, I'd enjoyed their company most when we ran races or played catch-me-if-you-can games. I was one of the fastest in our small group, winning so many of our contests that being first lost its thrill. Now just being able to run again was a challenge. If competing against the other girls could help me achieve it, I'd spend every day with them.

They had other ideas.

I found them in front of Suzu's house. Suzu was the oldest of our small group, almost nine, and was usually the one who chose the games. The others never objected, because she had a nasty talent for using words as weapons. If a girl didn't feel like following her lead, she could make the rest of them turn their backs on her until she gave in and begged to rejoin the group. Suzu always made her wait many days for that. Until then, the unhappy little girl was treated as if she'd turned into air.

I was the sole exception to Suzu's absolute rule. The few times I wanted to play a different game than the one she'd chosen, she rushed to say that my idea was *much* better, or that the game I'd just mentioned was exactly the one she'd meant to choose in the first place. Though I didn't know why I got such special treatment, I was satisfied to accept it without question. As I approached the group, I saw no reason to suspect that anything had changed.

Suzu's parents weren't nobles. Their family home wasn't built on tall pillars, like ours, but was a deep, square pit with an artfully thatched roof over it. She was seated with her back to the low doorway, holding her baby sister on her lap. When she saw me, she smiled and said, "Look who it is, everyone. You're back, Himiko."

What was it about her greeting that made me stop short and feel a splinter of uneasiness slip under my skin? Why was her smile so tight and cold, a grimace that lifted only one side of her mouth and never touched her eyes?

"Hello, Suzu," I said slowly. "What are we doing today?"

"*I'm* taking care of Tami," Suzu said, hugging her sister so tightly to her chest that the baby squirmed and whimpered. "My friends are helping me."

"I'll help too." I was hoping the girls would be playing something a bit more active, but maybe that would happen later, when the baby napped. "Do you want me to hold her for you?"

"No." Suzu's unnerving smile twisted tighter. No one else said a word.

"Oh. All right." I wondered what kind of strange new game Suzu was forcing everyone to play that day. I decided to take a place with the other girls until I could find out. As soon as I sat down, they all sidled away, their eyes darting back and forth between Suzu and me.

"You can't sit *there,*" Suzu declared gleefully.

"Why not?"

"Because it's too close to *my* house."

"But why can't I—?"

She pointed one grubby finger at me. "Because you're bad luck, and we don't want bad luck to come near Tami, *that's* why! Go away, Himiko!"

Her reply left me too shocked to do more than gape at her, watching in stunned silence as her smirk widened into a full, gloating grin. She enjoyed every cruel word she poured over me: "What's the matter, Himiko? Did you break your head too? I told you, go *away.* I don't want you near Tami. I love my baby sister *so* much." To prove it, she gave the baby such a tight squeeze that the little one shrieked. Suzu glared at Tami, then at me. "*Now* see what

you did? She was fine until you got here. You're worse than
bad luck: you're *cursed*."

"I am *not*." Her bizarre claims let me find my voice.
"You're crazy."

She laughed, and the other four girls echoed her,
weakly but dutifully. "You're *stupid*," she countered. "Too
stupid to know you're cursed, but everyone else does! Demons follow you—big, ugly demons with tusks and warts
and horns and smashed-in faces. That's why you climbed
up the sacred tree—to hurt our clan guardian and make
your demons laugh—but it didn't work! The pine tree spirit
was stronger, and he threw you down. You should have
died, except *they* caught you and saved you. Stupid demons.
I wish you *had* died! My mama says you should've been
punished the way you deserved, but you got away with it
because you're the chieftain's daughter, and now the pine
tree spirit's angry at all of us, and everything bad that happens from now on is *your* fault."

"Oh, shut up, Suzu!" I shouted. "*You're* the stupid one.
I didn't make anyone mad. All I did was climb a tree."

"The clan *guardian's* tree!" Suzu shouted back, startling
her baby sister into earsplitting yowls. "You put your dirty
hands and feet all over him and his home, and—"

"*It's only a tree!*" I yelled louder, to make myself heard
over the baby's shrieks and sobs. "A tree like all the others!
A *tree!*"

Suzu's mouth hung open. The other girls looked
equally horrified. What had I said to get such a reaction?

I soon found out: "I'm *telling*," Suzu said. "You don't

believe our guardian exists! You just wait, Himiko. As soon as everyone knows what you said, it's not going to matter that you're the chieftain's daughter, you're going to be *punished*." She relished that word.

I leaned back on my heels and began to stand up. My heart was beating bird-wing fast. "I didn't say that," I replied, trying to keep my voice from letting Suzu know how deeply her threat had scared me.

"Oh yes you *did*." She wasn't going to let go. "We all heard it. Right?" She looked at the other girls, who nodded their heads obediently. "And we're *all* going to tell." They nodded again.

"But it's not true!"

Suzu laughed. "Go away, Himiko," she commanded. "We don't want you! No one wants you." She turned to her followers and barked, "Don't just sit there; *make* her go before it's too late! If anything happens to my baby sister on account of her, it'll be your fault too, and I'll get Tami to haunt you until you *die*!"

Dumbstruck, I watched my former playmates stumble hastily to their feet and come at me, their hands outstretched as if they intended to shove me all the way back to my house. I stood my ground. I didn't want to stay where I was, but I refused to let Suzu drive me away. I'd go when *I* said it was time to go. When the first pair of hands touched me, I made a fist and swung.

As Suzu looked on, bouncing her sobbing baby sister on her knees, I was surrounded by a cloud of flailing arms as my former playmates lashed out in a storm of slaps that wound up hitting one of them more often than me. I had better luck, jabbing my fists into the crowd, driving my attackers back a few steps, and actually managing to knock one of them down. The unlucky girl's name was Ume, and she was such a skinny, fragile thing that I felt a pang of regret the instant after I hit her. The sight of her, holding her bleeding nose and blubbering, made the other girls drop their hands to their sides and skitter away from me. Suzu was *not* pleased.

"Cowards! You can't do anything right. Here!" She got up and plopped her baby sister into the weeping girl's lap. I'd forgotten how tall Suzu was, and how big. Her body made mine look like a tangle of thread next to the gnarled roots of a full-grown cypress tree. She strode toward me, a mountain ogre hungry for my bones, her upraised fist a club, ready to strike me down. "I told you, *go away!*"

I punched her in the stomach before she could hit me. I put as much strength as I had into it, and was astonished to see how just one blow made my formidable enemy topple, doubled up on the ground. Suzu gasped, tears swimming in her eyes. Her face contorted into a mask scarier than any demon, and when she caught her breath, her sobs roared out like a windstorm.

I didn't wait to see anything else; I spun around and hobbled off as swiftly as I could.

"*Demon!*" Suzu screeched after me. "That's why you can't walk like real people, because you're a demon! The spirits hate you, and they hate your family for not punishing you, and *that's* why your baby brothers died! You're cursed, and your family's cursed, and it's all your fault that—!"

I pressed my hands to my ears and strained to go even

more quickly, to escape the words that burned my heart to ashes. It was no use; I couldn't summon up a faster gait. I was shackled by my injured leg, forced to endure Suzu's cruel accusations for almost longer than I could bear.

I drove myself on until I was beyond the reach of her voice. I hadn't consciously chosen which way to go, only to *go*, so that when I did stop, I found myself deep underneath one of the village storehouses. Alone among the piles of empty clay pots, I leaned against a pillar, panting. My injured leg ached so badly that I wanted to cry, but I couldn't. Suzu's hateful words throbbed in my ears and tied my belly into knots, but left my eyes hot and dry.

I remembered how she'd come to visit me when I was recovering from my accident. We didn't have much to say to one another, but she'd smiled sweetly and told me that all my friends hoped I'd get well soon. The rest of the girls smiled and added their agreement and nodded at everything she said.

They'd nodded even more energetically today, when she'd turned against me. What had changed? What had I done? If she hated me for climbing our guardian pine, why had she come to visit me at all? I felt dizzy. A huge storage pot lay on its side near my pillar. It was half sunk into the earth, so it must have been there a long time, discarded and forgotten. I sat down cautiously on its curved side and tried to figure out what had just happened, but not a single answer came.

"Himiko? Are you here?" A low, shaky whisper came from just beyond the shadows under the storehouse. I thought I recognized the voice, except it couldn't be—

"Ume?" Why had she come after me? She was Suzu's creature, and I'd bloodied her nose. *She's going to bring the rest of them here,* I thought, and prepared to defend myself a second time.

"Yes, it's me." She crept nearer. "I'm glad I found you."

"Did Suzu send you?" I asked suspiciously. "Are you going to tell her where I am?"

In the darkness under the storehouse, I could just make out Ume shaking her head. "When you ran away, she told the rest of us to let you go. When our parents come home, we're supposed to tell them that you don't believe in the gods, and that's going to be better than teaching you a lesson ourselves." She dropped her voice even lower and muttered, "I think she was afraid that if she chased you, you'd hit her again. You hit *hard.*"

She was trying to hit me, *Ume,* I thought. *And so were you.* But what I said was "Does your nose still hurt?"

She shrugged, and the shadows made it look like she was a huge, black bird lifting its wings. "Not much, now. Not enough to cry about." She paused. "I thought I heard *you* crying, under here."

"I wasn't," I said firmly. "I don't care how much you and Suzu and everyone else hates me, I'm not going to cry about it."

"We don't all hate you, Himiko," Ume protested. "Only Suzu."

"Why? I didn't do anything to her." *Not until today,* I thought. *And I'd do that again!*

"I know. I don't understand it. Her mama likes you. She's always telling Suzu how smart and pretty and special you are, and if Suzu can't be more like you, she should at least try to play with you every chance she gets, because you're going to be real important one day."

"Important? Me?"

"Oh yes!" There wasn't a flicker of doubt in Ume's voice. "The whole clan knows how much your brother Aki likes you. Everyone says that when it's time for him to marry, he'll pick a wife you like too, and when he becomes chieftain, she'll be the highest lady in the village. That's what makes you so important, see?"

I did see; I wished I didn't. "Suzu pretended to be my friend so she could be a chief's wife one day. How stupid! When he's ready to get married, Aki might listen to Father or Mama, but me?" I laughed bitterly.

"Suzu thought it was a stupid idea too," Ume said. "But her mama didn't." I heard her let out a long sigh. "Now Suzu's happy, because if enough people hear what you said—you know, about the spirits not being real—no one will like you, not even your brother Aki. You won't be important anymore, and then her mama won't want her to be like you or play with you or even talk to you at all."

"And that's exactly what Suzu's always wanted," I concluded.

Ume came closer. I heard her feet kicking aside pieces of broken pottery. "Don't be unhappy, Himiko; I'm going to tell my parents that you never said one word against the gods, and that you *do* believe in them, and that Suzu probably imagined the whole thing." Her hand closed over mine. "I want to be your friend. We can play whenever you want"— her voice dropped—"as long as Suzu doesn't find out."

"Are you *that* afraid of her?" I asked. "Because I'm not."
The only reply I got was an uncomfortable silence. Finally I
said, "All right, Ume. Do you want to come play tomorrow?"

"Yes, please!" She was overjoyed. "What would you like
to do? Should I bring my doll? Will it be early enough if I
come after breakfast?"

"Early enough for what?"

"For Aki to see that now *I'm* your best friend, not Suzu.
Ohhhhh, I wish I was older. By the time we can get married,
he might already have one wife, maybe two, and I don't want
to be a junior—"

I pulled my hand away from hers and staggered out
into the daylight. I heard her calling after me, but I kept
going, never looking back. I didn't stop until I was up the
ladder, inside my house, and curled in a corner, crying.

Mama and my stepmothers flocked around me, demanding to know what was the matter. I refused to explain,
and so they waited until Father and the boys came home
and begged them to discover the reason for my misery.

By that time, I'd stopped crying. Suzu's meanness and
Ume's offer of false friendship were buried, no longer a
sharp pain but a lesson and a memory. I was able to turn a
smiling face to Father when he sat down to question me
about my tears.

"It was nothing," I told him cheerfully.

"Ah." He stroked his chin. "All right, then. Let's eat."

"Is that all you're going to say?" Mama objected. "If you
could have heard how loudly she was sobbing when she
came home this afternoon, it would have broken your heart."

"Probably so. Children *cry*, woman. They cry and they

stop crying, and unless they're sick or injured, it's nothing for us to bother about. She's not crying now, is she?"

"It doesn't mean—"

"Then that's that. It's over." There was no further argument allowed when Father used *that* tone.

But it wasn't over.

In the days that followed, I stayed close to home. I wasn't afraid of encountering Suzu and the others, but I was scared of running into their parents. What if they had tattled about me to the grown-ups? *Himiko hurt our guardian on purpose! Himiko says the spirits don't exist! Himiko's going to make the gods angry and curse us all!*

Would any of our clanfolk believe them? And if they did, what would they do about it? What would they say to me if we met? In my mind, I conjured up one outcome after another, all of them terrifying. The grown-ups of my imagination did everything from scream at me to throw stones.

The worst part was knowing that some of what Suzu and the rest said was . . . true. Since my fall, I hadn't heard the voices of the spirits in my dreams. I no longer called the ancient pine Grandfather. I saw it as nothing more than just an old, empty tree.

If one of the grown-ups were to ask me straight out whether I believed in the spirits, what would I do? Tell the truth or take refuge in a lie? I didn't know, and that made me even more afraid. I chose to hide from the village instead, in my home or under it.

You can learn many things from a good hiding place. It

wasn't long before I had the luck to overhear Father confronting Suzu's parents when they came to tell him what I'd done. The three of them stood at the foot of the ladder leading up to our house's platform and never knew I was taking in everything from behind one of the pillars.

Father let Suzu's parents speak freely. Her mother did most of the talking. Her father put in a word now and then, but mostly he just nodded.

When they were done, Father spoke. "Is that so?" he said. "Your daughter tells you that mine rejects the gods?" He sounded calm, the way the air feels right before a thunderstorm breaks.

"We thought you should know about it," Suzu's mother said primly. "This is *very* serious. We're concerned about the child."

"You should be," Father replied. "She's a liar."

Suzu's father sucked in his breath sharply. "You can't mean it! A sweet-faced little girl like Himiko, a liar?"

"I'm not talking about Himiko," Father said, and without warning burst into a fierce rant, berating Suzu's parents for taking the word of an eight-year-old about something so important. "By the gods, do you let your *child* rule the house? Do her words drive you here and there, like chickens? Little girls quarrel all the time; even I know this! And when they do, they try to turn their enemies into monsters. But you took your daughter's wild words *seriously*? Incredible. Are you fools, or have you lost your minds?"

Suzu's parents fled. Her mother was wailing. I couldn't help hoping that things would go badly for Suzu when they got home, but I never heard anything about it. More days passed, and no others came to accuse me; that was all that mattered.

Winter drifted over our village with a light dusting of snow and a faint chill that turned breath to mist. I played alone, except for those times when Aki could spend time with me, or when Masa and Shoichi were so bored that my company was better than nothing. When the weather wasn't too cold and while sunlight lasted, I continued with my plan to exercise my leg, trying to walk more steadily, working hard toward the day when I'd be able to run.

That day didn't come, and no matter how diligently I practiced, I never quite lost a small hitch and hobble when I walked. At last I realized that if a broken walk was the best I would ever be able to manage, why should I even try to dance? I turned away from my dreams.

My home and my family became my world. They were all that I could trust to never let me down—not like my own body, or my so-called friends, or the supposed spirits. If I'd said such things aloud, other people might have thought that my life had grown empty and sad. The truth was, I felt relieved. Everything was simpler. Why break my heart trying to reach a goal that might always remain beyond me? It was better to enjoy the things I *knew* I could have. That was what I told myself, anyway.

I wasn't a hunter. I wasn't a dancer. I wasn't someone who wasted time fretting over the whims of beings who might or might not exist at all.

I was Mama's helpful, reliable child. I was Father's good, obedient girl. I was Aki's favorite. I was Yukari and

Emi's darling, indulged and cuddled and fussed over and told twenty times a day how pretty I was.

I smiled and laughed and sang and did what was expected of me. I didn't ask questions. I was Himiko, the chieftain's daughter, and someday I would be a Matsu nobleman's senior wife.

I was supposed to be happy.

4

SPIRITS OF THE FOREST

Two full turns of the seasons passed. I didn't miss having friends. After all, I hadn't spent much time with them before Suzu showed her true nature. If our paths happened to cross, I made sure to give my former playmates a smile that shouted in their faces, *Who needs you? Not me!*

I saved my real smiles for my family, Aki above all. When it became clear that I had no more friends among the village children, he took every opportunity to fill that empty spot in my life. I was so pleased to have more of my beloved brother's attention that I never told him how little I missed Suzu and the rest. I treasured each moment he spent with me, but some occasions were more special than others.

One morning of my ninth year, I awoke to a wonderful sight framed in our doorway: almost overnight the breath of springtime had blown the cherry trees on the distant hillside into a soft froth of blossom. I'd grown up witnessing this spectacle year after year, yet every time was as glorious as the first. When I saw them at their peak like that, a splash of wind-tossed pink against the new greenery, I clapped my hands, knowing today would be wonderful.

"Oh, so you've finally decided to wake up, eh, Little Sister?" Aki's familiar voice sounded behind me. My oldest brother dropped to one knee by the side of my bedroll, a quiver full of arrows on his back, his bow in one hand. "Everyone else is out of the house, and I'm about to go too."

"Not without me!" I cried, gesturing toward the doorway. "Look there, Aki: the cherry trees are all covered with flowers. You took me to see them up close when that happened last year, so you have to do it again."

"Oh, do I?" he asked, teasing.

"Yes." I was firm. "This is *our* day! I know it's a long walk to reach them, but I won't take much time to get ready, I promise." I reached for my clothes, spread out at the foot of my bedding, and slipped my tunic over my head.

My brother looked uncomfortable. "I'm sorry, Little Sister, *our* day will have to wait. You're such a good girl, I hate saying no to you about anything, but we can't do this today."

"Why *not*?"

"You know why, Himiko," Aki said soothingly. "You were here yesterday when Emi's uncle brought word that he'd spied a wolf pack near our fields. Luckily, most of our clan was out planting the new rice, and they made enough noise to send the beasts fleeing toward Cypress Mountain. You heard Father say we'd be sending a hunting party after them."

"*Wolves—that's all we need.*" Father's grim words ran

through my memory. *"A bad winter's left them hungry and much too bold. If we let them come so close to our village unchallenged, the next thing you know, they'll be over the ditch and inside the palisade. I won't allow it! We don't raise our pigs and chickens to feed wolves."*

"That doesn't mean *you* have to go, Aki," I protested. "Father has plenty of other hunters; he doesn't need you. He's not even here! I'll bet he's already left the village!"

"I know he has," Aki replied. "That's the plan. I helped him work it out last night, after everyone else was asleep. He's leading the older hunters up the eastern mountain trail right now, and I'm going to bring the younger ones around by the western way. It's steeper, and the winter's probably crumbled the path in places, but we have to be ready to outflank the wolf pack if they flee Father's men by that route."

He stood up and slung his bow over his back. "I'm *supposed* to be late to this hunt so that the wolves don't sense too many men on the mountain at once. We want them dead or driven far away, not scared into hiding. It'll be no good if they den up today and come back to our village tomorrow." His teeth flashed in the shadows of our house. "Don't you fret about any of this, Little Sister. I wouldn't want you to be afraid that a wolf will come prowling after you."

"*I'm* not afraid. I only want—"

He spoke on as though I'd never opened my mouth. "We shouldn't be gone more than a day or two. You be good and wait patiently"—he patted my cheek—"and, I promise, the two of us will have our day together soon."

I had no chance to say another word to him before he bounded out of the house. By the time I followed him onto the porch, he was down the ladder and racing through the village, summoning other young men to join him as he ran.

I knelt on the boards and watched him go. I had a fine view from up so high and saw my other brothers, Masa and Shoichi, join his hunting party. After two years, Shoichi had gotten better at handling weapons, but Masa was still unskilled. In spite of that, he was allowed to be a part of the wolf hunt, while I was left behind like a baby's discarded toy.

I tried to console myself. *Oh, so what? This doesn't involve me. I'm no hunter; I'll never be one. Why should I care if Masa—?*

But it's not fair! The words burst inside my head with such force, it was as though a mountain ogre had bellowed them in my ears. *I'm tired of being treated as if I were helpless. I hate being nothing more than the* good *girl, the* cheerful *girl, the* pretty *girl. Is that* all *I'll ever be?*

I turned my eyes toward the great pine tree. "This is *your* fault," I muttered, before I remembered that it was only bark and wood and fragrant needles. Still grumbling, I climbed down the ladder and began to walk aimlessly through the village.

At that time of day, in that season, nearly everyone was off working in the fields. Our village was like a land of ghosts, with only the smoke from the potter's kiln and the blacksmith's forge to show that people lived there. I paused on the path between those two places, wondering what to do. I thought about going to watch the potter at her work, but she was a sour-tempered woman. When she was in a bad mood, she'd order everyone to go away and leave her alone. If they lingered, she'd throw gobs of clay at them. The blacksmith was friendlier. He liked having someone there to chat with while he worked, but the forge was such a hot, noisy, smelly place that I always thought twice before paying a visit.

Rough laughter sounded at my back. "What do we have here? Has the earth given birth to fresh stones?" I spun around to see our shaman's grinning face. "You've been standing here long enough to take root, Himiko. Don't you have somewhere to be? Something to do? Or are you trying to make the Matsu clan into a smaller version of the Mirror Kingdom, where the princesses do nothing all day but sing?" The old woman forced her voice into a high, squeaky trill and warbled nonsense words, then laughed again.

"I—I don't know the Mirror Kingdom," I said, trying and failing to hide how nervous her presence made me feel. A shaman's magic came from her control over the spirits. Even if I doubted their existence, something about Yama made me hesitate to question her power.

"No, why would you?" Yama reached for her sash and untied a small bronze mirror hanging from it by a silk cord. "It's the name I've chosen for that vast land to the west, the place *this* came from, and many more like it." She offered me the mirror, but I made no move to take it. My timidity made her chuckle. "Afraid, Himiko? Not what I'd expect from you. You attack our guardian spirit, you break his old bones, you declare that he's nothing but a tree, that the spirits are smoke and dreams, that the gods are nothing more than stories, but you're scared to touch a mirror?"

She reattached it to her sash. "Well, I suppose you have a point. If you looked into it, you might see something *truly* frightening."

I was becoming more and more bewildered. "I didn't— I didn't attack the pine—I mean, our guardian spirit. I only wanted to show Aki that I could—"

Yama held up one hand to silence me. "No need to defend yourself, Himiko; I'm joking. Tell me this instead: Why are you standing here alone, little stone child? Why aren't you in the fields with everyone else? You look as if you like to *eat* rice well enough, so hadn't you better help plant it?"

I lowered my eyes, ashamed. "I want to, Lady Yama, but it's not possible."

"Ha!" Her bark of laughter made me look up sharply. "Try that excuse on someone who hasn't known you since you were born. Oh, *that* was a day full of impossibilities!"

Impossibilities? When I was very small, I'd asked my mother to tell me the story of my birth, but she'd never used that word to describe it. She did tell me that there had been an earth tremor, but such things were no rarity in our land, and most certainly *not* impossible. "What do you mean, 'impossibilities'?" I asked.

"I want to tell you"—a mocking smile curved her thin lips—"but it's not possible."

Her gibe stung. I turned my back on her and began to walk away.

"Where do you think you're going?" Yama's hand closed on my shoulder like a hawk's talons. She forced me to face her again. "Have I angered you? *Tell* me so!"

"I can't—" I began.

"*That* again?" she spat disdainfully.

"—because you are our shaman, Lady Yama, and my parents would be angry at me if I was rude to you."

Her frown faded. "I seem to remember a little girl who didn't worry so much about what would make her parents mad," she replied. "Unless she thought that climbing that pine would please them?" This time she gave me a friendly look that seemed to say, *You and I know better, don't we?* I couldn't help smiling shyly in return. Softening her voice, she said, "You've changed since then, Himiko. You used to be a bold child—not foolhardy, but adventurous. Now I seldom see you far from your house, and never at work in the fields. Is this my fault? Did I heal your leg so badly that you lost your freedom?"

I shook my head vigorously. "Oh no, Lady Yama! I can stand and walk and I *know* I can help with the crops, but—but Mama won't let me. She told Father that I'd wear myself out tending the plants. She reminded him that I can't run anymore and said field work would make my bad leg so stiff I wouldn't be able to walk, either. She wouldn't stop talking until Father agreed with her and forbade me to do it."

"May the gods bless your home with a new infant before your mother turns you back into one. Although"—she sighed—"maybe it's too late. Every part of a baby's life is controlled by her parents, but what choice does she have? She *can't* speak up, and you—" Her gaze pierced me. "Have you ever tried? In two years, have you *once* attempted to make your father change his mind?" I didn't answer, which made her nod and say, "That's what I thought. Your mother must have bragged to everyone in this clan about what a *good* child you've become." She shook her head glumly. "I wish she could call you a *happy* child instead."

"I'm happy," I said automatically.

Yama raised one eyebrow. "All alone in the middle of the village with nothing to do? Oh yes, *that's* happiness!"

"Well, I *would* have been happy today," I replied. "Aki and I were going to see the cherry trees." I gestured toward the distant wave of flowering trees and told Yama all about the wolf hunt, and our broken plans, and my disappointment. I was still in awe of her position and her powers, but something about our shaman made me also feel that here was someone to whom I could open my heart.

When I was done, the shaman rested her hands on my shoulders. "Why do you let your happiness depend on what others can do for you, Himiko? Soon you'll be grown up. Will you still spend your days then waiting for them to bring you what you desire?"

"I don't do that!" I protested.

Yama gave me a sad smile. "Then tell me: what are you doing now? Take the easy path too long and one day you won't even be able to tell the difference between what you want and what you're told you *must* want. Or has that already happened?" She clapped her hands loudly, the way she did at clan rituals when she wanted to command the attention of the spirits. "May the gods grant that isn't so!" she called out to the sky, and with that, she strode briskly away.

I wanted to follow her, but she moved too fast, slipping from my sight when she turned the corner of the nearest pit house. How infuriating! In my mind, I saw myself doing the impossible—running to catch up to her and tell her she was wrong, wrong, *wrong*! I wasn't an infant. I wasn't helpless. I *could* make my own choices, I *would* live my own life. Above all, I knew what I wanted, and I wouldn't let anyone—not Mama or Father or Aki—hand it to me as a gift or keep it out of my reach because they decided I shouldn't have it.

What I wanted most that day was to prove myself, to be more than someone's *good* little daughter, *good* little sister, *good* little girl. How would I do that? The answer called out to me from the distant hillside where the blushing petals of the cherry trees were dancing along the dark branches.

Two years of surrender vanished. My slumbering ambition awoke. I didn't need Aki to take me to see the flowers. I could—I *would* do it myself!

There was no one to stop me as I left our village. If the lone watchman in our lookout tower saw me, he must have assumed I was headed to the fields, where everyone else was hard at work. I certainly acted as if that were my goal. My heart began to beat faster as I crossed the wooden bridge spanning the ditch beyond our palisade. I wanted to turn my head to see if the watchman was looking in my direction, but I forced myself to keep my eyes forward. My plan was to continue a short distance down the road to the rice paddies, then make a sharp detour and duck into the shelter of a stand of young oak trees. Only then would I look back, when there was no danger of the watchman observing such suspicious behavior.

It felt like it was taking forever for me to reach the oak grove, but at last I stood in the cool shadow of the tender springtime leaves. I leaned against the largest tree there and peered at the top of the watchtower through the greenery. Our sentry was looking elsewhere, toward the snowy peak of that wondrous lone mountain I'd once seen from the top of the ancient pine.

"Thank you, beautiful one," I murmured, forgetting that since I'd set my heart against believing in the spirits, that mountain could be only soulless snow and stone. I turned my eyes toward the next step in my journey—passing through a field of tall, winter-stricken grass to reach the protection of the true forest—and set out as swiftly as my legs would allow.

The grass rustled around me as I walked. I kept my head low and hoped that the spring planting was keeping all my fellow clanfolk occupied in the paddies. So many things could happen that might send someone home early—a broken tool, an ailing baby, an accident—and the road back passed alongside the wind-rippled straw. What would I do if I were spied before I was safely hidden by the trees? Keep moving? Turn back? Freeze where I stood? My thoughts became a jangle of everything that could possibly go wrong. The only thing with the power to silence them was the blessed relief I felt the instant I emerged from the dry grass and stumbled into the sweet shelter of the woods.

I was a little out of breath, but I refused to waste time lingering at the forest's edge. The cherry trees beckoned. I could see them hugging a gentle curve of the hillside just a little farther away than Aki's maple grove. I'd walked that far many times, easily, on the path I'd shared with my big brother. Today I'd take a different path: my own.

I kept well away from the edge of the forest as I made my way toward the blossoming hillside. Sometimes I had to ascend the thickly wooded slope to go around places where the trees grew so closely together that my choices were go into the open or go higher up. If I could still see the sparkling water of the rice fields, I climbed, even if I had to pull myself along by clutching trunk after trunk. Other times the earth spread a soft path of lush moss before me, cool and comforting to my bare feet. Birds chirped and twittered from countless hiding spots among the branches of spruce and fir; I smiled to hear them.

I was well out of sight of our fields by the time the sun reached midday. Filled with confidence, I walked in the open along a strip of ground where the grass was new and green. The need for stealth was gone, and the way forward was clear. In next to no time, I was laughing among my lovely cherry trees.

As pleasant as it was to sit under a roof of flower-laden branches, my stay couldn't last. I'd spent most of the morning reaching this spot and I needed to be home before the sun set, or what would become of me?

At least it won't take me as long to go back as it took to get here, I told myself. *There's no more need to take a hidden trail. I've done what I set out to do; it doesn't matter if someone sees me. I want to be seen! Oh, wouldn't it be perfect if I met Aki on the path and told him what I've done, all by myself? Ha! I can do better than tell him.* I stretched out my hand and broke off a small twig thick with delicate pink flowers. *I'll show him!*

I imagined how Aki would react, then drifted off into more daydreams where he and Father looked at me with new eyes. I wouldn't be Himiko-the-good-girl anymore, but something better: Himiko-the-strong, Himiko-the-self-reliant, Himiko-the-free! Mama would squawk about it, and both Yukari and Emi would join in, but that wouldn't matter. In fact, I believed that they were happiest when they had an excuse to fuss.

Best of all, I'd bring my branch of blossoms to our shaman's doorway and call for her to come out and see what I'd accomplished. Let her try claiming I was an infant then!

A sudden pang in my belly jerked me back into the real world. "Oh!" I said out loud. "I'm hungry." I'd been so wrapped up in my fantasies that the uncomfortable sensation took me by surprise. Now the insistent rumblings from my stomach demanded attention. Unfortunately, there was nothing I could do to silence them. I'd set out on my own without pausing to take food or water with me. When Aki used to bring me to the maple grove, he'd taken care of such things. If I grew hungry or thirsty, rice balls and water were simply *there* for me, as if by magic. Now my hunger and thirst were no one's problem but mine.

I started down the hillside, grumbling. Why had I rushed out of our village so impulsively? I knew where I was going, so why hadn't I taken a little time to provide food and drink for my journey, even though it wasn't anywhere near as long as the wolf hunt that Father and my brothers were—?

The wolf hunt. A sharp awareness made me stop short. *I forgot about the wolves! I'm out here alone, I can't run, I can't climb out of harm's way, I didn't even think to bring a knife, and there are wolves roaming these mountains!* I covered my mouth with one hand, stifling a gasp of dread, and fought back the avalanche of panicky thoughts cascading over me. *What can I do? What can I do?*

I closed my eyes and, without thinking, began to pray to the spirits for help and mercy. When I realized what I was doing, I shook my head forcefully, as if that could free me from them. *Why am I doing such a silly thing?* I thought. *Silly and useless! If the spirits were ever there for us, why did they let me fall from the pine? Why did they give me a crooked leg and steal my dream of dancing? Why did they refuse to save my baby brothers? I brought myself here, and I can bring myself safely home again. I will!*

Anger crushed my wild fears of encountering the wolf pack and let me steady myself. "Aki said the beasts ran off toward Cypress Mountain. That's all the way on the other side of our village, nowhere near me!" I said out loud. The sound of a human voice, even if it was just mine, was a great comfort in the forest solitude. Holding my branch of cherry blossoms, I walked on.

The way home should have been faster and simpler than my path to the flowery hillside. There was no longer any need to worry about being discovered by one of my kinsmen. To tell the truth, I would have welcomed running into someone from our village, especially if he was carrying a clay flask of water. I was so thirsty! Finding food could wait, no matter how loudly my empty belly complained, but my parched throat refused to let me delay searching for something to drink.

I remembered seeing a narrow mountain stream on my way from the village. I'd come across it not too long before

I reached the maple grove. It wasn't much more than a trickle of water running among smooth black and gray rocks, but it would be enough to soothe my thirst. I wished I'd paid attention to the direction of the little stream as it followed its downhill course, but because it lay in my path, I'd only concentrated on getting to the other side without falling.

Aki's voice spoke in my memories from a time when he was entertaining me with tales of his exploits as a hunter: *"Up in the mountains, streams, creeks, and young rivers can play tricks on you, Little Sister. One moment they're in plain sight, the next they hide themselves behind a wall of trees, or lose themselves in a tangle of rocks or roots or undergrowth, or dive beneath the earth itself. Water can be the most elusive prey of all."*

Maybe so, I thought. *But I will find it.*

I wish it had been that effortless! If confidence had magical power, I'd have found the stream only a stone's throw from where I stood, but that wasn't how things happened. I had to try retracing my steps, which wasn't easy. There were places where my feet left clear prints over crushed moss, but others where the thick layer of fallen leaves and pine needles made it impossible to tell if that had been my path. I trudged on, sometimes hopeful, sometimes discouraged, and always growing more and more weary. If I saw a spot farther up the mountain where the trees grew more sparsely, I climbed, seeking a better view. If I heard a loud rustling in the brush ahead of me, I spun around and fled, imagining it was the sound of a wild boar, or a bear, or a even a mountain ogre!

In the end, I did find water, though it wasn't the shallow

stream I'd been seeking. As I emerged from yet another thicket of evergreens, I saw the most beautiful sight: a foaming waterfall plunging from a low ledge into a stone basin. The sound of those rushing waters was sweeter than any song. I'd heard it calling to me while I was still threading a path through the pines, but believed it was no more than wishful thinking. How glad I was to see that it was real! I sank gratefully to my knees beside the shining pool, laid my branch of cherry blossoms to one side, and scooped up handful after handful of cool relief, drinking until my stomach felt ready to burst. I splashed water over my face and laughed with joy at the welcome touch of the stray breeze that dried my skin. I didn't think I could ever feel happier.

As I wiped the last few droplets from my eyes, I saw a thick clump of mushrooms growing at the foot of a pine tree even larger than our clan's guardian. When Aki brought me to the maple grove, he often pointed out such plants before gathering them to bring home. "Look closely, Himiko," he said, holding one less than a finger's length from my eyes. "Remember what it looks like. Not all mushrooms are good to eat—some can make you sick, some can even kill you—but these are delicious."

I was almost certain that the pine tree mushrooms were the same kind Aki said were good to eat. I picked one and washed the dirt from its base before studying it closely, inhaling its woodsy fragrance, and popping it into my mouth. The rich taste reminded me of how hungry I was. I began to devour the mushrooms until I hadn't left a single one standing. How good they tasted! When I was done, I leaned against the pine tree and sighed, content. My belly was full, my legs were tired, the sound of the waterfall was lulling, and my eyelids began to grow heavy. Without meaning to, I was soon fast asleep.

I woke up to the light of stars peeping through the tree branches and the weak glimmer of a crescent moon. *What a funny dream this is,* I thought just before I realized that it was no dream. I scrambled to my feet and stood swaying as reality struck hard. *No! Oh no! This isn't happening. I can't be—* I let out a little moan of fear, which was swept away by the tumbling stream. *What do I do now?*

I stood there for some time, my blood pounding in my ears louder than the rumble of the waterfall. I could hardly breathe. Then, little by little, a strange sense of calm crept along my bones. *Why am I standing here like a lump of clay?* I thought as my eyes grew more and more accustomed to the meager light. *What good does it do? Being too scared to move won't help me. I need to think. I need to remember more of what Aki told me about the mountains. I'll never be a hunter, but for now I need to have a hunter's skills if I'm going to find my way home.*

I inhaled deeply and filled my body with the breath of the forest. The familiar sweetness of the evergreens steadied me. I looked to the pool beneath the waterfall and saw how it slipped over its bank at one point, becoming a thin stream that glittered by starlight. *Maybe this is where our clan's water comes from,* I thought. *If I follow it, it will bring me to our fields.* I paused long enough to pick up the flowering branch I'd plucked from the stand of cherry trees and set out.

It was a hard road. The streamlet I followed played cruel games with me, snaking through places where the trees grew so massive that they blocked all sight of the sky.

In that intense darkness, I couldn't rely on my eyes. Instead, I had to bend down to catch the slightest whisper of running water to guide me. There were also places where the stream split into two paths and I had to choose which one seemed more likely to lead me home. I chose badly, coming to a spot where the trail stopped and the water seeped into the ground. Retracing my steps took me over the same rocky ground twice, except now I was going uphill. I made a misstep and tumbled hard, scraping my arms on the stones as I broke my fall. I began to cry.

Stop that! I told myself sternly. *It's useless. You're wasting time. Get up! Go!* But I cried anyway, and felt a little better. At least the sound of my sobs filled the silence for a while.

I think that I must have tired myself out again, blundering through the woods that night. I remember waking up a second time, though I had no memory of falling asleep. The sunlit morning mists found me curled up in a hollow at the roots of a great yew tree, my head cradled on one arm, my free hand clutching the cherry branch. When I sat up, I saw a scattering of pink petals on the moss. Only a few flowers still clung to their twigs.

"Ugh, look at that!" I announced in disgust to no one but myself. "It's ruined. If I don't get home soon, all I'll have to show Aki and Lady Yama is a *stick*. And what will that prove?" I stood up, shaking dirt and dead needles from my clothes. I'd gotten my long-ago wish for a more vivid garment: there was hardly a spot of white fabric to be seen on my tunic, now streaked with all the colors of the forest floor.

I soon saw that I had a worse problem than the condition of my trophy branch. As keenly as I searched, I couldn't

find even a trickle of water anywhere near the place where
I'd spent the last of the night. Sunbeams striped the trees,
birdsong trilled through the countless shades of green surrounding me, brilliantly hued beetles lumbered past my
feet, but the stream I'd followed, lost, and followed again
was gone.

I closed my eyes and sighed. "It's all right," I said aloud,
to keep my hopes up. "I don't need the stream to help me
find my way. Our village and our fields lie at the foot of the
mountain. All I have to do is head down and I'll find them.
I'll be home before the sun sets."

I believed what I said; I had to, or lose heart. Starting
down the slope, I pictured our house. Mama would be half
mad with worry—I felt terribly guilty about that—but I was
sure that once she had me in her arms, she'd forget everything except welcoming me home. As the youngest wife,
Yukari would probably be sent to fetch water for my bath
while Emi would carry off my clothes and give them a good
washing. My mouth watered at the thought of the fresh, hot
rice I'd eat, topped with the nicest leftover bits of the dried
fish that had seen us through the winter.

My stomach growled. I was hungry again, and this time
there were no mushrooms along my path, nor anything else
that looked edible. I scanned the trees, hoping to spy a bird's
nest on a low-hanging branch. A few tiny raw eggs would be
better than nothing, but nothing was all I found.

My downward route was not a clear road. At one point,
the slope before me was covered with what looked like a
wide river of rocks, a place where the earth farther up the
mountain had slipped and brought down a tangle of young

trees and loose stones. I lost my footing trying to cross it and landed badly, on my weak leg. My cry of pain echoed hollowly through the trees. Shaken, I stayed where I'd landed for a long time, though in the end I had to reclaim the pitiful remains of my shattered self-confidence and get moving. I crawled back up the slope rather than risk another fall while trying to ford the rock slide. What if I broke a bone again? I wouldn't be able to move at all, and then what would become of me? I had no one to help me. The full, dreadful impact of how alone I was chilled my heart. I gulped hard to hold back my tears.

All that day I walked a weaving path that led me up and down and across the mountain. There were places where it cut like a knife between banks of earth and stone and tree roots looming more than twice my height. In spite of my desperate situation, I grew more and more drawn to the loveliness surrounding me. I never knew what each new step might reveal. Butterflies with sunrise colors on their wings danced past my eyes, swooping over thickets of slowly uncurling ferns. I caught sight of a tiny squirrel, bushy tail twitching as he watched me from the safety of a high branch. The stone I almost trod on turned out to be a turtle at rest, her ancient face slowly emerging from the shadowed haven of her shell to give me a reproachful stare. Still holding tight to my branch of fast-falling cherry blossoms, I saw its petals come to rest on the forest floor amid clusters of white and yellow flowers, dainty as raindrops.

I tasted beauty in the mountains, but the tang of fear was never far. A second setting sun caught me in a place where a slab of rock stood up on end at a steep slant from the ground. It looked like the thatched roof of one of our village's pit houses. I was tired, and I'd learned a hard lesson about the foolishness of trying to travel by night, moon or no moon, starlight or no starlight. I gathered armloads of fallen needles from the ground and heaped them as far back under the slanting rock as I could. With my makeshift mat in place, I broke some young, low-growing branches from the nearby fir trees and used them to screen off my refuge. As the darkness deepened around me, I curled myself up as small as possible, turned my face to the reassuring sturdiness of the stone, tried not to think of wolves, and fell into an exhausted sleep.

I wish I could say that the next day brought me home, but it only took me farther in my wanderings. At least I was able to find another patch of mushrooms, though not enough to do more than take the edge off my hunger. I grew so desperate for food that when I noticed a nest of ants working in the shadow of a fallen tree trunk, I lured some of them onto the broken end of my cherry branch and slid them into my mouth without thinking. Their taste was sharp and hot on my tongue, and the whole experience was so unpleasant I decided that I'd have to be not just hungry but starving before I tried it again.

That night I wasn't lucky enough to find a rocky stronghold. I did the best I could to protect myself, choosing a place where the trees grew thickest and making my nest in the small space in their midst. It was a bad night. The ground under me was lumpy with roots, in spite of the bed of branches I'd laid down once again, and the woods were weirdly quiet, as though a presence greater than the birds and beasts and insects was passing by and commanded their respectful silence.

Afraid to sleep, I sat with my back pressed hard against a tree trunk, my legs drawn up to my chest, both fists clenched so tightly around the cherry branch that for an instant I imagined I heard the tender wood beneath the black bark groan. I *know* I heard my heartbeat throbbing in my ears and the rasp of my breath sounding louder than the roar of a rushing stream in full flood. Peering into the blackness, my eyes glimpsed moving shadows darker than the outlines of the trees. Now and then I caught the flicker of lights that were the indescribable color of sunlight touching dewdrops, but they vanished before I could decide whether they were beautiful or terrifying.

In time, my heart calmed and my eyelids grew heavy. My head nodded, my weary limbs relaxed, and I slumped down to sleep with my head cradled on one arm there amid the tangled roots of the trees. A warm, moist breeze passed over my face just before I dropped entirely from the waking world. It felt like the breath of some monstrous creature, but it carried such a sweet scent of reborn grass and newly opening flowers that I shed my fear like an old cloak and slipped serenely into peaceful dreams.

Early light dappled my face with a pattern of shadows cast by the pine trees that had guarded me through the night. The morning was alive with birdsong and the bright chirr and hum of insects. My bones ached when I stood up and my head was a bit giddy on account of my empty stomach, but at least I was rested.

Much later that day I found a way beyond the dense

growth of evergreens into a more sunlit space where broad-leaved trees flourished. They were young oaks, not the grandfathers but the children of the woodland. I heard squirrels chattering in their branches and laughed to see the antics of a pair of the fluff-tail creatures chasing one another around and around a moss-stained trunk. I wished I could have moved half as nimbly as they, and that I had their knowledge of how to make the forest feed me.

I felt a brief surge of hope when I emerged from the oak grove and stood looking down into a flower-filled valley, scarcely larger than our village. There was something about it that lightened my heart. It reminded me of a cupped hand, freely offering up so much peace and beauty. A few deer grazed in the distance, their sleek brown hides stippled with white as though someone with more than human power had sprinkled them with stars. I sat down on the grass under one of the oaks to watch them and to rest awhile.

As I sat there, a strange feeling came over me. The short hairs at the nape of my neck prickled, and my skin tingled the way it sometimes did in the moments before a thunderstorm broke in fury over our village. There was another presence close to me—I sensed it, though I couldn't explain the sensation. I turned my head slowly and found the answer.

The sharp, red-furred muzzle of a fox was pointed directly at me from less than two arm's lengths away. The beast lolled in the shade of another oak tree, forepaws crossed, regarding me as calmly as if I were just another patch of moss. Suddenly he flicked his ears forward and sprang, pouncing on something in the grass. His snout dipped, and I heard tiny bones crunch. When he raised his nose again, I saw the body of the luckless mouse he'd caught. Three snaps of his jaws and the mouse was gone.

He looked at me again, his eyes glittering with mischief. *Envy me, little human kit? The world feeds us, when we know where to look. You starve in the midst of a feast!*

My mouth opened soundlessly. Had I heard that? I leaned toward him, but he flicked his tail and trotted away.

I *was* starving. How else could I explain having heard the fox speak? When I stood up, I had to lean against the oak tree for support. I laid my head against its bark and watched the deer herd. *They must know where there's water,* I thought. *Even the fox knows. How could any of them live without it? Maybe I can follow them. I won't get too close, just near enough to keep them in sight.*

As I gazed over the little valley, the stag who ruled the herd raised his head and looked at me. *Do I hear you rightly, little fawn? Have you finally grown weary of walking by yourself, of pushing us away?*

"No," I said aloud, beginning to shiver. "I'm not hearing this. I'm *not!*" The last word was a shout. All the deer lifted their heads and stared in my direction, but they stood their ground. Even with so much space between us, their eyes held mine.

My breath grew steadier, my heartbeat slowed. The longer I stared into their deep brown eyes, the calmer I became. My thirst, my hunger, my aching bones, and all my scrapes and bruises faded. The need to shout "No, no, *no!*" at what was happening to me became instead a whisper of words that swirled through me, body, mind, and heart, gently murmuring *Why not?*

There was a faint droning in my ears like insect song. The sound became a spiderweb of silver threads that I could see but also hear and touch. They drifted down over me with the sunlight, looped around me with the valley breezes, crept up from the warm springtime earth like newly sprouted vines. I couldn't move without feeling the tug of those countless threads.

The sensation of being tied fast scared me. *What is this? What's happening to me? I won't be captive, I won't! This is just a bad dream. Let me wake! Let me go!* I closed my eyes and fought to pull free, only to feel the web around me melt like a snowflake. I opened my eyes and raised my hands, turning them slowly. The threads that had held me had vanished, but were not gone. They were—as they had always been—a part of me.

In that moment, so much changed. My mind accepted what my heart had always known: no matter how loudly I denied that they existed, the spirits remained. When anger, bitterness, or sorrow filled me, when the world's unfairness overwhelmed me, I turned from them, but they never turned from me. They were not the cruel, spiteful beings that filled my father with so much fear and anger. They didn't send the fox to kill the mouse because the mouse had done something to offend them. I might never fully understand the reasons for their actions, but who could? Did I even understand my own?

None of that was important. The truth, the comfort

that I felt more strongly than my thirst or hunger or pain, was that they were forever as much a part of us and our world as we were a part of theirs. We shared balance and beauty, the soft breath of spring and the harsh cold of winter. If I was in the heart of my home, surrounded by my family, or here in an unknown land, far from Mama, Father, Aki, and all the rest, still I was not alone.

I never was and never would be alone.

I folded my hands more tightly around the nearly bare cherry branch and walked out of the forest.

5
PEOPLE OF THE DEER CLAN

The spell of wonder that had fallen over me at the edge of the woods lasted only until I'd half walked, half skidded down the green slope. The moment I set foot in the little valley, the stag tossed his head and snorted, then began to trot away. The does followed.

"Wait!" I called plaintively, stretching out my free hand toward them. "Don't go! Not yet!" When I'd shouted at them before, they'd stood firm, but this time my cry startled them into a run. I stumbled after them, begging them to return. They fled beyond my sight in a heartbeat, out of the valley, up the hillside, and into the forest, their white rumps flashing. I stood staring after them, hoping for one last glimpse of their dappled coats through the trees, but the woods had taken them.

I sank down in the grass to catch my breath. My mouth was dry as ashes and my head spun. Almost without my being aware of it, I tilted sideways and was soon stretched full length with my face pressed against the cool earth. My eyelids felt so heavy, I could hardly keep them open. Through the blur of my lashes, I saw that my fingers were still sealed around the branch I'd carried with me every step from the cherry grove. It seemed as though I'd been holding on to it for a dozen seasons. Not a single petal remained.

Oh, that's too bad, I thought dully as my eyes closed. *Now Aki will never believe me when I tell him I walked all that way. What a shame, what a shame, what a . . .*

I slid into unconsciousness as swiftly as I'd slid into the valley.

The sound of an unfamiliar voice woke me. It was low and strong, like the stag's, but there was something softer to it as well, reminding me of my mother. I blinked rapidly and breathed in the smells of dried herbs, steaming hot rice, and cooked meat. I was lying curled up on my side, my face no longer pressed against grass and dirt but the thin cushioning of a bedroll. The tunic I wore smelled very clean, but it was too big for me, and felt coarser against my skin. I squirmed and flipped myself over onto my back, eyes wide, and saw a strange woman's face hovering above me.

"Ah! There you are, little one." Bit by bit, the rest of her came into focus. She was a thick-bodied woman who didn't look much older than Mama, though her face was much more heavily tattooed and her hair was more elaborately looped and braided. Her unfamiliar accent was striking, but that was the sole difference between her speech and mine. "I was concerned that you'd never wake. Here, I want you to try to sit up and drink this." She slid one arm under my back and lifted me upright, setting a shallow bowl to my lips with the other. When I took it from her hand and sipped the thin rice gruel eagerly, she smiled. "Good, that's very good. So you were only hungry and thirsty, nothing worse after all. When I get my hands on Sora, I'll teach him to go spinning tales of demons!" The arm supporting me tightened into a warm hug. "Nothing demonic about you, is there, pretty one?"

I didn't reply right away. I was too busy gulping down the contents of that bowl. Once it was empty, I set it on my knees, took a deep breath, and said, "Demons?"

That made her laugh. It was a reassuring sound that made me feel immediately at ease. "Is *that* what you want to know? Haven't you got a few more important things on your mind, child?"

"More import—? Oh!" I gaped at her for a moment, then let loose a flood of questions: "Where am I? How did I get here? Who are you? How long have I been here? Am I very far from my home? Can you tell me how to get back? Do you know if I—?"

"Enough! Enough!" She raised her hands in surrender, still laughing. "I'll give you your answers, but one at a time, eh? And before anything else, you'll answer one question for me." She leaned closer, and her many necklaces clinked and clattered. "What's your name, my young guest? I can't go on calling you 'pretty child,' though it suits you. It makes you sound as though there's nothing more to you than *this*." She chucked me under the chin lightly.

I smiled at her shyly. "My name is Himiko. I belong to the Matsu clan."

"Matsu?" A faint crease showed between her eyebrows, then was gone. "I don't know the pine tree people. If our paths ever crossed, it must have been very long ago, before my great-grandmother's time. Of course, up here, we're so out of the way that most clans don't even dream we exist, and that can be a good thing. As long as the gods know where to seek us, it's enough." She smiled. "So, Himiko of the Matsu clan, how did *you* manage to find us? Did the gods show you the way?"

I told her all about my wanderings, from my decision to go see the cherry blossoms on my own to the moment when I'd seen the herd of deer go running away from me in the little valley. All that I held back was how I'd heard the wild creatures' words as clearly within me as if they'd opened their mouths and spoken our language.

When I was done, she pursed her lips and looked pensive. "A stag with does at *this* time of year? That's not right. Usually, they keep to their separate ways until autumn. I was joking when I asked if the gods guided you here, but they're the only ones laughing, and they're laughing at me. I need to consider what it means for my people, what *you* mean, Himiko." She gave me such a solemn look that she reminded me of our shaman at those times when she seemed to gaze beyond our world into another realm. It frightened me.

"I—I don't mean anything," I said. "I just got lost, that's all. I want to go home!"

My distress worked an instant change in her. Her arms encircled me, and she held me as tenderly as if I were her own child. "Poor little one, of course you want to go home," she crooned. "Of course you do. I'll do everything in my power to make it so." She hugged me and sighed.

I knew what she wasn't saying: *Everything in my power is nothing at all. How can I send you home if I don't know where you come from? How can I find the village of a clan I didn't even know existed?*

I pushed myself gently out of her embrace. "I know you'll help me," I said, forcing myself to speak calmly. "Thank you." It was the bravest lie I ever told.

Her chin lifted, and she regarded me as if trying to untie a stubborn knot. "You *are* a rarity. Tell me, Himiko, would you happen to be a shaman's child?"

I shook my head. "Lady Yama's our shaman, and she has no children. I'm our chieftain's daughter."

"Now, that's odd too. In every clan I've ever heard of, the chieftain and the shaman are one and the same, like me." She bowed her head slightly. "Well, who knows how many other ways the Matsu differ from us? I know nothing about your people. You'll have to tell me more." She looked at me with kindness. "For now, I owe you some answers, don't I? First, know that I am Ikumi of the Shika clan and you've been under my roof for two days. You were carried here by one of my best hunters, a man named Sora. According to him, he saw you running across a mountain meadow, calling out to the deer, commanding them to return to you. Your face and clothes were smeared green and brown all over, and you waved a black wand. That was enough for him to decide you must be some kind of demon, trying to cast evil spells over us by enchanting the guardian creatures who give our clan its name."

"If he thought that, why did he bring me here?" I asked. A darker question arose in the back of my mind: *Why didn't he just kill me?* I shivered at the idea.

"Luckily for you, Sora is a *mostly* sensible man—when he's not seeing demons in the wrong places. After you collapsed in the grass, right before his eyes, he reasoned that maybe you were human after all. He chose to bring you to me so that I could decide your true nature. If you were human, he knew I'd heal you. If you were a demon, he believed my magic was strong enough to overcome you." Her smile lit the house. "I'm very glad you're human."

"So am I!" came a girl's voice from behind me. I turned to where a small figure stood backlit by sunshine in the doorway of the house. "I'd hate to think I was taking care of a demon."

"Kaya, is that any way to speak of our honored guest?" Ikumi put on an exaggerated scowl, plainly done in jest. "Come here at once and apologize." Looking at me again, she added, "Please forgive my daughter Kaya, Lady Himiko. My other children are courteous, but this one has the manners of a badger."

The girl in the doorway came running in to kneel beside her mother and give the Shika chieftess an enthusiastic squeeze. "But a very *nice* badger, Mother; not the kind who bites." She grinned at me. "Not like you."

"I don't bite!" I protested.

"Then explain this." She thrust one plump hand under my nose. She was quite casual about it, but to my horror, I saw a semicircle of teeth marks. A few looked as if they'd bled.

"Did I do that?"

"Oh yes." She shrugged it off. "I was trying to get you to drink. Mother said you had to have water or you'd die, but you had your jaw clenched shut like *this*." She demonstrated, gritting her teeth and making a face so hideous I had to laugh. That pleased her. "It *is* funny, isn't it? And you did it all in your sleep! But you wouldn't wake up and you wouldn't open your mouth, and you *had* to, so I pried it open with my fingers and dribbled in a little water, the way Mother taught me—not too much at once, or you'd choke— and I thought you were going to wake up then, because your eyelids fluttered, but instead, you sat up straight and yelled, 'Come back! Come back!' and then you *bit* me." She paused, trying to catch her breath after that landslide of words.

The chieftess shook her head. "Tsk. My mistake. My younger daughter has the manners of a badger *and* the tongue of a magpie."

"I like magpies," I said quietly, and smiled at Kaya, who returned my friendly look eagerly. "Thank you for taking care of me. I'm sorry I bit you. I must have been having a bad dream."

"Better that than a dull one," she replied cheerfully. "So! Why is Mother calling you *Lady* Himiko? Are you important?"

That made me giggle. Kaya's mother answered for me: "She's the daughter of a clan chieftain. Of course she's important!"

"Well, then, so am I, but you don't call me *Lady* Kaya," she pointed out.

"That's because I'm still waiting to see if you're really a human child or a shape-shifting spirit," her mother returned, patting her head affectionately. "I can call you Lady *Badger*, if you insist."

"I'd like that!" Kaya exclaimed. Snorting and grumbling, she threw herself onto hands and knees to imitate the shambling walk of the beast. Her mother and I laughed until we couldn't sit up straight. "*Whoof-whoof-whoof.* Stupid humans!" Kaya declared.

It didn't take me long to recover from my experiences in the forest. After she saw that I was able to eat gruel without any ill effects, Lady Ikumi gave me a heaping bowl of rice with pheasant meat and mushrooms. I felt like I could have eaten three! When I finished it, I asked if I could get up.

"Can you?" Lady Ikumi asked. "How do you feel? Remember, it's been a couple of days you've been lying there."

I moved my legs tentatively. They felt rested rather than weak. "I think so, but—" I began.

"Then who's stopping you?" Kaya piped up. She offered me a hand to help me rise, then stood there, hands on hips, studying me. "My big sister's old tunic looks nice on you," she stated. "You can keep it. It's not pretty-pretty-pretty enough for *her* anymore. She's got to wear something to make the *boooooys* pay attention to her." She started mincing around the house, flirting with imaginary people, then made a disgusted face. Her mother just rolled her eyes.

"Kaya, my dear, why don't you take Lady Himiko outside so she can meet some other people? I don't want her getting the idea that we're all badgers."

"Don't be silly, Mother, she *knows* we're the Shika.

We're *deer* people, not badgers!" With that, she grabbed my hand and dragged me after her.

I stumbled a little when we had to clamber up to get out. To my surprise, the chieftess of the deer clan didn't live in a raised dwelling like my family and the Matsu nobles, but in a square pit house like everyone else in our clan. Once outside, I saw that it was much more elaborately thatched than the other houses nearby, with a high, flared roof that covered it cozily. It reminded me of one of those pines whose lower branches swept down to touch the earth and made a wonderful hiding place.

The Shika village occupied a mountain valley much like the one where I'd seen the deer. There was no moat, but the palisade was backed by thick stands of fir trees that scaled the steep slope. Golden daylight bathed the houses. I could almost see the sun goddess's smiling face in the heavens, but couldn't tell if she was still climbing the sky or already beginning her descent. Had I emerged from my long sleep in the morning or the afternoon? I shook my head; I'd know it all, in good time. Besides the cluster of pit houses, I glimpsed a single tall structure on pillars, half hidden in the trees.

Kaya saw where I was looking and proudly informed me, "That's our storehouse. Our fields are so rich that we always fill it, every harvest season. And we've got plenty of grain to trade too!"

"It looks like a giant version of my family's home," I said.

She gave me a mystified look. "You sleep in a store-house? Why? Do you have to do it, to keep the rats out of the rice jars?" My laughter only baffled her even more.

I was explaining the differences between our villages when we encountered three of the clan grandmothers. They were seated on the ground outside one of the pit houses, chatting and enjoying the fair spring weather. When they saw me, one of them got to her feet with surprising nimbleness and rushed away, calling out to anyone within earshot, "Come see! Come see! Sora's little 'demon' is up and about!"

My appearance stirred up a great deal of interest among Kaya's people. We soon found ourselves surrounded by the curious eyes of old and young. Kaya loved being in the midst of so much attention and made a grand business out of presenting me to everyone. She even showed off the place where I'd bitten her, but she did so with such good-natured pride that I didn't feel the least bit awkward about it.

Kaya took special satisfaction in being able to introduce me to Sora, the man who'd saved me. The Shika huntsman told me how glad he was to learn that he'd helped a lost girl and not some kind of ill-natured mountain spirit. "I've never heard of the Matsu clan, Lady Himiko, but I'll try to think of something to do to help you find your people again."

"Don't find them too soon!" Kaya cried. "I like her! I want her to stay."

"But how does Lady Himiko feel about that?" he asked, his eyes crinkling when he smiled.

"I . . . wouldn't mind," I said softly. "I like Kaya too, very much. But I don't want my family to worry about me."

"I'll go to where I found you and see if I can backtrack your path," Sora volunteered. "Perhaps the gods will favor me."

"Be careful, Sora!" one of the grandmothers called out in her reedy voice. "If you're successful, you might find the girl's village, but you'll also find yourself in unknown territory, among strangers! Who knows what these Matsu are like? My mother told me about a time we were attacked by another clan from over those peaks." She gestured uphill. "She was just a girl, but she remembered how the enemy came streaming down on us like a flood. After our men drove them away, we found that they'd stolen some of our children. Her little brother was gone, taken captive! It was the season of rains, and when we sent a war band to trail them, their tracks were washed away. My poor uncle lived and died as a slave." She glared at me as if I were to blame for it.

"Oh, for—!" Sora made an irritated sound. "And where is this girl now except in a strange land, surrounded by people she doesn't know? She'll think we intend to make a slave of her too. Are you *trying* to terrify her?" He put a protective arm around me.

"It's all right, I'm not afraid," I told him. "And when you find my clan, they won't hurt you. Once you tell them why you've come, they'll welcome you!"

The reedy-voiced old woman snorted. "Do what you like, Sora. I wouldn't be fool enough to trust people who aren't Shika!"

"Yet you trust the Kamoshika clanfolk every time they come here to trade with us," Sora teased. "There's a strand of their fancy beads around your neck that proves it!"

"That's different," she replied stiffly. "The Kamoshika were part of our own clan years ago, until they insulted the spirits and aroused the anger of a fire-breathing dragon who lived under this mountain. That's why we drove them away, because the dragon kept thrashing around underground. He was trying to get out and punish the Kamoshika, but he wound up destroying our homes. My mother said—"

"*My* mother told me that *your* mother liked nothing better than to tell stories, true or not," one of the other crones put in. "Especially stories to frighten children."

Sora looked a little embarrassed. "My ma was the same way. She did tell some good ones, but now I keep seeing demons behind every tree when I'm out hunting." With a rueful smile in my direction, he added, "Even when nothing's there but a nice little girl who needs some help."

"Are you saying demons *don't* exist?" Kaya asked, wide-eyed.

The hunter shrugged. "Oh, they exist! They're as real as the rest of the spirits. I'm just saying that I might be wrong about how plentiful they are. Now, when I saw this girl come running after the deer—"

It was the second time I'd heard one of the deer clan say something so impossible. *Running? Me?* I thought. My disbelief must have put a peculiar expression on my face. Kaya stared at me strangely and took my hand.

"I'm going to show Lady Himiko our fields now!" she announced, and walked away from the group of grown-ups so briskly that it was all I could do to call out my thanks to Sora before she dragged me from their sight.

She didn't take me to the fields, but just beyond the village palisade. Once out the gateway, she marched me a short distance before making us both squat down in the grass along the wooden wall. Her first words to me were: "Do you have a cricket up your nose?"

"What?"

"You looked like something crawled up there and you were going to try blowing it out. Why were you making that weird face at Sora?"

"Ohhhhhhhh." I nodded. Now I understood. "I just couldn't believe him when he said he saw me running. I can't run, Kaya."

"Why not? Is it forbidden because you're pine tree people? I guess that makes sense. We're the deer clan, so we only eat deer meat at special festivals, and pine trees can't run, so—"

I covered my mouth to hold down my laughter. When I could talk again, I said, "I fell out of a tree and hurt my leg, Kaya. That's why I can't run."

"But you *did* run," she argued. "Sora said he saw you, and he doesn't lie." She stood. "Come on, get up and let's see about this."

I'd known Kaya for less than a day, yet I already knew that there were times when you had no other choice but to do what she told you. I stood slowly. "I think he was just saying that he saw me run, because I really— *Whoa!*"

Like a hawk dropping onto a rabbit, Kaya grabbed my right arm with both hands and took off, racing over the grass. My only two paths were to run or to fall, and no one was more astonished than I when, instead of sprawling full-length, I ran.

I ran, I ran, I *ran*! She hadn't given me the time to think about it, to prepare for it, to ease into the idea of doing it, only to *do* it. And I did! I could! I wanted to shout out with the feeling of pure joy enfolding me. I wasn't graceful or adept—I lurched and stumbled often—but with my own weird gait, I managed to keep up with Kaya. The rush of cool air and the rich, sweet scent of the waking earth bathed my face. I rejoiced as every swift step I took brought me farther and farther along the path to reclaiming what my fall had taken from me. For the first time in many seasons, I felt free.

When she stopped, I wanted to keep going, but she was still holding my arm and brought me to a halt. Panting, she said, "See? You can run. I told you Sora doesn't lie."

"But I'm so clumsy!"

"Who cares? Running's about being fast. I'm a good runner and you didn't hold me back, clumsy or not."

"What if I'd fallen?"

She shrugged. "I'd've caught you. Or not. But you're not made of eggshells, are you? You'd get up again and then we'd go back and you'd tell Mother what I did to you and I'd get punished for it." She grinned.

"Oh, Kaya, I'd never do anything to get you in trouble with your mother!" I cried. "You just gave me the best gift I ever got. I can't thank you enough." I threw my arms around her neck and hugged her so hard that we lost our balance and toppled over. I sat up and looked at the grass and dirt staining my borrowed tunic. "*Now* who's going to get in trouble with your mother?" I said, giggling.

"You'll get in trouble with my big sister, Hoshi, first," Kaya told me. "It's *her* tunic, and if I've got the manners of a badger, she's got the temper of one."

I made a solemn face and said, *"Whoof-whoof-whoof!"* the same way Kaya had done when imitating the grouchy beast. We threw our arms around one another and burst into alternating *whoof-whoof-whoof*s and laughter until there were tears in ours eyes.

I think that was the moment we both knew that we were going to be friends.

Five days passed. Kaya and I spent them happily together, our closeness growing steadily until it felt as though we'd known each other from the time we were babies. I shared her chores in the house and in the clan's fields, getting dirty and achy and tired and more contented than I could ever remember being. Though I missed my family every day—especially Mama and Aki—I found comfort in the warmth shown me by the deer people. The adults, who'd begun by calling me Lady Himiko, soon forgot about that and treated me like just another one of the village children. What a relief *that* was.

Lady Ikumi's welcoming heart wasted little time in making me feel at home under her roof instead of like a visitor. When I asked her when I'd meet Kaya's father, she told me that he'd died of a fever three summers ago. It felt strange to live in a house without a grown man making the rules, but I got the feeling Kaya's father hadn't commanded his family like mine.

I took real pleasure in getting to know the chieftess's four other children—two brother-sister pairs, one older and one younger than my friend.

"I'm right in the middle." Kaya sounded quite satisfied about it.

"Is that good?" I asked.

"Oh yes! I'm too big for Mother to fuss over, and I'm too little for her to scold for not acting more responsible."

Much to my new friend's annoyance, I soon had a second favorite person in her household: her sister Hoshi. She was even prettier than Kaya had described her; however . . .

"Why did you say she's got a badger's bad temper?" I whispered to Kaya one night after the family had gone to sleep. "When I was helping her cook today, I made the same mistakes over and over. She kept having to fix my messes, *and* teach me the right way to do things, *and* do her own work on top of that, but she didn't get angry about it. Not once! She was sweet and patient and nice to me."

"Fine, so she's not a badger," Kaya grumbled. "Why don't you spend all day tomorrow with her if she's so sweet and patient and—?"

"—not my friend," I said.

"Why, because she's too old?" Kaya sounded a little mollified, though not wholly convinced.

"Because she's too . . . predictable. She's nice, but she's not surprising."

"Huh! What's that supposed to mean?"

"It means that if I told her 'I can't run; it's impossible,' she'd say, 'Oh, that's too bad,' and go back to washing rice. She wouldn't bolt off like a startled rabbit, just to prove me wrong." I turned onto my side, in Kaya's direction. "She's nice, but she's not you."

Kaya said nothing. I wondered if my words had insulted her somehow. I'd had no luck keeping friends back home, but to be truthful, Kaya was the first friend I'd ever cared about keeping. *Maybe she fell asleep,* I thought nervously. I edged closer, straining my ears to catch the slow, regular breath of a sleeper, when suddenly her whisper cut through the silence:

"I hope he never comes back."

"What—?"

"I said, I hope he never comes back," she repeated. "I mean, I *do* hope he comes back, but only if he's given up." After a pause, she added, "I'm talking about Sora. He left the village three days ago to try finding your people, and I hope he never does. *Never!*"

"Why? Are you worried about him? I heard your mother say what a good hunter he is. He knows how to take care of himself in the mountains, and I'll bet he can find his way to my village by backtracking my trail."

"Yes, but if he does find your village, he'll be a stranger. What do your people do when a stranger shows up out of nowhere?"

"What did *your* people do when *I* first came here?" I countered.

"You weren't carrying weapons."

"No, I was a demon, remember?" We both giggled. Then I added, "My people aren't demons, either. I'll bet that when Sora finds them, they'll ask him why he's come, and once he tells them he's got news about me, he won't be a stranger anymore. You don't have to be afraid that anything bad will happen to him."

"I'm not," Kaya said. "But I don't want him to succeed anyhow. Then you can stay here and we can always be friends."

I found her hand in the darkness and squeezed it. "When Sora finds my village, that won't change anything, Kaya. We'll still be friends. We won't see each other every day, but I can come back here sometimes and you can come visit me."

"How? Your clan's so far from here that we never heard of them!"

I thought about that. "Maybe we're not *that* far away. Maybe it's just that our people's paths haven't crossed until now. Do *you* know what's on the other side of every mountain you can see from here?"

"I guess not." My friend sounded reluctant to accept my reasoning, but I think her heart wanted to believe it even if her mind couldn't.

"Of *course* not." I was sure enough for both of us. "You know what? I'll bet that the spirits are behind all of this. They came to me when I was lost and guided me here so that our two clans could become friends like us. Once I'm back with my family again, our people can start trading with one another, and you and I can tag along on those journeys!"

I heard Kaya snort. "How many kids have you seen traveling with a trading party?"

My lips turned down. I knew she was right, but I didn't want to admit it and spoil my beautiful dream of the future. "Well, we're not going to be children forever, and when we're bigger, *we* can become traders! Then no one can stop us from going where we like."

"I don't want to wait that long, Himiko," Kaya said. "I

think I'll just go back to hoping that Sora fails. And we should *both* get up early tomorrow morning and make an offering to the spirits so they cause your trail to vanish. That would fix everything!"

Before I could reply, Lady Ikumi's irritated voice rang out: "If you two stop chattering and go to sleep before tomorrow comes, I'll give the spirits a thanksgiving offering so huge it'll be *next winter* before they want another!"

We muttered apologies to Kaya's mother and didn't say another word.

The next morning, Lady Ikumi sent Kaya and me to fetch water. When we reached the stream that ran through the Shika clan's valley, my friend set down her clay jar and clapped her hands three times, then reached into her sleeve and dropped something into the current.

"What's that?" I asked.

"My gift to the gods so they'll let you stay," she told me, and clapped her hand three times again, the way my clan also did when we wanted to make sure the spirits would take notice. "It's a piece of the dried fish Mother gave us with our breakfast rice."

I started to say *You made an offering of* fish *to spirits that live in a* stream? *They've already got all the fish they want!*

Then I thought, *What difference does it make* what *we offer the spirits? The gods, great and small, are so powerful, what can we possibly give them that they can't take for themselves?*

I remembered the first time I gave Mama flowers. I was very small, and it was the most bedraggled, broken-stemmed, crushed bunch of blossoms ever! She didn't need it, and she could have gathered prettier, fresher blooms for herself, yet she welcomed my silly little present as though it were the finest thing she'd received. I didn't give it to her to make her change the way she treated me. It wasn't a crude this-for-that trade. It was given for no other reason than love.

Giving things to the spirits wasn't about the offering itself, but what lay in the heart behind the gift. I put my arm around my friend's waist. "I know how much you like fish, Kaya. Thank you for giving that up, just for me."

"Thank Hoshi," Kaya replied with a look of pure mischief. "I took the fish out of her bowl when she wasn't looking." Suddenly, like a cloud blowing across the sun, a worried expression shadowed her face. "I just hope the gods don't mind that I didn't give them *my* fish along with *my* prayers."

"Why don't we come back here later on with some rice for them?" I suggested. "That should make it all right."

"Do you really think so, Himiko?" Kaya asked anxiously.

"Absolutely!" I spoke with confidence, wanting her to feel at ease again. "Now let's get the water and go home."

The next morning marked the fifth day of my time with the deer people. I'd gone to bed the night before feeling a little sorrowful. The Shika clan had opened their arms to me and made me feel accepted, but I *did* miss my family. In the hazy time between drowsing and true sleep, I recalled their faces, the sound of their voices, the special smells of our house, the matchless way food tasted when Mama and

my stepmothers cooked it, and countless other precious details. My dreams were filled with memories.

That night, I dreamed that I was home again. I sat on
the floor of our house with everyone around me and told
them the tale of my wanderings with the deer people. Somehow I hadn't lost the cherry branch I'd picked on the mountainside, and it was once again thick with pink blossoms.
When I proudly presented it to Aki, a wondrous, fearsome
thing happened: the flowers multiplied and spread, flowing
along the branch, swarming up his arms, pouring over his
body until he was completely swathed in them. A mask of
fragrant petals fell across his joyful face. The last trace of
him to vanish was his lips, which smiled, and parted, and in
his beloved voice whispered one word—*Himiko!*—with a
breath that scattered the blossoms in a whirlwind, leaving
not a single sign of him behind.

I woke up haunted, calling his name, but my eyes were
dry, and when Lady Ikumi worriedly asked if I'd had an evil
dream, I honestly told her no.

The morning passed with nothing unusual to mark it,
and the afternoon too seemed likely to slip past in the same
way. All of the Shika except the very old, the very young,
and those who had to care for them were cleaning the irrigation channels that brought water to the rice paddies. Kaya
and I were knee-deep in cold mud when a sudden shout
came from the rising slope behind the village. Everyone
looked up at once, in just the way a herd of deer will do
when an unfamiliar noise takes them by surprise. We all left
our work and went running to see what had happened.

We looked up the hill to see Sora loping down and in his wake, moving more cautiously, two men. I sucked in a deep breath and let it out in a cry that came from the depths of my heart:

"Aki! Father! Here I am! *Here I am!*" Hobbling and flying by turns, I ran to meet them.

6

A Bad Bargain

Father and Aki spent the next two days as Lady Ikumi's honored guests. The Shika shaman-chieftess saw to it that they received the best of everything her village had to offer, and urged them to stay longer. Father refused. His words were polite, his reasons believable, but his tone was curt and guarded.

He was also reserved with me. Some of the old coolness had seeped back into our relationship, and while our reunion began with a blaze of love and thankfulness, this soon winked out like a wisp of burning straw, extinguished with a single breath. He didn't chastise me for what I'd done, or even ask for an explanation, but I could feel anger smoldering behind his impassive face.

Sora became the center of attention for his part in bringing my kin into the Shika village. He wasn't the sort of man who thrives as a hero. A look of embarrassment settled over his face with the first words of praise from his clanfolk, and I never saw it leave. Every time someone reminded him of what a great thing he'd done and what an expert tracker he was, he squirmed and repeated, "But you don't understand: I didn't find them. *They* found *me*!"

That was true. Aki told Lady Ikumi and her family the whole story over dinner on the first night he and Father lodged in the chieftess's house. "We would have come for Himiko sooner, but we didn't even know she was missing for many days. Our village was troubled by a wolf pack, so all of our best hunters were deep into the mountains, seeking to kill the beasts or at least to drive them so far away that they'd never come back to our clan's territory. When Himiko didn't come home that first night, and my poor mother wanted to send word to Father, there was no one left in the village with the skill to track the trackers! She turned to our shaman for help, but all Lady Yama could do was tell us that the last time she'd seen Himiko, they'd spoken about the cherry trees."

He lowered his eyes and gave me a guilty look. I clasped his hand, silently trying to reassure him that none of what had happened was his fault. There *was* no fault to be found; I knew it. Aki had been needed on the wolf hunt, but I didn't *need* to go in search of cherry blossoms that very day. Lady Yama's words had stung me into setting out on my own, but I didn't *have* to let her sway me. I'd made my choices, and that was my responsibility. The consequences were all mine. No one should bear the blame but me.

"Yama . . ." Father growled our shaman's name so low that I thought I'd only imagined it until he added, "Useless leech." I turned questioning eyes to him, but Aki was talking again and drew back my attention.

"Our hunt was successful—two wolves dead and the rest driven far beyond our land. As soon as we were in sight of home, we saw our clanfolk come running to meet us. We thought it was a welcome, not evil news. Father wanted to set out on Himiko's trail at once, but it was almost sundown. He and I left for the grove of cherry trees the next morning, as soon as there was enough light to see by, and once we found clear signs she'd been there, we followed her traces." He lifted one corner of his lips. "We would have come here sooner if she hadn't laid down such a wandering path. It was like trying to track a butterfly's flight."

"I couldn't help it," I muttered. "I got lost."

"I don't know how much longer we would have been trailing back and forth through the forest if we hadn't met your man Sora," Aki went on. "It was pure luck, that encounter. He must be an excellent hunter: he moves so noiselessly that no quarry would know he was near until they felt his arrow."

"He said the same about you." Hoshi's sweet voice drew all eyes to her. Her smooth face and glossy hair seemed to glow with their own radiance, even in the dim interior of the chieftess's pit house. "He's been telling everyone in our clan that when he first caught sight of you, you moved among the trees without a sound, so easily and naturally that he was sure he was watching a forest spirit. I mean"—she shot an awkward glance at Father and dipped her head sharply—"I mean forest *spirits*."

"It's very"—a strange catch stole my brother's breath as he gazed at Hoshi's bowed head—"very kind of you to say so, Lady Hoshi. If anyone's worthy of Sora's praise, it's Father. He taught me all I know."

Hoshi lifted her face and met my brother's eyes. "Then you learned well," she said so softly that the words were hardly more than a whisper. I'd never seen anyone look at Aki so intently, and never seen him stare at another person as though there were no one else in the world besides the two of them. I wasn't sure if I liked it or not.

Father impatiently took up Aki's abandoned story: "Well, Lady Ikumi, the *real* forest spirits must've been the ones who put that broken nutshell right under your man Sora's next footstep. He didn't yelp, but he couldn't stop himself from sucking in his breath from the pain. As soon as he knew there was another human near, I shouted that we were peaceable and declared the reason we'd come searching the woods."

Father's words broke the spell between Aki and Hoshi. My brother made haste to finish his tale, saying, "Oh yes! Blessed gods, you can't imagine how we felt when we heard Sora call back from behind the leaves, 'You're Lady Himiko's people?' I thought I'd grown wings and could fly!"

Hoshi laughed, and the sound made my brother's cheeks blaze. While Father and Lady Ikumi spoke of other things, Aki and Hoshi settled into a strange, bewildering silence.

Two days is not a long time. Kaya reminded me of that every waking moment of our remaining time together. Her mother saw our shared melancholy and did what she could to help us deal with the coming separation, releasing us from all chores and giving us the freedom to enjoy those last, precious days together. We wandered through the village, ran races around the palisade, explored the land within a safe distance of the clan fields, and tried not to think about what was coming.

We failed.

"What am I going to do after you go home, Himiko?" Kaya said as we sat on the banks of the stream, watching minnows.

"You've got other friends," I said. That was true; she'd introduced me to them and we'd played together. *The real question is, what am I going to do without you?* I thought. I hadn't had playmates for years and it hadn't bothered me; forfeiting the companionship of girls like Suzu and her little toadies was a small loss. It was only now that I'd experienced what a real friendship could offer that I dreaded returning to my solitary, unshared life.

"I know," Kaya said. "But I'll never have another friend like you, Himiko. *Never.*" She thumbed a pair of tears from her cheeks and put on a brave face, pretending they'd never been shed.

I frowned. "I wish I were a hunter."

"Huh? Why?"

"If I were, I could leave my village and come here to visit you anytime I wanted."

"Oh. Like your brother's going to do so he can see my sister." Kaya spoke as if she were mentioning the weather rather than saying something that made my jaw fall open.

"What?"

"Well, *you've* seen how they are together," my friend said, still unaware that she'd dropped a boulder on my head. "The first night your family was here, those two kept sneaking looks at one another and trying to act like it was all one big accident. I've seen Hoshi blush before, but never *that* much, and I didn't know boys could do it too until your brother showed up. They're in *looooooove*." She stretched out the word sarcastically and made smacking noises with her lips.

"No they're not," I said firmly. I did remember how things had gone between Aki and Hoshi that night, but I'd pushed the memories aside on purpose, denying them completely. I didn't like the idea of anyone being more important to Aki than me. "They can't be. They only met two days ago!"

"I don't know," Kaya said, looking thoughtful. "Mother used to tell us stories about how she and Father got married. She said that there are all sorts of ways to know when you love someone. Some are slow, like ferns uncurling or buds opening, and some hit you *fast,* like . . . like . . . ummmm . . . like when you drop a pot and it goes *smash*! He was just another village boy until one day she looked at him and—" She clapped her hands together so sharply, the loud report made me jump.

"Smashed pot?" I asked. She nodded. "Hmph! Just because that's the way it happened to your parents doesn't mean it happened to *my* brother *at all*."

Kaya shrugged. "I think it did. I *hope* it did."

"Why would you—?" And all of a sudden, I understood

what my friend was thinking. *Aki's a hunter. He's at home in the forests and the mountains. Now that he's learned the route to the Shika village, he won't have any trouble finding his way here again, and if he is in love with Hoshi, he'll want to come back many times. And some of those times*—my heart beat faster—*maybe* lots *of those times, he'll bring me!*

"You figured it out, huh?" Kaya was grinning. "Good. Now you don't have to be jealous of my sister anymore."

"I'm not jealous," I said primly. I didn't mean a word of it.

No matter how much comfort Kaya and I took in the thought of my inevitable return to her village as Aki's traveling companion, we still cried when it was time for me to go. We both awoke early that morning, sat up on our bedrolls, exchanged a single look, and threw ourselves into each other's arms.

"Don't go, Himiko, don't go!" Kaya sobbed.

"I don't want to, but what can we do about it?" I asked, sniffling.

Kaya dropped her voice to a conspiratorial whisper. "Let's hide your brother's clothing."

I glanced around the room. "Too late. He's not here, so he must be dressed and outside already. Father too."

"Well, then let's hide *your* clothes!"

"Your mother will only give me new ones. But what if—?" I thought hard. "What if I pretended to be sick? We'd have to stay longer then."

Kaya considered this awhile before her shoulders slumped. "That won't work. My mother would know. She always does when I try that trick." Defeated, we hugged each other and let our tears fall.

In time, we managed to get up and dress, but we couldn't bring ourselves to eat a mouthful of breakfast or to step outside the chieftess's house. It was as if we were clinging to the false belief that if I didn't cross that threshold, I could put down roots in the beaten earth floor and stay forever.

In the end, it was Hoshi who had the power to comfort us. "Poor girls, this is breaking your hearts," she said. Her sympathetic eyes added the unspoken message, *I know it's breaking mine.* "Lady Himiko, your father and brother are waiting for you at the village gateway. Mother's ready to perform the leave-taking ceremony. Maybe it would be easier for you if Kaya stayed in the house and didn't have to watch you go."

The thought of saying farewell to my only friend was bad, but the thought of losing even one moment of her company was worse. Kaya must have felt the same way. We dried our eyes and hastened to assure Hoshi that we'd attend the leave-taking ritual on our best behavior.

"Don't let Mother make me stay inside," Kaya begged, clinging to her older sister. "I promise I won't cry anymore."

Hoshi sighed and put her arms around both of us. "I wish I could promise the same thing."

The whole Shika village turned out to see us off. Lady Ikumi appeared in what must have been her most elaborate shaman's garb and performed a dance that called upon the spirits to protect our homeward journey. Her two youngest children gave us parting gifts—food for the trail, a handful of gorgeous pheasant feathers, a pendant of green beads for me that I'd last seen around Kaya's neck. Father accepted these with cold formality and had Aki give Lady Ikumi the trophy wolf's tail from his belt.

"May the gods protect and guide your footsteps," the Shika shaman-chieftess said, accepting the return gift with a smile. "I hope that the next time our paths cross, it will be for a happy reason, not fear for a loved one. Perhaps we can begin to trade or—"

"The Matsu have nothing fit to trade," Father said brusquely. "We are not worth the time or trouble it would take to bring any of your people to our gates. You have our thanks for the care you've given to my undeserving daughter. May the gods grant that this experience has taught her the wisdom to value her own home."

"Ah." Lady Ikumi's expression chilled to match Father's. "Yes. It would be a good thing if we all prayed for such wisdom."

As we started out of the gateway, I heard a sob behind me. I knew it must be Kaya, but I didn't dare turn my head for fear that I would break down in helpless tears. I tried to distract myself by looking elsewhere. The sight of Father's flinty, unwavering gaze on the road ahead lent me a little self-control, but I came near to losing it all when I looked to the other side and was struck to the heart by the poorly contained pain I saw in Aki's face.

"Lady Himiko! Lady Himiko! Wait!"

We all stopped and turned to see Sora racing from the village. Father scowled as the Shika huntsman caught up to us. "There's no need for a man of your years and standing to call this child by a title she doesn't merit," he said by way of greeting.

"I meant no offense." Sora bowed to Father. "I thought that honoring her would be a sign of how much I honor you."

"Fine, fine, never mind all that." Father made an impatient gesture. "What business do you have with us that's important enough to delay our journey? I want to sleep under my own roof for a change."

"I'm sorry." Sora bowed again, more deeply. "I forgot to give this back to her."

Father's eyes widened as he saw what Sora was holding in his outstretched hand. "A *stick*?" He spoke as if convinced that the Shika huntsman had lost his mind. "You came chasing after us to give this girl a skinny, miserable, broken *stick*?"

"I—I—I thought it might be something important." Sora fidgeted. "Important to her, that is. She was carrying it when I first saw her, waving it at the deer. I thought she was using it to cast spells on them. If it was something powerful, I didn't want to risk trying to destroy it. Who knows what kind of evil magic that might release?"

"Did you seriously think a child like this could be a shaman?" Father's icy laugh was a slap in Sora's face.

"No, I thought she was—" The kindhearted hunter wisely stopped himself from saying that he'd first mistaken me for a demon. Oh, what an unjustly ugly reaction he'd have gotten from Father for that! "Er, that is, I didn't know *what* to think."

"Obviously." Father jerked his head in my direction.

"All right, give the 'shaman' her"—he snorted scornfully—
"*wand.*"

Chastened, Sora handed me the stick—my long-forgotten branch of cherry blossoms, now black and bare. I thanked him as warmly as I could, wanting to make up for Father's sarcasm, but while I was still telling him how much I appreciated all he'd done for me, Father's hand fell onto the huntsman's shoulder.

"Forgive me, Sora," he said, all the chill gone. "When my mind's burdened with anger and worry, my tongue goes rogue and works mischief. You deserve nothing but my praise and thanks for having saved this girl."

Sora accepted Father's apology eagerly, and the two men clapped each other on the shoulder before parting on good terms. Still, judging by how fast he ran back to the village, I think Sora must have felt glad to escape our company.

To my surprise, Father made no more comments about the barren cherry branch, not even when I carried it along with us instead of discarding it by the side of the path. In fact, his silence extended from the moment Sora left us to the time when we made camp for the night in the shelter of the mountain pines.

The way home was far more direct than my wandering journey to the Shika village. One of the few occasions when Father spoke during our trip was to declare that if he had things his way, he'd be home in less than two days, but that it would probably take us four. He gave me a pointed look when he said it. This had the effect of making me determined to prove him wrong. I not only kept pace with him and Aki, but there were some fairly level places along the way where I could summon up my peculiar, eccentric style of running and speed ahead of them. Aki was impressed and said so, but if Father felt the same, he kept it to himself.

To be honest, none of us were very talkative on that journey. I was expecting Father to give me a blistering scolding for my escapade. That first day on the road I walked with my impending punishment hovering over me like a hawk's shadow over a field mouse. When nothing happened and not a word was said by nightfall, I didn't know what to make of his silence, though I was deeply grateful to be spared a reprimand.

As things worked out, we reached home in two days. When we came within sight of the lookout tower, Aki stooped to sweep me off my feet and onto his shoulders. He shushed my protests by saying he wanted everyone to have a clear view of my safe return.

"The sooner someone runs to tell Mama that you're all right, the better it will be."

"But if they tell her you're carrying me home, she'll think I'm so injured I can't walk," I argued. "Put me down."

I gave him a playful swat with my "wand." The scrawny branch of cherrywood had been with me throughout my adventure, and I wasn't going to part with it now. Father had called it a wand in mockery, but he spoke the truth unaware: every time I looked at it, it conjured visions of Kaya and memories of the happy days I'd spent among the people of the deer clan.

Aki did as I told him, but only after he caught sight of people running across the village moat to welcome us home.

Shoichi and Masa were among them, leading the crowd at a full-out charge. They didn't slow their pace by even half a stride as they neared us but plowed straight into me, laughing and calling my name. I would have been bowled over if their embraces hadn't kept me on my feet. At a word from Aki, all three of my brothers picked me up and carried me the rest of the way among them, as if I were a quarry they were bringing home from the hunt.

At our house, Mama, Yukari, and Emi were all waiting in a row at the top of the ladder, tears streaking their cheeks and smiles lighting their faces. I was hustled inside, examined thoroughly for any signs of injury, chattered over, hugged, and alternately told that I was the worst daughter ever born and the most precious child in the world. The three of them took turns, so when one woman had to pause for breath, another stepped in. I doubt that they *wanted* to keep me from uttering a single word of apology or explanation, but that's the way it worked out. The hardest part was not knowing where to look. Each speaker wanted me to meet her eyes, to be certain I was paying attention to what she was saying, but what was I supposed to do when they all decided to speak at once? I soon gave up and fixed my eyes on the wolf skull someone had mounted on the wall, counting and recounting the beast's fearsome teeth and waiting for my ordeal to end. Father and my brothers remained on the porch. I didn't know what they were doing, but I wished I could have joined them.

Things only settled down when Father finally stuck his head inside and said he wanted dinner. Mama and my stepmothers scattered to make the needful preparations while my brothers trooped back into the house. I couldn't wait to taste familiar dishes again, but my appetite was soon ruined by the dark mood that descended over the meal. It sprang into being from the moment Mama began serving us. All through dinner, she kept trying to give me the best bits of our food, and Father kept stopping her with a grunt and a sharp, forbidding gesture. It worked immediately every time . . . until the next time.

Trapped between them, I squirmed and prayed for the meal to be over. The rest of my family looked just as unhappy as I felt, especially my brothers. Aki sat at Mama's other side, with Shoichi and Masa next to him, in the order of their ages. Yukari had the place beside Masa, and Emi was next to her, at Father's elbow. We should have been a glad gathering, taking pleasure in a good meal and celebrating my safe return. Instead, we ate under a storm cloud.

Aki tried to lighten things by filling the house with stories. He told me about the wolf hunt, about how Masa and Shoichi had carried themselves like true hunters.

"There was one young she-wolf who kept splitting off from the pack and prowling around us, just out of bow-shot," he said. "I'll bet she wanted to see if our group would separate so that she could catch one of us alone."

"Foolishness," Father snapped. "Wolves don't think that way. Their strength comes from acting together. Something was wrong with that one."

"Well, it *seemed* as if she had that sort of plan in mind," Aki said. "If that were so, she nearly got her chance. The strap of Masa's quiver broke and all his arrows spilled out.

We didn't know he'd stopped to gather them, or that the wolf was circling closer."

"Oh, please don't say any more, Aki!" Mama cried. "I can't stand it!"

"But, Mama, look, nothing happened," I said, stroking her hand. "Masa's here, safe and well, see?"

"So he is," Aki said. "And who do we have to thank for that? No one but our own brother Shoichi!"

Shoichi turned red and lowered his head, murmuring that he hadn't done anything worth talking about. I was surprised by his newfound modesty and looked at my second-oldest brother with admiration.

Aki gave him a hearty pat on the back. "Is that so? Then tell me, who was it who spoke up and asked what had become of Masa? Who was the first to go back for him? Whose ears were keen enough to realize that he wasn't the only one on Masa's trail?" He swept his arm to indicate the wolf skull on the wall. "And whose arrow saved our brother just when—?"

"*Enough!*" Father was on his feet, fists clenched, the muscles on his neck and jaw taut, an apparition more frightening than any wolf. "*This* is why your sister wandered off like a fool." He jabbed a finger at Aki. "You. You and your stupidity, turning careless, negligent mistakes into fine-sounding tales. If Masa had had the sense to examine his weapons before leaving the village, he wouldn't have left himself open to the wolf's attack. And as for Shoichi, his arrow only grazed the beast's shoulder before flying wild into the woods! A flea's bite would have done more damage."

I saw my two younger brothers cringe under Father's

bitter tirade. I wanted to reach out to them, to take their hands, to tell them to pay him no mind. I knew that was impossible.

Only Aki sat tall and uncowed by the spate of rage loosed under our roof. Lifting his chin, he said, "You weren't there. You don't know how it was. That 'flea bite' got the wolf's attention, turning her away from Masa. Until that moment, none of my party could get a clean shot at the creature. We were all too scared of the scorn that follows every hunter of this clan if he misses his target. Was it always this way? No. I've spoken to more than one of our clan's grandfathers, and they remember other times. When did the Matsu start caring more about what others would say about them and less about what they could—*should*— do? Whose tongue-lashings worked that change?" He stared at Father meaningfully. "Only Shoichi wasn't afraid of drawing ridicule. For that, yes, I *do* call him a hero."

"Then you're a worse fool than I thought," Father said grimly. "Your behavior among that outlander clan proves it. Do you imagine I didn't see you sniffing after that woman's milk-faced daughter? My eyes work, even if your mind is full of straw! What were you thinking? If you want to take a bride, there are plenty of suitable girls within our own village walls, pretty girls, well-mannered girls, girls who'd be honored to become the first wife of a chieftain's oldest son!"

Aki's cheeks flamed. "*That woman* is Lady Ikumi, and she's as important a chieftain as you. No, she's even *more* powerful; she's her clan's shaman!"

Mama whimpered. "Aki, son, my dear son, please don't

say such things." She plucked at his sleeve, but he ignored her and the venomous look in Father's eyes.

"Her daughter is a hundred times as suitable to be my wife as any of our Matsu girls. She outshines them in every way, in everything you say recommends them. She's beautiful, kind, charming—!"

Father turned his head aside and spat. "She's a new face, that's all; new and different. You didn't grow up with her, so you've made her into something special, like a piece of fruit that's growing just beyond your reach. Believe me, if you get your hands on it, you'll find it tastes the same as the rest."

"Well, if she is the same as our girls, why *can't* I want her?"

"Oh, you can *want* her all you like." A cold smile stretched Father's lips. "You just can't have her. Are you too moonstruck to understand? She's not one of *our* people. She isn't Matsu."

"Why does that matter?" Aki challenged. "So she's Shika, not Matsu; so what? Her people showed us nothing but hospitality, generosity, and respect. They wanted to begin trading with us. They treated Himiko like one of their own instead of saying, 'She's not Shika, so leave her to die!'"

Father's expression changed to one of pity. With a slow shake of his head, he said, "My son, you've grown to be one of our clan's best hunters and trackers, the equal—even the better!—of men many years older than you. My pride in you is beyond measure, but sometimes it makes me forget that you're still little more than a boy. Your face is marked with a man's tattoos, but your mind and heart are as untouched and ignorant as a baby's. You haven't experienced enough of life to understand the grim truth behind the Shika chieftess's ready smile.

"Times are good now. We've been favored with many seasons of plenty, free from hunger and want, but who knows when the spirits will decide we've lived easily for long enough? Hard, hungering times are when the truth comes out and when clan fights clan to survive. If you married your Shika girl and her people attacked us, could you trust her to stay loyal to *our* clan?"

"And what if *we* were the ones who attacked her people first?" Aki shot back.

Father ignored the question. "Look at your poor mother!" he declared. "Look at what your rebelliousness and disloyalty are doing to her!" He pointed to where Yukari and Emi had moved to take Mama into their arms as if their bodies could shield her from the argument raging between father and son. Mama's hands covered her face as she wept so softly it was nearly inaudible. Only the shudder of her shoulders signaled the force of her grief. I tried to reach out and comfort her, but my stepmothers' embrace separated us.

"How is this my fault?" Aki cried.

"You're the one willing to sacrifice your own clan for the sake of that girl. What's worse, we wouldn't be involved with the Shika at all if not for you!"

Aki gaped at Father as if he'd gone out of his mind and dragged the rest of the world along with him. "How can you say that? Himiko was the one who led us to the Shika."

"Because of *you.*" Father's voice dropped, sounding like the rasp of a snake's scales passing over stone. "She never would have strayed if not for you. From the time she was small, you bragged to her about your exploits as a hunter and reveled in the way she idolized you. We all saw how she tagged after you, as though she weren't your little sister but your companion! I never said a word about it, because I held on to the false hope that you'd grow up and act like a man, not a girl child's playmate. You filled her days with fine-sounding stories of adventures in the woods and her head with dreams of joining you someday. *You're* the reason she nearly died from that fall, years ago. Would the thought of climbing the sacred pine ever have crossed her mind if she weren't seeking your praise and attention?"

"Father, it wasn't Aki's—" I began.

"Hush, let your father talk, child," Emi said urgently, taking my hand and pulling me closer to the huddled women.

"You're also the reason she could have died, lost in the forest," Father went on grimly. "She never would have gone there except for your influence."

"This is mindless talk," Aki muttered. "Do you even hear yourself? I won't put up with being accused of hurting Himiko." He started to rise, but Mama shook herself free of her co-wives, dug her fingers into his arm, and dragged him back down.

"He doesn't mean it," she whispered desperately. "He's tired; he's been so worried about her, he has to blame someone. You know he's a good man. He can't help it if he believes that being gentle means being weak. That's her cursed doing—Lady Tsuki's. Wait, I beg you. He'll rid himself of this poison and apologize to you before another sun rises."

"How can I sit here while he says such things about me?" Aki protested. "Mother, how can you expect me to bear it?"

"It's not his fault that I went off and got lost, Father!" I cried. The good food I'd eaten had become a hard, burning lump in my belly. My first night home was turning into a nightmare. "He had nothing to do with it; it was all my idea."

Father's rage softened to amusement. "Pff! Ridiculous. You're my sensible girl, my good daughter. You'd never come up with the notion of leaving the security of our home and safety of our village for no reason."

"I had a reason," I maintained. "I wanted to go see the cherry trees. Aki was supposed to take me, but he had to help drive off the wolves. I didn't want to wait for him to return because I was afraid the blossoms would be gone by then."

"You're only saying such things to defend him."

"I'm saying them because they're true. And climbing the sacred pine was all my idea too! I thought that if I did it, it would show Aki I was as brave and strong as Masa and Shoichi so that he'd teach me to be a hunter as well."

"Is that so?" Father stared at me with an unreadable expression, then turned to Aki. "So it wasn't enough for you to have the child worship you; you had to have her prove how deeply she adored you by making herself over in your image. And now that you've achieved that, you turn your back on her and all of us, bleating after a girl whose people wouldn't think twice about destroying us if war came."

"Father, that's not how it is at all!" I cried, but he was past listening and acted as though I were no longer there. *He must have been holding all of this inside him since we left the Shika village,* I thought. *Maybe longer than that.* I would have sacrificed our peaceful journey home a thousand times if that would have spared me from hearing the hurtful, twisted things he was saying now.

"May the gods witness the truth, Aki; you've made it clear that you don't value the mother who gave birth to you, the family that raised you, the clan that fed you. You'd burn this house to the ground in a heartbeat if that simpering deer girl said so. You are my son, my firstborn, the next chieftain of the Matsu, but all that means nothing to you, next to her. Well, let her have you! She'll get a bad bargain if she expects love from someone who's never known the meaning of it. Go to her! But if you do, you go from *us* forever."

I gaped at what I was hearing. When had my home become such a tangle of wild claims and assumptions? How could our father find it in him to attack so ferociously, so *unjustly,* the son I knew he loved so much? I thought about what Mama had said: this wasn't the first time I'd heard Lady Tsuki's name. What awful powers had she possessed over my father? I looked at Aki, Mama's arms laced tightly around his neck, holding him so closely that he'd have to knock her down to move. There was no need for that: my oldest brother was too stunned to stir. Mama's haggard face streamed with tears. Yukari and Emi had moved to offer comfort to my younger brothers. The two boys crept into their arms as if they weren't nearly grown men but children cowering from a thunderstorm.

I looked at what I'd come home to, and the warm memory of Kaya's family taunted me with everything that mine was not. A strange realization touched my mind: *This is broken.* Another followed: *I need to fix it. I have to fix it! If I don't, no one will, and then—* I didn't have the courage to follow where that thought led.

But how?

I stood up. "*Listen* to me!" I shouted. "*I'm* the one you're angry at, Father, not Aki."

"Are you telling me I don't know my own mind, *child*?" he asked in a warning tone. It didn't stop me; I had too much at stake to heed it.

"You're angry because I went off and got lost. Why can't you just say so? Why do you have to do things like walk in near silence for two days, and stop Mama from giving me special helpings at dinner, and turn Aki's story about Masa and Shoichi's exploits on the wolf hunt into . . . into"—I threw up my hands—"into a war *you* started? I'm sorry for what I did! I'm sorry that I was the reason you had to deal with outlan— with people you don't like or trust."

"'Deal' with them?" Father echoed, still in that soft voice that was so much more chilling than his shout. "Better to say that I'm now trapped in debt to them. They saved my only daughter's life. How can I forget that?"

Slowly I sank to my knees before him and leaned forward, stretching out my arms until my forehead touched the floorboards. "If my life is the debt, let me pay it. Send me back to the Shika as a slave."

I felt strong hands grasp my wrists and yank me to my feet. Father's eyes blazed into mine. "Have you lost your mind, Himiko? How can you make such an outrageous offer?"

I fought the urge to squeak out that I hadn't meant a word of it, that it was all a joke, that I was sorry yet again, that I'd be good, and quiet, and never stand up to him anymore. It would have been so easy to do! All I wanted was peace in my family. I longed for the time after my accident when Father had been all smiles and kindness. I knew I could regain that if I went back to being the girl I'd been then.

That girl wasn't me. I took a steadying breath, silently bid her farewell, and said, "I mean it, Father. All this is my fault, not Aki's. Send me back to the Shika as their slave, to cancel the debt that *I* owe them for saving me."

"This is nonsense," Father snapped. "You're an infant. What do you know of slaves?"

"I know that people become slaves when there's war between the clans," I replied. "The losers become the captives of the winners and have to work for them forever."

"Exactly! And you'd still make yourself the Shikas' slave willingly, when there's been no war between us?"

"Does that mean war will *never* come?" I said calmly. "When it does, I'll end up as their slave anyway, so why should I wait for it to happen?"

"Even if there were a war between our clans, don't you think I could defend my people and protect my family?" Father's indignation was growing by the moment, the way a ball of mud gathers size rolling down a mucky hillside.

"And don't you think I would fight to the death before I'd let anyone lay one hand on you, Little Sister?" Aki's voice broke in. *"Anyone."*

I saw the look that passed between my father and my oldest brother, and it lifted my heart. Father was a man waking from tainted dreams, and Aki was waiting to welcome him back into the healing light of reality.

A last scrap of suspicion still held Father back. "What— what about the girl?"

"I love her," Aki said simply. "I was with her for only a little while, yet what I feel for Hoshi is still—"

"Enough of that." Father raised one hand to cut off Aki's declaration, but his tone was now weary rather than enraged. "Such things are possible; I know it." He looked at Emi, who blushed, while Mama's face showed no emotion at all. "What I need to hear from you, my son, is what you intend to . . . to . . ." He seemed hesitant, even fearful of finishing that sentence.

Aki stood up. This time Mama did nothing to hold him back. Three strides took him to Father's side. "I love Hoshi," he said. "But I love you too and our family. I am faithful to our people. If a war comes, no matter which clan brings it, I will live and die fighting beside you for the Matsu. I swear by all the gods and by the life you gave me, I will do this and whatever else is necessary to prove what I tell you now."

We all heard the dry sob tear its way out of Father's

throat. We all saw the two men embrace, tears bathing their faces. "Then I forgive you, my son," Father said.

Aki bowed his head. "Thank you."

I had never loved and admired my oldest brother more than in that moment. He should have been the one who granted pardon, not the one who humbly, gratefully received it. He'd endured so many undeserved insults and such ill treatment from Father, yet been able to set aside all of his hurt and pride in order to restore peace.

If I were in his place, would I be able to find the determination to do that? To my shame, I knew that the answer was no.

We resumed our meal. Father fetched a small jar from one corner of our house and filled our cups with the milky brew of last year's rice wine. The argument that had nearly ended in Aki's banishment was itself banished. Even though I'd been allowed just a dribble of the wine, I went to sleep with my head spinning and woke up joyful to be home again.

My happiness lasted only a little longer than the effects of the rice wine. At first, I was the focus of everyone's attention, both within my family and among the rest of the Matsu. People swarmed up to me whenever I went outside, wanting to hear about the deer people. Mostly they wanted to hear about all the ways they differed from us. Every difference I could recall—and there weren't very many—was seized upon and repeated as evidence that the Matsu way of living was much better than the Shika path, and that was why the gods would always favor us more than them.

"Did you hear that?" one of our young men asked the

crowd that had surrounded me. "They have a woman who's both their chief and shaman!" He spoke triumphantly, as though he'd discovered a great prize.

"And what's the matter with that?" Lady Yama barked. "The part about her being a woman, the part about her being chief, the part about her being a shaman, or the whole bale of rice?"

"Er . . ." The young man quailed before our shaman's fierce demand. "The part about her being both chief and shaman?" came his wavering reply.

Lady Yama snorted. "Does no one teach these chicks anything? Do they think the world began when they pecked their way out of the eggshell? You idiot! *We* were ruled by a woman who was both chief and shaman!"

"Oh." The young man bit his lip. "Long, long ago?"

"She was our chief's older sister. How 'long, long ago' do you think *that* was? No, don't answer. There's only so much stupidity I can listen to in one day." She stamped off, beads clashing.

As day followed day and the chores of springtime occupied our clan, people lost interest in tales of my journey. I was perfectly content with this. I never asked for the attention, never wanted it, and was glad to be free of it. I didn't mind testifying to the kindness of the deer people, and speaking about Kaya was the closest I could get to spending time with her again, but I was always afraid that I'd say *too* much. It wasn't such a big leap to go from describing Kaya's family to mentioning Hoshi, and from there it was a very small step indeed to saying, *She was so nice and so pretty that it's no wonder Aki liked her as much as she liked him!*

A very small step is all it takes to leave the edge of the riverbank and plunge into the rushing water. If I uttered one breath about my oldest brother's attraction to Hoshi, word of it would flash through our village like lightning and set Father's temper ablaze. If I even *hinted* that Aki had liked a Shika girl, evil tongues would become arrows flying straight into our home to slay our hard-won peace. I was happy to be liberated from worrying about such things.

That is, I *thought* I was happy.

Early summer turned the rice fields a brighter shade of green, and evening insect songs grew louder with every passing sunset. Ever since my return, Mama had stopped objecting to my going to work in the paddies with everyone else. She was probably afraid that if I didn't have enough tasks to keep me busy (and where most of the village could keep an eye on me), I'd wander away again. I didn't care *why* she'd changed her mind as long as I got to be as much a part of my own clan's life as I'd been a part of the Shika's.

That wasn't the only change I witnessed that summer. At the beginning of the season, Aki took Masa and Shoichi with him on his hunting trips, but as the weather warmed, he began taking only Shoichi. Poor Masa! I knew how he must have felt, but he didn't want sympathy, just an explanation. None came, and he never found the courage to ask Aki outright *why* he was being left behind. I think he feared that Aki would tell him, and it was something he didn't want to hear.

One morning, Aki stayed home while Shoichi went into the mountains on his own. He came home with the body of a kamoshika slung over his shoulders. The deerlike beast wasn't very big under its bushy coat of brown and white fur, but from the fuss our parents made, you'd think he'd killed a creature whose meat could feed our whole village. Masa gazed longingly at the face of his brother's first kill—the two small horns just above the death-glazed eyes, the ruff of white fur edging the jaw—and went into a sulk, refusing to eat anything but vegetables for as long as we enjoyed the kamoshika's meager meat.

He continued to mope about it until the day Father marched him to the blacksmith's and said loud enough for half the village to hear, "The Matsu have enough hunters, but a hunter is useless without a good blade and sharp arrowheads. We are blessed to have a master of weapon making like you among us, yet a true master must also pass down his secrets, to save them from being lost forever. I believe you have the skill to teach your art to this son of mine. Show me that I'm right!" The blacksmith grunted his assent and took Masa into the forge. To everyone's surprise, including Masa's, he turned out to love the work and to excel at it.

On a midsummer evening when the fireflies danced and the hum of the cicadas was loud from every tree, I sat alone on our porch, lost in thought. The house behind me was empty. Masa was still at the forge, which had become his second home. Shoichi had gone off with one of the many village girls who trailed after my handsome middle brother. Father was conferring with some of the other nobles about how the crops were coming along, and Mama and our stepmothers were visiting friends.

Friends . . .

I turned my face to the crescent moon, who smiled at me through the branches of the great pine. "Is Kaya looking at you too, Lord Moon?" I whispered. "Do you think she remembers me?" I dangled my legs over the edge of the porch and swung them lazily, calling up all my memories of the Shika village. Every day when I woke up and every night before I went to sleep, I took the withered cherry branch from its hiding place in my bedroll and whispered a prayer to the spirits, asking them to let Father see that the Shika were not our enemies. If that happened, I could go back and visit Kaya, and Aki could see Hoshi again.

"Little Sister, what are you doing up there?" Aki's voice reached me from the foot of the ladder. "If Mother saw you sitting like that, she'd die of fright!"

"I'm all right," I said. "I do this all the time . . . when she's not around."

He laughed aloud and ran up the ladder to sit beside me. "Why are you all by yourself? Are you the only one at home?"

I told him where everyone else had gone, then said, "Isn't it funny how happy Masa is, learning to be a black-smith? I never would have expected that. He was always so eager to be a hunter!"

"So were you, remember?" Aki replied. "But neither one of you was right for it. I'm glad you both found paths that suited you better."

"*Masa* did," I said a bit ruefully. "Not me."

"Of course you did. You're becoming the girl you should be. Before you know it, you'll have some lucky boy ready to give you a house of your own, and children, and then you'll remember my words tonight and say, 'This is much better than anything else I could have done with my life. Aki was right'"—he paused to wink at me—"'as always.'"

I sighed. The evening was too lovely to ruin with an argument. "Is that why you stopped taking Masa with you on the hunt?" I asked. "Because you knew what he wanted to be better than he did?"

In spite of my resolve to preserve the peace, I couldn't manage to keep a slight edge out of my voice. Aki arched one eyebrow at me. "Noooo," he drawled. "I did it because I saw that if he didn't find a path other than hunting, it was only a matter of time before he killed himself or someone else. I didn't want something like that happening to my little brother. He's a good boy, but it turns out he's better at making weapons than using them. The important thing is, both of you are happy now." He gave me a quick hug.

I said nothing.

Aki sensed something wasn't right. "Himiko?"

I didn't answer him right away. I wanted to tell him, *I'm not happy, Aki. I try to be, so that Mama won't worry and Father won't try to shout me into cheering up, but I'm not. I miss Kaya. She was the only true friend I ever had and ever will have. I know you miss Hoshi too, maybe even more than I miss Kaya. You smile, but your eyes are always sad. You go away hunting for days at a time, even when we already have more meat than we can use, as if it's too painful for you to stay near us. If I asked you about it straight out, you'd deny it, but I never see you courting any of the Matsu girls. What am I supposed to believe, your words or your deeds?*

I'm glad that there are no more fights under our roof, and that you and Father are on good terms again, but why did we have to accomplish that by giving him everything he wanted? When did we make his temper into a god? Why do we have to be the ones who make the sacrifices?

I don't want to see you so sad. I don't want my own sorrow. Isn't there a way that we can keep the peace and have our own happiness too?

That was when the idea came to me. It seemed like a good one, the solution to all our problems, but if I simply blurted it out, Aki would reject it as impossible. *I* was sure that it didn't have to be impossible and that it was up to me to turn his thoughts in the same direction as my own. I reached for my brother's hand.

"Aki, when Father changes his mind about the Shika and you can visit Hoshi again, will you take me with you to see Kaya?"

He blinked, startled. "What are you talking about, Himiko? Father will change his mind when water runs uphill."

I shrugged. "You never know. He might. He hasn't been in a bad mood for a long time, not since that awful fight on the day I came home. Remember that?" It wouldn't be a pleasant memory for my brother, but I needed to guide him back to it if I was going to help us both.

"How could I forget?" Aki was grim. "I was nearly banished."

"Would that have been so bad?" I asked. "You could have gone to live with Hoshi's people."

"And never see my own kin again? I couldn't have lived with that. It's one thing to leave willingly, knowing you can return, but to be thrust out and the gates barred behind you?" He shook his head. "Perhaps I'm weak. Someone else might say that if I truly cared for Hoshi, I'd give up everything for her in a heartbeat. And what would that show her?"

"That you loved her?"

"That I loved convenience more than keeping faith. If she saw that I could cut all ties to our family and clan so easily, how deeply could she trust me not to walk away from *her* without a second thought someday?"

I linked my arm through his and leaned against him. "You could never do anything like that, Aki. That's why I like you best."

He gave me a wistful smile. "Better than Kaya?"

Clearly and deliberately, I replied, "Yes, because I'd never offer to become a slave to help her. I wouldn't have done that for anyone but you."

I felt his body tense. "You shouldn't have taken such a chance, Little Sister. Father was lashing out in all directions that night. He might have taken you at your word."

"I wasn't afraid to risk that for you, Aki. You don't think I can be a hunter and face wolves, but I want you to know that I *can* be brave, for your sake." I took a breath and added, "Wouldn't you do the same for me?"

"For the bold girl who faced the wrath of the storm god himself? Of course!" My brother chuckled and tweaked my hair. "You made him stop blowing up a tempest and got him to *listen*. That was what helped him and me mend our quarrel."

"*And* that's what got him to stop talking about sending

you away," I put in. I wanted him to keep that in mind when I made my proposal. I leaned against him. "I was brave for your sake, because I love you, Big Brother, and I hate to see you sad."

"I don't like seeing you sad, either, Himiko," he replied affectionately. "And I'm grateful for the way you saved our family."

"Good. Aki . . . I did something *really* important for you. Now I want you to do something for me."

"Ah! So it's time to pay my debt to you, is it?" My brother laughed. He must have thought I had something childish in mind. "All right, what's it to be? I can go into the woods and find you a honeycomb as a treat. I can give you a ride on my back all the way around the village—no, all the way around the *fields*! I can—"

"Take me to the Shika," I said.

"What did you say?"

"Oh, please, Big Brother, I know you can do it!" I clung to his arm so violently that I nearly sent the two of us toppling off the platform.

"Himiko, be careful!" Aki sprang up and hauled me away from danger. We stood swaying unsteadily on our porch. "Have you lost *all* sense?" he demanded.

"I'm sorry, I shouldn't have grabbed you like that. I only wanted to—"

"I'm not talking about that; I'm talking about what you just asked me. You were joking, weren't you?"

"No, I wasn't, Aki," I said, my voice rising and the words coming from my mouth so fast that I had no time to think about exactly what I was saying. "I want you to take me—to take both of us back to Kaya's village! It's not so far from here after all. You know the way, and I've proved that I can travel almost as fast as you—sometimes even faster! Oh, Big Brother, you *miss* Hoshi; I see it in your eyes every day! And I miss Kaya. She's my only friend. None of the girls here likes me—not really. Suzu hates me, and Ume's a nasty, scheming thing, and the rest of them— Agh! You're smart, Aki. You can find a way for us to go visit the deer people without Father ever knowing about it, or even suspecting. Who cares what *he* thinks of them?"

"Himiko, I gave him my word—"

I was too caught up in my own desperation to let my brother speak. "You shouldn't have to keep such a promise. Why should we be miserable just because Father has the wrong idea about Lady Ikumi and her clan? We know the truth! If you don't do this—if *we* don't find a way to be with the people who mean the most to us—what will our lives be like? Friendless! Loveless! Do you want to live that way? I don't; I *won't!*"

"Little Sister, please, lower your voice," Aki said urgently. "This isn't possible. I can't go back to the Shika village, and even if I could, there's no way I could take you with me. You have to accept that."

"*No,*" I retorted. "If I 'accepted' things so easily, I wouldn't have said one word when you and Father were tangled in your quarrel. I would have stood by and let him throw you out of home, village, clan, and family! You wouldn't be here now if not for me. You'd be—"

I stopped. A dire change had come over my brother's

face. It wasn't the warning look of one of Father's outbursts, or even a stern scowl. Rather, it was the silent, swift, unstoppable closing of a door made of iron and stone.

"Is that why you helped me, Himiko? So that you'd have a debt to hold over my head? To force me to play this-for-that with you?"

"Aki, no, I never—!"

"Forgive me. What I owe you will remain unpaid forever. There's no remedy that I can think of for my shame but silence."

He placed a cold kiss on my brow, climbed down the ladder, and shoved it over so that I couldn't follow him when he walked away. I called out after him, but my frantic cries were just one more cicada's piping song. I fell to my knees, sobbing because I thought he'd left forever.

My fears were groundless. He returned later that night in Father's company, before any of our other family members came home. I had laid out my bedroll, vainly trying to sleep, and heard them joking as they set the ladder back in place. I decided to keep quiet, hoping that everything would be healed by morning.

But the next day, Aki didn't speak to me at all. When our eyes met, his gaze went vague, as though there were nothing at all to see in front of him. When I spoke to him, telling him I was sorry, he turned aside, brushing my voice away like a stray gnat. That night I tried to change things by asking him a direct question at dinner, with the whole family present. With a frosty glance that flashed at me and was gone before anyone else could notice, he made a loud business of needing to leave the house to relieve himself. On his return, he started an earnest conversation with Father that allowed for no interruptions.

It was like that the following day as well, and the next, and the next, until I stopped pounding my fists against the wall he'd built between us and sank into the darkness of its icy shadow.

7

SHELTERING MOUNTAIN

"I swear by the gods, Lady Yama, I don't know what's the matter with the child," Mama said, fluttering one hand in my direction. We were seated on the beaten earth floor of the shaman's house while the eyeless skulls of a dozen small creatures stared at us from the walls. "She scarcely eats. She's the last one to get up in the morning and the first to go to bed at night. She sits by herself in the house doing *nothing*."

"Is that so?" The shaman peered at me, then looked back at my mother. "And how do you find the time to accomplish *anything* if you're always busy watching her do all that *nothing*?"

Mama looked indignant. "Don't you think I can take care of my household duties and watch over my daughter at the same time? I'm telling you, she hasn't left the house willingly since early summer, and I'm worried to death about it!"

"Not yet," the shaman said dryly.

"Do you think this is *funny*?" Mama snapped at her.

"I haven't decided what I think about this at all," Yama replied, calm as still water. "If I'm going to help Himiko, I need information, not exaggeration."

"I'm not exaggerating!" Mama slapped the ground.

"My own eyes tell me that's not so. The girl does go out. I see her helping you and her stepmothers in the paddies every day."

"Fine, yes, true," Mama said grudgingly. "She still does her chores, and works in the fields, but it's not like before. She used to be so enthusiastic about helping us, even when the task was difficult or tedious or grimy. Now she only does what she's told when she's told to do it. Once she's done, unless we give her another job, she goes straight home and just *sits* again."

"Some parents would be grateful for that kind of obedience," Yama said without a flicker of emotion.

"Well, *I'm* not!" Mama cried. "And on top of everything, there's something I've noticed that's very strange. . . ." She hesitated.

"What's strange? Go on, tell me."

"Well, it's as if . . . as if she isn't really there. Her hands move, her legs move, she answers when you speak to her, but otherwise it's . . . it's like talking to a doll."

"I see." Yama nodded and turned her penetrating eyes from Mama to me. "You should go now." I started to get to my feet. "Not you," came the crisp command. "Your mother's the one I want out of here. You're staying." I plopped down again like a cast-off bundle of clothes.

Mama stood up. There was a faint trace of hope in her

expression. "Should I wait outside, or do you want me to come back for her in a while, Lady Yama?"

"Neither. Himiko is going to remain here with me."

"Oh?" Mama's voice wobbled. "All . . . all right. Do you want me to have someone fetch her when it's time for dinner, or will you just send her home?"

"*If* I think she should go home, she'll be able to find her own way. But as for *when* that will be— Don't bother cooking this girl's dinner for a long time." She studied Mama's shocked expression and added, "Have someone bring her bedroll. That's all I won't be able to provide for her. Let it be a woman who does that."

Mama turned her head and gazed at me, her yearning eyes on the verge of tears. "Lady Yama—" Our shaman's name was hoarse on her tongue. "Lady Yama, I respect your knowledge. You speak to the spirits of this world and the world of the dead. Your arts have brought the gods' favor to this village. I don't question your wisdom, but . . . but is this the only way to heal her? To keep her here for so long that even you can't tell me when she'll come home again?"

Yama's thin-lipped mouth softened into a compassionate smile. Standing, she took my mother's hand between both of hers. "My dear friend, don't tell me you fear for Himiko while she's under my roof? No place is safer. Remember, I was there the day she was born. I brought her into this world more than once, and I witnessed the moment when the spirits set their mark on her. I have every reason to protect her. I want to say that she's even more special to me than to you, but you'd probably knock me down for that, wouldn't you?"

"You're right, I would. *Hard.*" Mama smiled, and the two women shared a laugh.

Yama clasped Mama's shoulders. "Trust me. I won't fail her, or you."

"I know." Mama sighed. "It's only that— Please, Lady Yama, do all you can to heal her quickly. If she stays here too long, you know that my husband will drag her out of here before she's well and forbid me to bring her back, and what will become of her if she's still like this?"

The shaman made a scornful sound. "He wouldn't dare. He's afraid I'll find a way to bring *her* back." She cackled. "That would serve him right, eh? But it would be hard times for the whole clan as well if Lady Tsuki walked among us again."

"The gods forbid it," Mama mumbled. She thanked the shaman profusely, promised to send Emi with my bedroll, and left.

Yama sat beside me and cocked her head. She looked as if she were settling down to scrutinize me in mute contemplation, but almost immediately she announced, "All right, girl, I'll give you three. If you want more, you'll have to earn them."

"I— What?" I was taken so strongly by surprise that it jerked me out of my sealed world of misery.

"Oho, so it talks!" Yama looked pleased. "Good, good, that's one thing I won't have to worry about."

"Three *what*?" I asked.

"Mmm, and listen to *that*: she's actually still able to be *interested* in something. Interested enough to be annoyed with me for keeping her in the dark. Dolls don't do that, do they? Even better!" She rubbed her hands together. "There's still a spark in you, Himiko. It's tiny now, but with the spirits' help, I'll fan it into a flame!"

Our shaman must have set a spell to work on me because her cryptic words roused me from my listlessness enough to spread my hands and protest, "Lady Yama, I don't understand."

She leaned forward until we were so close that I could see every mark the years had made on her face. "No, but I do, little one," she said in a voice so full of sympathy that it seemed as though my pain were her own. "I didn't need your mother to come here and tell me that something grave's been troubling you. I've known that a long time. I've been watching you for longer than you know, ever since the day you were born. I've watched you, and I watch this village. That's my job and my calling. The spirits wouldn't let me rest if I didn't walk the borderlands between the Matsu and the darkness. But sometimes the darkness slips past me and comes to rest *here*." She tapped my chest gently. "What is it that's turned you into a living ghost, child? Tell me your grief."

I shook my head. "Nothing. I'm just—I'm just tired."

She sighed and sat back on her heels, gaunt hands resting on her thighs. "Himiko, my life has taught me that we can win nearly every battle, but only if we know what we're fighting for. When fears and sorrows cling to us and drag us down, we have to call them by their true names if we ever hope to break their hold and defeat them. I can't do that for you, and I can't compel you to do that until you're ready. That's why I told your mother you'd stay here for as long as needful. I didn't tell her that only you could determine how long that will be.

"I said I'd give you *three,* and you want to know what I mean by that. I give you permission to ask me three *questions,* Himiko. Ask anything, and if I have the answer, I'll give it freely and honestly." She paused for a moment, then raised her brows and smiled. "Ah, if you could only see your face now. Such disappointment! Until I told you what I meant by *three,* my gift could have been anything: three pretty necklaces, three magical charms, three dragons! Well, that's good, that's a start. You can't be disappointed if you've forgotten how to hope. And now—" She slapped her thighs. "Now ask me anything."

I considered her words. Part of me wanted to go back to my detached existence, not caring about anything in a world where caring always seemed to end in loss. However, a different part of me was . . . curious. There were many things I'd just overheard in the conversation between the shaman and my mother that had aroused my interest. When I cast my mind even further back, I recalled other times I'd heard hints about the same mysteries, particularly what was said about—

"—my birth, Lady Yama," I said. "You once told me that when I was born, it was a day of . . . of . . ." I couldn't recall her exact words.

"Impossibilities?" the shaman suggested.

"Yes! But you wouldn't tell me anything more. And just now, you said that you were there when the spirits put their mark on me. What did you mean by all that?"

Yama pressed her palms together and touched her

fingertips to her lips. "Mmmm, a good question. Let me ask one of you before I answer: Have they come back to you at last, child?"

"They?" I echoed.

"Forgive me, that question was ill put. How can the spirits ever leave us? I should have asked you if—no, *when*— when did you open your eyes and heart and mind to them once more?"

She knows, I thought. Memories of my lonely wanderings swept over me like a great hawk's wing, but there was no menace in its shadow. Once again I heard the fox speak to me, and the deer, and then all the other voices that dwelled in every tree, every stone, every rushing stream and quiet pool. I stared at Yama, my blood pounding so forcefully that my whole body began to shake. I couldn't tell if I was trembling with fear or joy. *She knows!*

And even though I was convinced that there was no need to tell the shaman what she already understood, I closed my eyes and let the whole story fly from my lips. When I was done, she put her arms around me and said nothing. I don't know how long she held me like that, the way Mama did when I needed comfort. She was still holding me close when Emi came into the shaman's house with my bedroll.

Yama released me to speak with my stepmother. Apparently, Emi had some business of her own with the shaman, because the two of them drew away from me to confer in low voices. I waited patiently for them to finish. I hoped Emi would leave soon; I'd revealed so much *to* Yama, and that felt good, but I still needed to talk *with* her about what I'd experienced on my journey. I also wanted the answer to the first of the three questions she'd granted me. What *was* it that I didn't know about my birth? How did it involve the spirits? How had they marked me?

Probably with a curse, I thought, resigned. Given my friendless state and how thoroughly I'd managed to destroy Aki's brotherly affection, it struck me as the only likely answer. All that remained was for Yama to confirm it as soon as my stepmother was out the door.

But Emi still delayed her departure, and Yama didn't seem inclined to hurry her away. The shaman gathered an array of small clay pots from the packed-earth shelf that ran along the wall and sprinkled different amounts of their contents into a wide-mouthed bowl, then picked up a spouted vessel and poured a trickle of water over the mixture, chanting all the time. Emi cast an apologetic glance my way and shrugged as if to say *This wasn't my idea,* but we both knew that was a lie. When Yama commanded Emi to hold her face over the bowl and drink a handful of the liquid, I took petty satisfaction in hearing her gag on it.

Go home, Emi, I thought. *Why did you have to bother Lady Yama with your problems now? You're keeping her from answering my question!*

I tilted my head back and stared at the little animal skulls again. Where were the spirits that had once lived as that rabbit, that badger, that fox? They must be lingering nearby. Where else would they go? I closed my eyes and wondered if I'd be able to sense their presence, or if they'd speak to me the way the living creatures had done. As I waited in my self-made darkness, I heard Yama begin a slow, rhythmic chant. Metal struck metal in a deep, repetitive chime.

She's calling to the gods, I thought. I didn't know what Emi wanted from them, but my prayer was simple enough: *Go home, go home,* please *go home!*

When I opened my eyes, my plea had been answered: Emi was gone, but only because I'd fallen asleep in the midst of Yama's incantation and now it was morning.

I sat up yawning. I discovered that I was in my bedroll and my clothing was laid out at my feet, just the way it would have been in our house. Yama lay nearby, curled up on the bare ground. Snoring gurgled and bubbled from her throat. The sound made me laugh out loud.

"Is that all it takes to heal you? The chance to make fun of an old woman?" The shaman sat up and spoke so abruptly it was like a snake's strike.

"I'm sorry, Lady Yama," I said, ashamed of myself.

"Don't be. The more we laugh, the better we live. It's good to hear you laugh again, Himiko. You haven't done that since your brother turned his back on you."

"How did you—?"

Yama waved away my question. "I told you that I watch this village, didn't I? I don't know what happened between you and Aki, but the results are plain to see. If your mother weren't willfully blind to the ills under her own roof, she wouldn't have needed to bring you to me. I suppose she's one of those people who's convinced that closing your eyes makes the demons vanish." She shook her head. "Tsk. There's no mystery about what's made you curl up like a grub under a log. The whole clan whispers about it, though they're all quite careful not to do it where your father can overhear. Tell me, *has* he noticed?"

I bowed my head and didn't reply.

"That's what I thought," the shaman said. "Although I'll wager my finest mirror that he's only acting as though nothing's happened, nothing to be *too* concerned about. Everything will be all right if he leaves it to fix itself. He and your mother are well matched that way. Show him a shattered jar and he'll say, 'Oh, it can still hold water. It just has to *make an effort.*'" She laughed without mirth.

She was right. The nearest Father had come to acknowledging that something was wrong was to tell Mama how pleased he was that Aki was finally acting like a man, staid and serious, and to ask her, *When do you think Himiko will snap out of this ridiculous* mood *of hers?*

I looked up at the shaman. "I miss him," I said in a broken voice. "I miss him so much! Lady Yama, I beg you, make things right between us again. Call on the spirits, cast a spell, do whatever it will take to make my brother care for me again."

"Is that what it will take to make you a girl and not a living ghost?" she asked. There was no mockery in her tone. I nodded vigorously, which seemed to gratify her. "Then I give you my word that it will happen. But enchantments to change a person's heart are difficult to perform. If I work alone, unaided, it will take a very long time."

"Could I—?" I hesitated, then forced myself to take courage and ask: "Would you let me help you?"

The shaman tilted her head to one side, like a bird.

"That would make things go faster, and I think the gods would approve. Unless you lied to me last night, the spirits have spoken to you, and you certainly spoke to them clearly enough. 'Go home, Emi,' indeed!" When I gaped, she patted my arm. "Pull your jaw up, child, or a toad will leap into your mouth. There's no magic at work. You talk in your sleep."

"Oh." I blushed.

"Your stepmother needed my help with a serious matter. What it's about doesn't concern you. I know it kept me from answering your question, but you've already waited nearly twelve years for the answer. How much difference does one more day make?"

"That depends on the day," I replied.

Yama threw her head back and cackled. "That's true, isn't it? You're a smart one, under all that gloom. Smart enough to learn many things, including patience. No one enters my house unless they *must*. I think they fear what they might find. When someone does come to me, seeking help, I give it to them immediately. Will you ask the spirits to send *them* home too, every time that happens?"

"No, Lady Yama," I said, chastened. "I'll wait as long as . it takes, and I won't make a sound."

She nodded approval. "You'll wait, you'll be quiet, and you won't go bearing tales about anything you see here. If someone needs my help, it's no one else's business except for the spirits themselves." She made a wry face and added, "Of course, if even one pair of eyes catches sight of someone entering my house, the whole clan will soon be gabbling and guessing about what brought him to me. Your stepmother is lucky: she can excuse her visit by saying she only came to deliver your bedroll."

"Do you think the people are talking about me being here?" I asked.

The shaman clicked her tongue. "Aren't you a little young to care about village rumors?"

"Father isn't."

"That father of yours . . ." Yama muttered something under her breath. "A fine leader, a good man at heart, a much better chief than his predecessor, but—" She sucked on her teeth. "Don't worry about him, Himiko. He's more than a match for any gossip, and the people know it."

"I just don't want them pitying me."

"Then let's arrange things so they can't, eh? Let's see to it that they don't dare." She winked. "You said you'd help me with my spells. True?"

"Yes, Lady Yama. Anything to make things heal faster between Aki and me."

"Well, helping me makes you my apprentice, and who's going to be fool enough to get on the bad side of a future shaman?"

"Your apprentice?" I hadn't felt happiness for such a long time that the sensation was like a blow. "Really?" I was overwhelmed with excitement, but excitement marred by doubts. *Can I do this? What if I make mistakes? Lady Yama thinks I'm smart, but what if I'm not smart enough? What if I harm instead of help? What if I offend the gods?*

"Yes, child, my apprentice, but"—she dropped her voice to a comical whisper—"we won't use that word. Your father doesn't have pleasant memories of women who work magic. If he thought that I was training you to follow me as the Matsu clan's shaman—" She rolled her eyes in mock terror but spoke in earnest.

"Lady Yama, if you don't call me your apprentice because of Father, how will the villagers know I'm going to be—?"

"You're not going to be *anything* if you don't get out of bed," the shaman snapped. "Perhaps I ought to be glad to hear you talk about the future instead of lying there like a dead fish, but right now it's just annoying. We have many steps ahead of us, Himiko, many paths to explore, and I have many, *many* things to teach you before you can do anything useful when we serve the gods. But we're not going to accomplish the smallest bit of that on an empty stomach. Get up, get up! Today I'll show you how to cook our meals, tomorrow you'll show me you've learned that lesson, and in the meanwhile, we've got to help our people with the crops or there won't *be* anything to cook at all! *Go!*"

I scrambled to get dressed while Yama calmly went about making breakfast for us. I watched her carefully, in case the shaman had some special trick for making rice porridge with the spirits' help. I was disappointed when she followed the same method Mama and my stepmothers used.

"I could have done that," I told her. "I can make dinner too. Mama taught me."

"You haven't been my apprentice for half a day and already you're doing badly at your lessons," Yama retorted.

"What lessons? You wanted to show me how to cook, but it's something I already know."

"I *wanted* to show you how to pay attention, to observe, and to listen to me." She handed me a full bowl. "So much for that. We'll try it again tomorrow."

I expected to be punished for my unintended impudence, but Yama made no further mention of it. Instead of a scolding or resentful silence, she chattered pleasantly about the day's work ahead, the new babies she'd delivered, her hopes for a good harvest, and her concerns about the health of one of our older men. Her cheerfulness spread to me. I was no longer embarrassed by my misstep, and I didn't feel like my accidental error made me a complete failure in her eyes. Yet though she said no more about it, I knew I'd remember never to make the same blunder again.

Just before we set foot out of her house, I had a sudden misgiving. "Lady Yama? How do you think I should behave when we're working in the fields?"

"*That's* an odd question. Do you want me to count it as one of the three I permitted you?" she teased. "Don't worry. I haven't forgotten that I still owe you an answer to the first one. You'll have that tonight, provided you don't fall asleep too soon."

I fidgeted, favoring my bad leg. "I *am* worried," I said. "Mama's going to be out in the paddies with everyone else. She'll see me!"

"I should hope so! See you and talk to you and work beside you and flutter and fuss all around you too. Nothing new there."

"But she'll see that I'm—that I'm better. She'll want to take me home. What should I do? Should I pretend I'm still sad? Should I act as if I don't see her, or anyone else? Should I—?"

"Should I toss you in the stream until I wash all that nonsense out of your head, silly child?" Yama exclaimed. "You're not going home today. We have too much to do before I'd even *consider* sending you back."

I breathed a sigh a relief. "Thank you, Lady Yama."

We were late reaching the fields. Some villagers were tending the rice, others were seeing to the yams and other vegetables, and a few were hard at work repairing broken tools. Unlike the busy planting season of springtime, it took fewer people to work the crops at that point in the summer. Someone in the rice paddies began to sing a comical song about an old man and a lizard, and soon everyone joined in. I heard Mama's high, sweet voice rise above the rest and saw her working beside Suzu's mother. Emi and Yukari weren't there—probably in a different field or taking care of chores at home. I couldn't see Father or my brothers, either. Masa would be at the forge, of course, and the rest of them might be hunting. I wished them well but thanked the spirits for their absence. The thought of how they might react on seeing me made my stomach burn.

I needn't have worried. Mama saw me and waved, but when I went into the flooded paddy to join her, she only asked, "Did you sleep well, Himiko?"

"Yes, Mama."

"And you've eaten?"

"Yes, Mama. Lady Yama's rice porridge isn't as good as yours."

"That's all right; you'll get used to it." She bent back to her work.

Minnows and small frogs swam through the sparkling water where the rice grew. I thought I spied an early dragonfly, hovering on rainbow wings above the nodding stalks of grain. Mama and I moved through the field without speaking to one another, though every time she glanced my way I saw a sad smile on her lips.

Yama stayed out of the water. As always, she took a position on higher ground, where she'd be visible to as many people as possible, and began to summon the spirits to make our fields fertile and our harvest plentiful. First she clapped her hands, then turned her face to the sun, invoking the glorious goddess of warmth and daylight. A flock of cranes flew across the heavens, and she shouted for the Matsu to look up and behold what a good omen we'd received. My heart beat faster at this proof of our shaman's favor with the spirits: a crane had brought the first grains of rice to our land from some mysterious country across a great stretch of wild water, though some said it had been a heron. At certain times of the year, Yama would clothe herself in a cape and headdress of crane feathers and perform a ritual dance to call upon and honor the benevolent crane spirit.

We worked until the sun was directly overhead and it was wise to escape her power. Mama climbed out of the paddy and turned homeward. Without thinking, I began to trail after her, but we hadn't gone more than twenty steps before she turned and said, "Go back to Lady Yama, Himiko. Tell her Emi is in the woods today, gathering berries as a gift to thank her for her help." She hadn't said outright that I wasn't supposed to go with her any farther, but she managed to make that message clear to me.

She walked on toward our house, and I went back to give Yama her message. The shaman was kneeling in the shade of a small stand of pines, examining the bronze mirror she wore around her neck along with many strands of beads. She greeted me with, "I thought you didn't want to go home today."

"I don't," I replied, taking a place beside her. "I didn't. It was an accident. Mama says to tell you Emi's going to bring you some berries today."

"Ah, that will be nice! And someone else has promised me a fat chunk of honeycomb, if the bees cooperate." She smacked her lips, then gave me a second look. "What's this? You're drooping like a heat-struck flower. You didn't wear such a melancholy face when your mother brought you to me. Tell me what's wrong."

"Nothing." I shrugged and tried to force a smile, but it was a weak one.

"Himiko, digging answers out of you is like digging kernels out of hazelnuts. I can hit the hazelnut with a rock, but I don't think that's the way to handle you. From now on, you'll tell me what I want to know without this back-and-forth dance. I'm going to find out the truth eventually, so what's the point of delaying it?"

"It's silly, that's all."

"*What* did I just say? How do you expect me to teach you anything if you won't learn to listen?" She sounded in no mood for anything but my obedience.

She learned at once that I was in no mood to give it. "If I wanted to tell you what's bothering me, I *would*," I said sharply. "Why won't you let *me* be the one to decide when or if I talk about it? That day, when I went by myself to see the cherry trees, you were the one who told me to act for myself. If that makes me unfit to be your apprentice, send me home now."

Yama's eyes opened wider at my outburst. "That's a good idea," she said. She took the gleaming mirror from around her neck and gave it to me. "Go home and put this on the shelf, in the corner farthest away from our rice bowls. Then fill the biggest jar in the house with fresh, lively water. Oh, and while you're there, see if we cleared aside our bed-rolls. We were in such a hurry this morning, we might've forgotten to do it."

I leaned back on my heels. "You're not angry at me for saying all that?"

"If you're afraid of making me angry, think *before* you speak," she replied amiably. "But, no, I'm not. You've just shown me that you *can* listen to me. Even better, you can remember! Now go."

I spent the rest of that day in Yama's house. The errands she'd given me weren't difficult, not even filling the big water jar, which stood half as tall as me. I wasted some time trying to wrestle it toward the door before realizing that using a smaller jar to fill it little by little would be easier, even if I did have to go back and forth to the village well many times. *I wonder what she meant by "lively" water,* I thought as I poured in the last drop. *There are always lots of frogs in the well. They're lively enough! Should I have plopped a few of them in?* I giggled, imagining the shaman looking into her cup and seeing two tiny eyes looking back.

My work was interrupted once by a little boy who came by with the honeycomb his father had promised the shaman, and again when Emi arrived with a wooden tray piled high with berries. "Oh, Himiko, you're smiling again; wonderful!" she exclaimed, gave me a quick hug, and dashed out before I could respond.

Yama came home shortly after my stepmother's departure. As she surveyed the house, which I'd tidied without disturbing her things, I was delighted to see approval spread across her face. It grew even stronger when she asked me how I'd managed to fill the big water jar and I described my method. She dipped a cup inside and took a sip. Her look of satisfaction faded. "This water's dead."

"I'm sorry, Lady Yama. Next time I'll remember the frogs."

As soon as she stopped gawking at me as if I'd turned into a frog myself, the misunderstanding came out. "It's a good thing that this village has a well, even though we've got a fine stream running nearby," she said. "Streams can run dry, but wells hold deep water and last longer. A well inside the wall also lightens the burden of having to carry jars so far." She sighed. "But well water is lazy. It goes nowhere, just lies there like a pregnant sow. When we make magic, Himiko, the ingredients we select to attract the spirits must *all* be pleasing to them, even the water."

I thought this over. "We need *lively* water—water that rushes and swirls and tumbles along—because the spirits rejoice in *life*. Am I right, Lady Yama?"

She patted my head. "Mostly. There are some spirits that— Well, let's not talk about them now. I'd rather they didn't mistake our chat for an invitation." She shivered.

As we ate our dinner that evening, I pushed away my bamboo plate and blurted, "Why didn't Mama say anything about it?"

"About what?" Yama asked calmly, not looking up from her food.

"About my coming back with her. She didn't mention it once the whole time we were working together in the fields, or when we—when she was walking home."

"*That?* You were afraid she'd insist on it, and when she didn't, you were heartbroken!" The shaman took another bite and spoke through a mouthful of food: "Do you want to stay here or don't you?"

"I want to stay," I said in a small voice. "But I want *her* to want me home. Why didn't she?"

Yama reassured me: "Your mother loves you, Himiko, and she does want you to come home, believe it! But because she loves you so much, she doesn't want you to leave my care until you're healed."

"Amn't I?" I asked. To my consternation, she shook her head. *Is she joking?* I thought. *I feel better! The instant I knew she could restore my bond with Aki, my sadness fell away like a butterfly's abandoned cocoon.*

"Don't misunderstand me; you've made a start," the shaman said. "I'd say you're somewhat better, the way baked clay's somewhat softer than stone. Healing the body takes time—I don't have to tell you that." She flicked a finger at my mended leg. "Healing a person's spirit is no different, except that it can take longer still and it's often hard to tell if you've succeeded." She stretched her arms over her head and groaned at the popping sound her joints made. "If only there were a way to heal old age, eh? The only one I know is to put your bones in a jar or to lie under the earth for a hundred seasons. It works, but I can't say I'm eager to try it." She showed me a crooked smile. "You didn't care for being buried, either, Himiko."

"Buried?"

"I think you know what I mean. Have you ever felt trapped, child? As though the earth itself were rising up around you to hold you down when you know you were born to fly?"

Her words hit home. I'd seen what lay past the boundaries of our village. My dreams were filled with images of the beauties and mysteries of the forests and the mountains as well as the faces and voices of people who were not Matsu—men and women, boys and girls I *hadn't* known all my life. What else was out there, beyond our lands, even beyond the Shika territory? I longed to know.

But I never would. I was tethered to the pillars of my father's house as certainly as though there were a rope around my waist and my feet were sunk ankle-deep in mud. I'd tried to break free, to set out again—even if it were only another journey to the deer people's valley—but I'd gained nothing for my efforts and lost . . . too much.

"If I'd been born to fly, I would have hatched from an egg," I said, trying to cover my bitterness with a joke.

"Don't be so quick to brush away that notion," Yama cautioned me. "You are a bright girl, but unless you have the gift for visions, how do you know what the gods have in store for you? If the crane spirit favors you, he might lend you his wings! I do know this much: you were born for something more than an ordinary life. The signs of this were upon you from the day of your birth. I still owe you that story. Bring me those berries from your stepmother and I'll tell it to you."

"There's honeycomb too."

"Even better."

As we feasted on the sweetness of berries and honey, Yama answered my long-delayed question at last: "Your father brought me to his house when it was time for you to be born. On the way there, he joked about how he was only doing it because it was customary for the shaman to be present at a birth. He said that your mama had already brought five children into the world and that he expected you to be out already, howling for milk, by the time we climbed the house ladder." She snorted. *"Men."*

"Five children?" I repeated. Infants died—I knew that much too well from the grief Emi and Yukari had suffered—but I had no idea that Mama had lost children of her own.

"Before Aki was born, she gave birth to a girl, and another one after him. You're very precious to your mother for many reasons, Himiko, but the sisters you never knew are two of the most important." Yama popped the last berry into her mouth. "As it turned out, your father was right. I had one foot on the ladder when I first heard you yowling. I was glad: the louder the crying, the healthier the baby. I rushed into the house and called out, 'Well, who is it that's come into this world so boldly? Is it a young hero for the Matsu

clan, or do we welcome a little princess?' But before your
mother could tell me whether she'd given birth to a boy or
a girl, the gods spoke."

"The tremor," I said. "Mama told me that."

"Is that what she called it, a tremor? Then that makes
our ancestral pine tree a blade of grass!" The shaman chuckled. "I can laugh about it now, but on that day, no one in the
Matsu clan was laughing. A great dragon was stirring from
his underground sleep. We'd felt him move before—the
faint scratching of a claw, the quiver of his tail—but this was
different. This time he arched his back, reared his mighty
head, and stretched out his neck in a roar fit to shatter
heaven!

"Oh, that roar! I hear it in my nightmares. The handi-
work of its echoes is painted in fire across my memories.
The earth didn't just tremble; it quaked, heaved, and buckled. Houses were flattened, and the flames of the blacksmith's forge broke free to devour everything they could
reach. The rice paddies were drained dry when the ground
opened a hundred mouths to gulp down their water. I was
lucky that when the first shock struck, I was thrown forward, into your house, instead of backward, off the platform. Your father was partway up the ladder, and he was
flung to one side as though he were an ant a giant *oni* had
flicked off a piece of straw.

"How your poor mother screamed! How *I* screamed
when the house lurched all around us. And then, with the
marks of childbirth still on her, so much of her strength
spent to give you life, your mother thrust you into my arms
and commanded—yes, *commanded*—me to save you. Oh,

you should have seen her on that day, Himiko, wild-eyed and fierce as a swarm of demons flying off to do battle! But her battle was all for you. One look at her face and I knew that if I didn't guard your life with my own, she would destroy me. Even if she died in the earthquake, her wrathful ghost would return to hunt me down and tear the flesh from my bones!"

"Mama?" I was amazed. "*My* mama?"

"She was fighting to save what she loved." Yama spoke as though it were something so evident that it didn't need to be said. "She would have carried you if she hadn't felt too drained to trust herself with your safety. I was afraid she was so weak that she wouldn't be able to move from her bedroll, but the gods saw her devotion to you and took pity on her. Somehow she found the strength to follow me out of the house and down the ladder—still standing, for a miracle!—before the next twitch of the dragon's back.

"If I close my eyes, I see it all again: your father's house was split, the pillars toppled, the roof fell. The ladder *did* fall then and went rolling away. The ruins swayed before pitching toward us. We turned and ran—your father on his feet again to help your mother, and I, carrying you. You had gone silent, and for a moment, I feared that your newborn spirit had been so shocked by this rude welcome to the world that it had taken fright and flown away. My dread was so great that I didn't dare to look down at you, to see if it was so. Instead, I turned my face to where the great mountain stands—you know the one I mean, Himiko?"

I nodded. She could be speaking of only one mountain,

because all others were anthills beside it. Anyone with eyes knew that peak, awesome and holy, its shining majesty rising in the distance. I still treasured the memory of seeing its light-crowned summit from the top of the sacred pine.

"On the day I was born, my mother named me *mountain*. When I was older, she told me she'd had *that* mountain in mind. It's not a very dainty name for a girl, but she wanted me to have endurance enough to stand alone, and strength enough to spare for helping others. 'Be steadfast and let your shadow be a shelter for all,' she told me." The old woman looked thoughtful. "She was no shaman, but there must have been *some* reason that she gave birth to two—my half brother Michio and me. Even though she never walked our path, I think the spirits whispered to her too.

"Well, I can tell you that I didn't *whisper* to them on that day. I *bellowed* my pleas against the sound of crackling flames, crashing houses, groaning earth, and the screams and shouts of our people! I called out to all the spirits of that sacred mountain and begged them for your life." She sighed. "I've never been very good at begging. Everything that comes out of my mouth seems to sound like a demand. As I stood with you clasped to my chest, the earth reared up beneath my feet. The ground tore itself apart, I lost my balance and my grip, and you fell from my arms into a crack that pierced the heart of the world. I saw you plunge into the darkness, and I shrieked helplessly as the next shudder of the dragon clapped the sides of the fissure closed over you."

I tried to speak and realized I'd been holding my breath

during Yama's story when I had to gasp for air before asking, "If—if—if that happened, then why am I—*how* am I here now?"

"Didn't I once say that you were born on a day of impossibilities? But all things are impossible until they happen. You are proof of that. I thought you were gone forever. I lay on the ground, pounding it with my fists, howling like a wounded animal. I heard your mother calling out for me in anguish, your father commanding me to answer, but all I could see was dirt and stones. I clawed at them like a crazy thing, trying to dig my way into the dragon's lair until my fingers were stained with blood. And then, when the dead-weight in my belly told me it was over, that there was no more I could do, in that very moment, the earth moved again and there you were, alive and blinking in the sunlight! I scooped you out of the ground and curved my whole body around you. I'd stopped shaking by the time your father reached us, but I hadn't stopped weeping. I bet he thought I was just another silly woman, crying in terror. He couldn't know that I was shedding tears of joy—no, of something greater than joy! I had witnessed a miracle, a child born twice in a single day, and in your tiny hand, this!"

Yama reached for a small pouch hanging from her belt and tipped the contents into her cupped hand. I couldn't see what she held until she took my wrist, gently pulled it toward her, and dropped something into my palm. I looked down and saw a captive star, a shimmering golden stone whose surface had been polished smooth as the face of still water, but whose core held countless sparks of rainbow fire.

"This has been my secret since that day," Yama said

solemnly. "I took it from you and hid it before your parents reached us and snatched you from my arms. I kept it to myself until I could decide what it meant when an infant was buried and brought back into the light holding a prize wrenched from the very talons of the dragon. I have been keeping it from you and for you, waiting for the right moment to give it back. Guard it, Himiko. It is proof that you are chosen to be the spirits' own, but only if you choose to consent."

I gazed into the stone's cold golden fire and felt a wondrous warmth envelop me. I made my choice.

PART II

GATEWAY

8
The Heart That Listens

I remained in the shaman's house for seven days. I didn't go back to the fields during that time. That was her decision. She announced it to me the next morning as we ate our breakfast.

"Yesterday you saw your mother, and the meeting upset you. Next time, she might be the one whose heart would suffer for it. Also, if you return, there is the chance that you'll encounter other members of your family. Who knows what harm such an experience might do to you or them?"

Especially if I meet Aki, I thought sadly. *That's who she means, I'm sure of it. She won't mention his name to spare me pain.*

I inclined my head slightly. "I'll do as you say, Lady Yama."

"Good. That will save us from wasting time wrangling over trifles. I can't keep you here forever, Himiko, and I shouldn't. Your mother brought you to me to be healed, but I can only do so much to make you well again. The most important part of your healing must come from your own efforts. Unless you put yourself to the test, you'll never know if you've succeeded."

"Or failed," I said.

Yama gave me a funny look, then got up and fetched something from the shelf holding the supplies she used to make her potions. "Here." She dropped the item into my empty rice bowl.

"What's this?" I asked, picking it out carefully for examination. It looked like a smooth brown pebble, the size of my smallest fingernail.

"A seed, a special seed. The gods gave it to me when I first became the shaman of this clan. They came to me while I was deep in trance and offered it to me. The trouble was, they'd had it for so long that they'd forgotten what sort of plant might spring from it. Some of them swore that if I planted it, it would become an enchanted tree whose branches would bear every kind of fruit throughout the year. But there were others who shook their heads and said it would be unwise to plant it, since they were certain it would bring forth a weird, straggling, scrawny bush covered with sickly yellow buds, and that every few moments, those buds would burst open with the sound and stink of . . . a fart."

I giggled. "That's not true."

"Want to find out?" Yama said. "Plant the seed. Or don't. Why should the gods care if you're too timid to reach for success because you're too afraid of failure? But don't ask me to tell you what to do. I don't give a fart."

This time I fell over backward laughing at the shaman's

salty language, and the "magic" seed was lost. I think it was just a pebble after all.

The seven days I spent in isolation under Yama's roof were divided among the same household chores I'd done at home, lessons in the various skills the shaman had mastered, and times of much silence and little talk, when she guided me in my first steps along the path that led from the noise and bustle of the human world deep into the veiled and dreamlike kingdom of the spirits.

It was not an easy path to follow. Like a firefly, it showed me only small, erratic glimpses of its presence. At times, I would sit in silence, my sight turned inward, my mind cleared of all distracting thoughts, only to remain gazing into emptiness. Other times, I'd no sooner close my eyes than an otherworldly scene would reveal itself to me with such force and beauty that it made me gasp, but before I could take one step into that place of shimmering mists, unimaginably brilliant colors, and half-heard whispers of mysterious song, my eyes would snap open and everything was gone.

On our sixth day together, I asked Yama to explain why my attempts at seeking out the spirits had such erratic, unsatisfactory ends. I did my best to keep from sounding like a spoiled child whining because dinner wasn't ready when he wanted it *now,* but I don't think I succeeded.

"If that's how patient you are, thank the gods you were never a hunter," she said curtly.

I blushed. I didn't *think* she'd known about my aspirations to join Aki on the trail of game, but then again, our shaman did say she was always watching her people. She might have seen the longing in my eyes whenever Aki or the other hunters marched out of our village and returned in triumph, to feasting and praise.

"I'm sorry, Lady Yama. I'll do better."

"You *are* doing better, Himiko," she told me. "Better at listening to me, and to yourself. If I've done nothing else for you, I can take pride in that, at least. If it's any comfort to you, you should know that neither I nor my half brother Michio was immediately able to master the art of listening. In fact, it took him longer than me, though I believe he was better at it, in the long run."

"Michio?" I vaguely recalled her mentioning him, but knowing there was no Michio in our village, I concluded that there could be only one reason.

"Why are you looking at me with such melancholy eyes, child?" the shaman asked curtly. "Michio's not *dead,* he's just"—she waved one hand—"following his path elsewhere. Who ever heard of a village with two shamans?"

"Don't you miss him?"

"Not when I can summon him back with a memory. For instance, if he were here right now, I can hear exactly what he'd tell you about learning how to listen: 'No one likes to speak and be ignored. That's a poison strong enough to eat its way through friendships, marriages, families, even clans. Always listen, but above all, hear yourself.'" She smiled. "That's what my half brother would say, and we'd all do well to heed him."

The following day, our shaman handed me a cloth sling and led me out of the gates, away from the fields, and up the forested slope that rose behind our village. A light, warm, steady rain was falling, and when I looked back downhill at the rice paddies, I saw scraps of haze drifting lazily over them. I thought we were going to collect ingredients for Yama's healing brews, but to my surprise she kept climbing the mountainside, never even pausing at clumps of plants whose flowers, or leaves, or roots I'd seen carefully arrayed on the shelf or hanging in bunches from the ceiling.

She stopped at a small clearing where the trees out-lined a crescent of grass. A flat, moss-furred rock lay in the center of that miniature meadow, and for an instant I thought that the round white object atop it was a human skull. A step closer and I saw that the rain had played tricks on my eyes: it was only another rock.

"Scary-looking, isn't it?" Yama said, chuckling. "Those cavities in it complete the illusion a little too well. It scared *me* the day I found it. We'd had a bad year—far too many deaths, including our chieftess, Lady Tsuki—so I'd gone into the burial ground to appease the dead. When I saw it lying so near her tomb, I was afraid she'd sent it as a warn-ing. Hmm, no, more likely as a *threat,* considering that one's ways when she was still alive. A more envious creature never lived. She's the one who 'suggested' that my half brother leave the village, and— Well, never mind. I soon saw my mistake"—she gestured toward the white rock—"and felt very foolish. Now I keep it to remind me that anyone can be deceived and humbled, and also that the gods can have a wicked sense of humor." She smiled at me. "So can I. I was sure you'd squeal when you saw it, but I'm glad you didn't.

You'll put me to shame yet, Himiko. Now go closer and see what lies beneath that . . . 'skull.'"

I did as she said, feeling the rain-soaked grass underfoot, then the gentle caress of moss. Bending forward, I lifted the uncanny-looking rock with both hands and saw a flash of iridescent gold, sparkling and bright even under those thickly clouded skies.

"My dragon stone!" I exclaimed, for that was how I'd named it in my heart since the night Yama gave it back to me.

But it wasn't the same. Now the shining stone was set into an artfully wrought charm made of clay and twined with wires of silver and gold. A skilled hand had molded the figure of a beautiful woman whose arms cradled the dragon stone. The whole talisman was no bigger than the circle made when I touched my thumb to the tip of my forefinger, yet every detail of that splendid lady's face and form was exquisitely made.

"How did you do this, Lady Yama?" I breathed, entranced. "I kept this stone with me always—"

"—in your bedroll with that sprig of cherrywood you treasure," Yama concluded. "I took it from its hiding place twice—once a few days ago to make an impression of it in a bit of wet clay, and once yesterday, when it was time for it to be placed in its proper setting. You never suspected it was missing either time. Our village potter does good work, doesn't she?"

I studied the serene face of the woman cradling the golden stone and felt the same sense of awe as when I gazed at the heavens and saw the sweep of the scattered stars, the cool tranquillity of the moon, or the glorious light of the sun in all her majesty.

And here in my hand I held a woman who held the sun.

"Yes," I said quietly. "Very good."

We walked back to the village, gathering the plants that Yama had ignored on the way up the mountain. I did most of the work because her hands were full, carrying the grisly-looking white rock. "I hope the rain lets up," she confided in me. "I want lots of our people to be able to come out of their houses and see *this*." She tapped the "skull" right between its fake eye sockets.

I couldn't imagine why, and said so.

"Why else? To let them remember who it is that stands between them and the spirits of the angry dead. When you become a shaman, my little Himiko, you should remember that a thousand healings won't earn you as much respect as the threat of a single curse."

I frowned. "I'd never do that. It sounds too much like what—" I paused, searching for the unfamiliar name I'd heard so recently. "It sounds like something Lady Tsuki would do!"

"Ah. And you don't want to be like her, eh? If your father could hear that—hear it *and* believe it—we wouldn't have to worry about how to go on with your training."

"Then why don't I *tell* him?" I said. Oh, how marvelous it would be if I could come and go as I liked to continue my studies! These past few days had awakened a deep, true calling in me. Now I could no more abandon dreams of my apprenticeship with Yama than I could give up the hope of winning back Aki's affection or of seeing Kaya again.

Yama took a deep breath. "Himiko . . ."

Suddenly I realized my mistake. I stopped in my tracks and bowed deeply to our shaman. "I'm sorry, Lady Yama. I know that I can't do that. You said he had to hear that I didn't want to be like Lady Tsuki and *believe* it. We can't depend on that, can we? I'll say nothing, I swear."

The disappointed look fled Yama's face. "You *have* learned how to listen! Now the rest of what I have to teach you will be nothing but details."

That evening, she insisted on preparing a dinner that was more lavish than usual and heaped my rice with the best pieces of meat and vegetables. There was even some leftover honeycomb, though not enough for two. She wouldn't let me refuse it. Afterward, she produced a clay jar of rice wine and poured us two small cups to celebrate my great achievement. Though I didn't quite understand why learning how to listen was worthy of so much fuss—it was important, yes, but *that* important?—I accepted the wine and her praise joyfully. I can't say which of the two made my head spin more.

In the morning, she told me to pick up my bedroll and my few belongings. "You're going home."

"Now?" I was dumbfounded. I'd been given no hint, no warning. Had last night's festive meal actually been intended to celebrate my departure? Tears blurred my eyes.

"Oh, little one, don't look at me like a motherless fawn," Yama chided gently. "You'll be back under this roof many times. Your studies must and will continue."

"How? Father won't—"

"You let me worry about him. You have your own task

ahead: the completion of your healing. I've given you the tools to attain it, but you must be the one to use them. I don't pour out good rice wine for nothing, you know!"

I started to object. I wanted to exclaim, *But* you're *the healer, Lady Yama, not me!* Instead, my thoughts once again curbed my tongue. *Listen, Himiko! I told myself. She says that you'll return, that you must go on learning the way of the spirits. Believe it! Put your faith in her words. Try to be the one who heals your own sorrow.*

I smiled wholeheartedly. "It will be good to go home."

And it was. Yama walked me back to my father's house and announced our arrival by shouting from the bottom of the ladder. Emi came rushing to the edge of the platform. When she saw me standing beside the shaman, my bedroll tucked under my arm, her face was transformed with joy. She flew down the ladder and embraced me as though I'd been gone seven full turns of the seasons instead of only seven days.

"Is it true, Lady Yama?" she cried. "She's well enough to come home? To *stay* home?"

"Well, I doubt you want her to stay home *forever*. You know that won't happen with a pretty little thing like her," the shaman replied. "But she's well enough to return for now. There was a dark spirit weighing her down, one that stole all the pleasure of life from her. I like to think we sent it so far away it will never come back to trouble her. What do you say to that, Himiko?" she asked, patting me on the shoulder.

"I hope so," I replied, smiling.

"Oh, this is marvelous!" Emi exclaimed. "I can't wait for the rest of the family to come home and see you. They're all in the fields today, even Masa."

"Oh no! Did he do something wrong? Did the blacksmith send him away?" I asked urgently. I prayed it wasn't so. Masa loved the forge dearly! I could understand his feelings better now that I had found the place where I belonged and the path that had always been right for me to follow.

"Dear one, don't worry," Emi said, pressing her cheek to mine. "It's just that today's field work needs every hand available. The canals have grown thick with sediment and plants. They must be cleaned or the rice will die of thirst. I'd be there myself, except . . ." Her voice trailed off. She turned her head aside, but not before I caught the look of sadness in her eyes.

Yama drew Emi toward her. "It didn't work?" she asked quietly. Emi shook her head. "Then we will try again, when you're ready. Bring me no thanksgiving gift until you hold something in your arms worth thanking me for."

"Can I go to the paddies?" I asked. "I want to help clear the canals."

Emi stared at me, pleased and bewildered. I understood: it had been a long time since she'd seen me so lively. She hadn't been there on my lone day in the fields with Mama. "Why, yes, Himiko, I think that would be all right."

"So do I," Yama put in. "We'll go together. Emi, please take Himiko's bedroll inside."

"Let me do it!" I cried, and even with my lopsided gait, I was up the ladder before either of them could stop me.

Father was the first to see us. He wasn't knee-deep in the irrigation canal but up on a slight rise, directing the work. When he saw me, his expression became guarded.

"Here's your daughter," Yama said.

"She's well?" Father asked, eyeing me uncertainly.

"Why not talk to her directly?" the shaman said dryly. "You might be surprised by how well that works."

"I'm fine, Father." I rushed to reassure him, and to banish the glare he aimed at Yama. "Can I help? I'm ready to work."

He regarded me for a while, then shook his head. "You won't work here today, Himiko. Tomorrow will be soon enough for you. Go home and see if you can share Emi's chores, but first go down into the paddies and tell your mother that you've come home."

Yama gestured downhill. "I think she knows."

It was so: Mama had abandoned her work in the canal and was hurrying up the hill to greet me. "What's wrong, Lady Yama? Why are you here? Is Himiko all right?" she called out as she left a trail of muddy footprints on the grass.

"Why are you shouting about it?" Father rumbled as Mama caught me up in a hug that smeared mud all over my tunic. "Stop distracting everyone from their work. The whole clan is goggling at us! Of course she's all right. You act as if she were truly ill instead of just another moody girl."

"As if *he* knew all there is to know about girls," Yama remarked to the sky.

My father gave her a withering look but kept his tone almost *too* civil when he said, "Thank you for your efforts,

Lady Yama. You will receive proof of my family's thanks at once, and more after the harvest."

"I don't think I want to wait that long," the shaman drawled. "I'm an old woman. I won't die as soon as *some* people would like, but I'm not going to live as long as I'd prefer. Other Matsu will bring me gifts of food. What I'd have as my gift from you, my chieftain, is that your daughter come to my house every third day from now on to keep it tidy, to run errands, and to perform other small services for me."

"You want my child, a chieftain's daughter, to become your *servant*?" Father gritted his teeth.

"Why not say *slave,* while you're spouting nonsense?" Yama was cold as snow. "I gave your daughter help and now I want help in return, but not without your consent. Give it or let the debt between us remain unpaid forever."

Father's face paled. An unpaid debt to a shaman was an unpaid debt to the gods. It was nothing any wise man would risk. "Pardon me, Lady Yama," he said, dipping his head slightly as he bit off the words. "I didn't understand your request. It will all be done as you wish. Himiko"—he turned to me—"you will go back to Lady Yama's house in three days."

"Yes, Father," I said, fighting back a smile.

That evening, Mama and my stepmothers marked my homecoming from Yama's care with enough food to fill the bellies of a family twice our size. I ate heartily, which only made them heap my bamboo plate with a second serving, and a third.

"Be careful, Himiko!" Masa said, poking me in the side

with one callused fingertip. "If you get too fat, I'll have to set iron bars under the floor to keep our house from collapsing."

"Don't be so hasty to keep our sister thin just because you like skinny girls, Little Brother. If you ask me, there's no such thing as a woman who's too fat," Shoichi said. He gnawed the last scrap of flesh from the pheasant leg on his platter and held up the bare bone for all of us to see. "Hugging something like *this* isn't going to keep you warm at night!"

"No, but if they're thin enough, the rattling of their bones will keep the wolves away all winter!" Masa countered.

Everyone laughed—everyone but Aki. The only words he'd uttered throughout the meal were a stiffly formal "Welcome home, Himiko," and the thanksgiving prayer we all offered to the gods before we ate. He hadn't looked me in the face once, even keeping his eyes lowered when he gave me that cold greeting.

His indifference pained me, but the pang I felt wasn't as sharp as before. As much as I suffered from his silence, I could see that he was suffering more. Shoichi and Masa were still young enough to enjoy lots of flirtations, but it wouldn't take too many seasons before they each chose their first bride and started families of their own. There was no such future for Aki, by his own choice. His brief visit with the Shika had changed him forever. Those few days had been enough to place his heart in Hoshi's hands as firmly as the woman in my amulet held the glimmering dragon stone.

Oh, Aki, you're so alone! I thought. *Even here, in the midst of our family, you're living behind high walls. If you'd only speak to me—*

I was about to break the silence, to let my sympathy for Aki speak out, demanding to know what I had to do so that he'd let me share his life again. My mouth opened, but before I could speak, a calming presence filled my mind with a single word: *listen.*

So I said nothing, and let that evening's silence between me and my beloved oldest brother stay unbroken.

In the days that followed, little changed. Aki avoided me when he could, shut himself away from me within a palisade of silence when he had to be in my presence. I accepted this the way I accepted a storm or a splinter or any of the countless aspects of my life that lay beyond my power to affect or control.

Even as I accepted his silence, I refused to accept that it would last forever. And even though it seemed futile, every day I turned my face toward his silence and *listened.*

Now that I was home again, my world returned to what it had been before Aki had rejected me. I ate and slept well, I sang when I felt happy, I helped in the house, I worked in the fields, I kept my distance from Suzu and her little flock of chattering, pecking sparrows. And every three days, I stepped into a different world.

How often did I bless our shaman for bringing me under her wing! The days I was able to spend with her were precious. With every lesson she taught about the way of the gods, a new pathway revealed itself before me. I learned how to make medicines, how to bind broken bones, how to tell when a person who claimed to be sick in body was really sick in mind or spirit. When I had first come under her roof, she'd told me "Ask anything" and promised me three answers, but we soon exceeded that. She welcomed my questions, even when they were as numerous as summer raindrops.

Yama taught me the chants to use when it was time to praise the gods or to implore their mercy, to ask them for favors or humbly request that they leave us in peace. She also showed me the dances she performed, each with its own purpose, each sacred to a particular event or season, but when I tried to imitate her steps, my broken leg turned her graceful movements into a stuttering series of missteps and stumbles. Whether she set the beat fast or slow, whether she clapped her hands or struck a drum or one of the sacred bronze bells, I couldn't keep in time.

She finally gave up. "If you weren't doing so well at your other lessons, I'd take this as a sign from the gods that you're meant to do something else with your life."

"If I can't dance, can I still become a shaman?" I asked anxiously.

"Maybe it's a matter of time." She dodged my question, which to my ears sounded the same as giving me the answer I didn't want to hear. "You might not be ready to master the dances. That could—that *will* change. Now let's work on improving the talents you *do* have and waste no more breath wondering why you can't teach a duck's egg how to fly."

Sometimes Yama took me with her when she was summoned to help one of our clanfolk who was sick, injured, or in need of help delivering a baby. These opportunities didn't come often, and when they did, I couldn't accompany our shaman unless Father was far from our village on a hunting trip. Even then, Yama always was prudent enough to justify my presence with a glib reason.

"Don't pay any attention to Himiko. She's just here to spare an old woman a burden by carrying my things."

"Oh, Himiko? Such a good girl. She visits my house every few days to grind herbs for me, now that my hands look like a pair of ginseng roots. I had her come along so that I'll be able to mix your child's medicine faster."

"What did you say? Why is *who* with me? Oh! Himiko! I didn't see you. Did you come in here tagging after me? Tsk, that child. She must be bored. You'd think her parents would find some work for our little princess to do. Very well, if they can't, I can. Since she's entered your house uninvited, she might as well lend me a hand. Come closer, Himiko, and make yourself useful!"

Yama's efforts to crush any gossip before it got started were successful. The last thing either of us wanted was for some villager to tell Father, "Your daughter was such a help when Lady Yama came to tend my poor wife. We're all happy to know what a fine shaman she'll be someday!"

The days passed, and my clanfolk grew accustomed to seeing me accompany Yama whenever someone needed her aid. Yama had excused my presence at her side so many times that eventually nobody saw it as extraordinary. If they said anything, it was only to praise me for being so willing to help our aging shaman. No one suspected that the turning seasons were bringing me closer and closer to Yama's level of healing knowledge as well as her mastery of rituals for appealing to the gods and placating the spirits of the dead.

It was good to learn how to bring healing and peace of mind to my clan, to ease pain, to calm fears, and to restore balance between the worlds of the living, the dead, and the immortals. I felt a great sense of accomplishment with every lesson I conquered, but what gave me the most pleasure was something I never spoke of to anyone, not even my teacher.

How to explain the gift of silence? *Listen,* Yama told me, and I did—in our house, in our village, in the fields, everywhere. But most of all, whenever I could find the freedom and the time to do it, I sought the refuge of the forest. I left behind the noise and chatter and commotion of life within the Matsu lands and stole away into the shelter of the trees. I drank in their ancient air of peace and ageless contemplation, and in that haven of my soul, I closed my eyes and *listened* to myself.

Such times were precious to me. I could have spent an entire day with no other company but the sound of leaves rustling in the breeze, the song of birds, the hum and buzz and click of insects, the rumor of animals in the underbrush as they went about the frantic business of survival, the whisper of a distant stream rushing over its rocky bed, and the deep, subtle breath of the earth itself. It was in those moments that I once more heard the voices of the spirits.

I loved to walk among the trees, but I always turned my steps homeward. The voices of the spirits would always call to me, but the loud, exciting, tantalizing cries of village life had a bright, attractive magic of their own.

In my thirteenth year, I received my first tattoo from Yama's hands. It was given to mark my entrance into womanhood, according to our traditions. As soon as Mama, Yukari, and Emi saw the unmistakable sign that I was no longer a girl, they quickly cleaned me up, showed me how to care for myself during those times when the bleeding would return, had me change out of my stained tunic into Yukari's best garment, and hustled me to Yama's house.

"About time," Yama said, looking from their radiantly proud faces to my stunned expression. "How does it feel?"

"I'm not sure," I replied vaguely. "My head's spinning."

"Good enough." Yama clapped her hands ceremonially. "The spirits have spoken through your lips. Let's honor this day of transformation according to their words."

With that, she handed Emi a small clay jar and snapped, "See that she drinks it all!" before darting over to her shelf and bustling among her supplies. I wondered what she was looking for, but when I opened my mouth to ask, Emi set the jar to my lips and gave me the biggest swallow of rice wine I'd ever had in my life. Next, Mama grabbed me from behind and made me sit in her lap, as though I were still a little girl. Yukari and Emi placed themselves to either side of us, held my arms, and told me not to move or be afraid. Before I could flinch, Yama was pricking my chin over and over again with a sharp needle, pausing only to rub soot on my skin. She worked so swiftly that she was done before I could say "Ouch!"

"There." She wiped away the extra soot with a damp scrap of cloth. "Done." She held up the mirror she wore around her neck. I blinked to see the delicate spiral pattern she'd tattooed onto my chin, the lasting sign that would always commemorate one of the great changes in my life.

All of this happened just two days before the wine-making festival. The harvest had been good and there was more than enough rice to eat, so our clan could spare a generous portion to be made into wine. Huge jars were rolled into the center of our village and partially filled with water. Containers of raw rice were placed nearby as the Matsu formed groups and took turns chewing the hulled grains into a paste and spitting it into the water jars. When one group tired, another took their places. There was a great deal of laughter, song, dance, and comic storytelling. Unmarried young men and women flirted madly while the adults teased them mercilessly. Many couples took advantage of the festive air of confusion to slip away in search of a little privacy.

I'd been looking forward to being a part of all that. I hadn't told anyone—not even Yama—but there was a boy in our village who'd caught my eye. His name was Ganju, and he was one of Masa's age-mates. He was very good-looking and had a ready laugh, but he'd been just another of my clanfolk until the day Yama and I went to help his mother with a difficult birth. Things took a bad turn, and the shaman chased everyone out of the house, so he and I passed the time in conversation. Afterward, when the baby was safely delivered and I was packing Yama's gear, Ganju knelt beside me and said, "I'll look for you at the wine making." I blushed so deeply that my cheeks burned all the way back to Yama's house.

But on the morning of the festival, Mama dropped a boulder on top of my hopes.

"I'm sorry, Himiko, but you can't help with the wine making. In fact, you mustn't go anywhere near the rice or the water jars."

"What? Why not?" I was stunned by this news, but not half as stunned as when she explained the reason for her decree. No matter how attentively I listened, I could *not* believe what I was hearing. *"Unclean?"* I echoed. "But I'm doing everything you taught me to make sure I *keep* clean!"

She shook her head and explained again that making rice wine was a delicate matter. It could go wrong in any number of ways, leaving our village with nothing to show for our labors but a lot of wasted rice. Over the years, our people had made a series of rules that covered every step of the process, both what should be done ("If you want the wine to be sweeter, make it only from rice that's been chewed by unmarried girls") and what must *never* be done.

Apparently, the same life change that had made Mama so happy was now going to keep me as far from the wine-making festival as possible.

"Maybe it would be best if you stayed in the house, Himiko," Mama said.

Where else would I go? I sighed, but I didn't object any further. I could have chosen to shout my defiance. Instead, I chose to listen, and what I heard behind Mama's gentle suggestion that I stay away from the festival was something more than her blind obedience to a stupid rule. I listened with my heart, and heard her unspoken, fearful plea: *Please don't make a fuss, Himiko! Everyone in the village knows that you've entered womanhood and that you're still marked by that change. I don't like this any more than you do, but if you go against our traditions, you'll ruin the festival for everyone. I don't think that even Lady Yama herself would take your side in this. And you know how your father will react!*

I did, and I wanted to spare Mama another of his rages even more than I wanted to go to the festival and see Ganju.

"I'll stay inside, Mama," I said with a smile.

She embraced me. "You're a good daughter. The gods bless you."

After she left, I turned my hand to filling the time until the wine making was over. With three other women under our roof, there wasn't a lot of housework left undone. I decided to take all of the family's bedrolls out onto the platform and give them a good airing, but just as I was unfurling the last one, I heard footsteps on the ladder. The next thing I knew, Aki's face popped into sight.

Our eyes met, and I must have looked as surprised as he was. Unless you were forbidden to attend, as I was, *everyone* was supposed to help with the wine making. This was especially true for younger villagers who had good, strong teeth and plenty of endurance for chewing raw rice into paste. I was about to ask him why he'd come home, instead of participating in the festivities, when I remembered that he wouldn't welcome anything that came from me, even a simple question. As if to prove it, he scowled, made a small sound of irritation, and began to climb back down.

I have walked with the spirits. I know that this world holds the threads of many different kinds of magic. In the heartbeat that it took for Aki to take a single backward step on the ladder, I learned that one of those threads governs time.

Listen, Himiko.

Was it the voice of a spirit or the echo of Yama's teachings that filled my mind with those words? Perhaps it was only me. The source didn't matter. The important thing was, I listened.

I listened, and time stretched itself out like a spider's silken thread, so fragile-looking yet so strong. Though an unwholesome silence lay heavily over my brother and me, I wasn't listening for his words or mine. I used the lessons that I'd learned in my times of solitary forest contemplation and listened to the ghosts of the people Aki and I had been on the day that everything turned to bitterness.

I listened to the past, and I gasped as all of our long-lost words surged up around me in a storm of shining images. I heard, but I also *saw,* and saw so clearly, so keenly that it was like stepping out of the depths of a cavern to meet the dazzling face of the sun goddess.

I realized what had happened on that day, what had *really* happened to make my brother shut me out of his life. I understood why simply saying I was sorry wouldn't be enough, and I also knew what I would have to say to restore the way things ought to be between us.

Once my path was clear, time began to race away at its old pace once more. Aki was climbing down the ladder quickly. When his feet touched the ground, he'd dash off as fast as he could. I wouldn't be able to catch him, and what I had to say couldn't wait.

"Aki! Don't go!" I leaped to stop him, running so heedlessly that my bad leg betrayed me. I let out a cry of pain as it folded under me, sending me tumbling. The edge of the porch rushed to meet me, and I shrieked as I pitched over it headfirst, into emptiness.

"Himiko, *no!*"

Strong hands grabbed the back of my tunic. I gagged as the neckline cut into my throat and made choking noises as I was hastily pulled back to the comparative safety of the ladder. Dark blue stars whirled before my eyes. Too many seasons of sadness fell away at the sound of Aki's voice asking tenderly, "Little Sister, are you all right?"

I couldn't answer right away. He shifted awkwardly so that my feet could touch the steps of the ladder beneath him and watched as I slowly made my way to the ground. He followed, but as soon as we stood facing one another, the horrible coldness came flooding back.

"Still a fool," he snapped, and turned on his heel to stride away.

"*You owe me nothing!*" I shouted. My voice rang out so loudly that it blotted away the sounds of the wine-making festival. Aki stopped and looked back over one shoulder, his face contorted with surprise.

"What did you say?"

I stood my ground. I wouldn't be the one to close the gap between us. "I said, you owe me nothing. There's no debt for you to pay, and there never was." I dropped to my knees. "I was wrong, Aki. I'm sorry."

He looked down at me as if seeing a worm. "You said that before, many seasons ago. Why again? Why now?"

"Because now 'I'm sorry' means what it *should* mean to

me, to you!" I spoke quickly, casting my words like tethering cords to keep him from walking away. "Because now I know *why* I should apologize for what I did. That night, when you and Father argued so bitterly and he spoke of banishing you, all the things I said to him came freely. I didn't want anything in exchange except peace in our home. When I spoke to you about returning to the Shika and you refused, I was—I *was* a fool. You never owed me anything, Aki, but I behaved as if you did, to force you to do things my way. No wonder you looked at me and saw a shameless schemer, a selfish manipulator, a deceitful girl who never did anything for others unless she'd get something in return. I don't blame you for shutting someone like that out of your life."

I placed my hands on the ground. "I'm sorry, Big Brother. I wish there were a way for me to prove that *this* apology is more than words. This comes from my heart." I bowed to press my forehead to the earth. "Forgive me."

I barely felt the touch of soil and pebbles on my brow before I was whisked from hands and knees into Aki's arms. Laughing and crying at the same time, he twirled us around. "Little Sister! Oh, my dearest Little Sister, forgive me too!" he cried. "Let the gods punish me for my stubbornness and stupidity! Why did I wait for you to speak? You were a child; why did I act like one?" Sighing, he set me down. "I know the real fool here."

The rest of our clan was too deeply immersed in the various distractions of the wine making to notice when Aki and I slipped out of the village gates. We strolled down to the banks of the stream that fed the irrigation canals, and stood in the shadow of a lone willow whose leafless branches trailed in the water. We spoke of many things that day, serious and silly. I took him into my confidence, telling him all about how Yama had made me her apprentice, and how happy I was to be learning the way of the spirits. It felt so good to be able to share my greatest joy with someone special to me! He wanted to give me his promise to keep this secret safe from Father, but I said, "If he suspects anything, I don't want you oath-bound to lie to him."

"Then I promise nothing," Aki replied solemnly. "But keeping silent about it isn't the same as lying."

He wasn't so solemn when I made the mistake of telling him about Ganju, teasing me gently but relentlessly until I scooped a handful of water-chilled pebbles from the stream and dropped them down the back of his neck. By the time the sun began to set and the first bats flitted through the dimming sky, I had my brother back again.

"You know, Aki, I should thank you," I said as we returned to the village.

"Thank me for what?"

"If you'd given in to me that night, I wouldn't be studying with Lady Yama now." I sighed. "Isn't it strange? I regret that it took so long for us to mend our quarrel, but not the quarrel itself. It led me to my proper place in the world and to the work I was meant to do."

"I regret much more than that, Little Sister," Aki said. He stopped and looked away from me. "I went back."

"What?"

"I went back," he repeated. "I returned to the Shika lands. More than a year had passed, and it was autumn. I was hunting in the mountains and suddenly found myself at the edge of the trees, looking down at Hoshi's village. I told myself it was an accident and blamed the prey I'd been tracking, but if so, it was an accident I repeated many times since then."

"Is that—is that all?" I asked. "You never went closer? You never tried to see Hoshi even once in all the seasons since then?"

He kept his face averted, but I glimpsed a flush of red on his cheek. "I didn't want to risk it. I was afraid that if I saw her and spoke to her again, I'd never be able to leave her. So I haunted those woods the way her face haunted my thoughts and dreams. Sometimes the gods favored me: I caught sight of her walking through the village or going out to work in the fields. Mostly, it was enough for me to know that she was *there*."

My throat tightened. An angry voice within me wanted to shout, *You went back to the Shika village after all! You cast me aside when I asked you to bring me there, but you went back! May the gods punish—!*

No. A second voice, calmer than the first, banished it before it could utter any curse against my brother. *Himiko,* listen. *Listen to the pain in Aki's every word. He knows he did wrong. He knows he acted unjustly toward you. He suffers for it. He doesn't need you to reproach him; he has already condemned himself.*

I laid my hands on Aki's back. "My poor brother, it must have been terrible for you."

There were tears streaking his face when he looked at me. "Every time I went back, I wondered what I'd discover. Would my next sight of her be in company with another man? Would she be carrying his child? Would she be holding a baby that could have been ours if Father wasn't such a—" He bit his lower lip. "No. I can't blame Father for everything. I'm responsible for the life I've lived, and I've lived it as a coward. I deserve to die alone."

I hugged his neck the way I'd done when I was small. "Never, Aki," I said. "While I live, you'll never be alone."

9
WALKING WITH THE DRAGON

Autumn ended and winter was endured. If anyone in our house noticed that Aki and I were friends again, nothing was said about it. Our former closeness was back, though somewhat changed. No matter how carefully he hid the sorrows of his heart from the rest of the family, I always saw the shadow of yearning in his eyes and shared his pain. As for Aki, though he still teased and joked with me, he no longer spoke to me as if I were just a carefree, thoughtless child.

I continued my once-every-three-days lessons with Yama and began the most dangerous part of my studies, the summoning of the dead. More and more frequently, our footprints on the frost made a trail back and forth to our clan's burial place, where the shaman taught me the songs that would draw ghosts from their wanderings. I knelt beside her on the frozen ground, a thick cape pulled tight around my shivering body, and did my best to keep my teeth from chattering as I repeated Yama's chant.

My best was bad. The shaman laid one hand on my shoulder and gave me a pitying look. "We don't call the dead close often, Himiko, and never without good cause. Too many of them bear grudges against the living and would love nothing more than the chance to punish us for the crime of enjoying the pleasures of taste and touch and all the other things that now lie beyond their reach. We *never* summon them timidly. We must show them from the start that *we* are the ones in control. If you keep on c-c-c-c-calling them that way"—she did a fine imitation of my chill-shaken voice—"I'm afraid they'll think you're weak and overwhelm you."

"B-b-but doesn't it take more th-than words to bring them close?" I asked. There was no question that I believed in the spirits of the dead, in their feelings of envy and resentment for the living. I felt their presence as surely as that of the gods. I sensed them lingering at the edges of life, hungrily watching us.

"Sometimes we don't even need words. Often they don't wait to be summoned, but come uninvited."

"Why—" A fresh attack of shivers shook me, but I forced myself to speak without stammering from the cold. "Why summon them at all?"

Yama's mouth was a hard, straight line. "Because there are people in this world who heed fear more than honor. They won't do what's right, but at least they can be scared away from doing what's wrong. Summoning the dead has the power to do that. This is why it's something you should learn, but nothing you should abuse."

"Ah." I shifted my freezing body and sat up straighter. "I promise, Lady Yama. Please teach me how to call them. I'm r-ready now."

The shaman leaned forward and laid the back of her hand against my cheek. It felt very warm, which probably meant my face was ice. She looked mildly worried. "I'd be wiser to teach you the ritual for sending them on their way first, and we can do *that* indoors beside a good fire. This lesson is over." And that was the last business I had with the unquiet spirits of our departed clanfolk for several days.

We were fortunate that year. The winter turned mild and spring came early, once more strewing the far hillside with cherry blossoms. I was the first one awake and about on the morning they revealed themselves. I stepped out of our doorway into the clear, sweet air and was caught up in a sudden rapture when I saw that swath of pink blossoms in the distance. When the rest of my family woke up, they found me kneeling on the porch, gazing happily at the springtime's beauty.

"Uh-oh, this looks bad," Aki joked. "You're not going to run away to see the cherry blossoms again, are you?"

"You needn't worry, Big Brother," I replied. "I'm old enough to know the way there *and* the way home."

"I'm not so sure of that," he said with mock concern. "I'd feel much better if I went with you."

"Don't bother." I pressed my lips together, trying to keep from smiling. "You must have many other things to do. Many, many, *many—*"

"But if I don't go with you, I'll miss the pleasure of seeing the blossoms myself."

"No, you won't," I said, gesturing toward the mountains. "There they are."

"It's not the same as seeing them up close, and you know it."

"Maybe so. I'll tell you what, Aki, you stay here and I'll bring you back a branch of cherry blossoms to admire."

"That would be all right, provided that you've learned the difference between a flowering branch and a bare stick." He laughed. "How long did you hold on to that thing?"

I didn't answer. The truth was that I still had that relic tucked away in my bedroll. It was almost as precious to me as the amulet Yama had given me. I was never without my lady of the dragon stone, but I often carried the bare cherry branch with me too. I always wound up taking it to my lessons with the shaman, though I couldn't say why I felt compelled to do so. Once, I mentioned this to Yama in a small, embarrassed voice, as though I'd been up to something shameful. She gave the leafless twig a long, searching look, then patted me on the back and said, *"There are times we all do things for no other reason than it feels right to us. I believe the spirits have a hand in it, guiding us with whispers onto a path they can see before we do. If no harm comes of it—to us or others— why should we resist?"*

"What's the matter, Himiko?" Aki persisted, tugging one of my hair loops in his old way. "Nothing more to say? Did an owl swoop by so fast I didn't see him steal your tongue?"

"Don't tease your sister." Mama didn't even look up from combing Yukari's hair.

"Never mind Aki, Mama," I piped up. "He can't hear you. His head's so hollow, a pair of woodpeckers nested in his ears." Even Father laughed at that.

"Oh, caw, caw, caw," Shoichi grumbled, blinking sleepily in the sunlight. "Why don't you two crows stop clacking your beaks and go look at the stupid trees?"

"*This* crow wants breakfast first," Aki said cheerfully. "After that, I'm ready to fly. What about you, Little Sister?"

"I'd better come along," I said, deliberately sounding as reluctant as if I'd been asked to carry three storage jars on my back. "If you got lost, I'd never forgive myself."

Aki and I burst into sputtering laughter, and Shoichi rolled his eyes.

"You can go, Aki," Father said gruffly. "But see that you take good care of your sister and that you bring back some game for our dinner. I don't care what you get as long as it's nice and fat." He glanced at Emi with a rare smile and added, "I want this family to be well fed and healthy."

Emi giggled and folded her hands over her swelling belly. The baby she carried would be born in the summer and was already a lively one. We'd all felt it kicking heartily.

"Anything you catch will be good, Aki," Emi said. "And if there's nothing worth your arrows, don't worry about it. We all know there won't be many fat animals to be found now. It's too soon since winter."

"Ha! You're talking to the young man who kept our rice topped with meat all through the lean season," Father replied, his pride in Aki plain to see. "He'll do it. Right, my son?"

Aki dipped his head. "As you say, Father."

We left as soon as breakfast was over. Aki carried his bow and quiver; I took my bare cherry branch stuck into my belt like a sword. Aki's eyes widened when he noticed it.

"Is that the same—?"

"It's good luck," I said, holding my chin high, and refused to say another word about it, despite Aki's inquisitiveness, until he gave up and changed the subject.

"Things will be quite different at home soon, Himiko," he said as we walked out of the village gateway.

"I know. Do you think Emi will have a boy or a girl? I'd like to have a little sister." Every time I thought about the coming birth, I was filled with happy anticipation.

He shrugged. "You're the one who's so close with our shaman. You should ask her to implore the gods for a little girl."

"It doesn't work that way."

"I know; I was only joking. But her prayers must have *some* effect. We all saw how often Emi visited the shaman's house with gifts, and now, after many years, she's finally pregnant again."

"Lady Yama likes gifts, but she would have helped Emi even if she'd brought her nothing," I said.

"Is that so?" Aki raised one eyebrow. "And yet, when she forced Father to let you help in her house every three days, she called it a debt."

"Can you think of a better way to make him give in to

her? How could he preserve his honor if the village heard he'd failed to respect what he *owed* our shaman?"

"Ha! Clever woman. I hope she's not teaching *you* all that cleverness. You'd grow up to rule the world!"

"Oh, I'd never want to do that on my own, Aki. If Emi has a little girl, I'll let her share my power. It's the least a sister can do," I replied lightly.

"I wasn't thinking of Emi's child when I said things will be different at home, Little Sister. Everyone else will know this soon enough, but yesterday Shoichi took me aside and said that he wants to get married."

"Shoichi? Impossible!" I cried.

Aki found my reaction *much* too amusing for my taste. "Himiko, you're goggling like a frog! You may see Shoichi as just another miserable brother who does nothing except torment you, but he's old enough to take a wife and make a home of his own."

"Why did he tell you first?" I asked. "Why not Father?"

"Why do any of us keep secrets from Father?" Aki answered, his good humor suddenly extinguished. "He wanted to know if I thought Father would approve of the girl. I said yes, so our brother's going ahead with it."

"What would he have done if you'd said Father wouldn't approve?"

"Do you need to ask that?" Aki's expression went from rueful to grim. "What have *I* done for so many years? Kept away from the girl I love because of him. I should have had a home of my own by now. I should have been my own man. Instead, I'm still nothing more than *his* son. Did you hear how he spoke to me just now? *'You can go, Aki.'*" He mimicked Father's intonation perfectly, but in a voice steeped in bitterness. "Do I *need* his permission? Do I have to die to escape his control, or does he?"

"Aki, don't say such things!" I grabbed his arm and dug in my feet, bringing us both to a dead halt at the edge of the fields.

A fresh change came over my beloved brother's face. He was no longer downhearted, but determined. The rich smell of the reviving earth was all around us, a scent heavy with the magic of new beginnings. "Himiko," he said quietly. "How would you like to see your friend Kaya again?"

I held my breath for three heartbeats. If this was a dream, I didn't want to do anything that might blow it away. "You heard what Mama said, Aki," I replied at last. "Don't tease me."

"I'm not teasing. I'm going back to the Shika village. I'm going back, and this time I'm not going to haunt the forest, waiting to catch sight of Hoshi. I'm going to walk through their gates and see her face to face. I don't know how she'll react, or if she'll even remember who I am, but I'm not going to leave this unfinished any longer." He took my hands. "Come with me."

"Aki, how can we—?" I stopped. Old words from the argument that parted us whispered through my mind: *"You're smart, Aki. You can find a way. . . ."* I smiled. I'd been right. "I will come with you, Big Brother. Tell me what we'll do."

We walked on, but though the beauty of the blossoming trees before us was like a wonderful song, my ears were deaf to everything but Aki's plan. His part in it was simple:

who'd question another hunting trip? I had more complicated steps to follow: I'd need to get our shaman to send me with him. *"She's told everyone what a help you are to her, how your young eyes are better at spotting the plants she uses for her potions. Here's her chance to spare herself a hard trek into the mountains! She can trust me to protect you and trust you to fetch whatever she needs. She might be reluctant at first, but that won't stop you, will it, Little Sister? I know how persuasive you can be."*

I promised him that I'd do my best. He was so pleased with himself for coming up with that plan! I didn't want to steal his glory by saying I wouldn't need to persuade Yama at all. I intended to tell her everything, knowing that she'd recognize this journey for what it was: a healing. She'd do all she could to help us.

"I'm so happy, Aki," I said as we walked on. "I can't wait to see you and Hoshi together again. She's going to be overjoyed, I know it!"

"You have brighter hopes of that meeting than I do, Little Sister. I think she's only going to be confused. I'll have to do some hunting on the way so that she'll welcome me for the gift, at least."

"She'll welcome you even if you arrive empty-handed," I said. "I do wonder what Kaya's going to say when she sees me. Probably, 'Who are you?' I hope Lady Ikumi will do something to save me too much embarrassment." I kicked a rock out of our path. "Whatever happens, it'll be worth taking this chance. How soon can we go?"

"How soon can you talk to our shaman about—?"

Aki's words died. My brother turned to stone. His eyes were fixed on something in the distance, and it wasn't the cherry trees. I followed the direction of his gaze and saw a sight that was completely new to me, and completely terrifying: a company of armed men coming toward us on the road that led to our village. I couldn't tell exactly how many of them there were, but the sun goddess's light was reflecting off the metal bosses of their shields and the blades of their towering polearms.

"Go home, Himiko," Aki said in a strained voice. "Go as swiftly as possible, but don't run—don't let them *see* you run—until you're within sight of our gates. Then *race*! Alert the sentry, sound the alarm—"

"Aki, what about you?" I clung to my brother's arm desperately.

"I'm staying here. This might not be anything more than a trading party. They travel armed too. Whatever business those men have with the Matsu, I'm going to delay them while I can. Now, *go*!" He shoved me away so roughly that I staggered.

I did as he said, walking quickly without breaking into my ungainly run until our village was in sight. *I've got to do better than this!* I groaned to myself, lamenting how badly my mishealed leg was hampering me yet again. *I can't be this slow: I have to warn our people!* Clenching my teeth, I put all my strength into a fresh burst of speed. It was more of a high-speed stumble than a run, but though it felt like I was going to trip over my own feet at every second step, I closed the distance to the gate faster and faster.

The first of our clanfolk were heading out to the fields, but when they saw me racing toward them, the work songs died on their lips. Some of the men dropped their farming tools and rushed ahead to meet me, demanding to know what was wrong. I told them, and the next thing I knew, I was being swept back to my house between two men while all around us the Matsu made ready for battle.

My escorts had their arms linked through mine and were moving so fast, my feet nearly left the ground. "Stop, please stop!" I cried as we passed under the shadow of the sacred pine tree. "I'm all right; I can get home on my own."

"We only wanted to help you reach safety, Lady Himiko," one of them said.

"Thank you, but you don't have to worry about me. You're needed elsewhere." They bowed and ran off to arm themselves.

I leaned against the venerable tree and caught my breath while I watched every able-bodied man in our village swarm past, feet pounding thunder from the ground, swords or bows or polearms in their hands. Father and Shoichi ran by without seeing me, coming so close that I could have reached out and touched them. I couldn't see Masa, but he was probably working frantically at the blacksmith's side, searching the forge for usable weapons.

As the men rushed to close our gates and defend the palisade, women, children, and the old were moving as fast as they could away from the wooden walls, taking shelter in their houses.

I should go home too, I thought. *I should, but I don't want to. I should go, so that Mama, Yukari, and Emi know I'm safe, but then what? They'll want to know what happened to Aki, and once I tell them that—!* I shuddered, already hearing their wails of grief. Mama would be devastated, and who knew how much harm such a shock might do to Emi's unborn child? The news of the armed strangers had put my poor mothers under enough stress; they shouldn't have to handle more just yet.

Suddenly I had an idea that would relieve their minds about me but shield them from hearing of Aki's fate for as long as possible. I emerged from the shelter of the pine and looked around until I saw one of our village boys, too old to cling to his mother, too young to help defend us, but just the right age to hope he could be a part of all the excitement. I called him to me at once.

"Yes, Lady Himiko?" he said, clearly thrilled to be needed.

"Listen, I have a very important job for you. Go tell my mother you saw me and that I'm going to Lady Yama's house. Above all, tell her not to worry because Aki said the men coming here are probably a trading party. They carry weapons too."

"Really?" The boy looked disappointed.

"Yes, *really*. Now please, remember everything I told you."

"Trust me, Lady Himiko!" he said, showing a gap-toothed smile, and sped away.

I watched him go, then headed in the other direction. *It wasn't a lie,* I told myself. *It* wasn't, *but it wasn't the whole truth, either. I* am *going to Lady Yama's house. What's the harm if Mama believes our shaman sent for me? I don't want to go home yet. How can I help our clan if I'm hidden away, cowering like a baby mouse? Lady Yama must be preparing to call on the spirits to protect us. Maybe there's something I can do to aid her. Oh, gods, punish me for lying if you must, but let me save my people!*

I was only a few steps from Yama's house when I heard my father's voice ring out from high overhead. I looked to the watchtower and saw him gesturing with his sword to the massed men below. "Open the gates!" he bellowed. "My son is coming! Open the gates!"

I forgot all about seeing the shaman. Instead, I hurried toward the village gateway in time to see the great doors swing out just wide enough to let Aki come running in. His face was flushed, but he was smiling ear to ear. He opened his mouth to speak, and the men surrounded him, cutting off my view. I couldn't hear what he said, but their reaction told the tale: loud cheers filled the air, and every face shone bright with happy relief.

Father pushed his way through the roaring crowd. He'd descended from the watchman's post so swiftly that I wondered if he'd jumped while partway down. "Stand aside! Where's my son? Aki, are you all right? What happened?"

"They've come here peaceably, Father," my brother replied, giddy with his own good news. "They don't want a fight. As soon as they told me that, I ran ahead to tell you. They'll be here shortly."

"They, they, *they*?" Father barked. "You keep saying *they* as if I would know what you're talking about. Who are *they*? What do they want here? To trade with us? To ask our help? What?"

"I—" Aki began. His face fell into confusion. "I don't know why they've come. They're from the Ookami clan, the wolf people, and their chieftain is with them."

"The Ookami . . ." Father's face became impenetrable. "I have heard their name." He turned to his men and began giving orders for the village to prepare for a ceremony of welcome instead of a battle. Aki might as well have become a drop of water sinking into parched ground without a trace.

By the time the Ookami party reached our palisade, the gates were wide open and Father stood ready to greet them, attended by his fellow nobles. My brothers were there as well, summoned by his command. Shoichi and Masa stood next to Aki at his right side while Yama remained a few steps back, at his left. Our shaman was an imposing presence, her neck hung heavily with beads, a crown of dried flowers on her silvery hair. Her hands were crossed over her chest, one holding a mirror, the other a bronze bell. A second mirror hung from her neck and flung reflected shafts of sunlight in all directions at her slightest move. More mirrors dangled from her belt, girdling her with brilliance.

On Father's orders, most of our clanfolk had laid their arms aside—out of sight but near at hand, just in case. However, he'd also commanded five of his brawniest men to stand in a row by the gateway, bearing polearms. When the Ookami entered, it would be under the shadow of our weapons. I observed all this from my own place, at Yama's back. I carried a bamboo platter laden with the things our shaman would need to perform her ritual of greeting, as well as a small clay bottle of rice wine as a welcome gift for our guests. If Father noticed my presence at all, he must have shrugged it off as part of my continuing "service" to our shaman.

The Ookami party crossed our moat and stopped just outside our gateway. Now that there was no immediate danger, I was avid for my first close look at them. I peered around Yama and saw a group of eight men who didn't look all that different from us. Five of them carried polearms, like Father's guards, and wore swords at their sides. Two more— a thickset, gray-haired older man and a lean, handsome one who looked about Aki's age—were richly dressed and armed with swords alone. The last man in the group wore a tunic that was badly stained and tattered. His back was bent under a pile of bundles that must have contained supplies for the Ookami party's journey. His face was thin, his eyes were empty, and an awful air of weariness hung about him.

No one had to tell me what he was. I knew I saw a slave, and the sight was bitter.

The gray-haired man and Father regarded each other steadily for the time it took me to draw five breaths. Then our uninvited guest pulled back his shoulders, stood taller, and bawled, "I am Nago, chieftain of the Ookami clan. I come with open hands and swear in the sight of the gods that all I seek are words with your own chieftain." He then shouted orders to his escort to disarm themselves. They all laid down their polearms but didn't remove their swords.

Father returned Nago's formal greeting in a strong, carrying voice. "If you come to the Matsu for words and nothing more, I welcome you!" He clapped his hands, and Yama stepped forward, lifting her voice in an eerie chant that bored its way into my bones. As she sang, she swayed like a tree in a high wind and slowly traced the tightly woven pattern of a brief dance. When she was done, she struck the bronze bell and held the mirror above her head so that sunlight stabbed the eyes of the Ookami chieftain. He stood his ground, never flinching or raising his hand to shield his eyes. When Yama lowered the mirror at last, she nodded, then beckoned me to offer Nago the wine. He drank deeply and passed it to the younger man, who sipped it as if he suspected a live snake were lurking at the bottom of the jar. It was then passed to the remaining free men, and the ceremony was over.

"Well done, Himiko," Yama whispered to me as we watched Father lead the Ookami away. "Now come help me store these things." She started toward her house.

I lingered, devoured by curiosity. "Why isn't Father taking them to our house?" I asked.

Yama shrugged. "I'd guess he doesn't want their presence to upset Emi. It could be that, or else— Does your family still have that trophy? The one your brothers brought home from the wolf hunt, years ago?"

"Oh!" I understood what Yama meant. It would have been a very bad thing to invite the wolf clan men into a house that displayed a wolf's skull. "We do. No wonder Father's entertaining them in someone else's house."

I must have sounded disappointed because Yama smirked and said, "Don't worry, Himiko, you'll have your chance to get a good, long look at the strangers when it's time to feed them. Smell that smoke? Our women are all busy cooking a feast for the visitors, to impress them with how rich and strong we Matsu are. No doubt our chieftain will want our prettiest girls to serve them, and that's when he'll call for you."

But Yama was mistaken. Father sent for me much

earlier than that. We had just reached her doorway when Masa came running up to us, calling my name. "Come with me, Little Sister. Father has something important for you to do."

"What is it?"

"Baby tending." My youngest brother laughed, then made a sour face. "The Ookami chieftain's son has already grown tired of listening to the older men talk. He's been shifting and squirming in his place this whole time, like an impatient child. His own father either doesn't notice or doesn't care, because he hasn't said a word about it, but our father looks ready to *bite*! He took me aside and told me to fetch you. He wants you to take the child for a walk and distract him until it's time to eat, but said if doing that makes you feel ill at ease, he understands and you don't have to—"

"It would be my pleasure to help Father." I spoke so demurely that Masa gave me a profoundly skeptical look before leading me to the house where the chieftains were meeting.

Father presented me to our guests. "You remember my daughter Himiko, Lord Nago?"

The Ookami chieftain chuckled. "The pretty one who greeted me with such excellent rice wine is your girl? Are all of your daughters so graceful and lovely?"

"I have no other daughters."

"Then you're a lucky man to have this one, isn't he, Ryu?" The Ookami chieftain turned to his son. The younger man nodded, and a thin smile parted his lips.

"I asked Masa to bring Himiko here," Father said. "As

my daughter, it's her job to make our visitors feel at home by making our village as familiar to them as their own." It was a half-truth to rival the message I'd sent to Mama, since this was the first time we'd ever *had* visitors. "You've said you want to be on your way again before sunset, and we have much to talk about, but could you spare your son from our discussions? Himiko takes such pride in what she does that she'd be horribly disappointed if she couldn't escort at least one of your party through our village."

Lord Nago's grin was a little unsettling. "It's bad luck to disappoint a beautiful girl. The gods give us so few of them. Ryu! Go with Lady Himiko and thank all the spirits for the gift that's fallen into your lap." With a barely perceptible bow, his son obeyed and followed me out of the house. I could almost hear the sighs of relief from Father and my brothers.

I decided that it might be best to show the chieftain's son our fields first, then return inside the palisade so that we'd be easy to find when it was time to eat. As we walked, I was pleased to notice that Ryu was listening carefully to my every word. After what Masa told me about Ryu's constant fidgeting, I'd expected a bored and reluctant companion. Instead, I never once sensed his eyes wandering away from me. Since I wasn't talking about anything more fascinating than the crops and the weather, so much attention was especially flattering. When he spoke to me about his own village, I was free to study his face, so very strong and handsome.

I wonder what he thinks of me? I mused, drifting off into a daydream. *His father said I'm pretty, but he was just being polite. And yet . . . does Ryu think so?* It did no harm to let my mind wander that way. Any fantasies I'd had about love were empty. Ganju was the only boy in our village who'd been bold enough to approach a chieftain's daughter, but when I wasn't able to meet him at the wine-making festival, he'd looked elsewhere. The next day, every gossiping tongue in our village was wagging over how shamelessly he'd flirted with Ume that night—Ume, of all people!—and how she'd wrapped herself around him like a damp petal ever since. I told myself that if he was that shallow, I was fortunate to have lost him. But to *Ume*? That hurt.

Oh, I do hope Ganju sees me walking with Lord Ryu! I thought. *Ganju* and *Ume!* I imagined their reaction and bit back a giggle.

As I guided our footsteps toward the gates once again, I said, "Thank you very much, Lord Ryu. You're a gracious guest."

"Am I?" The Ookami chieftain's son seemed amused. "What makes you say that?"

"You've spent all this time humoring me, tramping all around our fields when you've already had a hard day's march and more to come. I can't believe you're going to leave us before sunset. My father must have misunderstood—"

"He didn't. We're the wolf people. We sleep in our own dens or under the sky, nowhere else." A proud note came into his voice, hard and sharp as an arrowhead. "It keeps us stronger than the other clans."

We were crossing the simple wooden span over the village moat, but his arrogant words checked me where I stood. By that time of day, everyone was already at their work. Unless our tower lookout happened to glance down, there was no one to witness me confronting Ryu.

"The Matsu are strong too!" I cried, leaping to defend my people.

"I know that. If it weren't so, my father wouldn't be wasting his time negotiating with yours right now."

"Negotiating?"

"For an alliance. That's why we've come. Your people do have a reputation as good fighters, even if you've let your warriors' swords rust for years. Your father could stand a lesson from his predecessor, Lady Tsuki. Now *there* was a chieftain! If she hadn't died, she might have led *you* to conquer *us*!" He laughed harshly. "When the Matsu join the Ookami, there won't be any clan that can stand against us. We'll be so rich and powerful that our lands will reach all the way to the sea, our people will wear silk, and even our smallest children will have slaves to serve them. Everyone will benefit." The corners of his mouth lifted lazily. "Especially you."

"Everyone but the slaves," I said coldly, remembering a pair of bleak eyes and a forlorn face. "You're talking about war. How would that benefit *me*?"

"As a chieftain's bride, you'll have your choice of every luxury. I'm sorry that I'm already married. Chizu's a nice enough girl, even if she's got a face that's plain as rice gruel. You're much prettier than she is. I wish I'd met you first. You deserve a higher rank than junior wife. Who knows? If you please me enough, I might consider demoting Chizu, or setting her aside altogether. You can help me decide." He spoke as casually as if he were juggling horse chestnuts instead of human lives.

I no longer hoped that Ganju and Ume would see me in this man's company. I wanted nothing more than to be free of him and his cold arrogance.

"Fine," I said. "I'm good at making decisions. In fact, I've made one right now. I've decided that if the gods ever force me to choose between marrying you and swallowing a live salamander—" I tilted my head back and pantomimed gulping down the wriggly creature.

He slapped me. When I cupped my hand to my stinging cheek, he grabbed me by the wrist. His fingers dug in so deeply, it felt like they were grinding my bones. I sucked in a deep breath, but before I could shout *Let me go!* his lips covered mine. Fighting to free myself from that loathsome kiss, I took a few lurching steps sideways, to the very edge of the bridge. The instant he felt himself teetering, Ryu released me and jumped away.

"Be careful, you clumsy turtle!" he barked. "You almost made us—"

I rushed at him with outstretched arms and struck him directly in the center of his chest with both fists. The impact threw him off his feet and over the edge of the bridge. I paused just long enough to hear the satisfying thud he made when he hit the bottom of the ditch, then ran.

I didn't head back through the palisade gates. Our moat wasn't deep enough for Ryu's fall to do him any lasting harm. He'd be clambering out of it all too soon, and when he did, I was certain he'd assume I'd run home. While he went hunting me within our village walls, I planned to be well out of sight in a hiding place he'd never suspect.

Once I'm there, all I'll have to do is outwait him, I thought as I put distance between myself and the Ookami lordling. *It will be safe for me to return when the feast is ready. He won't dare say a word about any of this in front of so many people. At best, he'd be humiliated because I beat him, and at worst, his father and mine would make him pay with his hide for how he treated me!* I was breathing hard but grinning with triumph as I stepped past the boundary stones that marked the borders of our burial place. *Even if he realizes I'm not in the village, he'll never dare to look for me here.*

I moved among the low mounds with reverence. All of Yama's lessons about the summoning and dismissal of the dead were with me. I didn't fear their presence, knowing I possessed the lore that would keep any angry spirits too far away to harm me. Still, I found that one hand strayed to my sash, where my cherry tree wand was tucked, and the other to my chest, where my dragon stone amulet hung from a cord long enough to keep it secret from everyone but me.

Most of the grave sites around me were no higher than my ankles, their original height worn away by the turning of the seasons and the slow shifting of the earth. I recognized the places where we'd buried Yukari's and Emi's infants and wondered where my family's other lost children lay. I clapped my hands to call out to the gods and whispered prayers for the spirits of our dear ones to rest undisturbed.

There was one mound there that stood out from all the rest. I'd noticed it every time I'd come to the burial ground, but whenever I'd asked about it, I was told to find better things to occupy my mind. Even Yama refused to speak of it, shaking her head and saying, *"Another time, Himiko. That one's listening—I sense it. Remember what I taught you? For some spirits, just to mention them is as good as an invocation. I'd rather not deal with banishing the uninvited today."*

The mound was almost as tall as me, a raised square of soil surrounded by its own narrow moat. The sweet, new grass of springtime that covered every other grave grew only sparsely over this one, the waving blades a sickly shade of green. I felt a qualm as I gazed at the desolate tomb, but tightened my grip on the reassuring shape of my amulet and it passed.

It doesn't matter who lies there, I thought. *I know the chants by heart for sending ghosts away. I know them even better than the chants for summoning! This place is as safe for me as any.* I circled the mound until I found a spot where its surrounding ditch had collapsed inward and settled myself down to wait for the day to pass.

The sun was warm on my face, and a gentle breeze carried the scent of newly turned earth from our fields. I rested my chin on my up-drawn knees and idly watched the comings and goings of insects at my feet. Somewhere birds were singing, declaring their courtships and challenges from tree to tree. I fished my amulet from its hiding place and let my lady of the dragon stone drink the light.

I was enthralled by the play of sunbeams on the gold and silver web embracing her, but not so absorbed that I didn't hear a new sound invading my peaceful retreat: a stream of curses slashing through the air, their brutal ugliness coming closer with my every breath. I shifted into a crouch and crept on hands and knees to peer around the corner of the tomb.

I knew what I'd see before I laid eyes on him, but I had to confirm my dread: it was Ryu, filthy and battered from his fall, striding toward my hiding place. His mouth spewed oaths and threats of what he intended to do once he caught me. Would he *dare*? Had I enraged him so much that he'd give no thought to my clan's retaliation? I didn't want to find out. He was coming closer, his long legs devouring the distance between us. His eyes were fixed on the ground, a hunter on the trail of his quarry. I'd hidden myself, but not my footprints in the dirt.

If I remained where I was, he'd find me. If I broke away and ran, he'd catch me. If I screamed, no one was close enough to hear it. I closed my hand over the dragon stone, tightened my fingers around the black branch that had once been sweet with flowers, and stepped out of the shelter of the tomb.

"Stop where you stand, Ryu!" My shout echoed so loudly over the place of the dead that the sky itself pulsed with the sound. The Ookami lordling froze, astonished, but not as astonished as I. *What just happened? Did that voice come from me?* I pushed my amazement aside. I wasn't out of danger by any means, and I had to build on this unexpected advantage while I could.

"Don't come any closer!" This time, the power that had possessed my voice was gone. It was still loud and forceful, but there was nothing extraordinary about the sound. "This ground is sacred! This is where the spirits of our people rest. You will not profane it!"

Ryu's awestruck expression withered and hardened into his old, self-assured sneer. "Listen to you chirp, you puny cricket! Playing grown-up, are you? But grown-ups know the meaning of good manners. What do you think will happen when I drag you back into your pathetic village and tell your father how you attacked his honored guest?"

"What do you think will happen to you when I tell him and *your* father how you attacked *me*?" I countered.

His scornful laughter was as cold as his eyes. "You call that an attack? A kiss? You *are* an infant. A woman would feel grateful."

"Then I'm glad to be an infant! The only thing I feel for you is disgust, and for your wife, nothing but pity."

"What you *feel*?" he repeated. He laughed again, the lifeless sound of dead leaves rattling on the branch. "Better learn to *think*. Do you know what an honor it is for you if I even *consider* taking you as my bride?"

"You're right; I wasn't thinking." I smiled as I spoke. "That proves I'm not worthy of such an 'honor.' Thank the gods for that!"

"Is *that* what you're thankful for, little fool?" Ryu took a step toward me, and I saw how abruptly a handsome face can turn ugly. "You're a rude child, and it's time I taught you respect!"

"Stay where you are!" I raised my arms like a hawk's mantled wings. "This place is forbidden to you!"

"Who forbids it? You?" He showed his teeth, and the image of the wolf's skull flashed across my sight. "Try."

He moved forward, his expression taunting me. He was

in no hurry. I think he expected me to run and was relishing the thought of the chase and the capture.

I didn't feed the wolf what he wanted. I took a single backward step, and stamped down hard on the earth that covered the Matsu dead. In that place where so many of my clanfolk's bones were laid, I lifted my voice to the spirits.

I didn't use the chant that Yama had taught me for summoning the dead. She'd warned me that my skills were still too new, too untried to begin such a potentially devastating spell. *"The words are only part of what controls our ghosts,"* she told me. *"Our hands, our feet, our bodies, must all be a part of the dance that weaves this great enchantment, and you, Himiko—"*

She didn't need to say it: no matter how many times I tried to copy the shaman's steps and motions, I failed. I couldn't dance, and so I mustn't chance setting loose powers I'd be unable to command or dismiss. Words were not enough to bind the dead.

That was so, but words could still command the living. Ryu was an outlander. He didn't know our ways, or the ways of our shamans. All that I had to do was make him *think* that I was calling the hostile spirits to help me, and that would be enough to send him fleeing. I pitched my voice low and threatening, rolling with its own thunder, then high and shrill, like the edge of a knife scraping over stone. I swayed, and made grand gestures with my black branch, aiming it at the sun, at the tomb beside me, and at Ryu's heart.

"What are you doing?" He stood still, caught between anger and uncertainty. "What nonsense are you jabbering?

Do I have to slap you silent? I will! I swear by all the gods, I—!"

A shiver of motion rippled under my feet. I swayed again, this time without trying. He felt it too. His eyes opened wide, and his mouth was a circle. The tremor shocked the chanting from my lips. The hush that hung between us was heavy with a presence I could not name but also could not deny. I inhaled a breath that prickled over my tongue and made my whole body burn.

I drove it out of me in a screech that would have frightened demons.

Ryu ran.

I watched his retreating figure, but felt no sense of victory. I was too drained to feel anything. My legs folded under me, and I dropped to my knees, hands hot and dry as they clung to the amulet and the wand. I don't know how much time passed before I was able to stand up and go home.

I didn't attend the feast. All of the cooking was already done, but there were plenty of other fetch-and-carry tasks I could use as excuses for my absence. Our clan potter's bossy, quick-tempered nature made her an excellent supervisor for the event, since Mama and my stepmothers couldn't be absent without insulting our guests. After the Ookami left, she made it a point to seek out my parents and tell them about what a wonderful help I'd been.

"So that's where you were, Himiko?" Mama hugged me. "I'm so proud of you."

"Hunh!" Father was taken aback by the potter's report. "Praise that comes from that one is something special. She doesn't like anybody."

I felt like a fraud.

That night, when everyone was supposed to be asleep, I overheard Father and Mama talking about our visitors.

"An alliance?" Mama whispered. "We're joining the wolf people? When?"

"Never," Father replied, and I nearly yelped for joy. "Lord Nago *wants* us to join his people, but he also wants to go out and look for wars to fight. I don't."

"I'm glad. I didn't like his looks, and that son of his—! A good-looking young man, but there's something nasty about him."

"A pig dropping covered with gold." Father chuckled.

"He was covered with filth, anyway. Did you see how ragged and dirty he looked at dinner?" She clucked her tongue.

"He didn't look like that when Himiko took him to tour the village. Believe me, dear one, as soon as I saw how unkempt he looked when he rejoined his father, I sent someone to see what had become of her. That wolf puppy doesn't know how fast I'd have clipped his tail if anything had happened to our girl. Lucky for him my man reported that she was already helping with the feast, safe, unrumpled, and clean as a washed egg. However our Ookami prince managed to get himself into such a mess, Himiko had nothing to do with it."

They fell silent. I thought they'd gone to sleep, but then I heard Mama say, "Did the nobles agree with your decision not to ally with the wolf people?"

"Eventually. After Lord Nago and his men departed, one of my lords confided that he was worried. 'If we're not their allies when they make war on other clans, how long before they come to make war on us? At least if we sided with them, we'd be safe.'" He sighed. "I told him that I'd known overly ambitious people like Lord Nago before. Their word of honor means nothing. They make countless promises to win over others—friendship, riches, power, security—but keep their word only as long as it suits their purpose." Father's bedroll rustled. "A mouse that makes a bargain with a viper is safe only until the viper gets hungry." I heard them kiss, and then I fell asleep.

10
THE HEALING PATH

Aki and I never did go to see the cherry blossoms that year. The days following the departure of the Ookami were taken up with too much work for both of us. Father called his most trusted counselors together to talk about the possible consequences of his decision to refuse Lord Nago's offer of alliance. He insisted that Aki be present and listened attentively to everything my oldest brother had to say. Aki found this new mark of favor immensely flattering and gratifying. Nothing would keep him from attending those meetings.

"You wouldn't believe it, Himiko," he told me when the two of us were working in the fields. "Father asked *me* what I thought!"

"It's about time," I said a little grumpily. We'd spent all that morning bent over row after row of seedlings, and my back was stiff and sore. "You're going to be our next chieftain. He should have included you long ago."

Aki straightened up and looked away from me. "Don't

blame Father, Himiko; he tried. I was the one who was too busy. Going on a hunt always seemed more exciting to me than sitting in a circle listening to a bunch of old—*older* men talk on and on."

"It *is* more exciting," I said, wiping sweat from my brow with the back of my arm.

"Only sometimes. And it's nowhere near as important."

"Bringing home meat to feed your family's not important?"

"The decisions we discuss in council affect *every* family in our clan. I don't know if I'll make a good chieftain—and I'm in no hurry to find out—but I have to prepare. It's time I grew up, Himiko."

I stood and stretched the kinks out of my spine, then slapped dirt from my hands. "Aki, if you're not grown up, no one is. Look at how old you are! There are boys in our village younger than you who've already got wi—" I bit off the end of what I'd been about to say—*wives and children*—and cursed my hasty tongue.

"You make me sound older than Lady Yama," Aki said lightly. If he'd guessed what I'd nearly said, he didn't show it. "Even if I were, it wouldn't carry any weight. Growing up is more than a matter of counting years. There are plenty of old fools in the world."

And young ones, I thought, regretting how close I'd come to hurting him. Without another word, I went back to work. If I kept my hands busy, maybe I wouldn't have the time to say anything else stupid.

Aki bent to his own task, but not before stooping near me and murmuring in my ear, "It's all right, Himiko. I know you didn't mean to say that." My cheeks flamed as he went on: "If anyone should be embarrassed over what my life lacks, it's me. And if anyone can mend that, it's me too."

Day followed day, and I watched the distant flourish of pink blooms dwindle away, branch by branch, tree by tree. *There will be other seasons,* I told myself. But a nagging whisper of doubt kept asking, *And will they be any different from this one? Branch by branch, tree by tree, life is passing. How long before nothing is left for you but a bare, black twig in your hand?*

If Aki's days since the Ookami visit were occupied by his new importance at Father's side, mine were filled with the ongoing business of study in Yama's house. She no longer supervised me when I compounded salves and potions, but trusted me with the entire process, from gathering the ingredients to sealing the finished medicines in their jars. She took special pride in seeing how clearly and cleverly I marked the wet clay stoppering each container with symbols of my own invention.

"Excellent," she said, kneeling at my side as she watched me put the finishing touch on one project. "Just see to it that you don't forget to add *my* symbols to yours, or I'll have to come running to you every time I forget what each jar holds. My half brother Michio taught me this method years ago, to save time and waste. I've never had to risk breaking a good jar to find out what's inside. By the way"—she squinted at the simplified images of a flower and a house I'd used to label one remedy—"what *is* inside this one?"

"The syrup for treating too much stomach gas," I replied, and we both laughed.

My brother might have missed the season of cherry

blossoms, but he hadn't forgotten our plan for a far more important journey. One evening, as spring was waning into summer, he took me aside and said, "When can you speak with Lady Yama about accompanying me into the mountains? I don't want to put this off any longer."

"I'll ask her tomorrow," I said. "Emi will be giving birth soon. I'm going to suggest that I go gather plants that give strength to infants and nursing mothers. They aren't growing plentifully near the village."

My brother beamed. "Perfect. Lady Yama's certain to approve." He didn't say what we were both thinking: *And Father won't be able to object. He'll do anything to make sure that, this time, the child thrives.*

As I'd expected, I didn't have to resort to ruses or persuasion when I sought Yama's aid for our plan. As she and I worked together, tying herbs into bunches for drying, I told her exactly what Aki and I had in mind. Our shaman was fully in favor of it.

"There's no greater pain for a shaman than being unable to ease suffering," she said. "I've had to watch your brother's grief for so long, it's become my own. He's been carrying an arrow in his flesh for many seasons, and I'm glad that he's ready to pull it out. Whether it leaves a wound that heals cleanly or it tears his heart, it's better than bleeding away a little every day."

"I wish there were another way," I said. "I don't want him to be hurt anymore."

"Not even if he has to be hurt in order to become well? Ah, I can see you don't care for that idea, but when you're a healer in your own right, you'll understand."

"When I become a healer, I'll find new ways to take away pain," I declared, tying a tight knot around the last bundle of greens. "Ways where the cure doesn't hurt worse than the sickness!"

For some reason, Yama seemed amused by my announcement. "Nicely said, but not so easily done. Your training is coming along well, but there are many things you still need to learn, and some lessons that you'd better perfect under this roof before you try them on your own. It would have been a tragedy if you'd summoned the wrong ghost on the day we welcomed the Ookami. *That* one wouldn't have been satisfied with scaring off their chieftain's loutish son, and she wouldn't have been so easy to send back afterward."

"That one—? Which—?" I was thunderstruck by how glibly she spoke of ghosts. *"How did you know?"* I blurted.

"Not through magic, Himiko," she said. "I've taught you to listen. Now learn to *look* as well. I was at the feast that day. I didn't see you, but I saw the Ookami creature. He looked like a man who'd witnessed fearsome things. He guzzled rice wine, only picked at his food, and jumped at the slightest unexpected sound. We'd all felt the earth tremor that afternoon, but I couldn't imagine why such a mild one would turn a healthy young man into a nerve-racked rabbit! When I asked what was troubling him, he denied anything was wrong. His eyes told another story. I pretended to take him at his word.

"I encouraged him to talk. I asked him about his journey, about his family, and finally about you. He changed the subject quickly, but not quickly enough. His father overheard. 'See what a ragged mess this boy is!' Lord Nago said scornfully. 'He goes off with the prettiest girl in this village and comes back alone, looking like *that*. What, Ryu, did you fight a wild boar bare-handed to win the Matsu chieftain's daughter? No, that wasn't your way. *You* tried to impress her by turning into a coward right before her eyes!'"

"Why would Lord Nago say something like that?" I asked softly.

"Maybe he'd had too much wine. Then again, maybe he simply likes bullying others, but calls it teasing so he'll have someplace to hide if they fight back. He mocked his son for running away and leaving you behind when the earth shifted. 'Poor little Lady Himiko, abandoned!' he bawled. 'Forsaken, helpless, defenseless—!'" Yama dropped her imitation of the mean-spirited chieftain and gave me a pointed look. "*That* was when Ryu shouted, 'Defenseless? Abandoned? *Her?* Ha! Not when she could call for so many ready to protect her. I wish you had been there. I wish you'd seen them. I wish you'd join them!' And he burst into a drunken laugh that lifted every hair on my head.

"His father looked ready to choke the life out of him. He ordered him to leave, and Ryu was happy to obey. I think he went off to be sick; no surprise there." Yama looked lost in thought. "He said you could call for so many ready to protect you. So many . . . So many *what*, Himiko? He didn't say. I believe he didn't dare." The shaman folded her hands in her lap. "That was when I knew what you had done." She stared at me severely.

I didn't look away. "Why did you wait so long to tell me?"

"I should ask you the same question," Yama replied. "Except you weren't going to tell me at all, were you? And I got tired of waiting."

"You know what I did, Lady Yama," I said. "You don't know why I did it." And I told her the whole story of what had happened between Ryu and me, ending with our confrontation in the clan burial ground. "Ryu made it sound like I gathered a host of angry spirits around me. How could I have done that? You taught me the incantations, but you know I still can't perform the dance. I conjured nothing more than whatever haunts Ryu's imagination. It wasn't the real summoning ritual, but the earth shook enough to make it seem real to him. I was lucky," I concluded.

"Then why conceal it?"

"I'm not ashamed of what I did, if that's what you're asking. What good would it have done to tell my family? If I'd mentioned it while the Ookami were still in our village, there would have been trouble, and if I'd said anything after they left, there would be trouble over why I'd waited to speak," I replied.

"Fair enough. But why hide it from *me*?"

I bowed my head. "Because I was afraid you'd end my training if you thought I'd tried summoning the dead." I looked up at her again. "Even if that wasn't what I did."

Yama looked grim. "I ought to end your training here and now."

The dreadful words hit me like a blow to the belly. This was worse than any earthquake. I forced myself to speak: "If that is what you want, Lady Yama, I'll go." I began to stand up, holding back tears.

"Stay where you are!" the shaman snapped. "I want no such thing! There's a difference between what we *want* to do and what we *should* do; remember that!"

I dropped back to the ground. My head spun. I was dazed by how close I'd felt to losing something precious. "I don't—I don't understand."

"Why did you fear telling me? Did you believe I'd dismiss you without hearing your explanation? Do you think I'm that unfair? Do you trust me so little? If so, I'm not the one to train you. Without trust between us, how can I truly teach, how can you truly learn?" She clasped my hands. "Himiko, if I can't be your teacher, find another, but if you love your people—your people and yourself—never leave the spirits' path."

My flimsy self-control crumbled; I began to cry. It came over me like a summer rainstorm, gust after gust of tears. I threw my arms around the old woman's neck, weeping with relief and sobbing that I would never even *pretend* to use a shaman's powers until Yama declared I was ready to do so.

"Oh, my dear, don't make a promise you can't keep," the shaman said fondly, wiping away my tears with her fingertips. "I won't be the one to declare you've mastered all the lore of the hidden ways; *you* will."

How will that be possible? I thought. Yama was the one who guided me through my lessons, pointing out my mistakes, telling me when I'd done things correctly. Why would she step back from pronouncing the final words of approval? Even if the ultimate decision was mine, how could I make it? How would I know when I was good enough?

Yama believed in me, and I loved her for that. Yet in spite of how deeply I trusted and respected my teacher, this was one thing I could *not* believe.

I chose to keep my self-doubt silent. I sat back on my heels and smiled. "May the gods grant it." It was something safe to say.

I left Yama's house soon after, bearing her assurance that she'd clear the way for me to go off into the mountains with Aki the next morning. I was so happy at the thought of what lay ahead, I scarcely noticed the sliver of a nagging question at the back of my mind. What was it that Yama had said? *"That one wouldn't have been satisfied with scaring off their chieftain's loutish son, and she wouldn't have been so easy to send back afterward."*

That one. Why speak of any spirit in such a veiled way? To name could be to summon, but Yama had complete command of the proper rites for banishing the unwelcome dead. Was there a ghost so terrible that even our shaman held back from speaking her name? I had my own suspicions about who that hostile spirit might be, but I wondered if I'd ever know for certain.

That evening, Yama came to see Father, to tell him that she wanted to have certain plants on hand in preparation for Emi's childbirth. "They don't grow around here, so I'm going to have Himiko fetch them for me." She spoke as casually as if she were sending me to bring her a jar of water.

"What? Send her where? How can you—?" Father began to bluster, but Yama quickly put a stop to that.

"Do you honestly think I'd have the girl go by herself?

I may be too old for such a journey, but I'm not feeble-minded. Have one of her brothers accompany her! Better make it Aki; he's reliable, and a more experienced hunter than Shoichi. You'll have some fresh meat for the pot, I'll get my herbs, and your wife will have a safe birth and a healthy baby. Do you object to any of that?"

Of course he didn't. Father grumbled a bit at the shaman's brash way of speaking to him, but he promptly gave her what she wanted. "Aki, you will go with your sister."

"As you wish, Father." He acknowledged the command with a deep, respectful bow, but I still glimpsed his smile.

We set out the next morning before the sun goddess showed her face. The sky shimmered a deep silvery blue with the first thin line of pink beginning to tint the edge of the world. By the time the life-giving light drove off the last of the darkness, Aki and I were well on our way, the clear heavens no more than shards of brightness caught among the branches of the trees.

It had been some time since I'd last taken this road, or ventured so far into the mountains. My legs were longer, but my off-kilter stride held me back on the steeper inclines. Aki didn't chide me for slowing us down, but he didn't need to: I scolded myself.

Why didn't I exercise more? I knew we were going to do this; I should have prepared! I thought furiously. *Even one day would have made a difference.* I peered ahead to where Aki was already almost a bowshot away. When the ground first turned steep, he'd offered to walk beside me and let me lean on him. Smiling, I'd refused. Now I realized I'd made a mistake.

I've got to go faster. I have to catch up. I can't let him think it was a mistake to bring me. He might insist we turn back. No! Never! I'm going to do this. I'm—

I forced myself to walk at a brisker pace, climbing the hillside, striving to reach my brother. Suddenly a harsh twinge shot up my leg. I sucked in my breath through clenched teeth, biting back the pain, and hoped Aki hadn't heard.

"Himiko? What's wrong?" My brother stopped and looked back down the slope.

So much for hope. "Nothing. I'm all right. Keep going."

He scrambled down the slope to my side. "This isn't a race. We don't have to reach the Shika village in a hurry. Let me help you."

I tried to divert him by joking. "How? By carrying me on your back again? I'm too old for that."

"Not too old to lose your stubborn streak, I see," he replied.

"I *told* you, I'm fine. I can do this."

"I don't doubt it. I never would have undertaken this journey with you if I believed you weren't strong enough. I'm just saying that there's more than one path we can take and more than one way for us to follow it. I don't want you hurting yourself just because you decided you had to outspeed the sun goddess. It won't make any difference if it takes us two days or four or even more to get where we're going. Father knows you're safe with me, and he also knows my hunting trips can keep me away from home for a long time. No one's going to worry about us."

"That's not why I tried to run," I said. "We're in this together, Aki. I want to be your equal on this journey, not your burden."

He tugged my hair in his old way. "I never saw you as anything but my equal, Little Sister."

The rest of our trip to the Shika village went more slowly, but if Aki was impatient to be reunited with Hoshi, he gave no sign of it. I wondered whether he was afraid of what sort of reception might await him at journey's end. As for me, the worst I might expect was that Kaya would stare at me and not remember who I was, or that we were ever friends. If that happened, I could live with it, but how would Aki's loyal, loving heart endure it if Hoshi saw him as no more than a stranger? If her heart had gone elsewhere during the years since they'd last met, he would be hurt, but I thought he'd understand. Time passes, people change. But what if he was nothing whatsoever to her, not even a memory? That would crush him. I prayed to the gods to spare my brother that.

It took us three days to reach our destination. I don't know whether we would have gotten where we were going sooner if I'd been fit to match my brother's stride or if the trip took that long because of the route Aki chose. I was glad he'd gone back to steal secret glimpses of the girl who held his heart. It meant he knew the way to the deer people's settlement very well. I wouldn't have been able to remember it on my own.

As much as I wanted to see Kaya and her family again, I had to admit to myself that I was enjoying the trip through the wilderness for its own sake. Aki knew all the secrets of living off the gifts of the forest. We'd brought some food from home, but when our rice balls were gone, we didn't go hungry or thirsty. He taught me which plants were safe to eat, how to raid the remains of squirrels' hidden stores of nuts from last autumn's harvest, and even to turn over dead logs and rocks to find fat white grubs. I made a revolted face the first time he held one of those squirming things before my eyes and challenged me to eat it. What choice did I have? I decided I'd rather stomach the insect than my brother's teasing and let him pop it into my mouth, biting down hard to put an end to that sickening *wriggling*. I swallowed it so quickly that if my life depended on it, I couldn't say what the thing tasted like.

"Well?" Aki regarded me curiously. "How was it?"

"Eat one yourself and you tell me."

"I meant how did *you* like it?"

"Delicious," I replied with a straight face. "The best thing I've ever eaten. A delicacy like that should be reserved solely for clan chieftains. Thank you, dear brother, but I'm not worthy to enjoy such a marvelous treat again. *Ever.*"

Aki snorted with laughter.

On a day when the sky was strewn with clouds and the sun goddess darted in and out of hiding, we emerged from the forest and gazed down at the village I hadn't seen for almost five years. Aki and I stood with our backs to the trees, not saying a word. We had a clear view inside the palisade, though the cultivated fields were mostly out of sight, concealed by a curve of the land. We watched the people of the deer clan come and go through their village gateway, saw smoke rising from their cook fires, listened to their voices on the cool, damp breeze. Neither one of us moved.

At last, I took a deep breath and began walking down the hillside. I paused after about twenty steps and turned. Aki hadn't moved at all. He remained where he was, still as a stone.

"Do you want to wait for me here?" I asked gently. "I'll find Hoshi, but I won't tell her you're here until I've talked to her and found out if she . . . if she . . ." I hesitated.

"If she still knows who I am?" Aki finished the thought for me. "Thank you for your offer, Little Sister. Your courage shames me. The gods should have let you be born first. You'd make a better chieftain for the Matsu." He looked wistful. "Father is always telling me that a good chieftain leads by example. Lead me, Himiko."

I stretched out my hand to my brother and waited for him to come away from the shelter of the trees and take it. I squeezed his fingers as hard as I could. "You will be the best chieftain our people ever had," I told him. "And *you* will lead us all."

We walked through the late-spring grass until we reached a narrow path of beaten earth that merged into a wider way. This broader road would have brought us across the moat and into the village, but we had no chance to follow it: we'd been seen. A trio of Shika men came running out to meet us. Their swords were sheathed, but their hands clutched the hilts, ready to draw iron in the time it takes to blink.

Aki and I stopped where we were. He dropped my hand

and stood with his arms spread, palms out, showing the men that he was not a danger. I did the same, even though I doubted they'd view a girl as a threat even if I'd been carrying a bow and arrows on my back, *two* swords at my side, and a polearm in my hands.

The man in the lead slowed his pace and squinted hard as he drew closer to us. He came to a halt and signaled his companions to do the same as he shielded his eyes to peer at us. "I know you," he said, though with a slight note of doubt in his voice. "You're that little girl I found years ago, in the field where the deer graze."

"Not so little now, eh, Sora?" one of the Shika men said, chuckling. "That's a nice-looking fawn you saved."

"Think she's come back to *thank* you?" a second man said with a snicker that made my ears burn.

"Shut up, you frog brains!" Sora barked. "These are our honored guests. Do you want me to ask Lady Ikumi if you're showing them the proper sort of respect, saying such things? Or maybe I should just let him"—he swept his hand in Aki's direction—"have a little time alone with you, to teach you the right way to talk to his sister?"

The two rude men swore they'd only been joking, babbled apologies, and begged Sora not to tell Lady Ikumi anything. He snorted and turned his back on them. "A fine welcome for you, after all these years, my friends," he said to Aki and me. "But I hope you'll find a better one under our chieftess's roof. Come."

We walked through the gates of the Shika village and soon found ourselves in the center of a crowd of curious faces. Some studied us closely and smiled as they recognized us; others remained baffled. There was a lot of whispering, including any number of attempts to recall our names. In the five years since I'd last set foot within that village, the deer people had had more important things to bear in mind.

Then a well-remembered voice rang out to silence the murmurs: "Himiko! Himiko! You came back!" Her clanfolk scattered as Kaya dashed through their midst to greet me. I'd grown much taller than my friend, but the years had made her far sturdier, with wide hips, strong legs, and arms that held me pinned in a breath-stealing hug.

"Is it true?" Lady Ikumi arrived at a more dignified pace than her impetuous daughter. The Shika chieftess looked much as I remembered her, though there were some threads of white running through her shining black hair. "Lady Himiko! Lord Aki! Welcome back." She opened her arms to us, and her face shone.

I wanted to laugh out loud. I wished I could dance. I longed to do both at once because I felt that nothing else was good enough to express my happiness. *Lady Ikumi knows our names! Kaya remembers me! Aki and I haven't been forgotten! Oh, gods, grant that Hoshi still holds Aki in her memory too.*

As if in answer to my heartfelt hope, Kaya's older sister Hoshi came trailing in her mother's wake, accompanied by the rest of the chieftess's children. She was still as pretty as I recalled, yet with a familiar sadness in her eyes. I recognized it far too easily: it was the same expression that had haunted my brother's face ever since we'd parted from the deer clan.

I looked at Aki. My brother's face was pale and his lips were parted, but he was unable to make a sound. His eyes

were fixed on Hoshi, and as their gazes met, I imagined a
ribbon of light encircling them, becoming a glowing shell
that held them both in a place no one else could go. My skin
tingled with warmth: I knew that I stood in the presence of
wondrous magic.

I was so fascinated watching the two of them that I paid
only vague attention to what was going on around me. Lady
Ikumi's more formal greeting, her prayers of thanksgiving
to the gods for having brought us, Kaya's carefree chatter,
the good-natured laughter of the deer clan—all these
blended into one soothing current of sound, like the rustling of windblown leaves.

A sharp tap on my shoulder snapped me back to reality.
"Wake *up*, Himiko," Kaya said, nudging me for good measure. "Didn't you hear Mother? We're going to our house
now." She linked her arm through mine and strode away so
abruptly that I stumbled along at her side.

"I'm sorry," I said, with a backward glance to where Aki
and Hoshi still stood unmoving just within the gateway.
Many of the villagers remained watching them. I could hear
them laughing, but it wasn't a mean-spirited sound. "I was
distracted."

"By what?" my friend asked intently.

I didn't want to respond. I felt that I shouldn't have
stared at Aki and Hoshi after all, no matter how pleased I
was by their reunion. I could offer only a shrug.

Kaya was *not* satisfied with that.

"Hey, *answer* me! What are you doing, turning into another Hoshi? *Wonderful.*" Her sour-faced sarcasm shocked
me, totally out of keeping with her usual cheery nature.

"She didn't talk a lot before, but ever since you and your family left, she hasn't said a word unless we pried it out of her. She doesn't talk and she doesn't listen, she just stares at *nothing*. We're all sick and tired of having to repeat everything we say to her at least twice, and the sighing—! *Awful*. I wanted to dump a jar of cold water over her head to see if that would wake her up. The only reason I didn't was Mother said it wouldn't fix anything, and besides, Hoshi's too tall. I can't *reach* higher than her head unless she's sitting down, and I don't think pouring water on her feet would work, do you?"

I had to grin. "I think you won't have to worry about any of that now, Kaya. And neither will I." As we walked on, I told my friend about my brother's long, sad separation from her sister. "That's all over for both of them now, thank the gods. At least he went out hunting instead of sitting around and sighing. I don't think I could have stood that."

"Lucky you." Kaya stuck out her lower lip, then giggled. She just couldn't hold on to a bad mood if she tried.

We couldn't stay long among the Shika. Aki explained to me that we could spend no more than two or three days there. "Don't forget, besides our stay, it's a journey of at least two days each way," he said as we went to gather kindling wood, our small effort to thank Lady Ikumi for her hospitality. "We don't want anyone back home to become concerned about our absence. Father might send hunters on our trail, and if they discovered where we are and told him—" He shook his head. "We can't take that chance, Himiko. I want to be able to come back here."

"I do too." I took my brother's hand. "For you."

We made the most of the time we had. Kaya and I had countless things to tell each other. My friend was impressed when I showed her my dragon stone amulet and told her the story behind it. She was also spellbound when I spoke about my training with Yama.

"I wish I could become a shaman too," she said.

"Why can't you? Your mother's chieftess *and* shaman. She could train you."

"She won't. She says that she could teach anyone the words and the songs and the dances you need to cast spells, but unless the spirits choose you, it's like pouring rice wine into a cotton bag." Kaya sighed. "At least I'm pretty good with the bow and arrow. Sora says I've got a sharp eye and a steady arm."

I laughed. "You want to be a shaman, and I once wanted to be a hunter. Too bad we can't trade dreams like dresses."

"As long as they both fit," said Kaya.

The night before Aki and I were to set off on our homeward path, Lady Ikumi asked me to walk with her after we'd eaten. It was a clear night, with the moon nearly full. A warm breeze lightly stirred my hair and carried sweet scents from the fields and forests, but I couldn't relax enough to enjoy it.

Why does she want to talk to me? I wondered, casting nervous sidelong glances at the Shika chieftess's serene face. *What does she have to say that couldn't be said indoors, with others there to hear? Did Kaya tell her about my training? She's a shaman; maybe she doesn't think I'm worthy to become one. She can't interfere, but what will I say if she tries persuading me to stop my studies? Oh gods, I hope she won't—*

"Is your brother a good man, Himiko?" Lady Ikumi's abrupt question startled me out of my thoughts.

"Aki? Yes. I think—I know he is," I replied, wondering why she'd ask such a thing.

"What makes you say so? If he weren't your brother, would you still believe that?"

My uneasiness disappeared. Lady Ikumi's question became a spider dropped down the back of my neck. "Of course I would!" I knew I should speak respectfully to the Shika chieftess, but I failed to keep the irritation out of my voice. "Why ask *me* such a thing? Has he done something wrong? Talk to *him* about it!"

She rested one hand on my shoulder. "I would, but I've hardly seen him since your arrival, except at meals and when it's time to sleep. Sometimes not even then."

"Oh." Now I understood, and I probably would have done so earlier, if she hadn't taken me by surprise. "He's spending all his time with Hoshi. He waited so long to see her again! Please forgive him if that's made him a bad guest."

"I know where he's been. He doesn't need to ask my pardon for his absence, and for being with Hoshi. I bless him for that." Lady Ikumi smiled sadly. "He loves my daughter very much, I think. I know that she loves him. When he left, she cried for two days. It's torture for a mother to watch her child in pain and be helpless to heal it. I told her everything I could think of, trying to make her feel better. I'm afraid I told her many things that weren't true or right. I said she shouldn't pine over someone she'd never see again. I scolded her when she turned away from the young men in our clan. I insisted that if she married one of them, it would solve everything. I was stupidly cruel enough to say that Aki would probably forget all about her. I told her she was too young to know her own heart." The chieftess sighed. "In short, I was a fool."

"He didn't forget her," I said softly. "And once we got home, he wouldn't look at any of the girls in our clan, either. He even—" I hesitated, then decided to speak on, no matter what the consequences might be. "He even came back here secretly, to catch sight of her. That must have hurt, but he was willing to bear it. He'd rather see her and feel that pain than pretend she never existed and feel nothing."

The Shika chieftess nodded slowly. "For two people to meet for such a brief while and yet know that their lives should be linked eternally . . . My mind rejects it, but my eyes tell me it's true. Is there anything that the gods can't do?"

"He'll come back again," I murmured. "Now that he knows Hoshi loves him too, he won't linger to watch her from a distance. He's one of our best hunters, so he's got an excuse to go into the mountains as much as he likes."

"So I hoped." Lady Ikumi looked at me. "And what about you, my dear? Will you come back with him?"

"I will, but not as often. I'm happy to see Kaya again, but my excuse for leaving our village is much more fragile than Aki's. If I overuse it, it would look suspicious and I could wind up ruining everything for both of us."

The chieftess lifted her gaze to the moon. "So your father is unchanged?" I muttered something under my breath and shook my head. "That's too bad."

"Maybe Aki will change enough to stand up to him," I offered. I told her about how Father had threatened my brother with exile from the Matsu clan, and how Aki had submitted. "If he does, will you let him join the Shika?"

"Certainly, but I hope it won't come to that. To lose your family, to lose your clan, is to lose a piece of your soul. If the piece is big enough, you become a ghost long before your body dies. I wouldn't ask your brother to do such a thing. Neither would Hoshi. She loves him too much to let him sacrifice himself. And I would never be able to live without grief if I were responsible for taking away another woman's child."

I thought of how badly Mama would react if Aki left our clan for good. "Thank you, Lady Ikumi," I said quietly.

We left the Shika village the next morning. On the way home, I took care to gather an impressive number of roots, leaves, blossoms, and fungi. Aki justified his reputation as a hunter by bringing down some fat birds and a rabbit. When a very young boar crossed our path, my brother put an arrow into it and finished the kill with his knife before I could blink at the unlucky animal.

"If this isn't a sign of favor from the gods, I don't know what is." Aki's teeth flashed as he slung his prize over his shoulders. "No one will be able to call this a wasted journey once they see everything we're bringing home. And *that* means you won't have to get Lady Yama to justify your next trip quite so forcefully."

My brother's words proved true. I couldn't accompany him every time he left the village on one of his "hunting" trips, but after he'd made three of them, Yama once more informed Father that she needed me to go on another distant herb-gathering expedition. Before Father could even think of objecting, our shaman reminded him that it was nearly time for Emi to give birth.

"The plants I need won't be at their best for much longer," she said. "If I'm going to brew enough of my fire-cough remedy in time for winter, someone has to harvest the blossoms before they wither. If I go myself— Well, the flowers won't wait, but neither will your baby. Do you want me here for the birth or not?"

As it happened, by the time Aki and I returned, we had a new baby brother. The birth hadn't been easy, but Yama used all her arts, practical and mystic, to help Emi's son Sanjirou safely into the world. The child was big and healthy. Father proudly declared that when his newest son demanded milk, it wasn't an infant's wail but a warrior's battle yell that burst from that sweet, toothless mouth.

Father never raised any further arguments whenever Yama wanted to send me into the mountains with Aki. "He'd *better* not," she said as the two of us picked through my latest harvest. "He knows that I'm needed in the village, not wandering the wilderness. If I hadn't been here when Emi needed me, her arms would be empty now. I stay close to home, you bring me excellent ingredients, and your brother no longer walks under a cloud."

"But wouldn't you like to go deep into the forest again?" I asked. "Don't you miss it? It's so beautiful!"

"I've walked this world for longer than you can imagine, Himiko, and I've seen more of its beauty than these mountains hold. These days, I'm happier relying on my memories than hiking over rough ground and slippery rocks. I like to sleep with a bedroll under my back and a roof over my head. I wasn't lying when I told your father I'd grown too old for the sort of journey you and Aki undertake without thinking twice."

"Lady Yama, you're not old!" I protested.

She waved away my words with a hand whose wrinkled fingers made it look like a hawk's taloned foot. "Why deny what I am? You can't deceive the gods. These sags and creases, this thinning hair and scrawny body, don't make me especially pleasant to look at, but I don't mind. I was ugly when I was young too, so I'm used to it." She guffawed at her own joke. "Besides, if I were still young enough to do all my own work, what excuse would you have for your travels? The gods fill our world with hidden blessings. Did you ever think that a fall from our sacred tree would bring you *here*?" She spread her arms. "We have to learn how to see them, Himiko, even when they're hidden so deeply that we're sure they don't exist. A cherry pit looks like a barren stone no bigger than your fingertip, but in its heart, it conceals a living world."

11
TOO MANY BLESSINGS

Our shaman never claimed to have the gift of prophecy. Her vision was fixed on the here and now, and when she did speak of the future, it was purely about practical matters: new marriages, new babies, new houses to shelter new families, and how we of the Matsu clan would adjust our individual lives to accommodate these changes. She also dealt with sadder things to come, and often warned our potter to begin work on a funerary jar a few days before the need for it arose. Even so, our people regarded Yama with as much awe as if she had the power to see what lay a hundred seasons ahead.

It was just as well that my teacher wasn't endowed with supernatural foresight. If she'd predicted what lay ahead for my family and our clan over the next two years, no one would have believed her. How she would have hated that!

I can understand how people turn away from prophecies that foretell dreadful things. No one wants to hear that they're about to meet disaster, but at least they're ready to believe it. We learn soon enough that bad things happen. Who has ever come through childhood without experiencing at least a hundred misfortunes, great and small?

But if we're told that our lives are about to be flooded with good things, we turn away for a different reason: we can't believe it. We don't dare. How can we enjoy what we've been given when we keep looking over one shoulder for the catastrophe that's sure to follow?

It was so much better that those two years of countless blessings came to us unannounced. Food was plentiful. Our fields yielded enough to feed a clan twice our size. Our hunters never came home empty-handed. Our pigs and chickens thrived.

There were other blessings too, blessings that touched my family. Emi's son Sanjirou was a loud, sturdy two-year-old who took turns enchanting us and driving us wild with worry. His favorite trick was to rush headlong out the door, showing no sign he intended to stop before plunging off the edge of the porch. Of course, he *did* stop, along with our hearts. He always said he was sorry, but I could tell that the demon inside him was already plotting Sanjirou's next nerve-racking exploit.

Things might have been easier if there had been four pairs of hands to keep him under control, but it was solely up to Emi and me. Mama and Yukari couldn't move fast enough to keep up with the child because they were expecting children of their own.

"I hope they're both girls," I confided in Aki as we

walked in the woods near our village. With *two* family births about to happen, we were all staying close to home in case we were needed.

"Why do you want a sister so badly?" he asked. "Aren't you happy being our only princess?"

"I'd give it all up if it meant a little more peace around here. One Sanjirou in the house is enough. Can you imagine *three*?"

"Maybe the solution is for you to get *out* of the house," Aki said. "I've had my eye on you, Little Sister, and I've counted at least three young men trailing after you like ducklings. It's almost as much fun to see the lovesick looks on their faces as it is to see the ugly scowls you get from some of your friends."

"I haven't had a friend in this village for years, and you know it," I replied sternly. But I couldn't help smiling as I added, "Did you see Suzu's expression when all three of the boys got into a fight over who was going to carry Lady Yama's water jug for me? She got two deep creases right *here*." Gleefully, I tapped the space between my eyebrows. "It looked like she was hit in the face with a hoe. Twice!"

"Oh, I don't blame her for glaring at you. You're being greedy, holding on to three possible husbands. Choose one, get married, move into your own house, start having babies of your own, and let poor Suzu scavenge your leftovers!"

"All that? Right now? I was hoping I could have some dinner first."

"Fine, make fun of me." Aki pretended to take offense. "That's the thanks I get for having your best interests at heart and giving you good advice. It'll serve you right if Mother and Yukari each has twin boys and all four of them turn out to be worse brats than Sanjirou!"

"Why don't you take some of your own advice and marry a nice Matsu girl?" I joked.

"You know I could never do that, Himiko." Aki looked so sad that I felt a sharp pang for having taunted him.

"Forgive me, Big Brother. I know that you love—"

"Oh, love hasn't got anything to do with it," he said. A hint of mischief crept into his voice. "It's just that my wife would object."

"Your *what*?" I gawked at my brother. He gave me a smug grin in exchange.

"Hoshi and I were married last autumn."

"And you didn't tell *me*?" I wanted to push him into a ditch the same way I'd treated Ryu.

"I didn't think you could keep a secret." He was teasing, but as soon as he saw that I was in no mood for it, he changed his tone. "I'm sorry, Little Sister. I was hoping to tell you when Hoshi and I told everyone in our families. Her mother's the only one who knows." That made sense. As shaman of the deer people, Lady Ikumi would be the one to call for the gods' blessings on the new couple.

"At least that explains why Kaya never said a word about it," I remarked.

"The secrecy wasn't my idea. I love Hoshi, and I was sick and tired of hiding it like something foul that needed to be buried. I told Lady Ikumi I was going to confront Father. If he still gave me no choice but exile or renouncing my beloved, I'd go to the Shika and never look back."

"She convinced you not to do that, didn't she?" I recalled my conversation with the Shika chieftess: *"To lose your*
family, to lose your clan, is to lose a piece of your soul."

My brother nodded. "And Hoshi agreed. She's willing
to wait for the day when she and I can live together openly.
I only hope it comes because Father has a change of heart,
not because he—" Aki didn't finish his sentence, but I
could: —*not because he's dead.*

I kept my thoughts to myself. Kaya's sister was a sweet,
gentle girl, with more patience than I would ever have. She
was willing to take a husband who couldn't acknowledge
her as his wife, who had to hide her from his kin, who was
little more than a visitor whose comings and goings were
unpredictable and whose stays were brief.

I couldn't live like that. Try as I might, I couldn't com-
prehend how Hoshi was able to do it. What would she say
if I dared to ask her for an explanation? Most likely *"I love*
him." That might be a good enough reason for her, but not
for me. Perhaps I didn't understand Hoshi. Perhaps I didn't
understand love.

What I said was, "Maybe when you and Hoshi have a
baby, Father will be more ready to accept her as your wife."

Aki agreed. "That's what Lady Ikumi said. It's easy to
reject the person your son or daughter marries, but to turn
your back on the grandchild who carries your blood? Not
even Father could do that." He paused and added, "I hope."

"So do I, Big Brother, with all my heart."

Yukari gave birth to a little boy who was every bit as lusty as
Emi's son. Sanjirou didn't like his new half brother Takehiko

and made sure that all of us knew it. When the baby cried, he howled for attention. When the baby slept, he danced around the house, making the floor shake. When the baby needed to be cleaned, he— Well, some things are so obvious they don't need to be said.

Luckily for us, before the moon god's disk went through the full cycle of its changes, Mama delivered her baby, another boy. Sanjirou stared at my brother Noboru, screwed up his mouth as though he'd tasted something sour, and ran to bury his face against his mother's shoulder. From then on, he kept his distance from the infants, spoke in a hush, and walked softly in the house.

"Did you ever see anything like that?" Masa remarked as we all shared dinner. He indicated Sanjirou, who was casting suspicious glances back and forth between Noboru and Takehiko while he ate. "Remember how he used to be? I'm not complaining about the change, but I do wonder what caused it."

I shrugged. "After Takehiko was born, Sanjirou made a big fuss every chance he got, and what happened? Noboru. I think he's afraid that if he makes too much noise again, we'll get another baby."

Of course *that* was when Aki let out a whoop so loud it jolted dust from the thatch. Poor little Sanjirou jumped like a cricket and turned a terrified stare my way, as if he expected *me* to produce the next infant then and there. It would have been funny if Aki's holler hadn't scared the babies too. A three-way chorus of yowling shook our house, made worse by Father thundering at Aki for acting like a badly behaved child.

Masa looked at Shoichi. "Well! At least *we* know how to maintain our dignity, don't we, my respected Elder Brother?" He spoke so primly it would have made a turtle laugh.

"Oh, beyond a doubt," Shoichi replied, lifting his nose high. "We would never engage in such immature behavior, would we, my dear Younger Brother?"

"By no means."

"Never."

"We'd sooner die."

"*I'd* die first. I'm older than you. It's my privilege."

"Hey, I'll die first if I want to!" Masa gave Shoichi a light shove, Shoichi shoved back, and soon all three of my older brothers were rolling on the floor like puppies while my three younger brothers wailed on. Father ran out of threats before Mama and the rest of us managed to get the boys to settle down.

I loved my brothers, but at times like that there was no way to measure how very, *very* much I wished Mama, Yukari, and Emi had given birth to daughters.

Father was one of those people who could not enjoy good times wholeheartedly. As our clan chieftain, it was his responsibility to stay alert for trouble, but his mind was so filled with all the possible setbacks, accidents, and calamities that could overtake the Matsu that there wasn't much room left for his own celebrations and pleasures. Although he rejoiced over the births of his three new sons, his eyes were always anxious when he looked at them, as if he saw the ghosts of his lost children hovering nearby, waiting for the chance to steal their little brothers away into the darkness. When Shoichi married the girl he loved and moved into a home of his own, Father wished the new couple every happiness, but never visited their house without casting uneasy glances everywhere, as though fretting that the walls wouldn't stand and the roof were about to collapse any moment.

One early summer morning as I sat on our porch, holding Noboru in my lap, I heard Father's voice drifting up from below. He was walking with one of the other nobles. The man congratulated Father on all the new additions to our family and went on to rejoice over the happy days that had come to the Matsu clan.

"What a splendid time to be alive!" he crowed. "I can almost feel the gods embracing us. Not even the oldest member of our clan can recall better years than these. I can barely begin to count the blessings we've received, and no end to them in sight! How can we ever thank you enough for having led us into so much good fortune, my chieftain?"

"Don't thank me for anything," Father said in a flat voice. "Good fortune is as fickle as a songbird. It lands for long enough to let you glimpse it, then flies away."

"Er, as you wish," the nobleman said.

As they moved on, I heard my Father add, "You know, my friend, there's such a thing as too many blessings."

I didn't believe that at all. If good fortune really was like a songbird, Father was wrong to call it fickle. As a hunter, he'd spent more time in the woods than I, but his eyes and ears were tuned solely to the prey. He hadn't truly *seen*. He hadn't truly *listened*. I had.

A songbird, I thought as I looked into my baby brother's

sleeping face. *They're quick to take flight, but not always. They're true to their mates, build nests made to last, and stand guard over their hatchlings with their lives. If our clan's luck is that "fickle," we'll be blessed for many seasons to come!*

After the boys were born, I had to stay close to home for some time. Mama and my stepmothers were competent women, but caring for Noboru, Sanjirou, and Takehiko was exhausting for them. They needed my help, and I was glad to give it, especially on those days when Mama put me in sole charge of Noboru.

I'd prayed for a sister, but once I held my baby brother in my arms, I forgot all about those prayers. Noboru was a beautiful boy, with a round face, plump cheeks, shining eyes, and hair so thick and black it was astonishing. He was also the most charming infant I'd ever known. He had such a sweet disposition that it seemed as though he'd been born smiling. Even when he cried, he never sounded whiny or strident. It was the difference between listening to a person who politely asks for what he needs and one who complains he doesn't have *this,* and he doesn't have *that,* and *why* doesn't he have it, and he wants it now, now, *now!*

The one thing I couldn't do for Noboru was feed him. When he cried for his milk, I had to bring him to Mama and wait for him to finish nursing. At those times, I found myself longing to have him back in my arms and wishing he were old enough to eat solid foods so that I'd never have to give him up. Mama must have noticed how hungrily I stared at the baby because she said, "You know, dear, I wasn't much older than you when I got married."

"What made you say *that*?"

She smiled serenely at the baby. "I've seen you in the company of at least three of our young men, and I'm willing to wager that there are at least two more who are too timid to approach you. Any one of them would make a good husband."

"I don't want a—"

"And a good father." She wiped a last drop of milk from Noboru's sleepy mouth and handed him back to me.

My time with Noboru was precious, but so was my time with Yama. The problem was, the baby had more magical power in one of his smiles than the shaman had in all of her spells. I was carrying my baby brother through the village one morning when Yama came up to us and said, "So there's the little thief."

I raised one eyebrow. "Mama *gave* him to me."

"I didn't mean you, Himiko." The shaman looked down at Noboru and let him grasp one of her fingers. "I meant *this* sneaky thing. He can't walk, he can't talk, he's small as a wink, and yet he managed to steal away this clan's next shaman. How did he do it?"

My cheeks flamed. "I'm sorry. I was going to come back to my studies, but everyone needed my help with the babies."

"Everyone? I've seen you looking after Takehiko once or twice, and I can't remember ever seeing you alone with Sanjirou. Poor Emi! She could *use* an extra pair of hands to deal with that boy, but obviously she's not going to get yours." Yama smirked knowingly. "I've underestimated your mother. She's always been an intelligent woman, but I never suspected she could be so clever when there's something she wants so badly."

"What could Mama possibly want now that she has Noboru?"

The shaman gently disengaged her finger from the baby's grip. "She wants what all good mothers want: for her children to be happy. And what does happiness mean to her? A family. A home. Children of your own. All of those have brought her the greatest joys in her life, even if your father's been a bit of a . . . *challenge* now and then. She loves you and your brothers, Himiko, and she believes that what makes her happy will make you happy too."

"Lady Yama, I still don't understand."

"When you were small and your mother wanted you to try something new to eat, what did she do? Filled her own plate and let you have only the smallest taste. You were soon begging her for more!" She lifted Noboru's tiny fist to her mouth and kissed it. "Delicious." She grinned.

I had to laugh. "Well, Mama may be clever, but she's not subtle. She keeps reminding me about all the boys who'd like to marry me."

"Mm-hmm. Shall I begin the preparations for a marriage rite? It's not every day that a Matsu princess takes a husband."

"It's certainly not going to be any day *soon*," I said. "Mama wants me to share her kind of happiness, but first I have to see if it holds everything that will make me happy too."

"Does this mean you'll resume your studies soon?"

"Yes!" I shifted Noboru in my arms and delicately touched the dainty indentation just below his nose. He snuffled in his sleep. "I didn't like it when you called this little one a thief, Lady Yama, but when you said he'd stolen our clan's next shaman"—I smiled at her—"I liked *that* very much."

My lessons with Yama weren't the only part of my life interrupted by the birth of my new brothers. It was almost autumn by the time I next visited the Shika village in Aki's company. Mama looked a little disappointed when I told her I'd be going away again to gather supplies for our shaman. I think she'd had high hopes that Noboru's enchanting power would overcome Yama's presence in my life and that I'd be a bride before winter. She didn't realize that neither she, Noboru, nor Yama herself had any real influence on my decision. That was mine alone. *I* wanted to go. I wanted to see Kaya again, but what I wanted more than that was to see Hoshi and give her a sister's welcome.

Aki and I left our village well before dawn. We greeted the sun goddess's first light when we were already far into the forest. We were done with the days of my needing Aki's help to cover the distance between our home and the Shika lands. I'd grown stronger thanks to all the times I'd made that journey. Even my "bad" leg wasn't so bad anymore. If I fell behind my brother, it was usually in those places where the trail was too narrow for the both of us to pass, or at the very steepest parts of our route through the mountains.

We reached Kaya's village under an unwelcome cloud of cold rain. No one was outside except the watchman, huddled like a wet owl in his tower. We heard him announce our arrival in a phlegmy voice broken by hard coughing. Immediately, I began concocting one of Yama's remedies in my mind, wondering if he'd allow me to treat him. I'd reached that stage in my studies with Yama where I knew all the shaman's cures. I could do everything from identifying the right plant for each ailment to turning it into the potion or powder or poultice the individual case required.

What I *couldn't* do was practice healing. Yama admitted that I was more than ready for that responsibility, but still refused to let me try. "If you begin taking care of the sick, there will be no more pretending you only do my errands. The whole clan will know I've taken you as my apprentice, and that includes your father. I wouldn't mind seeing the end of that deception, but that must not happen until you feel you're in command of *all* my arts. I want you to be my successor, Himiko, fully trained. That can't come about if your father puts an end to your studies before they're done."

She was right, but accepting that didn't do a thing to relieve my frustration at being unable to *use* the lessons I'd already learned. Of course, now that I was far from our village and Father's hostile eye, there was nothing to prevent me from letting my healing knowledge do some good for others.

The weather was nasty, but Aki and I received a greeting warm enough to burn off the chilly drizzle. By the time we crossed the moat and entered the gates, Lady Ikumi and Kaya were waiting to embrace us. Hoshi was nowhere to be seen.

The Shika chieftess noted my brother's look of dejection and disappointment right away. "Don't worry, my son, she's well. In fact, she might be *better* than well. I told her to stay inside. If she is"—she paused and smiled—"as I *hope* she is, she shouldn't risk falling sick."

Aki's face brightened at once. "Do you really think that she could be—?"

Lady Ikumi spread her hands. "As I said, I'm hoping it's true."

Kaya snorted. "And *I'm* hoping you'll stop talking in riddles, Mother, and let all of us get out of the rain!"

It wasn't far from the gates to the chieftess's house, and Kaya made the distance shorter by pulling me along as she dashed for home. I still couldn't run gracefully, but speed was no problem. The two of us erupted through the doorway well before Lady Ikumi and Aki did.

Hoshi was busy setting out cups around an open clay bottle. The pleasant aroma of heated rice wine warmed me almost as much as the merrily burning fire in the center of the house. Aki's bride welcomed me cordially.

"I hope you didn't have to endure this rain all the way here," she said, placing a filled cup in my hands. "I'm so happy to see you again, Lady Himiko. It's been too long since you visited us."

"*Much* too long," Kaya said as she filled her own cup. "Why couldn't you come back sooner? Aki told us about your new brothers, and how you had to help take care of them, but wasn't there *anyone* else who could do that?"

"I like looking after babies," I said mildly. "Especially my brother Noboru. He's a darling. You'd like him a lot, Kaya."

For the second time since my return, Kaya snorted. "I

had enough of babies when those two were small," she said, indicating her younger brother and sister. The girl giggled, and the boy stuck out his tongue at her.

"Don't you want to have children of your own one day?"

"I guess so. But my husband had better marry a couple of extra wives. One of them can take care of the mess and the crying and the teething when the kids are babies, and I'll take over when they're big enough to be *fun*."

Aki ducked his dripping head as he came into the chieftess's house. "What's this I hear about fun, Kaya? What are you plotting n—" He didn't get the chance to finish before Hoshi ran into his arms.

Kaya snorted a third time for good measure and made an exaggerated kiss-kiss face at me, rolling her eyes, fluttering her lashes, and hugging herself until I laughed the breath out of my body.

"Ah, it's good to see our guests so happy!" Lady Ikumi said as she came in. Kaya's younger sister hastened to help her mother dry off while my friend's older brother handed the chieftess a cup of wine.

"Hey! Hoshi's supposed to be doing that!" Kaya pointed an accusing finger at her older brother. She glanced at Aki and Hoshi, still sealed in their embrace, and sighed. "It's like this every time he comes here. He might as well stay."

"Or else Hoshi should go live with the Matsu," Lady Ikumi remarked. Everyone stared, even the two lovers. The Shika chieftess lowered her eyelids and calmly sipped her wine.

"Mother, what are you saying? Have you gone crazy?" Kaya was frantic.

Her mother remained unruffled. "Well, the bride usually does go to live in her husband's house." She looked up into the startled faces of her children. "Yes, my darlings, your sister is married to this young man. I thought that it was time to share the news with you. After all, Himiko knows already."

Kaya gave me a look that was stormy enough to shoot lightning. "You *knew*? You knew before *me*? She's my *sister*!"

Her mother put her arms around my infuriated friend and crooned, "Hush, my dearest Lady Badger. You can't blame her for that. As Aki and I were walking here from the gate, he told me he'd shared the secret with her, but he didn't do it until after her last visit here. How could she have shared it with you?"

This explanation mollified Kaya a little, but the hint of a frown lingered on her lips. "This is just another reason why you shouldn't have stayed away from us so long, Himiko. That's your brother's fault."

"Kaya, you're not being fair," Aki protested. "I brought Himiko with me as soon as—"

"Not *you*." Kaya waved away his objections impatiently. "The *baby* brother, the one she's sure I'm going to like. Well, I don't! And I won't! Not now and not ever." She crossed her arms and looked haughty. "Lady Badger has spoken."

"*Whoof,*" I told her, and the two of us shook with silly laughter.

Hoshi came to kneel beside me. "I'm so glad to have you for my sister, Lady Himiko. I know how special you are to Aki."

"If I'm your sister, you mustn't call me *Lady* Himiko anymore," I replied, and hugged her.

"Does this mean you'll be leaving us, Hoshi?" Kaya asked. She looked upset.

"Not soon, Little Sister, don't fret."

"Who's fretting?" Kaya fought to look indifferent and did a bad job of it. "It's not as if I'm going to miss you; it's just that I'm the one who'll be stuck doing all of your chores once you go!"

"There can be no talk of Hoshi leaving us until we know she'll be accepted among the Matsu," Lady Ikumi announced. "And that can't happen until Aki's father accepts *all* of us. Once he understands that not every outlander is an enemy, there will be a great bond of friendship between the Matsu and the Shika. After all, I'm not about to send my daughter away if I'm not welcome to visit her whenever I like." She set her wine cup down.

Not every outlander is an enemy, I thought. *But not every outlander is a friend, either.* Memories of Ryu and the Ookami clan's offer of so-called friendship left me with a cold feeling inside.

"If you can visit Hoshi, that means I can visit Himiko!" Kaya cried. She clasped my hands. "Won't that be wonderful? I can't wait to see your village!"

Aki chuckled. "You might *have* to wait, Kaya. We don't know how soon Father will see reason."

Lady Ikumi rose from her place. "Oh, it might be soon enough," she drawled. "*Very* soon, perhaps." She shared a confidential smile with her eldest daughter.

Unfortunately, before we left the Shika village, Aki and Hoshi had sad proof that they weren't going to be parents just yet. Their hopes for a child who would soften Father's heart would have to wait, and Lady Ikumi's "*Very* soon, perhaps" became my brother's wistful "Maybe not now, but in time."

That winter lingered. The cold crept through our clothes and curled up in our bones, but the Matsu had plenty of food stored away after another abundant harvest. No one wanted to go outside, and there was no end to the grumbling when any of my clan had to leave the comfort and warmth of their houses. Whenever Father heard their complaints, it left him seething.

"This is what happens when times are *too* good!" he thundered as we all sat down to eat. "People get soft as piles of pork fat. Then, when the world returns to normal, they're too weak to cope with hardship. They crumble up and blow away!"

Little Sanjirou clapped his hands and squealed with delight. He always found Father's outbursts funny. His innocent glee never failed to annoy Father, but what could he do about it? A child is a child. Father's only option was to lapse into sullen silence.

I suppressed a grin and slipped Sanjirou an extra tidbit from my platter. I loved Father, but not his constant insistence that the gods' blessings were doing us more harm than good. Sometimes it seemed as though he'd welcome a catastrophe because it would prove he'd been right.

Was it really wise to speak so? Would the spirits become offended to hear their gifts insulted? Would they give us nothing more, or worse, would they take back what they had already given? The thought drew my gaze to my three youngest brothers. I looked at them and felt an anxious shudder run over my skin. I scooped Noboru into my lap, despite his squirming, and held him tight. I wished that I could hold all of my family close to me in the same way, and protect them from whatever was to come.

On a clear spring morning when the cherry trees in the distance had not yet bloomed, our shaman was summoned to the house of one of the Matsu nobles to help ease a difficult birth. I was with her, carrying all the things she might need for whatever lay ahead. I watched attentively as Yama guided the new life into our clan and rejoiced with the child's family when all chance of danger to mother and infant had passed.

The birth took a long time. The light was already beginning to fade from the sky when Yama sent me down the ladder of the noble's house. My arms were full with all the gear I'd need to clean and put away. I trod carefully. The steps on the ladder had been worn smooth by years of use, and it was a far drop from the platform.

I was safely down and heading for the shaman's house when I heard Yama calling out to me: "Himiko, you don't need to—!"

I turned in time to see our shaman rush to the edge of the platform, slip, and plunge to the ground.

12
CHANGES IN A SINGLE BREATH

"Well, if this doesn't prove that the gods have a sense of humor, I don't know what does." Yama sat on her bedroll and looked down at her broken leg. Her thin lips twisted into a wry smile as she turned her head to me. "I want to say that you did a better job of piecing my old bones back together than I did for your young ones, but I'm a vain creature. I can't admit the truth when it shames me."

"I only did what you told me to do," I replied. "I couldn't have done anything without your guidance."

I knelt at the shaman's bedside, my fists on my thighs. It seemed to me as though my hands had been balled up tightly ever since Yama's accident, except when I was actively using them. Every fiber of my body felt perpetually taut and ready to snap at the slightest touch. Even my voice sounded strained, pitched higher than normal, while my head never stopped echoing with an unending stream of prayers.

"Is that so?" Yama cocked her head and regarded me with the bright, dark eyes of a curious crow. "Then who was it who guided you while I lay senseless on the ground? My wandering spirit?"

"I didn't do anything *important* then," I argued. "Anyone in our clan would have known enough to have you carried carefully, to clean your wounds, to—"

"Enough, enough. Soon you'll be claiming that you don't know how to *breathe* without my almighty guidance." Yama shifted her weight and winced. "You know very well that you could have done everything necessary without a single word from me. The only reason I spoke up and began directing you through each and every step was because your father was hovering around. We can't have him know you're ready to take over my duties *quite* yet."

I clenched my fists even tighter. "I don't feel ready for that at all."

"And why not?"

"The same reason: the dances that we must perform to—"

"What's wrong with the way you dance?"

"That's just it, Lady Yama: I *don't* dance," I said miserably. "I've been doing what you said, practicing the steps, the motions, but I still hobble through them. My dances look nothing like yours."

"Maybe they will, after this." Yama indicated her broken leg and uttered a short, harsh laugh. "My dear girl, when you invoke the spirits, is your voice exactly like mine? When you grind dried herbs for medicine, do you hold the bowl in precisely the same way that I do? My own teacher told me that we dance for the entertainment of the gods, to please them, to attract their goodwill, even to make them laugh! If every shaman performed the sacred dances in identical fashion, I don't think it would be very entertaining."

"At least I know they'll laugh when they watch me," I muttered.

"Have it your way, you stubborn thing: you're as clumsy as a two-legged rabbit, and you can scarcely manage to walk from my house to yours without falling on your face at least three times. Now bring me something to drink without spilling it, and then fetch your father. I want to know if there's been any word of Michio yet!"

I smiled at the old woman's feigned grumpiness. "Yes, Lady Yama. I'll be back soon."

One of the first things that our shaman had done when she revived from her fall was to tell Father to send for her half brother, Michio. It seemed like an impossible task.

A shaman like his sister, Michio had left our village years ago for reasons Yama had never told me. Ever since I'd learned his identity, I'd paid closer attention whenever anyone spoke his name. By doing this, I discovered that even though he wasn't a part of our clan's daily life anymore, he was a mighty presence in everyone's imagination. His name was mentioned most often when my clanfolk were working in the fields, harvesting the crops, washing clothes, or waiting for a community rite to begin. People lightened their work or simply passed the time by making wild guesses about why he'd gone away, though they also wondered aloud about whether he was still alive, where he was, and when and if he'd ever return. Their idle chatter let me catch hints about the man, like wayward glints of sunlight glimpsed through wind-tossed leaves.

From what I could gather, Yama's younger brother was a big fellow with a ready smile. His strength was incredible. Everyone called it a misplaced gift from the gods, more suitable for a man who'd follow the way of the warrior rather than the way of the spirits. He had a huge appetite and a sense of curiosity to match it. Some claimed that the moment after Michio was born and placed in his mother's arms, the infant turned his eyes to the open doorway of his house and stretched out one hand as if to say, *And what lies over there? I should go and see.*

My clanfolk seemed to know everything about Michio except where to find him.

I didn't want to leave Yama alone for very long, so I ran through the village, seeking Father. I found him with several of our nobles, conferring about the rice planting. I clapped my hands together in a gesture of respect before I told Father my errand.

"Please excuse me, my friends," Father said gravely. "I'll be back when I can." The other men muttered assurances that there was no need for him to hurry. Any matter concerning Lady Yama's condition pushed all others aside. Her accident had been like a dash of icy water in the face, awaking everyone in the village to the hard, indisputable facts: our shaman might have great powers, know many secret arts, call upon the gods, and be able to summon and dismiss the spirits of the dead, but she was as human as the rest of us. She was old, her bones could break, and as far as anyone in our village knew, no one could take her place when she died. When that day came, soon or late, who would stand between the Matsu and the darkness? Who would weave spells of protection around our lives? Who would heal us, in body and soul?

Yama was lying down when I brought Father into her house. At first, I thought she was sleeping, and for one unbearable instant I imagined the worst. Then she turned her head in our direction, and the horrible illusion of death was gone.

"Well, has Michio been told?" she asked.

"I don't know, Lady Yama," Father replied, kneeling beside her. He sounded unnaturally subdued. "I gave your directions to my best men, including two of my own sons. Unless your brother has moved on, they'll find him."

"You *know* where to look for him, Father?" I was too stunned by what I'd just heard to keep from blurting out that question. "I thought no one did!"

"He knows because I told him," Yama said. "And I know because Michio told *me*. Before he left this village, he let me know where I would be able to find him. He said he was going to his father's people, the Todomatsu, on the sunset seacoast. Their clan is distant kin to ours, and we used to trade with them years ago." She gave Father a pointed stare. "Some of us remember the old knowledge and can find the road that leads to their settlement."

Father ignored her jibe. He'd isolated us from other clans, but had no obvious regrets for his actions. "I've done as you directed, Lady Yama. If the gods are willing, Michio will be back."

"Why did he leave?" I asked. Yama had once told me he'd done so because one village couldn't have two shamans, but I suspected that wasn't the real reason.

Father and Yama exchanged a grim look. "He felt his life was in danger," Father said. "And he was right."

Yama sat up a bit, propping herself on her elbows, and nodded. "The day before he left, he came to me and said, 'Yama, the Matsu lands might be a safe place for one of us, but not both. *She* sees you as a rival, but she sees me as a threat, and you know how she deals with threats.'"

"*She*?" I echoed. "Who is *she*?"

"Our former chief," Father said, and before I could ask another question, he snapped, "And the less said about her, the better."

"But, Father—"

"I said, *enough*!" He stood up and strode out of the shaman's house.

Once he was gone, I looked to Yama for more of an explanation, but the shaman sighed and lay down again. "I'm so tired. I think I want to sleep for a while." She closed her eyes and was soon deep in dreams.

One of the lessons Yama taught me over and over was that sleep is a great healer. The more we rest, the better the chances of our bodies drawing their broken parts back together, whether those parts be bones or the edges of a cut or even a disturbance in our minds. If someone suffers from a pain so intense that it has the power to drive sleep away, a good shaman knows that she faces an appalling enemy and that the battle will be one of life or death.

But there are other times when the shaman's enemy

disguises itself as her friend. Sleep that heals is a blessing, but sleep that is too deep can be something else entirely. A good sleep can be the gateway back to health, but a sleep that endures too long may be the subtle opening of another gateway, one that leads the spirit down a path from which there is no return. And because this ill-omened sort of sleep comes secretly, easily mistaken for its kinder sister, by the time the healer realizes what's happening, it's too late.

I didn't see anything wrong with letting Yama sleep as long as she could. While she rested, I kept busy by cleaning her house, checking on the level and freshness of the water in the big jug, and seeing if any of her most used remedies needed to be renewed. I paid special attention to noting how much we had left of those medicines necessary to take care of the shaman herself, and breathed easy when I found that there was a good supply of all of them on hand. I wouldn't have minded going into the forest to gather the ingredients for making more, but I didn't want to leave Yama alone, if I could help it.

Of course, I had to leave her sometimes. I had no choice. I could have had my meals and bedroll brought to me in her house, but Mama pointed out that I wouldn't be able to get the full benefit of food and sleep if I stayed there.

"You'd be constantly on edge, jumping at every sound," she pointed out. "How soon before you started asking poor Lady Yama 'Are you all right? Are you all right?' every few breaths? I know you're devoted to our shaman, Himiko, but it will be best for both of you if you allow others to help care for her."

I couldn't argue with that. I knew Mama was right,

whether or not I liked it. No one from our household could sit with Yama because my three younger brothers were too lively to let our shaman rest properly, but Mama organized a group of Matsu women who were more than capable of tending her. They all said how easy it was, although they never explained that the reason for this was that the old woman spent most of her time asleep.

The fever came four days later. It might have been lurking inside her before that, but if so, it didn't make her skin hot enough to the touch for me to notice its presence until then. I had also been careful to keep my teacher comfortable while she rested, which included wiping her face with a cloth dipped in cool water. Had that kept the burning at bay? I didn't know.

That morning I arose, ate breakfast, and was heading for Yama's house as usual. I had no qualms about how she'd passed the night. If something had gone wrong, our household would have been roused from sleep and summoned in an instant. Mama had taken the precaution of assigning the night watch at Yama's bedside to two women at once. If our shaman needed something, there was less danger of both of them dozing off at the same time. Also, though one watcher might be afraid while wakeful and alone in a house that held the possibility of magic, two could trade friendly whispers and keep their fears away. Mama chose those whose children were grown up and had families of their own. These older women were happy to feel useful and to be trusted with such an important task.

I was halfway to Yama's house when I saw two women rushing to meet me. Their faces were pinched and pale with terror. "Lady Himiko! Lady Himiko! Something's wrong; she won't wake up!" one of them cried. I didn't wait to hear more. My feet flew as fast as I could drive them. I raced right past the frightened women and into Yama's house, calling my teacher's name.

Yama stirred at the sound, muttering and grunting on her bedroll. I was never so glad to hear any other sound. I dropped to my knees beside her and put one hand on her brow. It was burning.

"Lady Himiko, what's the matter with her?" came a trembling voice from the doorway. The two women had caught up with me and hovered just outside, afraid to come in. I was younger than any of their children, but now they spoke to me with more respect than I'd receive simply for being their chieftain's daughter. It wasn't because I was the shaman's apprentice—nobody in our village knew about that—but because I was the one person close to her. I had spent many days, many seasons, in this house. No doubt the women believed that I must have absorbed some of Yama's knowledge, the way a piece of cloth hung above a fire drinks in the scent of smoke.

"She has a fever," I said sharply. I wanted to add: *Isn't it obvious? Did either one of you touch her even once last night? What were you doing all that time, gossiping?* The only thing that stopped me was seeing the ghastly expression on their faces and knowing that I wanted to lash out at them because I was just as terrified by Yama's condition as they were.

"Ohhhhh, this is all my fault," one of the women groaned. "She asked for water just before she went to sleep, and she drank so much of it, we all joked about it. I was helping her sit up to drink. I thought her back felt warmer than it should, but then I told myself it was just because she'd been lying down for so long. I should have checked her later! I should have, but she was sleeping so peacefully, I didn't want to risk having my touch wake her up. Oh, gods, forgive me!" She buried her face in her hands. Her friend tried and failed to comfort her.

"Please, stop crying," I said dully. "No one's to blame for this." That was a lie. I was certain that somebody *was* at fault: me. Somehow I had made a mistake, done too much, done too little, done the wrong thing, done the right thing in the wrong way. I couldn't accept that such a horrid turn of events could just *happen*. "Will you please bring some fresh water? I'm going to bathe her, to cool her skin."

The two women sprinted off before I could tell them that I'd also need more cloth, to rebind Yama's leg. They were so glad to escape, I could almost *taste* their relief. I sighed and looked at the shaman. "Do you think they'll come back?" I murmured. Her eyelids fluttered, but she said nothing.

While I was waiting for the women to return, I untied the bandages. I don't know why I decided to do that. It was an impulse, but such a strong one that I had Yama's broken leg half bared before I realized what I was doing.

When she'd fallen, she'd suffered a break high on her thigh. Despite what she'd said about trusting me to take care of something so serious on my own, I was privately happy that she'd talked me through the process of setting it. I remembered what she'd told me as I tied the last knot in the bandages: "Now we're going to leave that alone and let it heal in peace. If there's anything else that has to be done for me, I'll tell you." She hadn't given me any further instructions since then, so I'd done as she directed, letting her rest and never untying the wrappings.

Never until now. I worked quickly but with gentle hands. A nagging thought rode me mercilessly: *To drown the fire, find the source! To drown the fire, find the source!* It pounded through my head, and the only thing that would silence it was doing as it bid me. I pulled away the last layer of cloth and discovered I was breathing as hard as if I'd raced all the way up a mountain.

And now I saw the reason for my teacher's unnatural sleep, and for the fever that was blazing through her body. Even though I'd cleaned Yama's wounds before I'd set her bone and covered them with the proper mixture of honey and herbs after, the place where she'd landed hardest and snapped her thigh had become a swollen, ugly mass of scarlet. Bright red streaks branched out from the center, and a gruesome smell rushed up my nose with so much force that it left me reeling. How had it gone unnoticed for so long? Was it the thick, sweet-scented dressing I'd slathered over the site, the bandages, or the pungent aromas of all the herbs, powders, and brews stored under the shaman's roof?

Oh gods, I did everything she told me to do! I thought miserably as I stared at the horror I'd uncovered. *Why didn't it work? Why did this happen? Why—?*

And then I closed my eyes and breathed in slowly, deeply. *"Why" doesn't matter,* I told myself firmly. *The question that counts now is: what will I do to save her?*

I forced myself to look at Yama as just another one of

my clanfolk. If I let myself remember how special she was to me, I'd cry, and tears healed nothing. I went to the door of her house and called out to the first man I saw: "Our shaman needs cloth, soft cloth, as soft as you can find! Bring it! Hurry!" He stared at me, astonished, but only for a moment before the dire urgency in my voice sent him running.

Other people heard and came to see what was happening. Their fearful questions made the air buzz as if a swarm of bees had descended on our village. I wanted to grab each one of them by the arm and shake them while I shouted *Don't just stand there! Do something useful!*

Shouting won't help Yama, I thought. I took another deep breath and waded into the crowd. One by one, I picked out the faces of the people who would best be able to do what was necessary. One by one, I told each of them what to do, keeping my words and demeanor calm. I sent one woman to bring honey, our brawniest man to fill and fetch the biggest water jug in the village, someone else to get some rice wine, and one of our keenest-eyed hunters to gather a very special plant: "It's called hare's-ear. The leaves are curved, and it's got yellow flowers. I saw some growing at the far edge of our bean field. You'll have to dig up the whole thing; I need the root. Please hurry!"

Father arrived in the midst of this. His brow was clouded with worry that was fast turning into anger. "What's going on here?" he demanded, confronting me. "Himiko, what do you think you're doing?"

This wasn't the time to assert myself, and certainly not to reveal how much of Yama's lore I possessed. You don't use the same force to slice a peach as to chop a tree branch.

I lowered my eyes and spoke softly as I told him what I'd found awaiting me that morning.

"Father, you saw how Lady Yama instructed me to set her broken leg. You know I've been her helper for years. Under her orders, I prepared the medicines she needed for our clan, and I was often with her when she used them. I know— I mean, I *think* I know what has to be done now. I'm not a shaman, but—"

"The gods forbid it," Father snapped. "You're a smart girl, Himiko. I'd be surprised and disappointed if you didn't know how to care for our shaman. Do your best. Our whole clan will help." He turned to the crowd and bellowed, "My daughter's voice is mine! Do as she says!"

With Father's support, I was able to command even more aid from our clanfolk. I no longer needed to shout my orders and hope no one would waste time questioning them. I had everyone's instant obedience. I soon had one person grinding dried herbs to powder so that I could make fresh honey salve, another preparing hare's-ear root as I directed, a third boiling water to make that root into the drink I prayed would lower Yama's fever, several women turning cloth into strips that were the right size for new bandages, and so on. Even Father stood by, vigilant, making sure my words were heeded correctly.

All of this allowed me to duck back into Yama's house and give my full attention to my teacher's treatment. I soon had that hideous redness cleansed, salved, and delicately wrapped up, all without disturbing the setting of her broken bone. When the hare's-ear draft was cool enough to drink,

I had Father prop her up in his arms as I tried to make her swallow a few mouthfuls without choking. Midway through the process, her eyelids fluttered again, then opened. She drank greedily. I wanted to jump up and cry out with joy, but instead, I kept the shallow bowl to her lips until it was empty.

"Lady . . . Lady Yama?" I asked tentatively as I set the bowl aside. "How do you feel?"

"Dizzy," she replied. She sounded like someone speaking from the depths of sleep. She blinked and turned her head toward Father. "What do *you* want?"

He smiled dryly. "I've got it."

Yama frowned and looked confused. "No riddles. I don't like riddles. I don't think I like you so much, either. I'm old and I'm tired, and I don't have to like anyone. Go away." But she lay back against Father's arm and rested her head on his shoulder.

"Lady Yama?" I touched her bony wrist lightly with two fingers. "What should I do for you now?"

"Do?" she echoed. Her eyelids lowered and she sighed. "If you don't know what to do by now, what's the use?" She muttered something unintelligible, but when I tried to get her to repeat it, she stopped speaking entirely. Her breathing became more shallow and regular. Father and I exchanged a look that contained the same question: *Has she gone back to sleep?* I laid my palm to her brow. It was still hot, though not as hot as before.

"What should I do?" Father mouthed silently at me. With an expressive shift of his eyes, he indicated the bedroll. I

nodded: *Yes, help her lie down again.* He moved carefully, letting the shaman's body recline full length without disturbing her rest. Then the two of us stood up and went outside.

"She spoke to us," I announced to the mass of people waiting for news. A few happy murmurs ran through the crowd, but most of the faces gazing at me were stiff with anxiety. *They feel helpless,* I thought. *It will be a comfort if I can give most of them something,* anything *to do for her. They'll be able to feel like a part of the healing, and they won't have as much time to let their worst imaginings grip their spirits.*

And so I told the people that we'd need teams of three to take turns keeping watch over our shaman—two who would stay at her bedside and one posted at the doorway, ready to run any errands that might arise. I left it to Father to choose the members of each group and organize the order in which they'd look after her.

The sun goddess was at the midpoint of the sky when I trailed home. It wasn't even afternoon, but I was already exhausted. Mama was standing at the foot of our ladder, Noboru on her hip, when I arrived. She had the tense, strained air of someone who has been on watch for a long time. I told her everything that had happened. I was so worn out that my voice sounded like it was coming from someone else. Mama promptly shooed me up to our porch, ordered me to sit down, and put my baby brother in my lap. Noboru's fresh, laughing face lifted the weight from my chest, and soon I was singing funny songs to the baby, my mind happily distracted from darker thoughts.

Father came home shortly after that. He sat beside Noboru and me, but didn't look at us. His eyes were fixed on the deep green of the sacred pine tree's boughs, as though he were wordlessly communing with the guardian spirit of our clan. When he spoke at last, it was to say, "I hope they've found Lady Yama's half brother. The gods grant he's on the road back to us by now. We need him more than ever. You did well today, Himiko, and I'm proud of you, but you're not a shaman."

I pressed my lips together. With all my strength, I held back the urge to cry out, *No, but I will be! And I already know more of the shaman's lore than you think, Father, but I have to keep it hidden from your stubborn eyes. Why don't you want me to follow the path that was meant for me? When will I be able to be myself without worrying that you'll fly into one of your rages?*

Instead, I thanked him for his praise and was sinking back into silence when suddenly a spark of inspiration flashed through my mind. "Father, a real shaman could help heal Lady Yama better than I. You know that's true. We have no idea when Master Michio will return, or even if your men will find him. Lady Yama needs healing now. Send a man to the Shika clan! You remember their chieftess, Lady Ikumi, don't you? She's a shaman too, and she'd be happy to—"

"*No!*" Father's voice boomed. Noboru startled and opened his mouth in a shriek of terror so loud that Mama came rushing out of the house in a panic.

"What is it? What's wrong?" she cried, taking the howling baby from my arms.

"Nothing," Father said in a way that let us both know there would be no further discussion of the matter. He stamped down the ladder.

"Himiko?" Mama cast an inquiring look at me, but I let it slip past without responding. Cold anger had clapped its hands around me the way a little boy captures a firefly. I was afraid that if I said one word to her, I'd find myself screaming out my indignation against Father's unending blindness to the possibility that once—just *once*—we could treat the members of a different clan as human beings, not enemies. My teacher's need for another shaman's healing wisdom was not as important to him as keeping the Matsu isolated from the rest of the world.

Mama waited for a reply, got none, shrugged, and left me alone.

I checked on Yama's condition regularly that day and the next. She spent a peaceful night, and when I came by the following morning, I was told that she'd asked for breakfast. Who would have thought that my world would seem brighter just because a white-haired woman ate a bowl of rice gruel? She continued to sleep more than she woke, but I wasn't too worried about that. When my visits coincided with her wakeful times, I asked her if I should reexamine her leg under the bandages. She sounded almost chipper when she dismissed the idea.

"Let it be, child, let it be. You'll fidget the bone into fragments if you're forever unwrapping and rewrapping it. Not even the gods can hasten this sort of healing."

I touched her forehead and made a doubtful face. "You feel warmer. I think I should check to see if the swelling's any better, and if the redness—"

"Pff! I'm sure everything's fine. I'm warmer because it's warmer outside and this house is stuffy. Bring me another dose of hare's-ear tonic if you're nervous." She yawned widely. "But be quick about it. I'd like to take a nap." I turned to have one of her attendants bring me the jug of fever remedy, but by the time the woman found it and I'd poured out a dose, Yama was snoring. I left her to rest, and when I returned later that evening for one last check before my bedtime, I was told that she'd eaten and drunk heartily and was asleep once more. My fingertips on her forehead felt warm, but not too much. I went home for the night with my mind at ease.

"Himiko! Himiko, get up, she wants you!" My eyes snapped open to see Mama's anguished face by firelight. She was kneeling at my side, Noboru clinging to her chest, and when I sat up, I saw Yukari and Emi standing nearby, holding their sons. The children were sobbing with fear, and my stepmothers' faces were awash with tears.

I didn't ask what had happened; I didn't have to. My belly smoldered with the bitter certainty. Yama's pale face hung before my eyes like a film of moonlight on water. I uttered an inhuman cry of grief, thrust myself out of my bedroll, yanked my tunic over my head, and bolted for the door.

"Wait! Wait! You need a light!" Mama called after me. I only half heard her and paid no attention until a strong hand closed on my arm before I cleared our doorway.

"Let me go!" I shouted, trying to pull away. "She needs me! I have to go to her before it's too late! I've got to save her! Let me *go*!"

"Mother said *wait*." My brother Masa's hard expression made him look like a younger version of Father. "Wait for me to go ahead of you with a light or you'll miss the ladder. How will you help her then?"

"*Fine.*" I spat the word in his face. "Stop talking and *do* it. Hurry!"

Masa swallowed my harsh words without complaint. He was no fool; he sensed the dire forces that were rushing to engulf our village. Soon I was racing by his side as he lit the way to Yama's house.

Father was there before us. He knelt beside the shaman's still-breathing body, his sword across his lap. Did he believe he had the power to fight off death? It was a mad thought, yet anyone there to see that unyielding glint in his eyes would have to ask, *Is anything impossible if a man with this much courage and determination decides it* can *be done?*

I dropped to my knees beside him. Masa remained in the doorway, his mouth a taut line. Searing heat flared over my palm when I put it on Yama's brow. There was a bowl of water near her head and a wet cloth draped over the rim. I dipped the rag, wrung it out, and wiped her face tenderly before speaking: "When did this happen? When did she get so bad?"

"Not long ago," Father answered. Tension radiated from his body like ripples from a stone thrown into a pond. "The women tending her thought she was sleeping normally until she let out a terrible groan and her teeth started chattering. When they touched her, they felt the fire and had the guard come for me. I got here just as she began to thrash around."

"She did what?" I was aghast. "But her leg—!"

Father's grip on his sword tightened. "Every move she

made brought her fresh suffering, but she wouldn't stop. I don't think she *could*. The fire in her body burned away all wisdom. We held her down as well as we could without causing her further pain, but she fought us, arching her back, trying to kick free, and always wailing from the agony she was suffering."

Tears spilled down my cheeks. "Why didn't you send for me? I could have done something to calm her, to ease the pain, to—!"

"Do you think I didn't want to do that at once?" Father jerked his head toward me, and I saw my own tears mirrored on his face. "But who could I send? All four of us had to restrain her until the fit passed. I prayed that someone would hear her cries and come to help, but no one did. She finally lay still, and I was about to tell the man on guard to bring you here when she stirred and opened her eyes. Oh, Himiko, her eyes! They held the white-hot glow of iron in the forge, and when she spoke your name, her voice was the creaking groan of great trees about to topple in a storm. The guard saw, heard, and ran without waiting for any word from me. He hasn't come back."

I looked around the empty house. "And the two women?"

"They saw and heard as well, but they were too scared to move. I had to yell at them to make them leave. What good would it do to keep them here, poor things?" He nodded at Yama. "She looks as if she sleeps, but I can see a thread of white under her eyelashes. She's awake. She's listening. Speak to her, Himiko."

I leaned forward until my lips nearly brushed my teacher's ear. "Lady Yama?" I whispered. "I'm here. It's Himiko."

"Himiko . . ." My name rasped from her mouth. I sat back on my heels and dabbed her lips delicately with the wet cloth to moisten them.

"You're thirsty," I said. "Don't try to talk until I've brought you something to drink. I'll get you some honeyed water." I tried to rise, but her hand shot out and gripped my wrist hard, her cracked nails digging deep into my skin.

"Stay, my princess," she croaked. "Stay, my queen. I need no more water. I have put on a crane's broad wings and flown from here to the sea! I have bathed in the waters that surround this island and all the islands that our people know as home. Ah, Lady Himiko, where are your wings? Mine are white as the snow that cloaks the sacred mountain, but yours—! Yours blaze with the holy light of the sun goddess's own splendor."

"Gods be merciful to her," Father breathed. "Her mind is gone." He must have thought he was speaking softly enough so that she wouldn't hear him, but he was wrong.

A hoarse, distorted version of Yama's familiar chuckle echoed within her house. "Gone?" she said. "Oh yes! Gone far from here! Gone to behold sights that you never could imagine, you sad little mole, your eyes buried so far beneath the soil that you can't see the wonder that lives under your roof. Himiko? Child, are you there?" She squeezed my wrist so powerfully that I felt the bones grind together.

"Yes, Lady Yama," I said with a gasp of pain. "I—I promise I won't leave. Please, would you mind—?" I plucked lightly at her grasped fingers, urging them to release me.

"Ah, forgive me." She let me go and sighed. As if in response, a faint rumble of thunder sounded in the distance.

"Do you hear that?" For the first time since I'd come to the shaman's bedside, Yama's eyes opened wide. "The gods strike the drums of heaven to drive the demons from your path. They send a rain of stones to crush you, but your feet turn them to steps that carry you higher with every stride: from shaman to chieftess of the Matsu, from chieftess of the Matsu to ruler of countless other clans, from ruler to legend! You will conquer the secrets of wind and water, of human hearts and animal spirits, of life and its darkest reflection. Your name will cross the wide waters to reach the throne of a mighty empire in the sunset lands. You will hold the mirror in which our people will see our true, glorious destiny. Oh, my beloved queen, I see it all, and my heart dances!" A radiant smile bathed her face with such rapture that the cruel signs of sickness faded away.

"Madness, ill-omened madness," Father muttered. His hands shook, and the sword that he held trembled. Another roll of thunder reached our ears, closer now, and the first raindrops began to fall. Father looked sharply to the doorway of the shaman's house, where Masa still stood waiting. Despite the rain, he did not cross the threshold.

"Madness," Father said again, hunching forward. "If she were my eldest, if there were only the little boys and her, then— But no!" His voice rose sharply. "I have sons who'll rule after me; grown *sons.* Almighty gods, be merciful! Don't let this woman's ravings turn to spells of destruction! Strike *me,* and let my life be the wall to shield my precious children!"

"Father, it's all right." I laid a hand on his forearm. "She's sick, so very sick that she doesn't know what she's saying. *Aki* will lead our people, not me! I don't want to. All that I desire is—" I caught myself. *All that I desire is to fulfill my training in the way of the spirits.* But I couldn't say such things to him yet, and so: "All that I desire is to follow my own path, Father. I promise you, it won't lead me anywhere you need to fear."

"*Your* path, my queen?" Yama's words resounded above the rushing downpour of the rain. "You think you see it so clearly before you, cutting through the future like a wide, well-traveled road? Oh, Himiko, so wise and yet so young, you cannot know that even the best-cut path can be swept away by storms, and even stones—even stones"—she drew a deep, shuddering breath—"are sand."

The last whisper of life trailed from between her lips, and she was gone.

PART III
SPIRIT PATH

13
A Road
Leading Nowhere

I sat alone in the doorway of Yama's house, listening to the sounds of grief and fear sweeping through our village. The cries of lamentation rose from every house, countless voices calling out to the gods for help and mercy. I leaned my head against the doorjamb and slowly closed my eyes, drained of everything but complete weariness.

The rainstorm that had swooped over us and snatched away our shaman's life had dwindled to a few random spits of drizzle. There was a large puddle an arm's length from the threshold where I sat, its surface pocked now and again with the last lonely drops to fall. It showed me the reflection of a clearing sky, a scrap of white cloud, and then the faint image of Mama's face.

"Come home, Himiko," she said softly. "You shouldn't linger here."

I looked up bleakly. "Why not, Mama? Lady Yama was my friend. Her spirit won't hurt me."

"It's still not a good idea to stay too close to—" Mama cast a nervous glance over my head, into the living darkness biding under Yama's roof. "To a house of sorrow."

I shook my head. "Where do you want me to go? Listen: our whole village is a house of sorrow today," I said with a rueful smile.

Mama hesitated, then turned resolute. She straightened her back and glared at me as if I were little Sanjirou, caught doing mischief. "Himiko, go home *now*." Judging by her tone, she wasn't going to hear any argument.

I wasn't going to give her one. I merely looked at her calmly and didn't move.

"*Agh!* What's *wrong* with you?" she exclaimed at last, exasperated. "What do you think you're doing? Sitting in the dirt like that isn't going to bring her back! And if you get sick, will that change anything?" I remained silent. "Do I have to pull you to your feet and *drag* you home with me?"

Mama's hands reached for mine, as though she were about to fulfill her threat. Abruptly, she let her arms fall to her sides and went down on one knee. When she took my hands in hers, it wasn't to haul me away with her but to clasp them lovingly and draw them to her heart.

"You think you failed her," she said. "My poor child, you blame yourself."

"Oh, Mama, it's true!" I burst into loud, body-shaking sobs and flung myself into my mother's waiting arms. "I should never have left her alone! I should have been with her all the time! I should have looked at her wounds more often! I should have—"

"Hush, hush, my sweet baby." Mama stroked my hair

and whispered comfort. "She was never left alone, you know that. And even if you'd spent every moment with her, do you imagine that sleep wouldn't have overtaken you sometimes? You're holding yourself guilty for nothing. You were only her helper, following her directions. Do you want to blame our shaman for her own death?"

I lifted my face from her shoulder and shook my head. "No, Mama," I said in a small voice.

"So you see how it is." A fond half smile curved her mouth. "Lady Yama was this clan's treasure. She saved so many lives, young and old, that it would take days to speak of them all. Her skills were a gift from the gods. But there were also many lives she couldn't save. It didn't matter how hard she tried, or if her remedy was exactly the same as one she'd used successfully on someone else; she failed. I remember how my heart broke when—" Mama's gaze drifted to a place of past sorrow until she wrenched her attention back to me. "Well, never mind that. What's important is that you understand you're blameless."

I sat back and dried my tears with the heel of my hand. "I don't feel blameless, Mama," I said.

"That will come, dearest. Trust me." She helped me stand up and gently urged me to go home with her. As we walked, she said, "We'll all feel better once Aki, Shoichi, and the rest return with our new shaman."

"What if . . . What if they can't find him?"

Mama sighed. "I don't know what we'll do then. Lady Yama should have trained someone to take her place, but she never did. I think she was relying on her half brother to succeed her. I wish she'd done more than that."

She did, I thought. My heart fluttered with hope. Our clan couldn't survive if we had no shaman to perform the rituals, to ask the gods for their blessing, to ensure the benevolence of the earth. If Yama's half brother didn't come back, how long should I wait to reveal that I had been her student, her apprentice, her heir? *Father will have to allow it. The Matsu will need me, and what else will he be able to do then? Turn to another clan for help? Never. This is the design the spirits have laid out at my feet. I will wait, but I will walk the pattern and serve my clan as Yama always intended me to do.*

Even if I hoped that our search party came back empty-handed, I could see how deeply distressed Mama was at the notion of an uncertain future. I had to offer her some reassurance. "Don't worry, Mama," I said. "Aki's a great hunter. He can track anything *and* anybody. And Shoichi will help him."

Her eyes wandered again. "We wouldn't be in this situation if things were as they used to be. In the past, our chief was also our shaman, and our chief's heir was given the training he would need for both positions. If he had brothers and sisters, one or two of them would share those lessons, in case the chief's heir wasn't fit for his duties to the clan and the gods, or if some calamity claimed him. The responsibility was always handed down that way, parent to child, until Lady Tsuki's reign."

"Lady Tsuki . . ." I remembered that name very well. I'd heard it spoken in the past, and I'd also heard it deliberately *not* spoken, to keep her spirit at bay. Never once had I heard it voiced with love. "She was our ruler before Father became chieftain, yes?"

"Our ruler, our shaman, and our punishment." Mama's eyes lost their usually sweet look, turning to bits of flint. "She never served our clan the way your father does or the way Lady Yama did. She only used her powers to lift herself above us all. Too many of us lived our lives in terror because she had convinced us that she only needed to utter one accursed spell and the vengeful ghosts of a thousand generations would pour across our land. She had to be flattered, satisfied, and indulged at every turn, but above all, she had to be obeyed!"

"Lady Yama told me that she envied Michio—Master Michio—and that was why he had to go away."

"No doubt of that," Mama said with a sniff. "I heard that he showed remarkable gifts from a very early age. The thought of anyone having skills that might rival hers was poison in Lady Tsuki's belly. There was a rumor that she caused the death of another woman of our clan because that one was more favored by the gods than she. The dead woman was the mother of both Lady Yama and Master Michio, and before she died, she gave both of them the proper training to become great shamans in their own right. Lady Yama had the wisdom to pretend that her only talent was as a healer, and that the world of the spirits was closed to her. Master Michio made a different choice."

We climbed the ladder to our home. Yukari and Emi had dinner ready for us. Masa was doing his best to keep our younger brothers from getting into everything and looked worn out from the effort. He gave Mama and me a welcome fit for heroes!

"Thank the gods you're here! I'm ready to take all three

of them down to the forge and tie them to the anvil." He groaned. "Why couldn't I have had three more sisters?"

"Because your little sisters would be as much trouble for you as your little brothers, Masa," I replied. "I'd make sure of that." I swung Noboru into the air and made him crow with glee, then planted him on my hip and looked around the room curiously. "Where's Father?"

"Gone to the burial ground," Masa said. "There are many things to do before tomorrow." A heavy pall trailed after his words and settled over all of us except the little ones. Somewhere in our village, my teacher's body was being prepared by the old women who knew the right way to do such things. At the burial ground, our strongest clanfolk were making a grave. When both were ready, our shaman would be given to the earth and a square mound raised over her. Only then would Father summon the whole village to honor her spirit and say farewell.

And then what? I thought. *We have no shaman. Who will ask the gods to welcome Yama's spirit? Who will purify our clan from the touch of death?*

That evening, Yukari ordered me to give her my dress and to take one of her old ones in its place. "Look at how filthy it is," she said, pointing at the stains I'd gathered from sitting in the wet dirt in Yama's doorway. "And it smells. I'll wash it for you, but you need something suitable to wear tomorrow."

"It wouldn't look like that if Himiko hadn't been sitting in mud for so long." Mama looked at me with pity in her eyes. "My poor little girl, you thought you could have saved Lady Yama, and it broke your heart when she died. How awful it would be if you had to lead a real healer's life. I don't think you could stand it. It's easy enough when you succeed, but when you do all you can and people die anyway? Be glad that you won't have to deal with such a burden anymore." She kissed me and then turned her attention to Noboru, who wanted to be fed. I doubt she gave another thought to what she'd said.

I couldn't say the same about me. My mother's words haunted me that night, when I lay down to sleep and found that I couldn't close my eyes without seeing Yama's face in the darkness. *"How awful would be if you had to lead a real healer's life."* Mama's words rang like the ghost of a bronze bell, and Yama's phantom face opened its eyes to gaze into mine and say, *How long will you deny your true self, Himiko? I was wrong to tell you to slink into the shadows, but I feared too much. I should have brought you into the light, and never mind what your father would have said! But if you stay hidden now, it's your own doing, and if you stay hidden too long, you won't be a real healer, you won't be a real shaman, you won't be real at all.*

I lurched up from my bedroll, fully awake, staring at ghosts and memories. I was panting as though I'd run all the way home from the rice paddies, and my body was streaming with sweat. Somewhere out there in the night, Yama's body lay under the warm soil, her spirit already well on its way into the land that lay beyond the life we knew. She was free, and her soul had merged with the harmony of earth and water, wind and stars, but her death was the touch of a spreading sickness that would contaminate our clan unless someone acted soon to cleanse us.

I arose in the dark and found my old, soiled dress. Yukari hadn't taken it away quite yet. I slipped it on like a whisper and crept out of our doorway, feeling cautiously for the ladder. The village slept as I made my way to Yama's house. I paused for a while before going in, remembering my teacher, my friend. Raising my hands solemnly, I clapped them together twice, just enough to make· a sound that wouldn't reach the ears of those asleep in the nearest houses.

There was no light to guide me once I went inside. All that relieved the blackness was the faint glimmer of stars and the waning moon shining through the smoke hole in the roof. That was enough for me. The interior of Yama's house was as familiar to me as the shape of my mother's face. My hands had arranged all the shaman's possessions. I knew where everything was. Within those walls, I could have found whatever I wanted even if darkness in the house were absolute.

I moved as quickly as I could, gathered the few things I needed, and stepped into the open air again. I wasn't hurrying out of fear. An encounter with Yama's spirit would have been a comfort to me. Somehow I just couldn't picture her as an angry ghost, and I would have welcomed the chance of being haunted by the sound of her wry wisdom and familiar chuckle. But all that lingered under her roof were memories and loss.

Night was growing paler when I emerged from the shaman's house and put down the things I'd taken. I laid them out in an orderly row. One of the first lessons Yama had taught me was the importance· of honoring the balance of existence, and neatness was part of that balance. I had salt, a bowl, a little jug of rice wine, and one of Yama's bronze bells. I'd had to fill the bowl with water from the shaman's house rather than living water from a stream, because there wasn't time for that. Besides, I didn't want to risk being stopped and questioned by one of my clanfolk while trying to leave our village. I hoped the gods would understand.

The last thing necessary for my work was a branch of evergreen. That was close at hand, and soon I was kneeling before the shaman's gaping doorway with a fragrant twig from our guardian pine tree clasped tight in my fingers. Before I began the rite, something impelled me to take my dragon stone amulet from my neck and lay it on the ground just outside Yama's house. That same impulse had me draw the keepsake wand of cherrywood from my belt and bundle it with the pine branch. Putting them to one side, I clapped my hands softly to beg the gods to attend what I was about to do, and opened my heart to their presence.

I had to proceed as fast as I could, to avoid being caught, and yet I had to honor the sacred nature of purification by following each step of the rite with the proper reverence. At first, my thoughts darted here and there between *Hurry, hurry, hurry before someone sees you!* and *Peace, peace, the spirits can't be rushed. What you do here isn't some crime to be hastened into hiding, but a holy thing.* As I swept away the presence of uncleanliness with the fresh green needles of the pine branch and sprinkled earth and air with salt, water, and wine, I let go of my fear of discovery and gave myself entirely to the rhythm of the words I chanted for the gods.

At last, I reached for the bronze bell. I raised it to the heavens, where daylight was beginning to glow. The images of deer and wild boar circling it danced in the light, and my spirit danced with them. For the first time in my life, I had performed a shaman's ritual, and every step of it seemed to fall gently onto my shoulders like the sweet warmth of the sun. What I had done for Yama's spirit and for my people felt as right, as balanced, and as natural as breathing, or the sight of tranquil mountains bathed in mist, or love.

I held the bell in one hand, my wand in the other, and poised myself to strike a note whose echoes would cleanse and sanctify us all.

"Himiko! What do you think you're doing?" Father's voice boomed through the cool morning air. His hand closed on my shoulder, forcing me to turn and face him. Startled, I dropped the bell. It uttered a choked clang when it hit the ground. His eyes skimmed the array of vessels I'd laid out for the purification rite. "What is all this? Speak!"

An excuse began to form on my lips. My thoughts sped to create some plausible reason that would cloak the real purpose of what I'd done. If worse came to worst, I could always use Yama as a way to escape responsibility: *Our shaman told me to do this for her if she died. I don't know what it all means. I was only following her orders, because I was afraid that if I didn't, her ghost would punish me!*

I bit my lip and swallowed the cowardly words. With my eyes looking straight into Father's livid face, I said, "I was performing a ritual of purification for this place, the way Lady Yama taught me. Please let me finish it."

"A ritual? How can *you* perform a shaman's work?"

I kept my voice level and didn't drop my gaze. "I can because I *am* a shaman, Father. I have the knowledge even though I'm new to using it. But I do know what I'm doing."

"You're *doing* nothing. You're playing games, like a little girl with her doll!"

I ignored his barb. "This isn't play. Lady Yama took me as her apprentice years ago."

"Her apprentice . . ." Father's jaw was tight. His words were bones grinding together, heavy with the dark power of a curse. "Is it true? Did she go behind my back like that when she knew I'd have forbidden it? For her to do something so deceitful, so dishonorable, so *vile*—!"

I couldn't control myself any longer. "She was *not* vile!" I cried, bringing my face within a hand's span of his. "How dare you say such things about her?"

"Is that how you choose to speak to me?" His voice became the hiss of a serpent's belly passing over sand. "Did she teach you to regard your father, your *chieftain,* with so much scorn? May the gods repay her for turning my precious daughter into—into *this.*" He waved one hand at me as if banishing something shameful from his sight.

I sucked in my breath, ready to scream my indignation at him for speaking so cruelly about my beloved teacher. Before I could unleash my anger, a realization pulled me back: *What good will it do to answer his rage with more rage? If we both shout, who's left to listen?*

I dropped to my knees and bent my forehead to the earth. "Father, hear me, please. *Hear* me! I could never scorn you. You have my love, my gratitude, and my respect, now and always." I lifted my face. "But I must respect who I am too."

"Ridiculous," he spat. "You're a child. You sway like a willow branch in every breeze. You think you're a shaman because that old woman *let* you think it, telling you false tales that made you feel important. Don't you see why she did it? To tie you to her! If she'd had children of her own, she wouldn't have needed to steal my daughter and fill your ears with foolish notions. Get up, Himiko. Get up, put away this"—he gestured impatiently at the things I'd used to perform the ceremony—"this clutter, and go home. Go home *now*!"

I remained where I was, palms against the ground. Father's hard words grew louder and louder in my ears, but made no impact. *So much shouting,* I thought. *But he wouldn't need to shout at all if what he says were true. The truth can be told in a whisper. The truth is here.*

As I pressed my hands to the earth, I could feel the pulse of life running through the ground, the countless stirrings of seed and soil, of thriving plants, humming insects, the rustle of the mouse under the grass, the song of the mother for her infant. Go home? I was home. I knew it as surely as I knew that he was wrong: I was not a child, not anymore.

"The ceremony isn't finished," I told him calmly. "I'll clear away my things after I'm done." I reached for the bell.

He snatched it up just as my fingers brushed it. "You'll do as you're told!"

I got to my feet and stared at him. "Yes, I will." *But not by you,* I thought.

I turned away and ducked into Yama's house before he could react. Our shaman owned more than one sacred bell just as she owned more than one mirror. It was the work of a moment to lay hands on what I needed and to strike the concluding note of the ritual. I emerged from the doorway while the echoes of that rich, centering sound still hung on the air.

"I had to do that, Father," I said. "I am a shaman, whether you like it or not, and I can't walk away with a rite left unfinished. I don't know why the thought of my being Lady Yama's heir is so hateful to you, but that's what I am, just as you are our chieftain. Neither one of us can change that, and would we? Our clan needs us both. If something's happened to Master Michio, if Aki and the others can't find him and bring him back, what will become of the Matsu? Who'll look after our clanfolk, body and soul? I don't care if you hate what I've become, Father, but accept it. Accept *me.*"

Father glared at me. He didn't respond to what I'd said, but I could feel the heat of his stifled fury beating against me in waves. I didn't look away. I counted ten breaths until he broke the bond of silent challenge between us, dropped the sacred bell in the dirt, and walked away without another word.

I picked up all the things I'd taken from Yama's house, put them in their proper places, and went home. When I came in, Mama glanced up from nursing Noboru and gave me a questioning look, but I let it pass and began helping Yukari make breakfast. Father wasn't there. That was expected—daybreak had come, and as chieftain, he had many duties to perform. I decided not to think about our encounter until our paths crossed again.

That was a strange day for me, for my family, and for all our kin. We were a clan in mourning, our lives in suspension until we could be purified. No one dared to do anything but the most vital tasks, for fear that the taint of death would contaminate whatever we touched. We didn't work in the fields, we didn't hunt, we heard no sound of industry from the potter's house or the blacksmith's forge. Many people stayed inside, speaking in whispers. Those who had to leave their homes wore garments made of hemp, just as we'd worn when Yukari and Emi lost their other babies.

Sundown fell, and Father didn't come home. Mama and my stepmothers became more and more nervous as the darkness outside grew deeper and there was still no sign of him. Our dinner was laid out but untouched. When little Sanjirou began to whine, Emi scolded him so ferociously that the child burrowed under the nearest bedroll and chewed his fist, too scared to cry. I tried to comfort him, but all he did was quiver and try to creep farther away.

Masa watched my efforts and exclaimed, "That's enough!" He slapped his thighs and stood up. "I won't sit here like a rabbit in its nest while my little brother's so miserable. I'm going to find Father *now*." He stalked out of the house. We heard him grumbling all the way down the ladder.

He was back before we succeeded in coaxing Sanjirou out of hiding. One of the clan nobles was with him. Masa looked a bit sheepish as he explained that he'd run into the man about ten strides from our home. "Father sent him."

The noble wore the serious expression of someone who considers himself as important as the news he brings. "Our chieftain has gone from the village. He's taken a small escort and won't be back until he's found the first party sent to fetch our new shaman or until he has found Master Michio himself. While he is gone, Lord Masa is his voice within the clan. I have further instructions and commands for his ears alone, and for the council of nobles to hear tomorrow."

Having formally delivered the burden of Father's message, he relaxed visibly and added, "Please don't worry about your husband, ladies. He'll be back among us before you know it. If there's anything you need while he's gone, call on me." We thanked him and he took his leave, with Masa following.

Mama, Yukari, and Emi sat as if stunned. From his place under the bedroll, Sanjirou found the courage to whimper loudly enough to be heard. I glanced at our waiting dinner, now completely cold.

"Emi, your son is *hungry*," I said. "If you don't feed him now, I will."

"But shouldn't we wait for Masa to come back?" she asked timidly.

"He won't care if we eat without him," I replied. "And if he does mind, it's my fault. He can yell at me until his voice cracks. Now *please* give Sanjirou his dinner."

We were all eating when Masa returned. He looked shaken and made no remark about the fact that we hadn't waited for him. Mumbling his way through the prayer of thanks for food, he fell into a brooding silence, eating as if it were an unwelcome duty. Mama and our stepmothers darted so many anxious looks his way that he twitched every time he caught them at it, as though every glance were a flea's stinging bite.

"May the gods have mercy on us, Masa, what's the matter with you?" I burst out. "Are you keeping some nasty piece of news from us? Was that man telling the truth about Father, or has something happened that's so bad he thinks we have to learn about it gradually?"

"Of course not, Himiko," Masa said, trying to speak with confidence. "Why think that?"

"Because I know him. He's the same man who told Ume's mother that her first husband had been killed in a hunting accident. I was just a little girl, but I was there and I remember how he did it. He started by saying her husband twisted his ankle when he slid down a hill and kept 'remembering' fresh details until the hill was a cliff, the slide was a fall, and the twisted ankle was a broken neck! He thought he was being kind; he was wrong."

Masa looked like a little boy caught telling his first lie. "You're very smart, Little Sister—too smart for me. You've got Lady Yama's way of seeing through people. No wonder she took you as her apprentice."

"*What?*" Yukari's voice was the loudest, Emi's the shrillest, but Mama's was the most stricken when the three of them all exclaimed that single word in unison.

"So Father spoke about it," I said flatly. It was good to

have my secret out in the open, but I couldn't enjoy feeling free. There would be consequences. "Who knows this?"

"He went to all our nobles and told them everything," Masa said. "They're aware that you're calling yourself a shaman—"

"I'm not *calling* myself a shaman, Masa; I *am* a shaman. No matter what Father would prefer to believe, I've learned everything Yama could teach me."

Everything but how to dance for the spirits, a niggling inner voice reminded me. *Even if your clan does accept you, how will you serve them if your skills are flawed?*

I gritted my teeth and pushed the troubling words from my mind. *I'll worry about that if—*when—*they accept me,* I thought. *One step at a time.*

"All right, Himiko, all right, if you say so." Masa clearly didn't want to argue.

"No, it's *not* all right!" Mama exclaimed. "Himiko, tell me this is a joke, a game, even a lie! You can't be a shaman; you *mustn't*! So this is why your father's risking his life hunting Master Michio. He's desperate to find him so that you'll *have* to back down. No clan has two shamans. Oh gods, if anything happens to your father because of this, what will we do?" She began to sob wildly, and Noboru took fright and cried with her.

"It's no game, Mama; it's true that I'm a shaman. Why shouldn't it be?" I spoke soothingly, though her words hurt me more than I could say. This wasn't the time to shout or rant or fight for her acceptance. She was so distraught that I could feel her pain even more than my own. "I've sensed the spirits' presence in a special way since I was a little girl. Lady Yama saw that and nurtured it. I'll always be grateful to her for setting my feet on their proper path. Why do you and Father act as though I were walking barefoot over blazing thorns and dragging everyone else along with me?"

Mama looked at me and sniffled, her eyes already rimmed with red. "It's not me, Himiko," she said, slowly relaxing her hold on Noboru and letting the baby move to a more comfortable position on her lap. "I—I would be proud to see you as our shaman. You're a chieftain's daughter and granddaughter. Your ancestors led the Matsu to these lands so long ago that no one remembers where we used to dwell, but everyone knows that you come from the most nobly born family in our clan. A family"—she looked sharply left and right, as though fearing eavesdroppers in the shadows—"a family whose chieftains were also our shamans until—until *she* died." Her voice dropped to a whisper: "Lady Tsuki."

She lowered her eyes to my baby brother. "She was your father's half sister. I hardly remember her. I was younger than you are now when she died, but my grandma told me all about that woman. Lady Tsuki was our chieftain's only child for a long time. She lost her mother when she was five years old and became the center of your grandfather's existence. He lived for her, pleasing her, lavishing attention on her, educating her as our future chieftess and shaman. Whatever else people may say about her, she had a brilliant mind. She was barely out of girlhood when she mastered all the arts she'd need to guide and help our clan. She might have become the greatest leader the Matsu had ever known."

"What happened?"

"Her father took a bride. The years of loneliness finally conquered his devotion to his first wife's memory. Perhaps if he hadn't waited so long, he might have made a more sensible choice. The girl he wed was a pretty little butterfly, and young; *too* young. She might have been Lady Tsuki's sister! She did love him and bring him joy, but his new-found happiness blinded him to everything but her. She became his world. Nothing and no one else seemed to matter, not even his once-beloved daughter."

"And then Father was born," I said. How would that have made Lady Tsuki feel? She'd already been edged aside by her father's love for his new bride. Now that his adored young wife had given him a healthy son, was there any room left for her in her father's heart?

"Yes," Mama said. "He was welcomed into this world with so much rejoicing that my grandma claimed the feasting lasted for five days. His childhood was perfect, his every wish was fulfilled."

"That doesn't sound perfect to me," I said. "It sounds like a good way to spoil a child."

"Oh, he wasn't allowed to run wild. His parents saw to it that he was given guidance as well as gifts. And it lasted for such a short while." Her eyes turned sad. "In the winter of his sixth year, his father died and Lady Tsuki became our chieftess. That was the end of your father's happy days. Wherever she could, she put stones in his path. Whenever she had the chance to make him feel small and stupid and a burden to the clan, she did it. His mother did what she could to shield him from Lady Tsuki's sly attacks, but she was too good-hearted to grasp how a cruel mind works. You can't win if you're fighting an enemy you can't understand."

Why did you do it, Lady Tsuki? I thought. *My father wasn't at fault for the way your own set you aside. Why punish an innocent child? Did it help soothe your old sorrows? Did it undo even one moment of the unfairness and neglect you endured? You were wrong, Lady Tsuki, so wrong that you crippled your soul.*

"Father wasn't the only one she mistreated," I said. "Master Michio will testify to that, if he returns."

"*When* he returns," Mama corrected me strictly. "Your father will find him even if Aki and the others can't. He has to. He *has* to." Her voice trembled as her faith fled. "If he doesn't find Master Michio, he won't come back at all. What will become of us then?"

"Oh, Mama, of course Father will come back, and soon!" I didn't want her to start crying again. "He knows we need him. Even if he's empty-handed, he'll come home."

My brother was glum. "I hope you're right, Little Sister, but Father isn't the kind of man who can live with failure."

"He won't fail," I said. "He set out to bring us a new shaman, and he'll come home to find one waiting." I folded my hands on my chest and looked at my family with a triumphant smile. "He might not like it, but what choice will he have? And I promise I'll do everything I can so that someday he'll be glad Lady Yama made me her heir."

"No, Himiko." Mama's eyes were dry, and this time she shook her head most emphatically. "That will never happen. You may think you're following in Lady Yama's footsteps, but your father will only see you taking the same ill-fated path as Lady Tsuki. She used her power as chieftess *and* shaman to hurt him too deeply to be forgotten. He was only a little boy, and she terrorized him constantly. She relished telling him that their father's spirit despised him and threatened to summon the dead chief to haunt him. When I first became his wife, he still had ghastly nightmares. It was years before he could think of a shaman as anything but a monster in human shape. He'd die before he'd accept the thought of you becoming what *she* once was. What parent could stand to see his beloved child make a choice he sees as evil?"

"Did he think *Lady Yama* was evil?" I couldn't believe that.

"That was different. She wasn't someone special to him, and he knew that our people needed a shaman."

"We need a shaman *now*."

"We do." She sighed. "And we will have one. But as long as your father is our chief, it can't be you."

"Himiko, I'm sorry," Masa said, patting my back. "One of the commands Father left behind was that I must get you to swear to tell no one outside of our family about your formal training with Lady Yama."

"Is that how he described it?" I asked. "He didn't call it foolishness, delusion, rebellion, *stupidity*?" I realized how sarcastic I sounded, but I couldn't help it and I didn't want to. When Masa blushed and looked uncomfortable, I knew I'd hit the mark.

"Please, Little Sister, I know you're unhappy, but give me your word."

"Why? What are you supposed to do to me if I refuse?"

My brother squirmed even more. "Himiko, I'm not the

only one who's here to follow Father's orders in his absence. The noble council members know about you. They're the ones who'll react if you won't keep your training hidden. I don't know what they'd do if you reveal yourself to the rest of our clan, and I don't want to find out."

"This is madness," I said. "Did Father command his men to *kill* me if—?"

"Oh no, not that!" my brother exclaimed hastily, holding up his hands to reject the ugly thought. "Never that, *never.*"

"How can you think such things of your father, Himiko?" Mama asked, her eyes once more filled with tears.

I wanted to cry *How can he think such things of me, Mama? How can he behave as if all my seasons of hard work and study were some kind of atrocious crime? When Father was small, he suffered because his half sister had suffered. She used her power over him wrongfully, to avenge how she'd been hurt, even though he was innocent. He* knows *how unfair that was, so why doesn't he see that he's doing the same thing to me? Oh, Father, you're a better person than this! Open your eyes and see it!*

Instead, I kissed my mother's cheek and said, "I'm sorry. Our clan has enough problems now. I won't cause us any more."

A shaman stands between her people and the darker aspects of their lives. Lady Tsuki had betrayed that trust. Instead of making peace between the living and the dead, she'd conjured fear and left a legacy of pain. I wouldn't set one foot on that path. If it lay within my power, I resolved that I would banish the ghosts of fear, resentment, and family troubles that her life had summoned from the shadows to haunt us all.

Turning toward Masa, I added, "You have my word that as long as Father's gone, I won't let anyone else in our village learn that I'm a shaman. I swear this by the sun goddess in all her glory and by everything dear to me. I'll only break my silence if you release me from this oath, Masa. Otherwise, no one will know. Is that good enough?"

A bright smile broke across my brother's face. "Better than good enough, Himiko. The look in your eyes when you swore yourself to secrecy—! It was breathtaking, like facing Lady Yama at her most impressive, when she spoke for the gods! I guess you are a shaman after all."

He meant that as a joke, but I was in no mood for it. "Thank you *so* much for your approval." My icy voice could have withered whole fields of rice.

Masa recoiled, wounded. "Little Sister, what did I say?" His distress was real, and it made me repent my harshness immediately. He had my apology before he could draw another breath, and for the rest of that night, our home was restored to precious harmony.

Six days later, as I sat on our porch dandling little Noboru, I heard an ecstatic shout go up from the sentry in our lookout tower: "Our chieftain returns! He returns! He's coming back, and all our men are with him!"

The news shot through our village like a fiery arrow. Men, women, and children flocked out of the gates. Everyone cheered when they saw Father come marching up the road, Aki and Shoichi at his sides, but the real focus of their attention was the short, stocky, round-faced man who came walking behind them with a rolling gait. The front of his hemp robe was almost entirely covered with strand after strand of beads, charms, and pendants, and his belt flashed with half a dozen bronze mirrors.

My hopes of persuading Father to let me use my gifts were dead: Master Michio had arrived.

14
MAN ON THE
RIGHT ROAD

The first thing that our new shaman did was conduct a ceremony of purification at his half sister's tomb. This was something he insisted on doing even before settling into his new house.

"We've let the gods tend the rice fields while we've mourned my sister," he declared as he stood in the center of the welcoming crowd. "They're tired of doing all our work for us, so the sooner we're able to return to looking after our own crops, the better. It's never a good idea to test the patience of the spirits." He looked to Father. "How soon can you show me her tomb?"

Father was taken aback by the new shaman's request. "Don't you want to have something to eat and drink first, Master Michio?"

"None of us will have much to eat if I don't let our people get back to working the fields," he said with a jovial smile. "And as for drink, you can't make good rice wine without rice! Shall we go?"

Father nodded mutely and turned to lead Michio to the burial ground. The whole village came trailing after them. I was still holding Noboru, whose happy squirming had nearly knocked us both off the house ladder when I'd climbed down to get a closer look at the man whose arrival had destroyed my dreams. I balanced the baby on my hip and wriggled through the crowd to reach Aki, who had fallen in behind Father and the shaman.

"Ah, there you are, Little Sister!" he said happily when we caught up to him. "And who's this gigantic mountain ogre riding on your hip? I'd better watch myself around him. He's probably carrying a big club, and he'll smash my head like a ripe peach if I let him!" He snatched Noboru away from me and tossed him high into the air as we walked. The little one squealed with delight.

"Aki, tell me everything," I demanded. "Did you find Master Michio, or did Father's party do it? Where was he? How—?"

"What happened to 'Welcome back, my adored big brother, I was lost and miserable without you'?" Aki teased, flinging Noboru skyward and catching him easily.

"Welcome back and the rest of it," I said crisply. "Now *tell* me!"

"Oh, *very* eloquent, Himiko." He clicked his tongue in mock disapproval. "But I suppose I'd better take what I'm given before you snap my head off. It was my group that found Master Michio. We were escorting him home when we encountered Father's party on the road. That was a piece of luck! If we'd missed one another, we'd have had to send out a *third* search party to fetch the second one."

"And where was he?"

"Living among his father's people, the Todomatsu clan, just as Lady Yama said." Aki sighed. "Can you believe that there was a time when it was a simple matter of love for two people from different clans to marry? Hoshi and I were born too late to—"

"*Shhh!*" I cautioned Aki with a frown and a meaningful glance at Father's back.

"Ah." He nodded. "Anyway, we found the seacoast village he called home when he wasn't off on another voyage and—"

"Voyage? What voyage?"

"Little Sister, how am I going to tell you anything if you keep interrupting me?" He chuckled. "The people of the coast have grown rich from trading voyages. We heard that they've even gone all the way into the west, to the sunset land."

"The Mirror Kingdom?" I asked, remembering what Yama had called that mysterious empire.

"Not a bad name for it. Master Michio told me that all of his mirrors come from there."

"He was a merchant?" I pursed my lips. "If he didn't serve the spirits for all those years, he can't be much of a shaman."

"I'll tell him you disapprove," Aki replied dryly. "Except he wasn't a merchant, though he spent more time at sea than many a man who was. The Todomatsu have an interesting way of guaranteeing the success of a voyage. One man takes a vow to abstain from eating meat, touching women, and combing his hair, even if that means he gets head lice! And he can't change his clothes, either, no matter how filthy they get in the course of the trip."

"Ugh!" I shuddered in disgust. "And that was what Master Michio did? *Why?*"

"I had the same reaction when he told me about it. He explained that it was a way of serving the gods and protecting his kin. If anything went wrong during the voyage, if anyone died or was injured, the people believed it was because the chosen man must have broken his vows and had to be killed. Master Michio said that you could never be sure when the gods might decide to drop a bit of bad luck on a boat whether or not a fellow was keeping his promise—and his head lice! 'Better to let my life pay the price than put some other man at risk,' he said."

"Oh." Reluctantly, I felt the first stirring of respect for our new shaman.

"Of course, when the voyage *is* successful, the chosen man is buried in a heap of gifts, even given slaves!"

"*Ohhhhhh.*" So much for respect. *He only did it to enrich himself!* I thought. I sniffed disdainfully at Michio behind his back. "I suppose his slaves are coming later, carrying all of his wealth?"

"That would be difficult. He gave most of his gifts to the clanfolk who needed them. As for his slaves, he always seemed to receive an urgent message from the gods telling him to free them as a thanksgiving offering." Aki uttered a comical sigh. "Master Michio is *very* strict about showing

gratitude to the gods." He glanced at me sideways. "You
look disappointed, Little Sister."

I was, but I wouldn't say so. I was ashamed to admit
that I'd been hoping to find fault with our new shaman. I
failed. Worse than failing, I soon learned how hard it was to
dislike the man. When we reached the burial ground, he
had two of our boys go off to bring some things he'd need
to perform the ceremony. It wasn't a command, but a courteous request. In fact, whenever he spoke to anyone, it was
with the greatest politeness and consideration. If he was the
sort of man who'd abuse his status as shaman to dominate,
he was doing a perfect job of hiding it.

While waiting for the boys to come back, he stood gazing at Yama's burial mound. It was tall and square, its massive size a sign that the person within was someone
important to the clan. Tears rose in his eyes and bathed his
cheeks. Slowly he knelt and hunched over, rocking back
and forth with his face in his hands. The sound of his grief-
stricken sobs moved every heart that heard them, for when
he raised his voice to cry his sister's name, his lament was
echoed by all of us, even Father.

The two boys were quick about their errands. As soon
as they rejoined us with water, salt, rice wine, and an evergreen bough for Master Michio, he set his personal sorrow
aside and began the ritual with the grace and dignity such
an important ceremony demanded. His voice was clear and
strong, his movements poised and graceful despite his size.
Watching him, I imagined myself trying to perform such a
dance. My cheeks burned with embarrassment as I pictured

the clumsy mess my bad leg would make of it. I couldn't dislike the man, but I could envy him with all my heart. Not only was he more graceful than I could ever hope to be, he was free to serve the gods openly. What a difference there was between this public ritual and the secrecy of night and silence I'd had to wrap around the interrupted cleansing rite that I'd performed!

Once Michio had purified us from the taint of death, our lives returned to normal. There was a mercifully short time during which every able-bodied person in our village worked in the fields, frantically trying to undo all the days of neglect. The crops weren't the only things that had been left to look after themselves during our extended time of mourning. There were waterweeds to pull out of the carp pond, places along the village moat where the earth had slipped and filled the trench, and a number of houses whose thatched roofs were in want of repair. Father tried to be everywhere at once, supervising, directing, and putting his own hands to work.

While all of this was going on, Michio settled into Yama's former home. On days when I wasn't helping in the rice paddies, I saw him strolling through our village. He divided his time among healing the sick, renewing ties with people he'd known before Lady Tsuki's jealousy forced him into exile, and making the acquaintance of those who'd been too young to remember him or not yet born when he'd gone away. By the time the moon god's disk had passed through a full set of changes, he knew everyone within our walls and everyone knew and liked him.

Everyone but me. Day after day, I kept my distance,

bitter disappointment making me surly toward a man who'd never knowingly done anything to hurt me. If I saw him coming, I slipped away like mist. If he came into our home while I was there, I busied myself with countless unnecessary chores, leaving Mama or another family member to talk to him. Once they were deep in conversation, I'd call out some flimsy excuse and steal away from the house, day or night, and not go back until I saw him leave. I spoke and moved too quickly for anyone to challenge me and became an accomplished little liar. Once I even pretended to fall asleep in the corner while he was still in the doorway, talking to Yukari. Every time I did such things, I despised myself, but that wasn't enough to prevent me from doing them again and again.

One day, as I was in the forest hunting mushrooms for our dinner, my luck ran out. I hadn't gone too deeply into the shadow of the trees when I heard Michio's voice say, "Good morning, Lady Himiko. Have the spirits finally decided to favor me with your company? Usually, you do your best to avoid me, and yet here you are, tracking me to my secret lair."

The words seemed to come from all around me. I whirled sharply, seeking the man, but saw nothing. The sound of his kindly laughter danced through the branches. "If I'd known that the best way to meet you was to hide from you, I would have done it days ago."

"Where are you?" I called, still searching in vain for Michio.

"Why do you ask? To join me or to be sure you run in the opposite direction? Or do you plan to pretend you're asleep again until *I* go away?" He sounded amused, and not annoyed with me at all.

I pressed my lips together and felt the tips of my ears burn with shame. "I'm sorry for the way I've acted toward you, Master Michio. Please tell me where you are. I want to apologize face to face."

"Ah!" he exclaimed, elated. "Is it true? Then come here, my dear. I'm on the other side of the big oak, the one with the ferns around him. Join us. See what I've found."

This time there was no mistaking the direction from which Michio's voice came. I walked slowly around the great tree and found our shaman seated on the ground with his back against the trunk and his feet hidden in a thick patch of gorgeous blue bellflowers. He looked at me and scratched his head vigorously. I couldn't help staring. Unlike Father, Aki, and the rest of our men, he didn't wear his hair in carefully arranged loops over his ears. Instead, it was cropped short and shaggy, though it had grown out a little since his arrival.

He noticed my interest, and his smile grew wider. "Not what you're used to, is it?" he asked, holding one coarse lock between thumb and forefinger. "It used to be long, you know. It grew all the way past my hips, to the back of my knees. Whenever I said no and shook my head, my hair would lash through the air and blind anyone foolish enough to stand too close to me. What a horrible time for the Todomatsu clan! People stopped asking me questions, for fear that the next 'no' would hit *them* in the eyes! There were a few lucky folk who could still see, but they grew very tired of having to lead all the others here and there. At last, they came to me and pleaded for help. 'Oh, dear and wondrous Master Michio, shaman of shamans, hear our prayer! Share your wisdom! Heal our kin! *Heeeeeeaaallll* them! And if the answer is no, *please* give us a chance to stand back before you say so!'"

I began to smile in spite of myself. "So you cut it off to save anyone else from being blinded?" I asked, playing along.

"Sacrifice my wonderful hair for *those* creatures? Ha! Hardly. Instead, I just stopped saying—you might want to stand back for this—*no*." He shook his head violently, then plucked at his short locks again. "Oh dear, it just isn't the same." He gave an exaggerated sigh and made such a tragic grimace that I couldn't help giggling.

"Why did you really cut off your hair, Master Michio?" I asked.

"Well, you might've heard about what I used to do for the Todomatsu clan? Accompanying their trading voyages?"

I remembered what Aki had told me, and my revolted reaction. "You took a vow that while you were at sea, you couldn't cut you hair or remove . . . or remove . . ." I hesitated.

"Don't worry," the new shaman reassured me. "*Saying* 'head lice' doesn't summon them. As if those little pests needed an invitation! We never want them, but they show up anyway and burrow in." His expression turned serious. "I'll bet you're thinking the same thing about me."

I opened my mouth to disclaim that, but something made me hold back the torrent of false words and say, "I am. I'm sorry."

"Hmm. So you can be honest. That's good. I must confess, when I observed all of the ruses you used to escape my company and then learned how close you were with my sister, I had to ask myself, 'Why would Yama choose such a deceitful girl to be her apprentice?'"

I reacted as though he'd slapped a handful of cold mud in my face. "Who told you that?"

"You don't deny it?"

I stood a little taller and spoke with all the dignity I could muster: "I never would and never will. I know what I am."

"And what would that be, since your teacher is gone?"

"I'm a healer," I replied calmly. "And a shaman." I held his eyes steadily, daring him to contradict me.

"I'm glad to hear you say so," he replied with a pleasant smile. "Otherwise, I'd still be wondering about those traces of salt I found on the threshold of my sister's house, to say nothing of the way the earth there smells of spilled rice wine. I'd hate to imagine that any of the Matsu would waste such good drink. 'Now, who's been performing a purification rite here?' I asked myself. 'And why did my clan bring me home after all these years if they already had a shaman to assume my sister's duties?'"

My face fell. "Because my father doesn't want me to do what I've been trained to do or to follow the path I love. I've known it for some time."

"Yet he allowed you to purify that place? Surely he would have wanted the fields cleansed first."

"He didn't allow anything; he caught me. I studied with Lady Yama in secret. My father—" I sighed. "My father doesn't like shamans."

Michio tilted his head back and gazed into the sunlit branches of the oak. "Your father has a very good reason for that."

"Lady Tsuki," I said softly. "Yes, I know. But Lady Yama wasn't like that, and you're not, and I—"

"A child whose belly aches from eating a green peach won't want to taste a ripe one," Michio observed. "And you *are* his daughter. He thinks he's protecting you."

"From what? From living my own life?" I cried.

Michio shook his head. "No; from living *her* life."

I sat down beside the shaman and leaned forward to run my fingertips over the silky blue petals of the bell-flowers. "I wish he could trust me enough to know that I would never misuse my skills the way she did."

"So do I, Lady Himiko," Michio said softly. "My sister never would have taken you as her apprentice if she'd glimpsed the tiniest hint that you would follow your aunt's unhappy road."

I tilted my head and looked at him. "My aunt died years and years ago. Why didn't you come home sooner? You would have been safe, and Lady Yama would have been happy to have you back." On second thought, I added, "I guess she didn't have any way to send you the news."

"Yes, she did." He sighed. "She asked one of your

father's finest hunters to seek me out and let me know Lady Tsuki was gone. The man she sent was someone very special to my sister. I think that they were going to be married. I know he loved her dearly because he told me so when he reached the Todomatsu village with her message. 'Come back with me and we'll have the finest wedding you ever saw!' he said. But I'd made a life for myself among my father's people. I had a lovely wife, a dear daughter, and a reputation for bringing the best luck to any ship that carried me.

"I told him, 'I'm accepted here, but if I come back with you, can you guarantee that my family will be welcomed among the Matsu? Besides, what would I do? I'm no hunter, I'm too slow and clumsy to be much help in the fields, you don't need a luck-bringer for your ships because you have none, and you already have a shaman. You don't want two. It makes the people nervous, not knowing which one of us to trust. Give Yama my love, and may you be as happy with her as I am with my dear ones.'"

I frowned, puzzled. "I never heard that Lady Yama was married."

"Didn't she?" Michio sighed again. "He must have died. Judging by the way he spoke about my sister, only death would have kept him from sharing his life with her." He lowered his eyes and contemplated the flowers at his feet. "No matter how adept we are in the healing arts, the gods always have the last word. I learned that within the year."

"What . . . what happened?" But I could guess the answer even before he replied:

"They died. My sweet little girl and my beloved wife both fell ill, and nothing I could do was enough to heal them. I suppose I could have come back here that spring, after I'd lost them, but I was too broken. I told myself that I might as well stay where I was. Why burden the Matsu with a second shaman?"

"Do you really think it's a bad thing for a clan to have two shamans?"

"No, but why would they want to support two when one of them is useless? If I wasn't good enough to save those dearest to me—"

"Master Michio, you said it yourself: the gods have the last word." Without thinking, I reached out and slipped my fingers through his and squeezed his hand. All my envy, all my bitterness, had flown, leaving behind nothing but the urge to comfort this kindly man.

He placed his other hand atop mine. "So you are a healer after all. And as for your place on the spirit path—" He looked deeply into my eyes. "Yes. Yes, I think I understand why my sister chose you. You sense *them*, don't you? They speak to you whether or not you call out to them, they come to you whether or not they've been summoned. They know who you are, and they know that you stand in perfect balance on the strand that links you to them and to all the rest of us and this bright, beautiful, terrifying, awesome world."

I bowed my head, unsure of what to say. His words had confirmed my unvoiced feelings about my need to serve the spirits, to walk with them, to know that they were always with me. They were more than forces to be feared and placated; they were a part of me, comforting and welcoming, taking me for who I was. I didn't want to be a shaman because I yearned for power. I wanted it because I yearned to draw closer to them, and because that yearning was something I couldn't deny or set aside no matter how hard I tried.

Master Michio understood my silence. He let go of my hand and got to his feet, puffing out his cheeks as he stood up and brushed dirt from the back of his clothes.

"Well, what are we going to do about you now?" he said. "If you're performing rituals on your own, your studies are over."

"It wouldn't matter if I hadn't finished my studies," I said. "How would I be able to learn from you, Master Michio? I'd have no excuse to come to your house and study. Father knows I was doing more than housework and chores for Lady Yama. He wouldn't be fooled twice by the same ruse."

"Then it's a good thing you *are* a full-fledged shaman already, isn't it?" Michio said.

His overly cheerful manner irritated me. I didn't begrudge him his place as our shaman anymore, but I wished he'd show me more sympathy. He was a well-fed man living snug in a warm house, and I was a starving wanderer outside in the rain. When he saw me, he said, *Why such a long face, my friend? Be happy! Life is beautiful!* but left me where I was, wet and hungry.

"Oh yes, it's a wonderful thing," I said dryly. "I'm free to help my clanfolk by sitting home and doing nothing."

"Very good," he replied, matching my peevish tone exactly. "You'll be able to accomplish a great deal by grumbling and sulking."

Once more his humor was disarming. "You're making fun of me." I couldn't help giggling, then added, "I guess I deserved that, but this is so frustrating!"

"I'm sure it is. If it will help you, feel free to make fun of me when I need it." In a more serious tone, he said, "We have to hold on to laughter, Lady Himiko. We have a lot of work ahead of us, and a massive, steep mountain to climb. If we reach the peak, it will be thanks to laughter. Laughter will save us from despair, laughter will keep us from becoming discouraged, laughter will hold us back from tumbling into the darkness. If we can't laugh, we cry, and if we cry too long, we lose sight of what we're trying to achieve."

He looked at me very solemnly for a man who had just been speaking of laughter. "You know, it does help if you can give a name to the mountain you want to conquer. There's a world of difference between declaring *I must climb a mountain* and *I must climb* that *one*. Names have their own magical power. They can set boundaries, but they can also set goals. My mother knew that when she gave my sister her name. A mountain is strong but beautiful, and it always stands firm." He smiled. "The magic worked. Yama proved that many times when we were growing up together. What a stubborn woman!" The corners of his eyes crinkled. "Of course, if she'd been a man, I suppose I'd have to call her strong-minded."

"Father is *very* strong-minded," I muttered.

"So he's your mountain. Would you like to hear me name mine?" I shrugged, not in the mood for riddles. "You."

That got my attention. "Me?"

"Yes, Lady Himiko. If I can see you recognized as the next shaman of the Matsu clan, I won't need any more peaks to scale. And if that means I must return to my father's clan once more, so be it. I'll be quite content to live a restful life in your shadow or far from it."

I found his words to be incredible. "You're offering me a wondrous gift, Master Michio. But why? How do you know I'm worth so much trust?"

He spread his hands as if to show how obvious the answer was. "I don't. But my mother chose to name me *man on the right road,* in hopes that I would find the wisdom to make good choices in life. I never make such choices blindly. If I choose to believe in you, it's partly because I know my sister never would have wasted her time training someone without promise."

"Only partly?" I asked.

"Well, as for the rest, I *could* claim that I've had a mystic revelation and foresee a fantastic future for you, but that would be a lie. The gods have never once granted me the blessing or curse of prophecy."

I remained silent, recalling Yama's deathbed visions. "Maybe Lady Yama only trained me to be a healer," I said quietly.

"Then why do you call yourself a shaman?" he countered. "*That,* Lady Himiko, is what decided me. To be a shaman is to stand between your clan and the spirits, to stand undefended, with every eye upon you! No one lives their life without encountering failures along the way, but a shaman's failures are there for everyone to see. Who would be willing to take on such a burden, such a responsibility, such a chance to be the object of blame, humiliation, even punishment? You would have to be possessed by demons." A half smile curved his lips. "Or by the gods."

The days passed, and my friendship with Michio became stronger, though it was never the same as my bond with Yama. I had no excuse to spend as much time with our new shaman as I'd had with his sister—Father saw to that. I felt as if he was always watching me, making sure that I didn't cross paths with Michio unless it was absolutely necessary and unavoidable. I regretted this because even if Michio hadn't been a shaman, I'd have enjoyed sharing his company.

There were some times when even Father couldn't keep me from associating openly with our shaman. When my brother Masa married our blacksmith's daughter, I contrived to sit near Michio at the feast. Even though we couldn't speak about my future, I was simply glad to hear his booming laugh and applaud him just as wildly as everyone else when he got up to do a comic dance to make the newlyweds blush.

He wasn't the only guest out to embarrass someone else. The rice wine flowed freely, and some of our kin let too much of it flow down their throats. One man stood up, wobbled badly, and shouted, "First it's Shoichi, then it's Masa, but when are we going to see *you* get married, Aki? Better still, when's some lucky man going to take *that* pretty little thing home with him, hey?" He waved his cup at me, sloshing his neighbors' clothes.

"Why are you asking about Himiko?" Aki replied with good humor. "Do you have someone in mind who's worthy to be her husband?"

"Huh?" The man stared at Aki with bleary eyes. "Nah, nah, she's still got a few years to go before she'll need someone else to find her a man. But you—! What's the matter? None of our girls good enough for you?"

"Ah, my friend, you've hit the mark exactly!" My oldest brother was enjoying this conversation, probably because he'd had a few cups of rice wine himself. "I can't choose any of the Matsu girls because—can you keep a secret?—I'm waiting for a sign from the gods themselves telling me when I'll be able to have the only woman I'll ever love!"

"Ohhhhhhh." The man nodded as if he understood all of Aki's nonsense, then shook his head violently. "Wait, wait, so if the gods are gonna talk to you, does that mean they're gonna talk to *her* too?" He gestured my way again. This time his neighbors were able to lean back far enough to dodge more wine droplets. "That's not right. How do you know if they'll ever say anything to either of you?"

"I suppose that's a chance we'll have to take." Aki smiled. "Right, Little Sister?"

"Leave me out of this," I said. "Can't you talk about something else?"

I didn't care whether the villager persisted in asking when I'd become a bride. I could laugh at his questions, ignore them, or play along, but what I *had* to do was stop them before they got out of control and swerved back to why *Aki* had no wife. I wanted to silence the fellow's drunken foolishness before my oldest brother took his next sip of rice wine, the crucial sip that well might extinguish his lighthearted mood and inflame the bitterness smoldering in his heart.

I knew it was there, and I knew why. In the time since Father had found out about my training with Yama, I'd been unable to leave our village and accompany Aki on his continued visits to Hoshi and her clan. I'd noticed that when he came home from such excursions, he no longer looked content. Rather, the more time he had to keep his beloved bride a secret, the more irritable and impatient he seemed to grow with the arrangement. He might not resent Shoichi and Masa for being free to marry the girls they loved, but he had to envy them. I could almost hear him thinking, *Why can't I celebrate my wedding too? Why do I have to conceal it from everyone, as if it were a sin or a crime?*

I wanted to shield Aki from his own unhappy thoughts. I also wanted to keep Father out of this. While my oldest brother and the drunken man had been trading words, I'd glanced in Father's direction. The look on his face was too ominous for my liking.

Springing to my feet, I raised my own cup high and declared, "Good health and good luck to the new bride and groom!" It wasn't a very inspired toast, but I only wanted it to be a distraction. With luck, it would provoke other people to voice their own joyful wishes for Masa and his wife, and the tipsy villager's outburst would be lost and forgotten.

Unfortunately, the man in question proved to be persistent. "Good health, good luck, and lots and lots of babies! *Someone* better make our chieftain into a grandfather before too long, or who's going to be our leader when *my* kids grow up? Hey, Shoichi, you've been married long enough. Any of *that* news yet?"

Shoichi's wife stared down into her lap, looking uncomfortable, which made Shoichi angry enough to yell, "You sit down and shut up before you say something really stupid!"

"Stupid? *Stupid?*" The man was too far gone to be sensible. "Is it stupid to care about our future? If you ask me, Shoichi, your big brother's never getting married, who knows why, so you're our next best hope. But if you fail and Masa there lets us down, who's left? Himiko! The little boys, well, they're too small to do their part in time, right? Right? So I say we let Aki listen for the gods until he's old as a tortoise, but let's find Himiko a man who'll give her what—"

Father moved so fast it was incredible. His right hand closed around the back of the drunkard's neck, and he shook him until the poor man's knees buckled. Even then, he held on, his other hand clenching the fellow's jaw. A deathly silence fell over Masa's wedding feast as Father snarled, "You will call my daughter *Lady* Himiko. You will call my firstborn son *Lord* Aki. And you will remember that their lives aren't something for an insect like you to discuss. If you forget that again, I will make sure to remind you. Now go." He released his double hold on the man, who collapsed in a heap, then scrambled onto hands and knees and scuttled away.

Once the unlucky villager was gone, Father turned to the rest of us. "What are you looking at? It's over. That man shouldn't be allowed to drink. Are his wives here?" Two

young women identified themselves in voices muffled by
deep humiliation. "In the future, see to it that he stays sober
or stays home! Now, let's forget this happened and rejoice
with my son and his bride." It was more of an order than an
invitation, but it was swiftly obeyed.

As the party returned to normal, Michio stole to my
side. "I've heard stories that the greatest mountain in our
land was once a cone of leaping fire. It seems your father is
that sort of mountain too. Don't despair, my young friend.
You'll still be able to climb him. But you're going to have to
be very careful about choosing the right road."

15
SHAMAN'S FATE

Some people accept life with a smile, some with a scowl, and those who scowl claim loudly that they're the only ones being "realistic" about it. But life is just as real for both. The difference is, those who scowl seem to take grim pleasure in dragging others down into the shadows, while those who smile lift us up high enough to see that the darkness surrounding us isn't infinite. As Michio said, if you can name the mountain, you'll find it easier to climb.

Though I wished I could speak with our shaman more often, on a practical level, this didn't matter. He was my friend more than my teacher. There was only one thing that I wanted to learn from him: the sacred dances.

I didn't wait too long to ask for this favor. My inability to dance for the spirits had bothered me for a long time, since before Yama's death. If it took our fourth encounter before I requested his help, it was only because I wanted to be sure that we would be *able* to get together without being discovered. The oak tree among the bellflowers was our preferred meeting place, and the two of us became as clever as a pair of foxes when it came to letting one another know that we'd be there.

When I finally spoke up and asked for his help in learning the proper steps and gestures, Michio seemed hesitant. "Didn't my sister show you?"

"She did, but I made a mess of it." I told him all about my childhood fall and my imperfect healing. "If anyone can help me, it's you. You're so graceful! You must know all sorts of secrets that will help me make up for *this*." I tapped my troublesome leg.

"Oho, and why do you think I need any *tricks*? Is it because of *this*?" He patted his ample stomach. I hastened to apologize, but he waved it away. "There's no reason to say you're sorry; you haven't offended me. And really, there's no secret to mastering the dances. If you perform them with the proper reverence and purpose, that's all the grace you need."

"But I keep stumbling! How reverent does something like that look to the gods?"

"Ask them." He winked, then said, "Himiko, who was the first shaman? How did he or she discover the way to move between our world and the world of the spirits? Who taught that person the proper offerings to make, the right words to chant, the gestures that were suitable, and the movements that would most please the gods? No one. These things came from within, just as the dances do."

"But that must have been a long time ago," I protested. "Now we have established rituals."

"Yes, *we* do. It gives us comfort. But we are not the gods. Listen to me: I've traveled far, to countless places. I've seen many clans scattered along the coasts of our islands. There are even more who dwell away from the sea, like us. Wouldn't you imagine there would be more than *one* first shaman? Why wouldn't *each* clan have a first shaman of its own, man or woman, even girl or boy? Did they all create and perform the same rites? Did they all dance to the same tune with the same steps?"

"I—I suppose they didn't." The thought opened my eyes and my mind, leaving me astonished and excited. So many ways to serve the gods! So many paths, and none the only path!

"And yet the gods found all the different dances acceptable." He smiled warmly. "Just as different and just as acceptable as yours will be one day."

In spite of Michio's reassurance, I still insisted that he teach me the dances in the traditional way that he presented them. I promised him that I wouldn't scold myself if I couldn't reproduce his steps exactly. "It's your dance when you teach it to me, but it will be mine when you see me perform it," I said.

"You can't imagine how happy it makes me to hear that," he said. "You know, Himiko"—he had stopped the stiff formality of calling me *Lady* Himiko soon after our first encounter—"I believe that we're both very near the summit of our mountain."

"Our what?" Time had passed, and I'd forgotten his way of describing my situation, but he hadn't.

"The goal we both seek: to see you publicly recognized

as a true shaman. I'm going to dare everything to achieve that. I swear to you that before another winter comes, our clan will know that their welfare is in the care of *two* shamans."

"Two shamans?" I smiled at my friend. "So you won't go running back to the Todomatsu after all?"

"Ah, well, as for that—" He made a helpless gesture that didn't fool me for an instant. "I've gotten used to living here again, and perhaps I was wrong about two shamans being a burden on the people. If worse comes to worst, we can both find additional ways to earn our keep and help our clanfolk." He smirked and added, "Not that you'd ever need the village to support you. It doesn't hurt that you're our chieftain's daughter."

I laid hold of his arm, suddenly concerned. "It could hurt *you*. Master Michio, what if Father exiles you for taking my side in this?"

"Your father can be stubborn and shortsighted, but underneath it all, he's a sensible man," Michio replied. "He doesn't want you acting as our shaman? Fine. The worst—the *unimaginable* worst—he can do is send you away. He doesn't want me fighting for your right to be what you *must* be? Fine. The entirely possible worst he can do is make me leave this village again. But if we both take a stand against him and have the people behind us? Then the worst he can do is . . . nothing. Or grumble, I suppose. No matter how much the Matsu admire his leadership or fear his temper, they'd sooner turn against him than face a future with no shaman at all."

"That's what I thought, before you came here," I said.

"But Father wouldn't accept me as Lady Yama's successor even when it looked as if Aki and the others hadn't found you."

"*That* was a different time," Michio said, full of confidence. "And who was there to witness what he said?"

"No one. We were alone."

"Then there you are! What we're willing to say in private and what we're willing to say in public are very seldom the same, or even similar. If you and I act boldly, before the whole clan, the people will stand by us, and your father will have no choice but to swallow his disapproval and concede. You'll have your dream, Himiko!"

"Just like that?" Michio's enthusiasm was contagious, but I'd lived under the power of Father's temper too long to believe it could be vanquished so easily.

"Why not? It's up to you, isn't it? I'm just waiting here for you to tell me you're ready to take that final step."

"To tell the people I'm a shaman? Some of them know already." I'd told Michio of the nobles Father had informed about me. They'd kept the secret, but from that day on, they'd treated me differently. Venerable men who'd known me since I was a baby, who'd smiled at me, given me rides on their backs, taken joy in every step of my growing up, now gave me wary looks whenever we met and hardly said a word to me if they could avoid it. I grew glum recalling it.

"Some do know, and not one of them has spoken up for you, including your mothers and brothers," Michio said gravely. "You're afraid that when we present you to the people, it will divide the clan."

"They all think I'll turn out like Lady Tsuki," I said miserably.

He raised his hand as if to push back my words. "Your *father* thinks you'll turn out like Lady Tsuki. The others haven't been given the chance to decide *what* they think. He's forced his own fears on them and turned his wrath into a fire that burns away any opposition. We will give them back the freedom to make up their own minds about you."

"What if they agree with him?" I asked.

"I think you should answer that for yourself."

I thought about it for a while, then said, "I'm a shaman. I can't change or deny that. I only want to help my people. If they agree with Father and believe I'm going to use my arts to hurt them, I don't belong here. It would break my heart to leave, but it would destroy my spirit to stay." I gave Michio a weak smile. "Do you think the Todomatsu would want a girl to be the luck-bringer on their trading voyages?"

He patted my arm. "Let's hope it doesn't come to that."

In the end, Michio and I agreed that we wouldn't make our stand until I told him I had no remaining doubts about my ability to fulfill all of a shaman's duties. What it would take for that to happen was for me to decide I'd finally mastered the art of dancing for the gods.

"I'll wait for your word as long as it takes, Himiko," Michio told me. "Just don't let it take too long. I hope you're not the sort of person who never fails because she never tries."

"I *will* try!" I replied, indignant. "I'll tell you as soon as—"

"—as soon as you've fixed this tiny fault or that little

flaw? You can waste your whole life fussing over details. If infants refused to show their faces until they looked perfect, no one would ever be born!"

He made me mad, but he made me think. "I won't do that. If I don't use the skills that Lady Yama taught me, I dishonor her memory. Master Michio, I promise that before the next winter comes, I'll practice all that you can teach me about the dances and perform a complete ritual at her tomb, to venerate and comfort her spirit. I'll prove to you that I'm ready to be called a true shaman before all our people!"

"Himiko, you don't have to prove that to me," he said.

"Maybe not," I replied. "But I need to prove it to myself."

That year brought a bountiful harvest. Our village stacked away jar after jar of rice and barley, soon joined by many containers of rice wine. I stole every moment possible to practice the lessons Michio had taught me, concentrating my mind on seeing him perform the movements of the dance. Even though I knew I didn't have to imitate his steps exactly, I couldn't help driving myself to do just that. As I struggled to mirror his every move, I heard his voice gently chiding me, saying that my dance didn't need to be perfect, just *mine*. I heard him, but I heard another voice too: Father's voice, sneering at me when I'd told him I was a shaman, comparing my chosen work to a little girl playing games with dolls.

I didn't have to be perfect for Michio, or for myself, or even for the spirits. I couldn't dare to be less than perfect for him. He had to see that I made not one mistake, not one misstep, not even the tiniest fault. I couldn't do anything that would let him declare, *You see? She doesn't know what she's doing! She claims she's a shaman, but how can we believe that when our own eyes witness how badly she blunders through the rituals and tempts the displeasure of the gods?*

On the day that I no longer heard Father's phantom voice scorning my efforts, I knew I was ready. When I told Michio, he greeted the news with less enthusiasm than I'd hoped.

"Now comes the hard part," he said, resigned. "We have to wait for a time when we can go to the burial ground without attracting your father's attention. It's not as easy as slipping away to the forest, you know. The road is more open, and anyone who sees me heading in that direction could easily get worried that I'm going there on some grim errand concerning the spirits of the dead. You know how gossip races through this village. Your father would hear of it, come to see why I was going to the burial ground, discover you, and then"—he threw his hands in the air—"it would be all over before we'd have a chance to begin."

"You make it sound hopeless," I said.

"Not hopeless," he corrected me. "But not easy. Be patient, Himiko; be patient and keep your eyes open. Your chance will come."

Michio's words were fulfilled sooner than I dreamed. I was sitting at the loom, weaving new garments for my little brothers, when Aki came clambering up the house ladder to call out, "Great news! Excellent news! One of our hunters spotted a herd of wild boar, a *big* one, and signs of another as well!"

Mama, Yukari, Emi, and I all looked up from our work

at once. "Where is your father?" Mama asked. "Has he been told?"

"Of course! He was the first. He sent me here to fetch his weapons and some supplies for the journey. All the able-bodied men are gathering. We'll probably split up into two parties, to track the two herds. Wish us well, and we'll come home with more than enough meat to see us through the winter."

There was a great deal of bustle as the hunting party prepared to depart. Everyone was excited at the prospect of a successful chase. The old and the young men left behind looked wistful, as did the few others Father commanded to stay and keep watch over our village in his absence. While Michio invoked the gods, offering prayers for plentiful game and asking that all of our men come back alive and unhurt, I sought out my brother Masa. He stood in the doorway of the forge, his face crumpled up with longing and disappointment, and he never took his eyes from the hunting party, even when I greeted him.

"Look at them, Himiko," he said, nodding in their direction. "When they come back, they'll be heroes. Every mouthful of meat we eat this winter will be thanks to them. Why couldn't that have been me?"

"Because someone had to make the weapons they'll use to bring down the boars," I replied. "Your father-in-law is a skilled blacksmith, but I've heard Father himself say that he can tell the difference between that man's arrowheads and yours. He claims that the ones you forge fly true and strike more deeply. You should be proud of yourself, not miserable. Or is this just your sly way of looking for compliments?" I nudged him and smiled.

He smiled back. "You always know the right thing to say, Little Sister. I'll bet you could make anyone feel better just by talking them out of their troubles. Even if you're not a shaman, you're a fine healer in your own way."

I began to say, *But I am a shaman! You know it! I might not be able to serve as one yet, but it's still who I am!* Instead, I remained silent. Masa and everyone else in our village would know what I was soon enough. I'd gain nothing by making a fuss about it now.

On a strangely mild autumn evening a few days later, Michio came to pay our house a visit. "Pardon me for intruding," he said from the doorway. "I was wondering if there had been any news from the hunters."

Mama came forward to welcome him. "Come in, come in, Master Michio. They've been gone for only two days, so unless something horrible had happened, we wouldn't hear anything of the hunting party yet. We were just about to have our dinner. You must join us."

Our shaman looked self-conscious and uncharacteristically shy. "What was I thinking, asking such a silly question? Of *course* it's much too soon to know anything about their progress. You must think I used that as an excuse to show up on your threshold just in time for a meal! I swear, it's not so, though I wouldn't blame you for refusing to believe it."

"But I do believe you, Master Michio." Mama smiled to put him at ease. "Why would you make up such a story when you know you're always welcome to share our food whenever you like?"

"And such good food too." Michio grinned. "You are truly gracious to a lonesome man."

Mama motioned him into our house. Before he took three steps, he was set upon by my younger brothers. They adored our shaman because he was always willing and able to play with them. First he stuck two fingers up on either side of his mouth and charged them, pretending to be a wild boar. They shrieked with laughter and ran away. He chased them until the four of them came dangerously close to knocking a dish out of Yukari's hands as she and Emi worked to get our dinner ready.

"Watch where you're going, you unruly things!" Yukari shouted. Her scolding transformed the wild boar into a heavy-footed *oni*, and when that dreadful mountain ogre swung his invisible club and threatened to gobble up bad little boys, Takehiko and Noboru flung themselves into a corner, giggling as they begged for mercy, while bold Sanjirou stood firm, claiming he'd found a magic stone that would turn the *oni* into something harmless. Michio the ogre froze in midroar and cried out in anguish that he'd been struck by a horrible spell and was becoming a pine tree! That was all the invitation that the boys needed to latch onto his legs and try to climb him. They all toppled to the floor and rolled around like puppies until Emi announced that dinner was ready. She seemed relieved.

When we finished, Michio patted his stomach and said, "Thank you for an excellent meal. You must let me do something for you, to show my appreciation." We all tried to dismiss his offer, insisting it was an honor to share our food with the shaman, but he refused to listen. "Winter will be here before we know it. The cold and damp can be especially hard on the very old and the very young." He looked meaningfully at my little brothers. "I've been preparing medicines to care for our clanfolk who may get sick when the weather becomes harsh, but I've also tried to create a potion that might strengthen our bodies so that we don't fall ill in the first place. I wasn't able to make a lot of it, so it would be my pleasure if I could give some to you, for the little ones."

"Does it work?" Emi asked.

Mama nearly snapped her head off. "What a thing to say to Master Michio! Shame on you, Emi."

The shaman shrugged. "It's a fair question. The truth is, I don't know if it works or not, only that it won't do any harm. Your sons will be no worse off if they take it than if they don't. And if it does work, you'll have good cause to rejoice."

"That's what you think, Master Michio." Emi sniffed. "You've never tried to make my Sanjirou swallow something he doesn't want to."

"I'll give him his first dose myself. But before that"—Michio wore an apologetic smile—"I have one small favor to ask. I want you to have the medicine tonight, so that I don't forget to give it to you. I'm afraid that if I did, you'd all be much too polite to remind me. However"—he sighed—"your delicious dinner's left me so lazy that I shrink from the thought of going from here to home, home to here, and back home again." He turned a pleading face to me. "Dear

Lady Himiko, will you accompany me to my house and fetch the potion for your little brothers?"

I held back a smile. "If it will spare your old bones, I'll do it willingly, Master Michio."

As soon as we were away from my house, Michio snorted. "*Old bones,* eh?"

"Ancient," I said, grinning by the light of the torch in my hand.

"Hmph! That's the thanks I get for trying to help an ungrateful lizard like you."

"Is this why you invented that story about a winter potion?" I asked calmly. "To be able to call me names where Mama can't overhear what a bully you are?"

"It's not a story, you impertinent egg. I *do* have a tonic that will be good for the little ones, and I *am* going to give it to you." He sounded smug. "But that's not the real reason I wanted you to come along with me."

"That's what I thought," I said, matching his self-satisfied expression with one of my own. "And I don't believe you came to our house tonight just to get fed. What's on your mind, Master?"

"The same thing that should be on yours: your future as our clan's next shaman. Your father is well away from here—I wanted to confirm that—and now that I know for sure that he won't be back for many days, we can take the next step."

"So it's time," I said. My heart rose. "At last."

"At last," he echoed in agreement. "Tomorrow at dusk we'll meet at my sister's tomb. You'll perform the memorial rite, and then"—he stopped and clasped my hands—"then

I'll proudly call on the whole Matsu clan to witness and welcome my sister's true heir. Wear your best garments and your finest ornaments, Himiko. Find some autumn flowers to adorn your hair. I want the people to be awestruck at the sight of you when I lead you back through the gates, proclaiming your new place among us. By the time the hunters return, you'll be so securely installed and accepted as a shaman that anyone who objects will look like they're defying the will of the gods."

"Master Michio, do you really think our kin will support me just because you tell them so?"

"They'll do it because you'll begin your duties at once. You will perform every healing; you will call out to the spirits for every blessing; you will dance for the gods where everyone can see. I won't lift a finger or stir out of my house until the day the hunting party marches home. By then, the people will have all the proof they need that you truly are a shaman, because you'll have provided it. Your father won't be able to do a thing."

I could hardly sleep that night. My mind was bubbling with anticipation. All the lessons, all the dreams, all the yearnings I'd ever had to serve the spirits were about to be fulfilled. There was a cold snap before dawn, a chill that left a thin, treacherous skin of ice over every surface and made my brothers and their mothers huddle together for warmth in a huge knot of bedclothes. I didn't feel it at all. The memory of Michio's confident words rang through my head and brought me visions of a bright future. Soon I would be living the life I'd chosen, freely treading the path I knew was right for me. No one would treat me like a child again, not even Father, and if I wanted to travel through the mountains to see my friend Kaya, I'd do it openly, whenever I liked. Who could say no to a shaman of the Matsu? I burned with a fever of hope. How could I help but feel warm?

I don't know how I made it through that day. Dusk couldn't come fast enough for me. As soon as the sun goddess hid her face behind the line of peach and crimson clouds on the horizon, I picked up a basket and slipped out of the house before Mama, Emi, or Yukari could catch me.

The village felt deserted. Everyone was indoors, either preparing dinner or already kneeling down to eat. The only person who saw me leave was the watchman in the tower above our gates. I called out to him even though I knew he'd spotted me. I didn't want my departure to seem suspicious, so I acted boldly.

"And where are you off to at such a time, Lady Himiko?" he asked, leaning down and smiling. I think he was glad to have some kind of diversion from the boredom of being on a lookout for threats that never seemed to come.

"Can't you guess?" I held my basket high. *Let* him *decide what it is I'm supposedly venturing out to gather so late in the day,* I thought. "Mama asked me to help her. I'm not going far."

"Ah, well, that's all right, then. Your mother would sooner cut off her own arm than send you into danger. Just be sure to hurry home before it gets dark!"

"You sound just like her," I replied, giggling, and ran.

I reached the burial ground ahead of Michio. There was still plenty of light in the sky, though the moon was already a sliver of silver against the dusty blue. I wasn't afraid to be alone among the dead. I was a shaman. I knew the spells that kept malicious ghosts at bay. I could sing the songs that soothed unhappy spirits. I could even recite the chants that would summon phantoms, though I knew better than to try.

And these were *my* people, my kin, my ancestors, even my unknown sisters and the little brothers who hadn't lived past infancy. I could feel their nearness. It was almost comforting. I prayed that their spirits felt some consolation from my presence too.

"There you are!" Michio's voice carried through the fading daylight. He was also holding a basket, though his was full. Together, we found the tall, square mound that marked Yama's resting place. In the lengthening shadow of the tomb, he set down his basket, stepped back, and said, "Go ahead, Lady Himiko." It was the first time he'd used my formal title in a long while.

I knelt beside the basket and unpacked it. Michio had brought everything I'd need to perform the rite: salt and wine, a pair of ornate bronze mirrors, a pine twig heavy with crisp-smelling needles, a newly shined bell, a flask that contained water so fresh that when I poured it into the clay bowl from the bottom of the basket, I could smell the green scent of mossy stones from the streambed. When I had all these things arranged in their proper order, I added two items of my own: my wand and my dragon stone amulet. The ritual I was about to perform was intended to revere the memory of my teacher, but it would also mark a new day for me. It was fitting to have the amulet Yama had given me, the stone that had been my birth gift from the gods, and the image of the goddess cradling that sun-bright stone all be a part of this. I propped her against the side of the clay bowl, then on impulse picked her up again and let her slide from my fingers into the water.

I stood up and clapped my hands to draw the attention of the spirits, then began.

At first, I felt as though a great weight were dragging down my shoulders. When I scattered the salt and sprinkled the wine, my arms were heavy as stones. I understood that for secrecy's sake, it would be unwise to raise my voice too loudly when I chanted the words imploring the powers of heaven and earth to bestow their favor and protection on my teacher. Still, I should have been able to do better than a rasping whisper! What was wrong with me? Why was I failing at the one thing that mattered most, under the eyes of the one person who would judge me worthy to be called a shaman or nothing?

Judge me worthy ... judge me worthy ... The phrase nagged my mind and gnawed my heart. *Michio is watching, Michio is judging, Michio will notice if I don't do this right, if I fail ... fail ... fail ....*

I swayed, clutching my wand and the pine twig with both hands, as though an abyss had opened under my feet and those two slender bits of wood were the branch I clung to in order to pull myself clear of disaster. I heard a hoarse, rushing sound in my ears and startled when I realized it was the sound of my own breathing.

Fail ... fail ... fail ...

No.

I heard a voice that wasn't mine, wasn't Michio's, a voice that wasn't a voice at all. I sensed it as I'd always sensed the nearness of the spirits, a force as real as anything I knew. I looked down and saw the full moon shimmering over the surface of the living water in my clay bowl, and just below that glimmering circle of light, my amulet. The dragon stone that had burned for me since the day I was born added golden ripples to the moon's brightness, and at the stone's heart, I thought I saw a gateway open, waiting for me to step through.

I lifted one foot, set it down, made a sweeping gesture with my arms, and began to dance.

How long did I dance for the gods and to honor Yama's spirit? It felt like forever, but when I stopped at last, there was still the lingering trace of daylight in the sky. I sank to my knees and raised my face to the first stars. The moon's crescent smiled at me.

The moon's *crescent*? Then why had I seen the gleaming white disk of a full moon bathed in the water of my humble clay bowl? I gave a little cry of astonishment and scooped out my amulet, pressing it to my chest with dripping fingers. What had happened here, in the mystic time between day and night, in the realm of change between light and darkness? I was left breathless, awestruck, and afraid.

Michio's strong hand fell on my shoulder. "That was wonderful, Himiko. For a while, I thought you'd lost courage, but then—! I know it wasn't easy for you. You must have imagined I'd be appraising your every move. It's hard to do anything when you believe you're being watched that closely. Even the simplest task you've done countless times becomes overwhelming. You know, if we thought someone was examining us bite for bite when we ate, we'd all starve to death!" His laughter was as welcome as cool water under the blazing summer sun.

"You think I did well?" I asked.

"Tsk. Have you forgotten, my friend? My opinion has nothing to do with it. Yours is all that matters. So! *Did* you do well?"

"I—"

"She did *not!*" A monstrous, unearthly shape showed itself from around the corner of Yama's tomb. Twilight outlined a hulking body with two heads, a deformed and hideous *oni* come to life out of legend, a grotesque apparition from our worst nightmares. Its roar was so loud I was surprised that the earth didn't rock under the impact of all that wrath. "She did not do well at all, and *you*, shaman—? You did *evil.* Let the gods witness your treachery, Master Michio. *You* urged her on to defy me like this. I'll have you dragged before all the nobles of our clan for judgment, I'll see to it that you carry the blame, and I'll take joy in witnessing your punishment!"

If that well-known voice didn't immediately banish the illusion of a two-headed mountain ogre, the next moment did: I peered into the dusk and saw my father's rage-distorted face side by side with Aki's grieving one. "Put me down," Father snapped in my brother's ear. "I might not be able to walk, but I can stand. Put me down *now.*"

Aki obeyed. He'd been carrying Father on his back and now let him slip off. Father flinched visibly as soon as his feet touched the ground, but when Aki offered him a supporting arm, he slapped it away. "I said I can *stand!* Does no one listen to me? Am I *dead?*"

"Father, don't say such things," Aki murmured. "Not here."

"Why not? We can just have your precious sister shoo away any ill-natured spirits. Hasn't she got power over the dead? Can't she summon and dismiss them with a single word?" He teetered badly, struggling to stay steady on one foot alone while he ranted on. "Be careful to treat her with respect, my son! Better yet, with *fear*. You don't want to cross her. She'll call up a host of hungry ghosts to destroy you if you say one wrong word to her, or even if you say nothing at all!" He lost his balance and toppled into the side of Yama's tomb.

I rushed to help him up, but he jerked his arm away and grimly motioned for my brother to attend him. Michio remained where he was through all this, silently watching and waiting for whatever might come. Aki dropped to one knee and slung Father's arm around his neck. As the two men rose, my brother softly said, "We were heading back to the village when we heard sounds coming from the burial ground. He insisted we investigate. There was an accident this morning, ice on some rocks we were climbing in pursuit of the boars. He slipped and hurt his ankle, maybe broke it. That's why I've been carrying him and why we came home."

"*Home!*" Father exclaimed with bitter irony. "Yes, a fine home *I* have. Nothing but deceit, betrayal, disobedience—" He took a breath and glared at me. "Do your mothers know where you are and what you're doing?"

I should have been afraid. I should have quivered and shrunk back under the old, familiar assault of Father's

temper. I should have whimpered and begged for his forgiveness and sworn I was sorry and wouldn't do such a
thing again. I should have offered to sacrifice everything for
the sake of pacifying him and buying peace.

But I didn't. I was done with that. I looked him in the
eye and answered, "They know nothing. They didn't see me
leave. We should go home so that I can take care of your
ankle."

I was expecting him to refuse my offer, but I wasn't
expecting the killing frost in that refusal when he sneered,
"Like you took care of Lady Yama?"

His words were a spear through my heart. I recoiled,
dumbstruck, and didn't utter another sound as the four of
us went back to the village.

"Himiko? Are you in here?" Aki stood in the doorway of
our darkened house and called timidly into the shadows. It
was midafternoon of a day thick with clouds, the fourth day
since I had danced at Yama's tomb.

"Where else would I be?" I responded from my place
by the wall nearest the door. He wasn't expecting to hear my
voice so close and jumped a bit, startled.

"You don't *have* to stay inside," he said, squatting beside me, arms crossed over his knees. "It's not as if you're—"
He caught himself about to say *Master Michio,* but bit back
the name. He knew how much it pained me to think about
our shaman's fate.

He was right, but my other choice was to turn my back
on a friend. I would not act as though Master Michio didn't
exist. I'd rather endure the pain.

"How he is, Aki?" I asked. "How is Master Michio? Is he being treated well?"

My brother let his shoulders rise and fall briefly. "He's acting as though he *chose* to be shut up in his own house. His guards report that whenever he speaks with them, he brags about being the only shaman with a whole village to serve him. He spends a lot of the time laughing, singing, and telling funny stories in a loud voice. Most of the children gather near his house just to listen. So do some of the adults. I'm surprised you haven't noticed."

"I haven't gone anywhere near his house since the day Father ordered him shut away," I answered dully. "When I *have* to leave the house, I always walk as far from the center of the village as I can, along the palisade. Mama keeps sending me on one stupid errand after another. I get the feeling that she thinks she's doing me a favor, giving me an excuse to go see Master Michio. She's wrong, but she means well."

"You don't want to see him, to speak to him?"

I peered hard at Aki, whose face was visible in the watery light spilling through the doorway. "I can't *see* him because he's kept captive on Father's orders, and what do you think would happen if I tried to speak to him? Father's men would scurry to report it, Father would get even angrier than he is now, and Master Michio would be the one to suffer for it."

"You say that as if Father's going to have Master Michio killed." Aki patted my arm. "He'd never do that, Himiko. The whole reason he's imprisoned our shaman is because he wants to punish him but he doesn't know how. I just came from the latest meeting Father's called for the nobles.

He's still trying to convince them to send Master Michio away, back to the Todomatsu. His arguments don't change, they just get louder, and more threatening."

"I'm surprised the nobles haven't given in," I muttered. "Father's temper has always worked on them before."

"Before, they weren't facing the possibility of life with no Matsu shaman. That's all that's holding them back from giving Father his own way." Aki looked dejected. "I don't know how this can be resolved."

"And meanwhile, what's happening to the people who need Master Michio's arts?" I asked. "Is no one sick? Has no one been injured? He allowed our shaman the *privilege* of binding his broken ankle, but what are the rest of us supposed to do?"

"Whatever complaint you have against Father, he *is* a good chieftain," Aki replied. "No matter how much ill will he has for Master Michio, he's not letting our clanfolk go unhealed. Thank the gods, there are only a few sick people in the village right now. Our shaman isn't free to go to them, but their family can describe their symptoms to him, to get advice and medicine."

"And what will they do when it's something like a broken bone or a difficult childbirth?" I demanded. "Run back and forth with *descriptions*?"

Aki sighed. "It's the best that can be done."

"No, the *best* thing would be letting Master Michio go free and recognizing that *I* can be a shaman too without turning into Lady Tsuki!" I shouted, thrusting my face into his before bursting into frustrated tears.

Aki put his arms around me and held me the way he

used to when I was small. "Poor Little Sister, you'll break your heart if you keep fighting against things that you can't change. Our father is a good man trapped in a bad past. He may never change. We can, we must."

"How do you want me to change, Aki?" I said between sobs. "To give up everything I've learned? To go back to being Father's precious *good* daughter?"

"I know you'd never do that." My brother gave me a hug. "But maybe it's time for you to become something more than just a daughter. Maybe it's time that you became a wife." He must have seen my wide-eyed, incredulous expression even in the weak light from the doorway, because he quickly added, "Think about it, Himiko. There are plenty of young men in this village who've been trailing after you with lovesick eyes. You've just been too wrapped up in other things to notice them. Any one of them would bless the gods if you'd agree to marry him."

I managed a half smile. "Do you think my husband-to-be would be grateful enough to support me as shaman of our clan?"

"You're joking, aren't you?" Aki looked doubtful for a moment. "You're joking, but I'm serious. Once you marry, Father can't tell you where you can and can't go, whom you can and can't see. You'll be free!"

He sounded so happy, as though he'd found the magical solution to all my problems. I was deeply touched by how sincerely my brother could rejoice at the freedom marriage might bring me while he still remained the captive of his own supposedly "single" life. I couldn't bring myself to discourage him with the truth: any freedom that didn't let me follow the spirits' path openly and without limits was no freedom at all.

"Thank you, Big Brother," I said. "I'll think about what you said."

"That's all I ask." He kissed my brow and stood up. "And will you stop hiding yourself away in this house?"

I rose to my feet. "I can promise you that."

For the rest of that day and for many more, I kept that promise. Aki soon saw me spending more and more time in the company of several of our clan's best hunters. They were good friends of his, reliable young men who were always found at Aki's side when there was game to track. They'd all been part of the first search party sent out to fetch Michio, after Yama died. I spoke to each one of them about that, never failing to ask, "What was the Todomatsu village like? How many days did it take you to reach it? How did you find your way there? Did they welcome you even though you were strangers?" I think that they were all flattered and impressed by how intently I listened to them.

Good. I wanted them to remember that on the day I ran away.

16
THE BREATH OF WINTER

The harvest was over, but my clan's preparations for winter weren't limited to putting aside what we grew in the fields and paddies. There was game to be hunted, fish from the carp pond to be caught and preserved, and the natural bounty of the autumn forests to be gathered. Over the countless seasons since we Matsu had come to our land, this last task had changed from a chore to a minor festival, a chance for young men and women to go up the wooded slopes of the nearby mountains and enjoy each other's company while filling baskets with nuts, mushrooms, and berries. If I could persuade my parents to let me join this food-gathering party, it would be my best opportunity to escape. If not, I'd have to find another way to get out of our village, either without our watchman seeing me at all or without my departure making him suspicious.

Good luck was with me: I didn't need to resort to a second plan. When I asked Mama for permission to go along on the harvest outing, she said yes, then cast an anxious glance in Father's direction.

"It *is* all right, isn't it, my dear?" she asked him timidly. "There'll be so many young people there, including some of . . . some of her new friends."

"Let her go, by all means," Father said mildly. "It's good for her to spend more time with young people, especially some of Aki's fellow hunters. They're all fine lads—not that she needs me to tell her that." He smiled at me. The last time he'd done that had been before he caught me dancing for Yama's spirit. "I've heard that she's been taking a healthy interest in two or three of them. Maybe this little excursion will help her make up her mind."

"Father!" I exclaimed, sounding as mortified as I could. "Why are you talking about me as if I weren't standing right here? And what do you mean about making up my mind?"

"Forgive me, Daughter," he said with surprising benevolence. "I only meant that until our people allow women to have husbands the way men can have wives, you're going to have to make a choice among your suitors."

Yukari laughed. "Stop it, you're making the poor child feel awkward!"

"Yes, you don't want her to be too self-conscious tomorrow," Emi put in. "The boldest girls always get the best husbands. I should know!" She winked at Father. I turned away with a little yelp of embarrassment that I didn't really feel and hid my face in my hands so that my parents couldn't see that I wasn't blushing.

And so it was decided, as far as my family was concerned:

I'd go out with the group, I'd use the time to flirt and be courted, I'd come home with my future husband, and I'd settle down to a normal life, with plenty of babies to take my mind off the foolish notion of becoming our clan's shaman.

The next morning, I kissed everyone good-bye and hurried away to join the group of young people massing by the village gates. None of the girls were glad to see me, particularly Suzu, but Aki's friends welcomed me enthusiastically and began jostling one another aside for the privilege of carrying my basket.

"You'll have to wait until we go home," I told them. "My mothers filled it with lots of good things, and I don't want anyone filching any treats until it's time to eat."

"'Good things to eat'? I'll bet!" Suzu muttered to one of the other girls. She pitched her mocking voice just loud enough to be sure I'd hear her. "So that's what they're calling husband bait in Himiko's house!"

I could have ignored her, but this was Suzu, still trying to bully me after so many years. If I didn't make her pull in her fangs, she'd try her venom on other girls.

"Here, Suzu, why don't *you* use what's in the basket?" I said sweetly, though I made no move to hand it to her. "The whole clan knows you've tried every other way to catch yourself a husband. Maybe you should switch to offering the boys something *good*. At least my mothers' cooking doesn't turn any stomachs."

"And at least *I* don't try to summon up the dead!" she shrieked, fists balled at her sides. Everyone gasped. Many people darted glances back and forth between us. I couldn't tell if they feared or hoped to see Suzu and me go for each other's eyes.

I had more important things to accomplish than entertain our audience with a battle. With a slight smile, I replied, "No, you don't, Suzu. It's a shaman's skill. You wouldn't know how." I placed my free hand on the arm of the nearest young man and let him escort me farther into the forest, leaving Suzu to seethe in her own bitterness.

It was easier than I expected to slip off from the group. I thought that having so many of Aki's friends interested in impressing me would make it difficult, but their interest worked in my favor. The other girls were already resentful and suspicious of me, and that made them keen to "steal" my suitors. They used every trick they could think of to tug the young men's attention their way. They twittered and fluttered and pouted and posed. They begged for help doing the simplest things and wailed plaintively over countless small injuries. Every bruise became a broken bone, every scratch and splinter put their lives in danger. It was the most amusing thing I'd ever seen. If I hadn't wanted to get away so badly, I would have stayed to watch their antics.

Suzu's performance was the best of the lot. She let out a shrill squeal as she took a deliberate fall, then turned it into a scream of utter terror. "Snake! *Snake!*" she cried, pointing wildly at the base of a tree.

I glanced that way. Nothing was there—nothing but opportunity. "Snake!" I shrieked, and ran. Behind me I heard the other girls panicking wildly, the rasp of knives being drawn, and the young hunters grimly demanding, "Where is it? Where's the snake? Do *you* see it?" I didn't look back until the forest's stillness swallowed the last trace of their voices.

How long would it be before they began to look for me? Not *too* soon, surely. I could imagine several things that would delay a search. First, Suzu and the other girls would cling to their new heroes, lavishing flattery on them for having driven off the nonexistent serpent. It would take time for the young men to stop basking in all that praise and notice I was missing. Even then, they might not begin to seek me right away. One of the girls would make a *sensible* suggestion: that instead of scattering and risking more people going astray, everyone should stay put and wait for me to find my own way back to the group.

When at last my suitors decided that they'd played wait-and-see long enough, the early dusk of autumn would be falling and the other girls would whimper that they were cold, they were tired, they were frightened, they wanted to go *home*! Perhaps someone persuasive would even say, "I'll bet that's what *she* did: returned to the village. She's not a child; she knows her way through the forest, and we're not that far from home. We should go back and look for her there." And because that sounded so reasonable, everyone would agree to it and leave.

Was that what would happen? I didn't know; I could only hope. Meanwhile, I'd use whatever time I had to put as much distance between me and my clan as possible. They might not come after me right away, but they would come.

And they'd come by the wrong road. As I moved higher up the mountain, I took satisfaction in knowing I'd given myself the gift of time. *"What was the Todomatsu village like?*

How many days did it take you to reach it? How did you find your way there? Did they welcome you even though you were strangers?" I'd asked those questions so many times of so many people that someone would remember. While Father raged and Mama wept because they realized I hadn't gone missing but had run off rather than live someone else's life, at least one of Aki's friends would recall my eager inquiries about Michio's former home. What else could it all mean except that I was heading there?

But I wasn't taking that path to find my freedom. Like a hunted fox, I'd laid down a false trail to mislead my pursuers. I wasn't seeking refuge in an unknown land among strangers. I was going back to friends.

I was going back to find the Shika.

"Himiko?" Kaya stood in the gateway to her village, staring as if I were a ghost. Her face was very pale and much thinner than I remembered it. She was breathing hard, nearly panting. The Shikas' tower watchman who'd seen me approaching from a distance hadn't recognized me. He'd shouted, "There's a stranger on the road! Looks like a girl from here!" My friend must have heard him and come running. Did she know it had to be me, or did she only hope it? Whatever the case, she was badly out of breath for her effort.

"It's me, Kaya!" I called back, waving. My feet were sore, but I was so elated that it hardly mattered. I'd reached my goal, and my spirit was alive with joy.

She came forward to welcome me. I was surprised to see my normally lively friend walking so slowly and sedately.

What could have changed her? But there was no change in the warmth of the hug she gave me when we met.

"It's so good to see you again!" She smiled broadly, then tilted her head sideways to peer over my shoulder. "Where's Aki? Did you take off running and leave him behind?"

"I did leave him behind," I said. "But not the way you think." Seeing her perplexed look, I added, "I can't live there anymore, Kaya. I can't bear it. I need new air to breathe or I'll choke to death. Please, let me stay."

My friend put one arm around my shoulders. "As long as you like."

While Kaya brought me through the village, she asked about my trip through the mountains. "You look a lot better than the first time you tried to make that journey on your own," she said with a spark of her old humor.

"I'm a little older, I know the road, and it's autumn," I replied. "You'd be surprised what a difference that makes. I had a basket of food to start with, but even after it was empty, I found lots of good things to eat along the way."

"You're lucky nothing ate *you*." We both giggled. Then Kaya looked serious again. "I missed you, Himiko. Aki came here many times, but where were you?"

"Didn't he tell you?" I asked. She only shrugged, so I related everything that had happened to keep me a prisoner among my own clanfolk.

"So that was it." Kaya blew out a long breath. "All Aki said was 'Family troubles.'"

"He was probably too ashamed of the way Father was behaving to want to talk about it," I said.

"Or else he didn't want to waste time answering a lot of questions," Kaya suggested. "Whenever he comes here, he's always in a rush to see Hoshi. The rest of us are lucky if he says hello."

As we drew closer to Kaya's home, I heard the sound of loud coughing coming from inside. My friend stretched out one arm to keep me from crossing the threshold right away. "My older brother's sick," she said. "You might want to wait out here until I see if there's anything I need to clean up. It's a pretty messy illness. I know what I'm talking about: I just recovered from it ten days ago."

"So that's why you look so worn out and weak."

"Hey! I can't help it." She gave me a resentful look.

I shook my head. "I didn't mean to insult you, Kaya. I was worried when I saw you'd gotten so thin, but you're on the mend, so I'm happy. Why don't *you* wait and let *me* take care of your brother?" I stooped to enter their house.

"Himiko, it *stinks* in there," Kaya called after me. "Mother left me in charge today while she went to gather fresh herbs and things for medicine. If she comes back and finds out I made our guest do my nasty work, I'll be in trouble."

I looked back and smiled. "No, you won't; I'll talk to her. I may be your guest, but I'm a shaman first, like her. She'll understand. And if she doesn't, we'll sic Lady Badger on her!" I dashed inside before my friend could raise a fresh objection.

Kaya's brother was asleep, his breath harsh and labored. His skin was intensely hot and dry to the touch, and as Kaya had warned me, there was a dreadful, sour stench filling the house. A row of bowls was laid out beside his bedroll, each holding a thin dusting of a different compound. I raised them to my nose one by one and sniffed. The scents were faint and familiar—blended herbs and ground-up roots that were good for bringing down fevers, soothing coughs, and easing breath. There was also a bowl of cool water with a damp cloth draped over the rim.

"I've been wiping his forehead," Kaya said, kneeling beside me. "It's all I can do."

"And I can't do much more for him unless I can refill these," I said, gesturing at the empty bowls. "Where does your mother store her medicines?"

"That's just it: she hasn't got anything set aside. She used it all." Kaya made a helpless gesture. "That's why she's gone harvesting."

I frowned. Ikumi didn't seem like the sort of person who'd fail to provide more than enough healing supplies. Rushing off to gather the ingredients she'd need to heal her own son was not like her at all. "Kaya, what's been going on here?"

My friend's pallid face looked terribly tired. "Oh, Himiko, it's been awful! This sickness, it's struck nearly every home in our village. Some of the people seem able to throw it off without any effort at all, but others—too many others—can't stop coughing. They feel like their skin's on fire, but sometimes it turns icy cold and dank. They cough and shiver, shiver and cough, and they can't even get a good night's rest. Mother's been trying *everything* to help them.

She even performed a daylong purification ritual for the whole village, and another one to drive back any vengeful ghosts that might have brought this sickness down on us."

I didn't want to ask a painful question, but I needed to know: "Have many died?"

Kaya nodded. There were tears glimmering in her eyes, and she sniffled. "Mostly old people and . . . and babies. The little ones get so weak that they can't nurse, and that makes them even weaker. My sister—Hoshi, not the little one—said she never thought she'd be glad that she and Aki still don't have any children. She'd rather be childless forever than lose a child she loved."

"Kaya, your little sister and brother—I don't see them here. Are they—are they all right?" I braced myself for what she might reply.

"Oh yes, they're fine." Her answer made me utter a huge sigh of relief. "When I got sick, Mother sent them to live at Hoshi's house."

So my brother's wife is safe too. Thank the gods for that! I thought. *And may they also grant that Aki stay away from the Shika village until this sickness has run its course.* Now I had a fresh reason to be happy I'd left a false trail behind me. As one of our best hunters, Aki would be chosen to lead the search party Father would send out on the road to the Todomatsu village.

I did all I could for Kaya's big brother, making him as clean and comfortable as possible, wiping the heat from his brow and body. When the water grew warm, I left my friend to watch over him while I hurried to the nearest stream. There was a young willow tree there, stripped of leaves by the season. I remembered one of Yama's lessons about treating fevers with willow bark and peeled a branch. When I came back to Kaya's house, I steeped the shredded bark in boiling water and spooned sips of it between her brother's lips. I didn't know if it would work, but I had to try.

Lady Ikumi came home just before sunset. She was too worn out to be more than mildly surprised to find me there. After a few formal words of welcome, hastily mumbled, she said, "I think we'll talk about this tomorrow," and began to process the medicinal plants she'd brought back with her. When I stepped in uninvited and started helping, she nodded approval but didn't say a word about it.

The two of us worked until late that night, replenishing the Shika chieftess's supplies of remedy ingredients. Kaya gave us our dinner, which we gobbled. The only time either one of us paused was to tend our patient. By the time Lady Ikumi declared we should sleep, I was already moving through a waking dream.

Kaya's mother was gone by the time I woke up the next morning. As I sat up in my borrowed bedroll, my friend handed me a bowl of rice gruel and joyfully announced, "He's better, Himiko! My big brother's better. He's still coughing, but his skin feels cool without being clammy, and his breath doesn't sound so raspy anymore. You did it!"

"I didn't do anything," I said sleepily. "I wish I could say I used magic—then I could use the same spell to help the rest of your village—but that's not what happened. It was just time for his sickness to change. I'm glad it changed for the better."

"Oh, I know you didn't weave any spells to help him,"

Kaya said, beaming. "But you must have done *something*, even if it was only bring us some luck. I'd rather have good luck than magic any day!"

If I'd brought good luck to the deer people, it was fleeting. When I walked through the village that day, the marks of this merciless sickness were evident all around me. I couldn't tell whether the haggard faces I saw everywhere belonged to people who were just beginning to fall ill, to those who'd been sick and were struggling to recover, to those who were caring for ailing relatives and friends, or to those who had already lost the battle for their loved ones' lives.

I found Lady Ikumi in the shadow of the watchtower, deep in conversation with several men. From their fine ornaments, I guessed they were probably nobles. I stood a short distance away, waiting politely for her to finish speaking with them, and when she finally noticed I was there, said, "Please tell me what I can do to help here."

Her mouth became a thin line that turned down at the corners. "Walk with me, Lady Himiko." She steered us out of the village, down the road that led us along the Shika fields. I was enjoying the peace of walking together silently when all at once, she demanded, "What are you doing here? Why have you come alone?"

The questions were so abrupt, I was taken aback and could only stammer, "Wh-what did you say, Lady Ikumi?"

"Forgive me for my bluntness. With things as they are among my people, I haven't time to spare on niceties. You've never before come to see us without your brother, not since the first time. Why now?"

I understood the reason for her rough way of speaking and told her everything as concisely as I could. When I was done, she gave me a hard look and a harder response: "Your quarrel with your family isn't mine. You can't stay here."

"Lady Ikumi, I'm not asking for your support, or for anything but the chance to make a new life for myself. I won't be a burden to you or your people. I have skills that will help the Shika and relieve you of—"

"You *can't* stay," she repeated. "Sooner or later, your clan will discover where you've gone. Your Father won't give you up."

"I wouldn't depend on that," I muttered.

"You're *his* daughter!" the Shika chieftess shouted in my face. "*His!* Do you think he's the kind of man who'll let go of *anything* that belongs to him? For all I know, he's also the sort who'll blame *us* for your escape from his control. Your trick about fleeing to the Todomatsu lands won't distract him forever. When you can't be found there, he'll remember our village and come here for you. What do you expect us to do when *that* happens? Stand in his way? Risk a battle? You're dear to me, Himiko, but not as dear as my people's peace." Her look challenged me to dispute that.

I didn't want to fight with her. I'd come among the deer people because I'd had enough of fighting. "I understand." I looked at her steadily. "I'm sorry. It was selfish of me to try making your clan wage my battles. At least let me stay here one more day to rest. After that, I'll move on. Your clanfolk trade with other villages. Perhaps one of them will have a place for me, a place where I can serve the spirits openly, gladly, the way I've always dreamed of doing. And if the people can't accept me as a shaman because I'm an outlander, maybe they'll let me live among them and *help* their shaman. That's the heart of what I want, Lady Ikumi: to use my arts at last. To help."

"*Help* . . ." That word seemed to blow away the heat of her angry outburst. Lady Ikumi's expression softened. "I could use that help now, Hìmiko," she said quietly. "You offered it to me, and what did I do? I shrieked at you. How could I have done such a thing? How could I not have *listened* to you?"

"It's all right; I understand," I said. "You've had so much to worry you, and you must be exhausted."

"True." She looked beaten. "I'm afraid that a demon's crawled under my skin. He came riding into our village on the back of the sickness that's destroying us, and he's been twisting me like thread on a spindle ever since. I'm stretched out so taut, it feels like I'm going to snap any moment." Her hands cupped my face. "Stay with us as long as you wish, leave us whenever you desire, but know that if you linger too long and your clanfolk find you here, we won't stand in their way. Forgive me if I can't give more."

"Oh, Lady Ikumi, it's enough, it's so much, it's all I ever wanted!" I hugged her with my whole strength. We walked back to the ailing village laughing.

Laughter didn't survive long within the wooden palisade. My days were soon a whirl of looking after the sick, scouring the countryside for useful plants, making medicines, calling out to the spirits for help, leading the lucky families in prayers of thanksgiving, and serving the unlucky ones when Lady Ikumi and I danced for the comfort of the living and the peace of the dead.

Kaya did her part in all of this. She didn't have a healer's knowledge, but she was a quick learner with a hawk's eyes. If Lady Ikumi or I showed her a dozen different plants we needed, she'd never fail to find every last one and be back with a heaping basketful. She often watched closely when I crushed stems, shredded leaves, and ground up roots.

"You know, I've seen you make *that* brew a lot," she observed one day when we were alone in the house. Her older brother had recovered and was out seeing his friends, her two younger siblings were still living with Hoshi, and Lady Ikumi was going through the village to take stock of how her people's health was faring. "In fact, if you ask me, I've seen you make it so many times before, I think *I* could do it."

"I'm sure you could," I said absently. I was concentrating on adding boiled water to the mixing bowl. I was so tired that my hands were shaking and water was sloshing over the rim.

Kaya took that as an invitation, helping herself to the bowl and dribbling out exactly the right amount of water. She countered my astonished look with a self-satisfied grin. "Told you so."

Things became a little easier after that. Kaya was an adept student, and while she'd never be a shaman—or want to be one—she was eager to learn the ways of the healer. Now the Shika had three people working to rid their village of the great sickness. This became especially important on the day that Lady Ikumi herself fell ill.

Kaya and I woke up to find her suffering from the same symptoms she'd treated in so many of her clanfolk—the fever, the chills, the cough, the sweaty skin. Without waiting to be told, my friend began making a fresh batch of fever cure for her mother. We'd all learned that the sickness's other manifestations could wait, and that if we lowered our patients' fevers as soon as possible, they usually recovered quickly.

Lady Ikumi's violent coughing woke Kaya's older brother. "I'll get some fresh water," he volunteered, scrambling to dress himself.

"And I—" I began.

"You should go tell some of the nobles what's happened," Kaya said. She was right, of course. It was no small thing when a clan's leader was too sick to perform her duties.

As I was heading for the nearby house of a Shika nobleman I knew, I saw Kaya's little brother and sister come running toward me. Their faces were contorted with fear. Who had told them about their mother's illness? I bent over and spread my arms to offer them a comforting hug. "Dear ones, don't worry, your mama sounds sicker than she is. Kaya and I will make sure she gets better, I promise you."

The little girl sobbed against my shoulder, but her brother asked, "Mama's sick too? Then who's going to take care of Hoshi?"

That was how I learned that Aki's wife had fallen victim to the great sickness.

Kaya took charge of the children, bringing them to Sora's house. The huntsman and his family had all been doubly fortunate: their encounters with the sickness were mild, and their recoveries were long over. Yama taught me that whatever made people sick—spirit or demon—seemed to like variety. We seldom experienced the same illness twice. Sora's home would be a safe haven for the little ones.

As for me, I paused only long enough to prepare the medicines that had done the most good for the most people, then went straight to Hoshi's side. According to the children, she'd fallen ill just that morning, so I had great hopes of cutting off the progress of her illness before it had time to sink its roots too deeply into her body.

I did not enter her home until I had put on my brightest smile. Michio told me that he made it a point to speak cheerfully and even tell jokes whenever he went to heal someone. The sick needed to be strengthened in body *and* spirit, so that they could work with the shaman to battle what ailed them. Nothing stole away a person's will to fight more than seeing a grim-faced healer. "You don't want your patient thinking, *If he looks that glum, I must be doomed!*" he said. It was good advice.

"Hoshi, this is a fine way to treat your sister-in-law!" I called out lightly as I crossed the threshold. "If you don't want to see me, just say so."

"Ah, there's no fooling you, is there, Himiko?" Hoshi's hoarse voice answered me in the same joking tone. "And yet, here you are. Oh well, I suppose I'll have to"—her words were interrupted by a short burst of coughing—"have to put up with your company now that you've come into my house uninvited."

I knelt beside her bedroll and studied her closely. To my relief, she didn't look too bad. Her lovely face was a little paler than I remembered and there were dark circles under her eyes, but that was all. I was able to smile at her without forcing myself to do so.

"Too bad for you that you don't like my company," I told her. "You're going to have it for the next few days, until you're strong enough to throw me out the door. And don't imagine you can get your little brother and sister to help you get rid of me any sooner. They're safe and happy and won't be coming back here until you're well. There's nothing you can do about it."

"Terrible children, running off and leaving me in your clutches." Hoshi's eyelids began to droop, and her speech became slurred with drowsiness. "Glad that Aki and I don't have any of our own yet. Probably'd take after you. Terrible, terrible children . . ."

She drifted off to sleep. I knew that rest was a much better healer than I would ever be, and a much better medicine than any I could offer. There would be time enough later to give her a drink to bring down her fever and a soothing syrup for her cough. In the meanwhile, I tidied the house and had some hot rice gruel waiting for her when she woke up.

"Who told you that you could cook?" she teased as she devoured it all. Seeing her eat with such a healthy appetite was the answer to my prayers.

In the days that followed, I learned that sometimes the spirits answer our prayers in ways so overwhelming we might wish we'd never prayed for anything at all. I'd prayed for the chance to prove that I could be a shaman and a healer. Now I was both and more. I took great pleasure in being able to use my arts to help the Shika clan, but because of the tragic circumstances, I couldn't truly enjoy the opportunity the gods had given me.

My days among the deer people were spent reporting to the clan nobles about Lady Ikumi's condition, caring for her, nursing Hoshi, rushing from one villager's house to the next to look after the sick, and warning the healthy not to try to do too much and risk falling ill themselves.

I tried to take my own advice. Kaya was a tremendous help to me when it came to harvesting ingredients and making medicines. To my surprise, she soon had her older brother trained to find all that we needed for our potions.

"How did you manage to teach him to do this?" I asked her as I picked through the basket holding his first gleanings. The quality and quantity of what he'd gathered were amazing. "He's brought everything, even some plants I thought were already withered and gone for the season. I was driving myself mad trying to figure out what we could use as substitutes, but here they are!"

Kaya shrugged. "He knows where to look for things. Why wouldn't he? He's a hunter, like Aki. Plants can be his quarry as easily as animals. If he didn't have good eyesight and know the land around here, especially the secret places of the forest, we'd all go hungry." She grinned and added,

"You're not the only one who's got a special older brother, Himiko."

Now that I had two helpers, my life should have been easier. I was able to devote more of my time to those people who were in the most danger of losing their lives to the sickness. I worked confidently, even though I found myself with less and less time to look after my own needs. The hardest part of it all was remembering not to play favorites. Sometimes, it couldn't be helped.

The Shika nobles made it clear that I had to give more attention to Lady Ikumi. If she hadn't been lost in feverish dreams, she would have objected stridently to getting special treatment, but she was helpless as a newborn rabbit. Unless one of the other villagers was in immediate danger of dying, or if an infant or child was in peril, I followed the nobles' commands and took care of Kaya's mother first.

But how could I neglect my brother's beloved wife? Hoshi didn't seem to have a severe attack of the sickness, but there was something about her cough that bothered me. I alternated nights sleeping in her house and under Lady Ikumi's roof in order to catch any troubling symptoms, but more often than not, I fell into a deep, exhausted sleep. When I couldn't be with Hoshi, Kaya stayed with her sister. She always said that Hoshi had passed a peaceful night.

"You should relax a little, Himiko," she said to me as the two of us enjoyed a rare, warm autumn evening. "You're starting to look worse than some of the sick folk."

"So says Lady Badger, the newest healer of the Shika clan," I replied with a smile that became a resounding yawn.

"I'm enough of a healer for you to trust me and get some rest. If I can't take care of my sisters, what use am I?"

"I never questioned your ability to tend Hoshi, Kaya. You take very good care of her, and of your mother, and—"

"*All* my sisters." Kaya folded her arms and glared at me so intently that there was no mistaking what she meant. "For once, you're going to go to bed and sleep through the night. Mother's better. You saw that for yourself today. And I caught Hoshi trying to get up to use her loom. She says she wants to make Aki a new tunic, but I soon put a stop to that. I told her he had more than enough clothing, but only one wife."

"Well done," I said, pleased. "All right, I'll stay in my own bedroll tonight and you be with Hoshi, but if anything happens—"

"—I promise I'll drag you out of the house by your hair." Kaya rolled her eyes. "*Now* are you happy?"

I yawned again. "It will have to do. Badgers . . . stubborn beasts."

"I know one beast who's more stubborn than that," she muttered, and dashed away.

Kaya kept her word. When I came to Hoshi's house the next morning, I found the two sisters happily arranging each other's hair. I was delighted to see a bit of color in Hoshi's face, though I would have been more pleased if it had been an allover healthy tint instead of two bright red spots blazing high on her cheeks. It might have been the last traces of her fever or simply a sign of excitement at feeling better. I told myself I'd check it out as soon as possible.

"See, Himiko?" Hoshi said merrily when she saw me in

the doorway. "You don't have to hover over me anymore." She began to cough, but by a great effort managed to suppress it. "Never mind that. My throat's dry, nothing worse."

"Here, have a drink of water." Coughing herself, Kaya passed her sister a flask. "Everyone in the village sounds like us lately, sick or well."

"It's not just the sickness; it's the damp weather," I said right before my own cough made itself heard.

"Oh, were you feeling left out, Himiko?" Hoshi teased. She laughed, this time without coughing. It was a sweet sound. "And how is Mother?"

"Fully recovered. Not even the whisper of a cough all yesterday and last night," I said. "Now she's bothering me to let her come stay with you."

"To *let* her come here?" Hoshi's laugh was faint and breathy. I was concerned that she was putting too much strain on herself. It often happened when people were recovering from severe illnesses. At the first hint that their bodies were returning to normal, they tried to recapture lost time and wound up making themselves sick all over again.

"Mother must be sicker than we thought if she's waiting for *this* outlander's permission to see her own daughter!" Kaya snickered, and used a pin to anchor a loop of hair over her big sister's left ear.

I drew myself up with comical dignity. "This *outlander* is the only shaman you've got until Lady Ikumi is ready to resume her duties. I'll thank you to show me a little respect, young ladies!" My attempt at sounding haughty was cut off cold when Kaya threw a comb at me. I threw it back, she leaped up and dragged me down beside Hoshi, and soon the three of us were sitting in a ring, chattering gaily as we turned each other's hair into magnificent mazes of swooping curves. I was glad to be accepted as a shaman, but it was a great blessing to be able to be only a girl, only Himiko, for a little while.

I examined Hoshi carefully before I left. Her skin felt a little warm to the touch, though not warm enough to worry me. Her breathing was slightly labored, but I'd noticed such signs in other villagers who'd made full recoveries within no more than two days. It was as if the spirit of sickness couldn't bear to release his hold on his victims and clung to them by his fingertips until the last possible moment. Lady Ikumi's recuperation had gone exactly the same way, and now she was completely well.

"Lady Badger, you're a good healer after all," I told Kaya before I left.

"What do you mean 'after all'?" Kaya protested with mock indignation. "This is the appreciation I get for letting you have a good night's sleep!"

"And I'll have another tonight," I replied, hugging her. "Thanks to you."

That evening, Lady Ikumi insisted on making dinner. She looked like her old self and took great joy in piling food on my plate. Kaya only stayed long enough to take away dinner for herself and Hoshi.

"Big Sister's going to be glad to have *you* cooking for her again, Mother," she said before she left. "She'd probably be lots better by now if she didn't have to suffer through the meals Himiko and I were making her eat."

"She needed your care more than your food," Lady

Ikumi said. "Once she's well, she'll have plenty of time to eat good things. Give her my love, and tell her I'll come to look after her myself tomorrow."

Without Kaya, dinner was a quiet time. Lady Ikumi's older son wasn't much of a talker. The few times I tried to bring him into the conversation, he reacted with just a few words before withdrawing in silence, blushing as he concentrated on eating his dinner. He finished long before either of us, blurted that he was going to speak with some of his friends, and rushed out of the house as though wolves were after him.

"Did I say something wrong to him?" I asked Lady Ikumi.

"Of course not. You're imagining things." She picked up the dishes and quickly turned away, but I was almost sure I heard her chuckling under her breath.

"But the way he ran out of here—!"

She looked back at me. This time she made no effort to conceal her laughter. "Oh, Himiko, I do believe you've spent too much time studying and not enough living. Can't you *tell* when a young man likes you?"

It was my turn to blush, and I wasn't pleased to do it. "In my village, they were always straightforward about it."

"So what if my son's not as direct as your Matsu lads? Apparently, it doesn't matter if they were bold and he's shy; none of them's managed to capture your heart." She clicked her tongue. "Too bad. I wouldn't mind *that* much if I had you for a daughter-in-law."

"And I wouldn't mind marrying your son *that* much if it meant I could stay here."

I thought I was trading joke for joke, but the shocked expression on Lady Ikumi's face was like a slap. I hastened to add, "Oh! You didn't think I was *serious,* did you? Please forgive my foolish chatter. Even if that were the only way for me to live with your clan, I'd never use your son like that. He deserves a wife who'll love him as much as he loves her."

Lady Ikumi's gentle smile returned. "I'm sorry, Himiko. I should know you better than that." She took me into her arms with a mother's tenderness. Her sweet nature made me think of my own mother, and my heart ached. I began to cry.

"What's wrong, dear one?" Lady Ikumi asked, bewildered. "Did I hurt your feelings so badly?"

"It isn't that," I said between sobs. "I'm just—just missing Mama and—and hoping she's not too worried about me."

"But if she *were* that worried—if she were frantic with concern—wouldn't your brother Aki do something about it? Surely *he* must suspect where you are. He wouldn't have to tell anyone, just come here to fetch you."

I shook my head. "You already know about the false trail I left behind me, leading to the Todomatsu clan. Father would have sent Aki to follow that. I don't know how long it would take before he dared to give up and return home. And meanwhile, Mama—" My voice broke.

"I see." Kaya's mother nodded solemnly. "I'd like to say something to comfort you, Himiko, but we both know the truth: in these circumstances, how can your mother help but be worried, not knowing where you are, asking herself if you're safe, well, even . . . alive."

I sobbed more wildly. "I didn't think I had a choice, Lady Ikumi! I thought I *had* to run away or—or—"

"Or die?" she asked gently.

"*No.*" I spoke so emphatically I surprised myself. "Maybe I thought that once, but— No! I know it's not true. I wouldn't have died, but I never would have lived, either. And I couldn't do that."

She pushed my disordered hair out of my face carefully. "You thought you had no choice but to run away, and now you regret it. I'm not surprised. You and I follow the same path, Himiko, but to walk in the way of the spirits means to walk in the footsteps of other people too. You feel your mother's pain, you share her fear and her uncertainty. They all become a cord that binds you. You ran off in order to be free, but how free will you be until you untangle that cord and bring her peace?"

My face was wet with tears, yet felt as though it were on fire. "I should go back," I said in a voice that pleaded, *Tell me not to do it! Tell me to stay! Tell me there's another way to ease my mother's heart and still be true to my spirit!*

Lady Ikumi lowered her eyes. "Think about that," she said. "Be sure it's what you want, not what you think I want to hear. Remember, living your life to please other people is what drove you to run away. Go to sleep, Himiko. You'll have time to decide tomorrow, or the next day, or even the next. But you should make your choice before winter reaches us, because whichever road you choose, *my* decision remains unchanged: you can't stay here."

"I—" A sob snatched the words from my mouth, and a

cough followed it. I cleared my throat loudly and said, "I understand. Thank you, Lady Ikumi."

That night, I dreamed that I was home again. The first thing I saw as I mounted the house ladder was Mama sitting on the porch, playing a clapping game with Noboru. Neither one of them seemed to be aware that I was there. Then my little brother jerked his head toward me, stared, and let out a tremendous shriek before throwing himself into Mama's arms.

Please forgive him, she said. *He isn't used to strangers.*

Strangers? But it's me, Mama! I'm Himiko.

Himiko? she repeated as if sampling a new and unfamiliar food. *What a pretty name. If I had a daughter, I think I'd like to name her that.*

But I am *your daughter!* my dream-self cried. *I am—*

Himiko? A new voice sounded from the darkness inside our house. Aki appeared in the entryway.

Oh, Aki, what's happened to you? I stared at him, horrified by his appearance. His hair was tangled, his face was gaunt and wan, and he seemed unable to stand up without holding on to the door frame. *Tell me,* please *tell me, what's wrong?*

What's wrong? he repeated dully. *Don't you know? Didn't they tell you? She's dead, Himiko. Hoshi is—*

"—dead!"

I woke up to the flare of lights and the sound of a family's heartbroken wailing.

17
INTO THE MIRROR

No one could tell how it had happened. Lady Ikumi's grief-stricken screams woke the whole village, and when her clanfolk came running to see what was the matter, the first question all of them asked was "How?"

"I don't *know*!" Kaya groaned as she stood outside of Hoshi's house, head bent, her hands clapped tightly over her ears to shut out the never-ending questions. "I told you and *told* you, I don't know how it happened! She went to sleep and just—just didn't wake up, that's all." She looked up at the mob of villagers in front of her and shouted, "I don't know anything else, I swear it!"

I stood beside my friend, a steadying arm around her waist, my other hand resting on her shoulder. I struggled to be strong, for her sake, but the dream image of my brother's ravaged face lingered in my mind and filled me with sorrow. *Oh, Aki, this will break your heart!*

Kaya hadn't been the one to bring the tragic news to

her mother. When she awoke to make that awful discovery, she'd dashed to the nearest house to find a messenger. She wouldn't leave her sister alone, even now that Hoshi was gone. The young man who'd accepted the grim responsibility was a friend of Kaya's older brother. The two of them now stood to either side of Lady Ikumi, helping her stay on her feet.

Kaya's protests did nothing to stop the battering rain of questions. Hoshi had died at dawn, and in the growing light of a new day, I could see the crowd as more than just a featureless mass of people. I recognized every one of the villagers before me and realized that their relentless demands to learn the truth about Hoshi's fate wasn't mere idle curiosity. Many of them had loved ones who'd come through the worst of the great sickness and seemed to be on the mend, just like her. I could read their fears in their faces: *Lady Hoshi was getting better, and then, without warning, she died. Why? Can that happen to my kin? Will it? Must it? Tell me it was some random evil, something that won't cross my threshold! Say there's something, anything we can do to prevent it! Banish it! Destroy it! Cast it far away! Don't leave us like this, so helpless, so afraid.*

"Stop it!" I called out to the people in my loudest, most commanding voice. "Don't you *hear* what Lady Kaya's saying? It's *all* she knows. When there's more to tell, we won't hide it, I promise you, but for now—for now, please let there be peace." I cast a significant look in Lady Ikumi's direction. "For all our sakes."

The attack of questions died to a murmur of sympathy as Lady Ikumi was escorted into her oldest child's house. I remained outside with Kaya for only a little longer, then helped my friend go back in and join her mother. As we knelt in a row beside Hoshi's body, I heard the sound of someone clearing his throat behind me. Turning toward the doorway, I saw Sora waiting patiently.

"I've brought the children," he said. "I thought—I thought that she would want to hold them." He indicated Lady Ikumi.

I looked to Kaya, who nodded. The next moment, Lady Ikumi was hugging her two youngest children fiercely, defying the forces that had stolen her oldest daughter away from her, taking comfort from life in the face of loss.

Hoshi's funeral rites took place the next day. Lady Ikumi dressed me herself, seeing to it that I was arrayed with all the ornaments she wore when she performed such ceremonies. The Shika burial ground was somewhat different from ours. There were no tall, square mounds to mark the resting places of high-ranking people, only low rises where the soil had been piled over the earthenware jars holding the bodies of the dead. As I looked upon the site, I saw far too many new graves and prayed that the first snow would come soon, to hide them from sight until spring could cover them with flowers.

The spirits of wind and cloud took pity on Hoshi's family and sent us a day of clear skies and cool, dry weather. As we walked to the burial ground, the mourners' hemp clothing rustled as softly as the scarlet swashes of maple leaves on the far mountainside. Before I began the ritual, I turned to Lady Ikumi and asked her to bless my efforts.

"Hoshi was very dear to me," I said. "I'm afraid that my arts aren't good enough to honor her spirit as well as she deserves. When I dance, I—I'm afraid that I might stumble, the way I always used to do."

"If you stumble, you stumble." Lady Ikumi cradled my face with her hands. "It will be as the gods decide. They guided you here, years ago. They brought you back to us now because they knew we would need you." She kissed my brow and added, "That *I* would need you. Dearest one, I pray that you'll never endure the pain of losing a child, but trust my words: the pain of having to send your child's spirit into the darkness with your own hands is even worse. You've spared me that today. If you dance as lightly as a dragonfly or lurch at every second step, it won't matter. However you tread the path the gods have laid at your feet, you honor my daughter's life. Dance for her, Himiko, with every blessing."

Her reassurance filled me with serene confidence. I performed the burial rite with my mind free from any misgivings and my actions cleansed of everything but the desire to bring comfort to those who mourned and peace to the departed spirit.

We returned to Lady Ikumi's house after the ceremony. I changed out of my borrowed shaman's garb into my own familiar clothing. Lady Ikumi was sitting with her two youngest children, quietly telling them a story about some bit of mischief Hoshi had gotten into when she was their age. I knelt in front of them and offered her the pile of clothes and ornaments I'd used.

"Thank you, Himiko." The Shika chieftess smiled, but

her eyes were soft with melancholy. "Please put those in that corner over there, with the rolled-up bedding, but before you do—" She leaned forward and picked two things from the top of the pile I held out to her. "I want you to keep these," she said, holding up a necklace of curved green glass beads in one hand and a bronze mirror in the other.

"Lady Ikumi, I haven't done anything to deserve such rich gifts," I said.

She dismissed my protests with a gesture. "If every gift had to be earned, we would all be poorer. I want you to have this necklace because my Hoshi always admired it, but whenever I tried to give it to her, she refused."

"That's true," Kaya put in. "Hoshi always said, 'That necklace is for a chieftess to wear, not me.'"

"Then I shouldn't accept it, either," I said. "I'll never rule my clan or any other."

"You *should* take it, Himiko," Lady Ikumi corrected me. "Not because of what you are now or what you might become, but only because it would please me to know that whenever you look at it, you'll remember us."

"I'd never forget you, necklace or no necklace," I replied. "But since it will make you happy—" I ducked my head, and she let the glittering beads fall around my neck.

"Now, I do hope you won't raise any objections to my giving you *this*," she said, holding out the mirror. "I have several more. Put down that pile of clothing and look at it."

I did as she directed, first gazing into the gleaming surface that held a second Himiko's face, then turning the little mirror over to study the designs decorating the back. I saw

the image of a leaping woman so elaborately garbed that she
had to be a shaman. A pair of antlered deer flanked her.
They were rearing up, brandishing their forelegs so that the
three figures looked as though they were dancing together.

"Did this come from the Mirror Kingdom?" I asked,
awed by such a lovely thing.

"No, it was made here years ago, in this very village. My
great-grandmother was our shaman and chieftess then. She
saw the scene in a holy vision and had our smith re-create
it in bronze. Take good care of it, Himiko; it's very special."

"It *is* special—too special for me to take," I said. "Lady
Ikumi, this mirror is sacred to your clan, to your family, and
I—I don't belong to either one."

She didn't dispute what I said. We both knew that I
wouldn't be remaining among the Shika. The only question
was *when* I'd leave, and why. Would I go because it was my
choice, made to spare my mother further anxiety, or would
my departure be forced on me by Lady Ikumi's own un-
swayable decision, that I had to leave to spare her people
war with mine?

Meanwhile, she sat with her children clinging to her
neck, her hands folded in her lap, and ignored my attempts
to give back her great-grandmother's relic.

"Please, Himiko, no arguments," she said calmly. "You
did me a great service today. This is the most that I can do
for you."

I bowed my head a second time. I saw no point in fighting this battle. There were still sick people among the Shika,
and I had my work waiting for me.

"As you wish, Lady Ikumi," I said. I rose, put away her clothing and the rest of her ornaments, tucked the mirror into my sash beside my cherished wand, and left the house.

For the rest of that day, I couldn't take three steps without encountering a villager who wanted to know the details of Hoshi's death. I told them the truth—that there are times when the gods like to remind us that they *are* the gods. Even though we share this world with them, their powers are greater than ours will ever be.

No one liked the truth. They kept insisting that there must be something about Hoshi's illness that I'd overlooked, or had seen and forgotten, or was deliberately keeping to myself.

"I'm not hiding anything," I protested. "Why would I? These things just . . . happen."

Still the people kept at me. They didn't want to be told that things just . . . *happen*, especially bad things. What would prevent random tragedy from finding them? They wanted a magical reply—that if you do this or if you refrain from doing that, you'll be safe. I should have made up such a comforting lie, but I was too tired to think of one and too miserable over Hoshi's death to be able to deal with the same questions over and over again.

Finally, I couldn't take any more. "Why won't you believe me?" I snapped at an especially persistent villager. "I did everything I could to heal Lady Hoshi—*everything*! It just wasn't—wasn't—" I was so frustrated I was sputtering.

"It wasn't enough," the villager murmured. "You did so much for us that it's hard to remember you're only a girl. You can make mistakes. It's not your fault she died. Sorry to bother you." He walked away, never knowing that the words he'd meant to comfort me had left me sick at heart.

Your fault... The ghost that had been haunting my thoughts so timidly now leaped into the light, a monstrous thing. *Her death is your fault! It is! It is, and you know it! Your fault and no one else's!* The ghastly phantom howled with triumph.

I tried to reject it, to cast it out, but it anchored its claws in me and would not let go. My mind became a whirlwind of *I should have* and *If only* and *Why didn't I—?* My brother's haggard face emerged from the land of dreams to accuse me: *You saved so many other lives, Himiko. Why couldn't you save hers?* Memories of Yama's death brought their own ruthless ghosts. I *had* saved many lives. Why had I lost the battle to save two of the people who meant the most to me and to those I loved? I burst into sobs and ran back to Lady Ikumi's house.

Kaya was standing outside when I came stumbling up and collapsed on the threshold. She dropped to one knee beside me and tried to raise me from the ground, but I was too heavy with grief and guilt to be more than deadweight in her arms. I lay there until I felt three pairs of arms working together to lift me and saw the faces of my friend, her mother, and her older brother all staring at me with a mixture of confusion and concern.

The vengeful ghost inside me leered. *What are you going to tell them when they ask what's wrong? Will you confess that you're the one responsible for their mourning? That you didn't work as hard as you could to save Hoshi? You should have been tending her constantly, day and night! Instead, you left her care to others while you slept. You slept her life away! Tell yourself the truth, Himiko: Did Hoshi's death just . . . happen? Or did it happen because of your selfishness, your neglect, your failure? How does it feel to play at being a healer when someone else loses the game?*

The creature's cruel laughter was an echo in my ears as I sat up and faced Hoshi's family. Without waiting for their questions, I said, "I'm sorry, I don't know why I'm crying like this. I'm just very tired, and"—I coughed—"and I miss her, and I don't know how I'm going to be able to break the news to Aki, and"—I coughed again, my throat rough from so much sobbing—"and I think I should go home now. Soon. Tomorrow."

"There's no need to make a hasty decision, Himiko," Lady Ikumi said.

"Oh, I'm not!" I said quickly. "I've been thinking about this. I went around the village tonight and saw that things are much better. Your people don't need me anymore. I should go, before winter comes."

The Shika chieftess gave me a searching look. "Are you sure of what you're saying? You have *some* time. Winter won't come as soon as you imagine."

"I thought you'd be glad to know I'm ready to leave," I replied. A fresh bout of coughing threatened to interrupt me, but I held my knuckles to my mouth and fought it down. I didn't want Lady Ikumi deciding it meant I was too sick to travel when it was only the end result of all my weeping.

"I said that you couldn't stay, but that doesn't mean I'm

happy to see you go. Don't you know how deeply I regret having to send you back?"

I nodded, and took a long, hoarse breath. "Please forgive me. I shouldn't have said such a thing to you, especially now. I don't know what's wrong with me, why I'm so selfish. I should stay at least long enough to perform the purification rites for you, after the time of mourning's over."

"*You,* selfish?" My friend Kaya snorted. "You *must* be tired. Mother, tell her to go to sleep before she says anything else so ridiculous."

Kaya had the gift for being able to cheer anyone, in nearly any circumstances. Lady Ikumi was able to smile at us both and say, "There's the wisdom of Lady Badger again, always so sensible. Perhaps you should have a nap now, Himiko. Wash your face with some cool water first; you look a little flushed from crying, and I don't like the sound of your throat."

"It's nothing. I brought it on myself," I said. "I'll be fine if I can rest my voice."

"See that you do." She patted my cheek, and a momentary look of uncertainty flitted over her face. "We'll wake you up when it's time to eat."

"Thank you, Lady Ikumi," I said, and went to lay out my bedroll in the back of the house.

I slept deeply, so very deeply that when Kaya came to wake me up, she had to shake me for a long time to rouse me. When I did open my eyes, I couldn't get them to focus. Her face was a blur, and her voice seemed to be coming from the bottom of a well.

"Himiko? Himiko, what's wrong with you?" she asked. "You look strange. Why are you just lying there? Get up! It's time for dinner."

I wanted to answer, but when I tried to speak, all I could do was cough, a tempest of a cough that shook my bones and set my chest on fire. I struggled to sit up, and managed to prop myself on one arm for a few hard-won breaths, but then was swept away in a renewed fit of coughing. My head spun, my sight darkened. Kaya grabbed me before I could fall back onto my bedroll. I heard her calling frantically for her mother, though I couldn't make out anything she said except for Lady Ikumi's name. I wanted to tell her that I was fine and not to make a fuss. Didn't she realize that her mother shouldn't be bothered at a time of mourning? As soon as I woke up, I'd make a soothing potion that would relieve the hot pressure on my chest. I could take care of myself.

I opened my mouth to speak to my friend, but she melted from my sight. Her words trickled through the cracks in the world, and I went falling after them into oblivion.

Himiko?

The voice that called my name did not belong to Kaya. I heard it clearly, high and sweet on the cold wind that whipped through my hair and wound my dress tightly around my legs. The soles of my bare feet were chilled by the slick gray rock beneath them, but as I glanced down, I saw them suddenly buried in ghostly mounds of pale blue springtime flowers.

Himiko, are you there?

I tucked my hands under my arms and shivered, curling into a crouch to keep out the cold. Tears clung to my eyelashes, turning everything I saw into starbursts of captured light, but they weren't tears of sorrow. They were the children of the wind, which sent his clever, merciless, icy fingers probing into every unguarded gap in my clothes, seeking every exposed portion of my body to torment with frost.

And yet, at my feet, those flowers . . .

The flowers stirred and parted. I was gazing into a shallow pool of tawny water encircled by the nodding petals. A round black stone rested in the very center of the pool, glowing with its own enchanting light. I reached out one hand to touch it, but when my fingertips brushed the surface, the flowery banks snapped together sharply. I jumped, startled, lost my balance, and sat down hard among the flowers—flowers that now spread their petals into wings and flew away, a cloud of singing birds.

What are you doing, Himiko? The voice in the wind now bubbled up out of the pool, and the pool grew smaller as it floated up from the ground, turning slowly in the sunlight. *What are you doing, little fawn, so far from home?* The smooth black rock at the heart of the golden brown water was the center of a single eye, which rippled gently until it became two. *How long it's been since we have seen one another,* said the stag who stood before me.

You know how these people are, Cousin! The fox thrust his muzzle out from between the great deer's forefeet and looked up at him boldly. *Always so busy, always so sure they know how to master life that they forget how to live it.* His jaws parted in a rascally grin. *At least* this *one kept us in her heart. Welcome, Himiko! We've missed you. Can you play with us?*

Impertinent thing, the stag murmured, with an indulgent look toward the fox. *Not everyone wants to play.*

Ha! Maybe you don't, but I'll bet she does! And if she doesn't, she should. A fine time she'll have here if all she does is mope and freeze and wander without knowing which path to take. Let her play! Let her dance! Better if she lets her feet do the thinking, not her head! That old thing's too weary and muddled up inside to help her anymore. Better to go dancing down the path that pulls them than to stand fretting until she turns to stone. Dance with me, Himiko! He sprang from his haven between the stag's hooves and capered wildly on his hind legs, his bright eyes daring me to join him.

This isn't the time for me to dance with you, little one, I said quietly. *I've just come from a house of mourning. My brother's wife is dead.*

So am I, but does that stop me? The fox uttered a merry yelp and did a backflip, landing with his hindquarters raised and twitching. *Wind and fire, water and stone, none of these live the way you humans count living, but see how they all dance!*

He swished his tail, and it became a rush of countless colors that swept across my eyes and lifted me through the heavens. Silver lights glinted all around me, and I realized I was flying through the stars toward the crimson and gold line of the horizon. I raced headlong toward the dawning light. It shimmered and took the form of my amulet, the dragon stone's golden rainbow glow transformed into the glory of the sun, the woman's image reborn as the radiance of a goddess.

Welcome, Himiko! Welcome, O princess, healer, shaman! Her smile was as dazzling as her words of greeting. She reached out to me, and the sphere of light she held cradled in her arms became a cloak of undying brilliance that wrapped itself around us both until it overpowered my sight.

When I could see again, I was on solid ground once more. I looked down on rolls of white clouds that stretched away forever, then moved aside with the slow grace of grazing deer to reveal the immense shadow of the mountain where I stood. Beyond the shadow, I saw forests, fields, rivers, and farther off, mountain ranges dusted with threads of snow, veiled with drifting sheets of rain, wreathed with the rising breath of dragons.

I could sense the presence of the sun goddess all around me, hear her voice resound from earth and sky, and see her image overlaying everything my eyes beheld. Even so, at the same time, I felt she was at my side, her light around me, her hand on my shoulder, her words a tender whisper in my ear and in my heart.

Such things should never have been possible. They *weren't* possible in the waking world, but here—? The realm of the spirits set its own boundaries on possibility, and they are no boundaries at all.

Snow blanketed the summit, lapped itself around my feet, but the sun goddess's nearness shielded me from the cold. I turned slowly, sipping air that was sweet with the essence of evergreen forests, icy waterfalls, moss-furred stones, and from somewhere far within the great mountain's core, the darkly beautiful breath of ancient, smoldering fires.

This is Yama's mountain. I don't know how that thought came to me, only that I had no doubt about the truth it contained. *This is the peak I've seen so often in the distance from home. My feet are on sacred ground.* I closed my eyes and inhaled deeply, drawing the spirit of the mountain's strength and serenity into me. Then, with words I wove from dreams and love, I raised my voice in song and lifted my feet in dance.

I danced with arms wide, to hold the world, and with head flung back to let the sun bathe my face. I stamped on the snow, and my bare foot opened a zigzag crack from which streamed beasts and birds, silk-winged butterflies and jewel-eyed serpents, silvery fish and countless other creatures too wonderful to name. I heard the fox spirit call out to me, and I danced to meet him. We leaped into the sky and twined our steps through the eternal forests. We slipped beneath the earth as easily as we dove into the water, laughing when we startled drowsy moles and grouchy badgers in their burrows. We moved through water as easily as we danced through air. I was never so happy. I was never so free.

Himiko! Himiko! Where are you going? the fox spirit cried.

Where? I echoed, dancing through a tangle of winter-bare branches, a splash of springtime blossoms, a wealth of summer-shadowed grasses, and a glow of autumn-kindled leaves. *Everywhere! Oh, everywhere I can!* I closed my eyes in bliss.

But you're going too far. You're losing sight of the path to take you back again. You're caught in the winds of the spirit world and flying away from the land of the living!

What did you say? The fox spirit's words were a splash of cold water in my face. My eyes snapped open, seeking him. Nothing was there. Nothing. I was alone in a place that was no place, a void the color of smoke. *Where are you?* I called, but what I should have cried was *Where am I?*

All at once I was falling. I hit the ground with a jarring impact and sprawled on my belly over what felt like a serpent made of stone. When I caught my breath and pushed myself upright, I saw that what I'd thought was stone was actually the gnarled root of a gigantic tree. Looking around, half dazed, I saw that I was deep in a forest of looming evergreens. Their trunks were an otherworldly silver, and it would have taken five of me, with arms stretched to the limit, to encircle the smallest one. The air was damp and carried the wails, shrieks, and crazed tittering of vengeful ghosts.

Welcome, Himiko. Their voices swirled around me, mocking the goddess's greeting. *Welcome, O princess, healer, shaman. Welcome to your eternal home.*

This is not my home, I told the unseen phantoms, using all my strength to keep my body and my words from trembling. *I don't belong here.*

Don't you? Don't you? Their words piped and screeched like the song of cicadas. *Then why have you come?* The needles of the massive cypress and pine trees shook with ghostly giggles.

I don't know. I tried to lick the dryness from my lips, but my whole mouth felt parched. *But I'm going, and you can't stop me.*

Why would we have to do that when it's you who'll make the choice? The invisible ones hissed with the sound of a plunging waterfall. *How can you go back to the waking world now that you've tasted the marvels of this one? Here, nothing holds you down, nothing grieves you, nobody forces you to choose between who you are and who they want you to be. Don't you want to stay, Himiko? Don't you want to be free?*

I felt the brush of deathly cold fingers over my face, the dreadful imitation of a loving touch. My heart fluttered wildly. I took a deep breath to calm it and placed one hand on my sash. The comforting presence of my wand was there, and so was the weight of Lady Ikumi's mirror. It radiated an eerie warmth under my palm. I glanced down and saw the polished bronze glowing steadily through the cloth of my sash.

"I *am* free!" I shouted, drawing wand and mirror. My voice—my *living* voice—rang out across the spirit world. The ghosts shrieked, and I saw them as a momentary flare of tattered white shapes among the trees before they fled into the shadows. The silence rushed back to fill the forest after they were gone.

Holding the glowing mirror against my chest, I began to walk through the trees, tripping over the huge, upthrust snarl of their roots. The forest sucked away any sound I made, and aside from the evergreens, I saw no other life, not even a speck of moss or the flicker of an insect's wing.

I had no sense of time or of direction. No matter how far I walked, nothing looked different. Aside from undulations of the roots, there was no change in the flatness of the ground. I cried out into the hush surrounding me, calling to the fox spirit, to the deer spirit, to all the spirits I had known and seen and sensed in this place, and above all, to my lost lady of the dragon stone, my goddess. But no call answered mine, no sound reached my ear, my mind, or my heart.

At last, I sat down with my back against a pine tree. Had the fox been right? Had I wandered so far that I could never find my way back to the living world? And now that I was trapped within the world of the spirits, was I also doomed to wander here alone forever? I sighed and glanced at the mirror resting in my lap. At least my own reflection would be better than no company at all.

But when I gazed into the mirror, my image was not alone.

So you've come to me at last. In the gleaming bronze surface, a young man's face appeared just behind my left shoulder. I gasped and threw myself to one side, twisting sharply to face him.

Who are you? Where did you come from? What do you want from me? I demanded as I scrabbled to gather up my fallen wand and mirror. My mind reeled with shock and disbelief. There had been no room between my back and the pine tree's trunk for a lizard to fit, let alone a human being.

He knelt beside the monumental trunk of the pine tree, his long black hair cloaking a sky-blue tunic tied with gold, his dark eyes smiling. *Can it be that you fear me, Himiko? Just now I saw you defy and scatter a multitude of ghosts. That's not the action of a timid girl.*

He rose slowly and held out his hand, offering to help

me to my feet. I hesitated only a moment, then took it and stood. *I'm not afraid of you,* I said. I wanted to say more, but my speech deserted me. I was looking into eyes that spoke to mine, gazing at a face I'd never seen before but that I'd known forever. I was safely on my feet, yet I did not let go of his hand, and he did not pull it away from mine.

I didn't think you were, he said. *The abruptness of my appearance must have startled you, but now you remember how things are in this world. You danced above the clouds and into the dark warmth of the earth; I moved through the green heart of this forest. Can you accept that we both walk a path that's laced with magic?*

Who are you? I asked again.

Someone much like you, he replied. *Someone who feels the threads that bind life to life and who crosses the boundaries that keep world from world. Prince and healer and shaman.*

But your name—?

Do I need one?

You know mine.

Yes, Himiko, I do. He brushed a strand of hair away from my face. A delicious thrill ran over my skin. *Let me be Reikon, then, since you won't be happy otherwise.*

Is that who you are?

No, only my name. Who I am is someone who wants to purify your spirit of everything that troubles you, everything that's making you sink farther from the living world because it seems so much easier to surrender and let go.

I smiled at him. *But I didn't surrender,* I said. *You saw that for yourself when I faced the ghosts; you said so! And I'm not going to surrender now, lost in this forest. I'll find my way back to the sacred mountaintop, back to where my goddess waits, back to the realm of the living. I can do it.*

I know you can. He clasped his hands over mine so that both of us held my mirror and my wand. *And—with your consent—I'll help you.* I felt his lips touch my brow, and for an instant I forgot what it was to breathe.

Reikon raised my hands in his. The mirror we held glowed brighter, and a breeze sweet with the scent of cherry blossoms blew around us. I heard familiar laughter, gentle and loving. Hoshi's ghost floated above us, clothed in a gown of wind-ruffled petals. *Himiko!* she cried joyously, and pressed her cheek to mine.

Hoshi! Oh, Hoshi, forgive me! I wrenched my hands free, leaving Reikon to hold the mirror and the wand as I embraced her. *I should have taken better care of you! I should have stayed with you! I should have—!*

You did what was right, she answered serenely. *You did all that could be done. If you ever loved me, forgive yourself, for my sake. Not even you could have saved my life, not with all your skills nor all your magic.* She took my hand and set my fingertips to her chest. *I didn't die because you failed me, Himiko. Something inside me was weak and would have worn out sooner or later, sickness or no. My body simply . . . stopped. My spirit flew. It wasn't what you did or didn't do, it was* time, *only time, inescapable as an encircling fire, fragile and fleeting as this:* she plucked a handful of petals from her gown and blew them into the air.

They became a storm of pink and white, a cloud that hid Hoshi's spirit from sight. Her words had lifted the last weight of guilt from my heart, leaving my spirit so light that

I found myself racing up a path of nothing but petals and air, a path that spiraled into the heavens. I laughed, jubilant.

Wait for me, Himiko! Reikon's hand closed on mine. He drew me back a pace and encircled my waist with one arm. He matched me step for step in the dance until we balanced perfectly on the topmost blossom. *Have you forgotten these?* His free arm reached around me to offer back the mirror and the wand.

I turned within his embrace and for the first time felt warm, human breath from his lips touch my cheek. The shock of it dazed me. *Reikon, are you real?* I asked my spirit prince. *Are you alive, like me?*

"Real"? Which side of the mirror are you asking? he replied, his smile as mischievous as a small boy's. He placed my wand and mirror in my hands. *They are objects of great power, gateways to those who know how to use them. We hold the mirror and the mirror holds us. It can hold the world, and worlds are mirrors of each other. Look there, Himiko. See the truth of what I say.*

Still holding me close, he gestured with his free hand, directing my sight to gaze down from our place among the clouds. My eyes grew wide with wonder, my vision expanding to take in all that stretched beneath us.

This time I saw much more than the earth that lay in the shadow of the sacred mountain. I poised, breathless, to behold the great expanse of water that lay at the farthest reaches of the land. Craggy rocks lifted their ancient heads from the foaming crash of waves. Pine trees that had been twisted into fantastic, exquisite shapes by seasons of salty winds clung to the stones. In the deep waters, the sleek backs of titanic creatures curved above the surface and sank back beneath the foam. Gusts of mist spouted from their heads before they dove from sight. The waters where they danced went on forever.

Look back now, Himiko. Reikon's voice resonated through me. *There is the sea that gave us our home, but turn your eyes toward the land again.*

Hovering beside him, I looked down once more and saw that the land beneath me was not a single mass, but many. Four great islands spread their bounty over a sea that also cradled innumerable smaller ones. Somewhere among the marvels and blessings of this grandeur lay my home.

No, I thought. Not somewhere, *but everywhere. All of this is my home, and not just mine alone.*

Do you see those lights scattered everywhere? Reikon asked. *Those are the spirits of the living—mothers, fathers, children, the old, the young, the loved and the lonely, all! See how they cluster there! That is the home of your people, the Matsu clan. And there you see the lives of the Shika in their mountain realm, and on that sliver of coast, the Kamoshika, and there the Ookami, and there, and there, and there—!*

So many, I whispered, awestruck. *But . . . why so weak?*

It was so. The innumerable lights were very dim, and some were flickering low. For a reason I couldn't name, it made me apprehensive to see those countless sparks in danger of being blown into nothingness by the next faint breeze. Mothers, fathers, children, all, I wanted to cup my hands around their light, shelter it, make it strong, and turn it into a single flame burning with such pure light that nothing would have the power to extinguish it.

Is that what you want, Himiko? Reikon walked through

my thoughts, hearing them as surely as if I'd spoken aloud. *Then do it. Stretch out your hand. Weave the spell that will save your people, all your people and not just the clans you know.*

I heeded his words. I raised my right hand, holding the cherry branch, and swept it over lights burning low across the land. Light touched light and brightened. Clan met clan and each renewed the other. Old fears and mistrusts long aimed at outlanders were herded away into the ebbing darkness. I'd never felt such joy.

Well done, Himiko. My lady of the dragon stone rose before us, her beauty bright against the sky. Her presence had become so vast that she stood tiptoe on the summit of the holy mountain, now no more than a snowcapped pebble at her feet. My spirit fluttered on her breath. *Well done, O princess, healer, shaman, chieftess, queen!* She raised one hand, and the islands that were my people's home became a golden chain the sun goddess wore closest to her heart.

Chieftess? I whispered as her words and her image began to fade before my eyes. *Queen? But I'll never—*

Well done, my love. My spirit prince's human breath was on my lips in the instant before he kissed me and vanished as I woke back into the living world.

18
A ROAD OF DREAMS

"Are you sure you saw her eyes open?" Lady Ikumi's voice was muffled and indistinct, a confusion of sounds. I had to work hard to string them into words.

"I did!" Kaya declared. My friend's clear, assured tone brought my senses sharply into focus. "I'm not just making it up because I want it to be true. It is! Watch closely and you'll see, Mother. I told you it was a good idea to put her talisman in her hands!"

My fingers flexed. I encountered the familiar touch of my amulet. I lifted it slightly and was amazed to see my face reflected perfectly in the glittering golden curve of the dragon stone. Was that another face beside mine? I strained to see, but then I blinked and it was gone.

"Oh, I *did* see that!" Lady Ikumi exclaimed.

Kaya snorted. "*Anyone* could have seen that."

"Then she's out of danger at last. Thank the gods,

but"—Lady Ikumi's voice dropped—"now we'll have to tell her."

"Not right away!" Kaya protested. "Something like that is too—"

"Of *course* not right away. Do you think I'm a fool?" her mother snapped. "I'm worried about *how* to tell her, not when."

"Tell me what?" I shaded my eyes with one hand and looked up into the weary faces of Kaya and Lady Ikumi.

"Oh! Himiko!" The Shika chieftess was taken by surprise, just as I would have been in her place. It wasn't usual for a sick person to go from deep sleep to full wakefulness so abruptly. She leaned over me and wiped my brow with a damp cloth. "You've been very sick. I never saw a fever burn so hot without killing. We thought we would lose you."

"You were talking through your fever," Kaya said. "Sometimes it just sounded like a lot of nonsense, but sometimes you spoke so clearly that we thought the fever had broken and that you were awake again." She frowned and looked at me closely. "You *are* awake now, aren't you?"

"Yes." The word was not much more than a whisper. I let my hand drop to my side and lowered my eyelids. "I'm thirsty."

Someone put an arm under my back and helped me sit up. I opened my eyes as Kaya was putting a cup of water to my lips. I sipped it the way a bird does. When I was done, I smiled and shrugged off her supporting arm. "Thank you, Kaya. That was just what I needed. I can sit up by myself now."

"No, you can't," Lady Ikumi declared. She put her left arm behind me and laid her right hand on my shoulder, gently urging me back down. "I'm not going to let you overtire yourself. You heard me, Himiko: You were sick for many days. Your life was in danger. We heard you talking to people who weren't there."

I wanted to tell her that there was more to my rambling words than the tricks of fever, but I didn't know how to speak about all that I had seen and experienced in the world of the spirits. Instead, I clasped the Shika shaman's hand and said, "I heard you talking too, Lady Ikumi. You were fretting about *how* you were going to tell me something when I woke. Well, I'm awake now. What do you have to tell me? Just say it."

"Later, after you've had a *healthy* sleep."

"Not later," I said firmly. "Now."

She avoided my gaze. "You're not strong enough. It's too cruel."

"Mother, it's crueler to leave her wondering!" Kaya cried. "Himiko is strong enough to hear it. *Tell* her. If you don't, I will."

"All right. If I must." Lady Ikumi wound her fingers together in her lap. "The sickness took you with the violence of a landslide. I feared you'd be dead before the next sunrise. When that didn't happen, I gave thanks, but I knew that you weren't out of danger. When your fever rose even higher and you began to rave, I made a decision: as soon as our time of mourning for Hoshi was over, I'd send a messenger to your clan. If the gods were merciful, he'd only have to tell them that you were gravely ill; if not, he'd need to be eloquent enough to persuade your father not to hold the Shika liable for your death."

She sighed and waited a moment before adding, "He would also have to bring your brother the news that Hoshi was gone."

I took a closer look at Kaya and her mother. They were no longer wearing hemp garments. "How many days have you been out of mourning?" I asked.

"At least twelve," Kaya told me.

I was sick that long? I thought, astonished. *No, it must be even longer than that. They'd just begun the formal time of grieving when the fever took me.* "So many days," I murmured. "You kept me alive for so many days. . . ."

"It was Kaya's doing," Lady Ikumi said. "She found the way to make you drink and take a little nourishment without choking on it."

Kaya shrugged away her mother's praise. "It was no different than giving her medicine."

"At any rate, the time came, and I summoned one of my best men to bear the news to your clan. He was gone longer than expected. I began to fear that he'd suffered an accident while traveling through the mountains—a fall, an encounter with a wild beast, a snakebite. Then I worried that he'd reached your village and the news he brought was so ill received that he was made to suffer for it."

"My father would never do such a thing to an innocent messenger," I said, indignant.

"I know that, Himiko," Lady Ikumi soothed me. "But when you're responsible for another human being, sometimes you fret first and think sensibly later."

"Well, what *was* the matter?" I asked with growing anxiety. "Why was the man delayed? Did the great sickness strike my clanfolk too? Is my family all right? Where's the messenger? Let me speak to him! I want to know what he saw in our village. I have to ask him—"

"He never entered your village. He didn't dare."

My stomach knotted. "Why not?" I whispered. Kaya held my hand tightly as her mother went on.

"He told me that when he came down out of the mountains and began the approach to your village, he sensed that something wasn't right. There was an awful smell of burning on the air—not just the normal scent of cook fires or the blacksmith's forge, but an evil reek that warned him to keep his distance. Wisely he clung to the edge of the woods high on the mountainside, staying far out of sight until he could discover what had happened. He has good eyes, that man. He saw that the village gates were shattered and that the watchtower had been pulled down. Smoke was still rising from the smoldering ruins of many houses. Worst of all, he spied a train of people leaving the village two by two, each pair carrying a large storage jar slung from a pole between them. Armed men were overseeing them as they trudged away. There were—" She paused and took a shuddering breath. "There were rope halters around their necks, the mark of slaves. Himiko, war came to your clan, and . . . they lost. The Matsu have been conquered."

"No." I imagined I heard the throbbing of my heart trying to drown out those dreadful words. "It's not possible. Please, it can't be so."

But Lady Ikumi's expression held the grim truth as she

continued. "My messenger spent several days in hiding, hoping to find a way to learn the details of what happened. That was why his return was delayed so long. One night he was able to steal inside the palisade, but it almost ended badly. Two of the invaders came around the corner of a house and nearly surprised him. He clung to the shadows and was saved only by the fact that those men had been drinking heavily. They staggered past without seeing him and he fled as soon as he could, but not before overhearing them brag to one another about their chieftain's ruthlessness and the heroes' welcome waiting for them all when they returned to the lands of the Ookami clan."

I bolted upright at the mention of that name, though my head spun for it. "Are you sure?" It was the first I'd thought of the wolf people in years. The image of their chieftain's haughty, arrogant son, Ryu, flashed through my mind and brought back ugly memories. "Lord Nago of the Ookami came to us once, wanting to form an alliance with the Matsu, to take over other clans. Father turned him down. That was many seasons ago. If he was going to attack us, why did he wait so long?"

"Lord Nago?" Lady Ikumi repeated.

"The Ookami chieftain those drunkards were so proud to serve," I said bitterly.

"My man *did* hear them mention their chieftain's name, but it wasn't Nago; it was Ryu." She peered at me and frowned. "Himiko, please lie down. Your skin has just turned the color of snow."

Mutely I obeyed her. Ryu's handsome, leering face and casually brutal words came out of the past to turn my blood to frost. My cheek tingled as though he'd just slapped it again. I had a vision of my village, my people, helpless under his rule, slaves of a man who took what he wanted and showed blatant contempt for any human life except his own.

"Did your messenger—" I clutched my amulet tighter, taking strength from the goddess. "When he was inside our palisade, did your messenger happen to overhear anything else? Anything about . . . about my family?"

Lady Ikumi shook her head. "We know nothing. After his near encounter with the Ookami soldiers, he fled your village. He's brave, but how can I blame him for not wanting to test the limits of his luck? He brought no news at all about what became of your parents, or Aki, or . . . or . . ." Pity broke her voice. She began to cry.

I put my arms around her, too stunned to weep. Kaya hugged us both. We sat there together like that for some time, until Lady Ikumi recovered her composure enough to speak.

"You are now my daughter, Himiko," she said, her tone implying that the decision was made and not to be disputed or changed. "As soon as you're well enough, we will celebrate your adoption into the Shika clan. I want your cheeks to bear the same tattoo marks as mine and Kaya's. Your place with us will be secure, now and always. My older son has no real interest in ruling the clan when I'm dead, but Kaya will make a fine chieftess. When that time comes, you will serve your new sister as our shaman. Until then, I'll teach you any part of our lore you might not know. Were you ever taught how to read the future from the cracks in a burnt bone? We use the shoulder blades of deer, but perhaps the Matsu had another meth—" She stopped suddenly and looked ashamed.

I broke the awkward silence quickly. "My people aren't all dead, Lady Ikumi. The Matsu still survive. I thank you with all my heart for opening your home to me and wanting to make me part of your family, but I *have* a family—alive or dead, I have them. I must return home to learn their fate. When I have my strength back, I'll go."

"I forbid it!" Lady Ikumi's eyes flashed fire. "Winter is here. To cross the mountains now will kill you."

"Mother, please." Kaya clasped the Shika chieftess's wrist. "It's colder, but there's been no snow yet, not even on the high paths. If she's well, she can make the journey safely."

"I won't let her chance it." Lady Ikumi's face was dark and hard, rejecting any arguments. "If you don't care about her enough to protect her from herself, I do!"

"I'd never risk my friend's life if I weren't willing to risk my own," Kaya replied in a voice as steady and commanding as her mother's. "When she goes, I go."

"No! I refuse to allow—"

"Mother, are we your daughters, or are we your slaves?" Kaya asked softly.

The question struck home. Lady Ikumi was speechless. The struggle in her heart showed plainly on her face, but at last she regained the dignity befitting a clan chieftess and spoke: "You are my daughters. Go if you must, travel safely, come back alive and well, and walk with my blessing."

◆ ◆ ◆

Once she accepted the fact that Kaya and I were going to return to my village, Lady Ikumi became quite clever about finding ways to ensure I didn't set out on the road home until I'd recovered all my strength. She brought two tightly woven baskets into the house and filled them both with rice. They weren't as big and heavy as the clay jugs usually employed for storing grain, but when filled, they were weighty enough.

"The clan that conquered your people probably took most of their provisions," she said. "This rice will be a life-saving gift this winter."

Kaya hoisted one of the baskets onto her back. "I can carry this, but not both," she said. "I'm sorry."

"Your mother never intended for you to carry both," I said. I glanced at Lady Ikumi in time to catch the sly smile on her lips. "When I can handle the other basket, we'll be ready to go."

If the Shika chieftess thought she was putting an im-movable obstacle in my way by challenging me with the weight of the rice basket, she soon learned better. I turned her obstacle into my goal, eating heartily, exercising as much as I could without pushing myself to exhaustion, and forcing myself to sleep without worrying over what I'd find waiting for me when Kaya and I finally returned to my home. This last task was the hardest, and not one I accom-plished completely. At least my dreams remained untrou-bled, so that once I escaped from my waking worries, I rested well.

When the day of our departure came, Kaya's older

brother put up a strenuous argument with Lady Ikumi, insisting that she should send a party of Shika warriors to accompany us.

"Why? To protect them on the road?" she asked. "Your sister Kaya can do that for herself. You know she's a skilled huntress and can shoot bigger game than birds with her bow. It will be wiser for her and Lady Himiko to return to the Matsu village as unobtrusively as possible, not with an armed escort."

"It will also be best for your own people," I told him. "I know the new Ookami chieftain. He's greedy for conquest. Our village might not be enough to settle his appetite, and yours isn't that far away from mine. You want to have all your fighting men here, on the alert, if the Ookami should come."

Lady Ikumi hugged me. "I doubt they'll make another foray before spring, but thank you for thinking of us, dear one."

There were more hugs and kisses and many tears to see us off. We marched away from the Shika village not knowing what awaited us among my people or when we'd see Kaya's clanfolk again.

Our journey through the mountains was without incident. It had been a long time since I'd taken the path that I'd walked so often with Aki, but I hadn't forgotten the way. Kaya and I traveled as swiftly as we could, wasting little time over meals. It was all she could do to make me stop for the night. I wanted to get home now, at once, immediately! My anxiety for my people and my keen yearning to learn what had become of my family turned me into a boulder rolling down the mountainside, mindless and unstoppable.

Luckily for me, Kaya knew how to reason with stones. "You want to keep going after the sun's down? Fine, go ahead. I'll spend the night here and catch up to you in the morning. Just be sure to yell my name as loudly as you can so I can find you when I have to haul you out of the ravine where you've fallen in the dark. You *can* still yell when you've got a broken skull, right?" I grumbled, but I gave in.

Our last night on the road, we made camp in a grove of pines with low-growing branches. There was plenty of deadwood to feed the small fire Kaya kindled to comfort us. When we finished eating, we huddled together for warmth fully clothed, layered between our bedrolls. "I feel like a caterpillar," Kaya announced.

"Moth or butterfly?"

She giggled. "Only you would ask a question like that."

"Well, whichever one you turn out to be, you'd better come out of your cocoon early," I said. "We'll reach my home tomorrow."

She shifted onto her side and looked at me. "What do you think we'll find there, Himiko?" she asked softly.

"I don't know." I stared up at the canopy of pine boughs sheltering us. It was a clear night, and the stars were caught in a net of fragrant needles. "If I think about it, my mind swings back and forth. One moment I picture a scene of utter destruction, nothing left but bones and ashes. The next, I see my village exactly as it was when I left it. The gates are open, my family and kin are streaming out to welcome us, and everyone's asking, 'Whatever happened to that messenger the Shika chieftess sent us? Does she *know* what a miserable liar he is?'"

"I hope you're right about that second one," Kaya said. "That way, once you've seen your family again, you can go to him."

"Him?"

"Your sweetheart," she replied. "The one whose name you kept calling out when you were sick: Reikon. I want to meet him."

I laughed so hard that my friend must have thought I'd lost my mind. I laughed myself breathless, and when I was through, I found that laughter had freed my tongue. I no longer had to grope for the right way to tell Kaya about what I'd experienced while in the fever's grasp. Instead, I spoke of it candidly, naturally, without worrying whether she'd accept what I said. I told her everything about the journey that I'd made through the spirit world, and about encountering her sister's benevolent spirit, and about the prince who led me from the ghost wood back to the sun goddess's shining presence.

"And after all the amazing things that I experienced in that realm, Kaya, there's one alone that I still can't believe: I love him. He was a stranger to me, but almost at once I felt that our lives were bound to one another. I knew nothing about him—not even if he was real—yet I was so strongly drawn to him, soul to soul, that it didn't matter. It was uncanny."

"Maybe not so uncanny." My friend smiled. "You *did* say he was handsome."

"It was more than that," I said. "I've seen other handsome faces. They can mask ugly hearts."

"But not always," she pointed out airily. "At least, I hope not. I'd hate to think that every time I've fallen in love with a good-looking boy, I wasted my time flirting with an ogre in disguise." In a more serious tone, she said, "You're a shaman, Himiko. You walked among the spirits. You had a vision grander than anything I've ever heard. You stood in the shadow of the sun goddess herself. If anyone should believe that miraculous things can happen, it's you."

"You may be right." I sighed. "And if you are, what difference does it make? He belongs to the world of the spirits, not to mine."

"I thought that you belonged to both." Kaya yawned. "I hope that's true, but if you disagree, let it wait until morning. I'm tired. Good night, Moth."

I smiled. "Good night, Butterfly."

Dawn woke us, and we set out on the last small portion of our journey. As we walked on, the woods around us took on a much-loved familiarity. My feet trod a path that was part of me, flesh and spirit, and I breathed the air of home.

We didn't go rushing blindly out of the forest's concealment. I thought it best to take the same precautions as Lady Ikumi's messenger and observe my village from a distance first. It was likely that all of the Ookami war party had returned to their land with the spoils they'd taken from our clan, but it wasn't certain. If any of them lingered, Kaya and I would need to know and plan our next move accordingly.

I led my friend to a place on the mountainside that I knew would give us a good, extensive view of the village. My heart shrank as I saw that Lady Ikumi's messenger had told the truth. The harsh evidence of that lay plain before my eyes: broken gates and burned houses, the toppled watchtower and the great gaps in our palisade, the collapsed walls of our moat, and worst of all, the scorched and splintered trunk of what had been the Matsu clan's ancestral symbol, the sacred pine. The wolves had torn it down.

"Himiko? Himiko, Sister, are you all right? Can I help?" Kaya touched my hand gently. Her caring words brought me back from the edge of despair.

"I'm— I'll be fine," I said. "Look. It's bad, but not as bad as it could be. I don't see any sign of outlanders. I think we can go ahead safely, but first—first there's something that I need to do."

I stepped back into the shelter of the forest and knelt. I set out my mirror and the bare wand of cherrywood that I had picked from a blooming tree a lifetime ago. I took the smallest pinch of rice I could from my basket, scattered it over the ground, clapped my hands to call upon the spirits, and began a rite to purify my people from the wounds of war the Ookami had slashed across their souls.

Even with home in sight, I realized that I still didn't know everything that might be waiting for me at my journey's end. As much as my heart ached for the pain and loss my people had suffered, I knew nothing of how each person had been stricken. There would be wounds I couldn't heal, but I would try.

When I had walked into the mirror of the spirit world, I was granted a vision of great beauty and great hope. Both had the power to heal. I would follow where my vision led me, and I would share its magic to bring strength, faith, and comfort to my people. I would teach them what I knew, that all things were mirrored. What was destroyed could be rebuilt, what was broken could be made whole.

I rose with my mirror held to the sky, my wand sweeping back and forth to clear away the presence of any lingering evil.

"Himiko?" Kaya's voice was faint and trembling. She was standing a respectful distance away, pointing at me with a shaking hand. "Himiko . . . Himiko, look. Look at your wand, *look*!"

I turned my head. The dark, dead wood was ruddy. The bumps and nodes along the branch had burst into clusters of pink blossom. I blinked and shook my head, but what I saw remained. The fragrance of a vanished springtime wafted over me, cleansing the air of the stench of destruction.

"Is it real?" Kaya called to me. "We aren't dreaming this, are we? You see it too?"

"Yes," I said. "Oh yes, I see it." I touched the silky petals to my cheek. "It's real." *As real as hope,* I thought. *As real as love.*

If anyone should believe in miraculous things . . .

Holding the sun goddess's eternal light in my heart, I danced.

LADY OF THE "QUEEN'S COUNTRY"

May I have the pleasure of introducing you to Himiko? You might not have known much about her before opening this book, but I hope that you'd like to learn more. If you've read my other Princesses of Myth novels, you might be asking yourself whether she belongs to the realm of myth, like Helen of Troy, or to the pages of history, like Nefertiti.

The answer? A little of both.

I don't know how or when I came to learn about Himiko of Japan. Perhaps I first encountered her in a book about Japanese history, or about great women of the past. It might have happened when I was leafing through the *Early Samurai* volume of Osprey's illustrated military guides. Hers is the very first image in the plates showing an artist's rendition of Japanese warriors. But while Himiko was definitely a fighter, her weapon was not the sword or the halberd or the bow and arrow.

Her weapon was magic.

Himiko and her people, the Yayoi, lived in an age before Japan was united and ruled by emperors who claimed descent from the sun goddess, Amaterasu. Her clan was one of many, and the different clans often went to war with each other. There is much discussion about the identity of the Yayoi, where they came from, and whether they completely displaced earlier inhabitants of Japan (the Jomon, who might well have been the ancestors of Japan's Ainu population) or assimilated them through intermarriage. They were the first to bring paddy cultivation of rice to Japan.

The Yayoi were farmers, hunters, and merchants. They traded with the mainland through Chinese outposts in Korea. It is thanks to this international trade that Himiko's name enters history.

The *Chronicles of Wei* comes from third-century China and describes a journey to the land of the Wa people (the Chinese name for the Yayoi). It contains extremely detailed information about their appearance, dress, and customs, and the plants, animals, and minerals found in their country. Around AD 238, Queen Himiko of Wa sent an envoy with valuable gifts as tribute for the ruler of the kingdom of Wei, in northern China. This diplomatic gesture was intended to foster friendly relations between the two realms, and it succeeded. The ruler of Wei responded in kind, sending Queen Himiko many rich presents and issuing an imperial edict that said, "Himiko, queen of Wa, is designated a friend of Wei." It is most likely because of Himiko that the Chinese referred to Japan as the Queen's Country.

A delegation of royal representatives from Wei was dispatched to Himiko's court, and it is their description of the journey and what they found on arrival that provides nearly all our information about this astonishingly powerful woman and her people (outside of archaeological discoveries, of course).

Himiko's status as queen of Wa was established years before this exchange of tribute and the arrival of the Chinese envoys at her capital of Yamatai. The *Chronicles of Wei* says that until she came to rule, the land of Wa suffered "chaos as they fought each other." How was Himiko able to put an end to this time of war between the Yayoi clans? To find the answer, we have to trust the Chinese records, because the people of Wa did not yet have a written language. And what do those records say?

"She was skilled in the Way of Demons, keeping all under her spell."

"The Way of Demons" makes Himiko sound dreadfully sinister, but we should remember that the person writing about her was a foreign visitor who probably lacked a complete understanding of the Yayoi. From his description, it would be easy to picture the queen of Wa as an evil sorceress when she was actually a shaman.

We all tend to fear the unknown, especially when disaster strikes, and seek to deal with our fears by finding ways to explain what happened. If we can find a reason for floods, droughts, storms, famines, and epidemics—*whether or not it's the right reason*—we might feel less overwhelmed and terrified. We can even tell ourselves that since we know *why* these catastrophes happen, we're one step closer to being able to control and prevent them. The shaman's function is part of this very understandable human desire to make the world a little more manageable and a little less wild and frightening.

Shamans have existed in many cultures and in many times, including the present day. They perform a number of important roles to help and comfort their people. Some human societies believe that the world is filled with spirits. Plants and animals, earth and sky, fields and forests, anything can harbor them. Some are good spirits who help mankind and receive thanks, but some can be evil, bringing sickness or other harm, and are greatly feared. Among these are the spirits of the dead. Even today, when most people declare that they don't believe in ghosts, many others still do and are afraid of them.

The shaman helps people to deal with their fears about the spirits by acting as a go-between. Shamans are supposed to be able to speak to the spirits, to find out what offerings they want in exchange for their goodwill, to heal people and protect them from malicious spirits, and even to leave their own bodies and enter the spirit world. Some cultures believe that shamans also have the ability to control and command both good and evil spirits, and some shamans may take advantage of this belief because it gives them great authority and influence.

It is possible that this is what Himiko did, although her reasons for doing so were unselfish: she wanted her land to be at peace and used her sway as a spiritual leader to make it so. How did she do this? There's no way we can know for sure, since the Chinese chronicles don't go into detail about it, but we can guess. My own theory is that she reminded the warring clans about her powers over the spirits—especially the spirits of the dead—and warned them that if they didn't stop fighting, she would call up an army of ghosts to make them settle their differences. How could anyone hope to win a battle against the dead? Who would even want to *try* facing something so terrifying?

Whether or not this was what Himiko did to secure peace, something worked, and she went on to rule the land of Wa for many tranquil, prosperous years. Not bad for a young woman who never had to raise sword or spear to establish and hold her throne!

There is more to Himiko's story—in both my own version of her unknown girlhood and the Chinese records. I hope you'll enjoy discovering it all.

This is *not* the life one envisions
for a princess!

Himiko's exhilarating story concludes in

SPIRIT'S CHOSEN

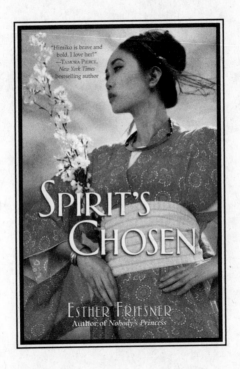

Available now!

Excerpt copyright © 2013 by Esther Friesner.
Published by Random House Children's Books,
a division of Random House, Inc., New York.

FROM *SPIRIT'S CHOSEN*

I began to weep without a sound. Tears bathed my face before I realized I was crying. When the first sob broke from my throat, Kaya already had her arms around me, my face resting against her shoulder.

"You're not talking about the blossoms, are you," she said. It was not a question. "I understand. Don't worry, Himiko. Whatever's waiting for you down there, you won't face it alone. Those flowers carried a message from the gods, and messengers don't linger once their job is done. The news they bring doesn't change after they leave. You called those flowers a *good* sign, right?" I nodded. "So we've *still* got favorable omens on our side. Don't you dare deny it!"

I raised my face and had to smile. It was good to hear my friend sounding like herself again: Lady Badger was back in all her gruff, stubborn glory. My distress let her set aside her own misgivings to help me through mine.

"I won't," I replied. "But . . . suppose I was wrong?"

Kaya snorted, sending the snowflakes flying crazily around us. "Next thing, you'll be claiming that none of it ever happened, that it was another one of your visions."

"It might as well have been a dream," I said. "There's no way to prove it was real."

"Oh, it was real enough, I'll swear to that. Maybe *you* could imagine something so fanciful, but not me, never. I'm a hunter, Himiko. I don't jump at shadows, and I only see what's there. Once we bring you home, you're going to tell everyone in the village about what we saw here. Who's better than their shaman to bring such cheering news? The gods know, they'll need it."

"I'm not their shaman, Kaya," I whispered. "Have you ever heard of any clan with two?"

"Maybe . . ." My friend took a deep breath. "I don't like saying this, but maybe your people no longer *have* a shaman."

"No!" I pushed Kaya away so violently that she staggered. "Don't say—don't even *imagine* such a thing! Master Michio's alive. The Ookami wouldn't dare kill a man who can command the spirits."

My friend looked at me with pity. "Himiko, it was war. The wolf clan wouldn't have hesitated to strike down anyone in their way, shaman or not."

"Stop it!" I cried, clenching my fists so hard that I drove the cherrywood wand painfully into my palm. "I don't want to hear this!"

"But you'll have to face it soon," Kaya said.

"I know that! I know, and I'll face everything—our plundered storehouses, our ruined homes, our wounded and . . . and our dead. I won't hide from any of what's waiting for me, but until I *must* do so—" I fought to calm myself again. "Until I *must* see who's missing, let me go on believing that everyone dear to me survived. *Please, Kaya.*"

She came back toward me and took my hand. "If that's what you want."

We continued our way down the hillside. As we walked, Kaya spoke about countless matters, great and small. I think she wanted to distract me from fretting over the fate of my clan. I had my own way of doing that. Though reason told me that each step I took brought me closer to a bitter reality, my heart persisted in believing I would find a fresh miracle waiting within our village gates: in the midst of war's destruction, my family would be untouched.

I pictured my welcome home exactly as I wanted it to be. Father would scowl when he saw me and give me a harsh tongue-lashing for having run away. Strange, how strongly I hoped he'd turn the full force of his temper against me. It would mean that the Ookami conquest had not broken him completely, that a spark of strength still glowed in his heart, and most important of all, that he'd survived.

As for the rest of my family, Mama's warm greeting would interrupt Father's scolding as she took me into her arms while his junior wives, Yukari and Emi, looked on, smiling. Our three little ones, Takehiko, Sanjirou, and my special favorite, Noboru, would try to swarm into my lap long before I could sit down. My older brothers would be there too, though someone might have to go fetch them from their work. Masa would enter the house still smelling of the smoke of the blacksmith's forge, but Shoichi and Aki would carry in a strong confusion of scents—the keen air of first snowfall mixed with the reek of sweat from their labors rebuilding our village.

There was only one part of my imagined return that filled my heart with pain: the inevitable moment when I'd have to tell Aki that his beloved wife, Hoshi, was gone.

When I'd first found the Shika clan, my father and eldest brother had come to bring me home. That was when Aki encountered Kaya's sister Hoshi and fell hopelessly in love. She returned his feelings with all her heart, but there was little hope that they could be together: Father nursed a burning distrust of anyone not born a Matsu, and would never consent to his heir marrying outside of our clan. In spite of this, Aki and Hoshi wed in secret and lived apart. He and I shared high hopes that a time would come when Father's hostile attitude changed, but before that day could dawn, a great sickness swept through the Shika village. I used the healing skills taught me by our former shaman, Lady Yama, and while I was able to help many recover, Hoshi died. As much as I blamed myself, I prayed that Aki wouldn't blame me more.

As I let my imagination dance, Kaya and I reached the road leading to the ruined village gates. I could see the rice paddies, bare and cold at that time of year. The harvest was gathered in, but how much of it remained with my people? I could tell myself that all my family were waiting for me, but I couldn't pretend that the Ookami had left without taking our stores of rice for themselves. The phantoms of imminent hunger and desolation loomed over the land, banishing the last of my comforting fancies.

No one challenged us as we crossed what was left of the moat, no one greeted us as we entered the gates, no one was there. The smell of smoke hung on the chill air, but not the welcome aroma of cooking fires or the sharper tang of the potter's firing kiln or my brother Masa's forge. This smell carried a hint of dreadful things, vague horrors whose ghostly voices whispered all around me. Their message was too faint to understand, but its meaning was somehow still starkly plain: *Lost, lost, lost! So much destroyed, so much gone forever, so much darkness left behind!*

I stopped about ten paces inside the village border and felt tears sting my eyes as I took in the sights. Some homes still stood—a random number of the raised houses belonging to the Matsu nobility and the thatch-roofed pit houses where simpler folk lived—but many were scarred by fire. A few were nothing more than blackened holes in the ground. I couldn't look at the charred ruins without picturing the people who had lived in each one and wondering—fearing—what had become of them.

Kaya took my hand and squeezed it. "You're seeing it the way it was, aren't you?" she asked. I could only nod. A fresh sob was rising in my throat, choking me. It was one thing to see my clan's fate from a distance, another to stand in the midst of it, where every toppled structure and every obliterated home was haunted by the faces of my kin. Whether they'd loved me or scorned me, they were still a part of me. How many of them were alive?

I hadn't seen a single person since entering the gates. Only the faint sounds of activity coming from the nearest remaining houses proved that some of my clanfolk still lived. But my family . . . where were they in all this desolation? The time for telling myself cheerful fantasies was over. Only truth reigned here.

"Come, Kaya," I said, forcing myself to speak firmly. "We're going to my house now. I have to see who—"

"Himiko?" A familiar voice sounded weakly from the shadows of a pit house. Master Michio peered out into the milky light of that snowy day. He took one uncertain step forward, then another. He looked haggard and exhausted, his eyes rimmed with red and sunk into dark circles, but once he realized he was seeing me and not a vision, his face became radiant with smiles. "Ah, it is you, my dear! You've come back to us, may the spirits be praised. How are you? Where have you been? When did you—?"

I raced to him so swiftly that my bad leg nearly tripped me up. I staggered, but he hurried forward to save me from a fall. My relief at finding him alive was so great that I couldn't help laughing, but my joy echoed strangely in the pall of emptiness hanging over our village.

I took a deep breath and steadied myself, then stepped back from him and bent to retrieve my wand. It had fallen from my hand when I'd stumbled. The twig so recently bright with miraculous blossoms was now covered with dirt. I brushed it clean before securing it in my sash. Only then did I clap my hands in the prescribed gesture of respect for greeting my friend and teacher.

Master Michio observed all of this and chuckled. "So

formal? That's not how things were between us. What did I do to offend you?"

"I am the one who has offended," I replied. "I went away because Father would never consent to my being a shaman, and when you spoke up for me, you suffered for it."

"Suffered? I wouldn't say so much myself. However . . ." Master Michio turned his face to the sky and peered up into the dancing snowflakes. "However, if we three stay outside in this weather much longer, my bones will suffer for it. Come to my house and let me offer you something to eat and drink." He gave Kaya a friendly smile. "Then you can introduce me to your charming friend."

"Master Michio, I think I should return to my own home first," I said.

He looked serious again. "There will be time for that. You're back, and your house is waiting. Be happy in knowing it still stands."

"And my family—?"

He spoke up sharply, cutting me off. "Himiko, I have never asked you for any favors. Now I do ask for this: let me be the one to bring you back to your kin. When the war came, I couldn't do enough to help our people. No matter how loudly I implored the spirits for aid, none came, and we were conquered. The Ookami spared my life out of respect for my calling, but that didn't stop them from pulling down our sacred tree. Every time someone looks at what's left of Grandfather Pine, I can almost hear them thinking, *What good is our shaman if he couldn't even save you?* That knowledge is a stone weighing down my heart.

"Give me the chance to redeem myself by taking credit

for your safe return. It won't be a *big* lie; I did pray daily that the spirits would guide you home again. Our clan's losses have been terrible, but if the people can believe my power over the spirits is great enough to accomplish *this*"—he made a sweeping gesture, indicating me from head to toe—"they will take hope for our future. Please . . ."

"Of course." I bowed my head, though my heart ached to rush home.

His smile returned, weary but warm. "Thank you."

Kaya and I trailed after him through the village. It was hard for me to see so many homes destroyed or badly damaged, but I took a bit of comfort from noticing that the Ookami had not devastated everything. Many houses bore only minor signs of harm, and a few remained entirely untouched. The thatch of Master Michio's pit house had been torn in a few places, but the structure was intact otherwise. Kaya and I stooped to follow him inside, and soon we were sharing a meager meal of cold rice and a few scraps of dried meat so tough it was impossible to name the animal that had provided it.

As we ate, I introduced Kaya to my teacher and friend. "The Shika clan, eh?" Master Michio's eyes twinkled. "I remember my mother speaking about the deer people, but she never said they gave birth to such beautiful daughters."

Kaya laughed into her fist. The shaman spread his hands and pretended to be confused. "Did I say something funny?"

"Well, *I* don't think so," I said. "But Kaya prefers to picture herself as Lady Badger: tough, stubborn, and always ready for a fight."

"Can't you be all that and pretty too?" the shaman asked Kaya in an innocent voice.

"Since when are badgers pretty?" my friend asked with good humor.

"Since the first day of creation," Master Michio replied. Then he added: "Just ask another badger."

We all laughed, and our laughter carried its own special magic. While it lingered, lifting our hearts, it pushed aside everything else. If that merry sound could have lasted forever, the world would hold only joy. But that was impossible. Like the tumbling petals that had once adorned a slender branch of cherrywood, the notes of laughter faded, fell, and were gone.

I was the first to fill the silence left in their wake. "Master Michio, thank you for welcoming us. It is good to be here with you again, but when can we go to my family? Do you want to speak with them first, before I show myself?"

"That might be the best idea," Kaya put in. "They don't know what happened to you, whether you're alive or dead. Happy tidings can be as big a shock as bad ones if it comes out of nowhere. You don't want your poor mother fainting because she thinks she's seeing your ghost."

"Little chance of that," Master Michio said under his breath. Before I could question him, he went on: "The pretty badger is right. Some news must be broken gently, gradually. It's the kindest way. I promise that we'll go to your house soon. Meanwhile, I could use your help. The battle with the Ookami left many men here gravely hurt. I met you just as I was leaving one of them. He needs fresh salve for his wounds and a potion to numb pain, but my supplies have been used up. The sooner we work together to make more, the sooner he'll have some relief, poor fellow."

What could I do but consent? With Kaya lending a hand too, Master Michio and I mixed dried herbs and other ingredients into medicines for our people. While I knelt to grind roots into powder, he chanted spells, seeking the spirits' assistance, calling on them to strengthen the plants' healing qualities. I had learned the same incantation from my first teacher, Master Michio's half sister, Lady Yama, but though I could have joined my voice with his, my throat closed. I was choking on a rising flood of questions, and if I let one slip out, the others would pour after, interrupting our shaman and perhaps making him lose the goodwill of the spirits.

At last he was done. A row of bowls filled with healing compounds lay on the ground between us. Master Michio looked content.

"Thank you, girls," he said. "Many people will bless you for helping their loved ones rest more comfortably tonight."

"How many?" Kaya asked. Master Michio gave her an inquiring look. "How many of your men were wounded? How many died?"

"Lady Badger has a blunt tongue." The shaman frowned. "Why do you ask such things? What good will it do to give you an accounting? Will it satisfy you to know that we lost *too* many of our people?"

"How many is too many?" Kaya replied. She held up both hands, her fingers spread. "This many? Less? More?"

Master Michio's disapproving look deepened. "Why

don't I take you with me through this village so you can ask the widows and orphans to tally their dead just to feed your childish curiosity? Or if you insist on an accurate count, wait a few days. A few more may die by then. Some wounds I'm treating won't heal, no matter how much I labor over them. Will that satisfy you?"

"Master Michio, she didn't—" I began.

"*Shame* on you." Kaya sat back on her heels and drew herself up with dignity. Her gaze did not falter as she met our shaman's hostile stare, and I heard echoes of her chieftess mother's commanding voice in every word she spoke. "I have good reasons for my questions. Himiko is my friend, my spirit's sister. Her pain is my pain; her clan's loss is mine! I didn't come all this way with her out of curiosity. I won't leave until I know that this clan can survive. I ask how many died because I want to know how many still live. Do you have enough food to take all of them through the winter? Will you have enough able-bodied people to tend your fields when the planting season comes? More important, how many of the Ookami are still here? How are they treating your chieftain in defeat? What will they do when they learn that another member of his family has appeared?" She seized my hand. "Himiko wanted to go home, but I won't leave her side until I know her home is *safe.*"

Master Michio's scowl softened. "A blunt tongue, but sharp teeth." He sighed, and that sigh melted into tears. I watched in horror as our shaman covered his face and sobbed like a heartbroken child. With a small cry of sympathy I rushed to throw my arms around him while he shook with weeping.

Kaya was stunned at the effect her words had produced. We had both grown up with the knowledge that a shaman must be as brave and strong as any warrior. It takes courage to confront the spirits, to entreat them, to command them, to summon and banish them. Some are kindly, but there are also malicious ones that need to be placated or even fought. Sometimes we shamans were all that stood between our people and the wrath of these powerful, harmful beings. Master Michio had stood guard for many years on the border between darkness and light. Why should a young girl's words, no matter how biting, reduce him to this?

"I—I'm sorry," Kaya stammered, her face pale. "I didn't—didn't know—didn't want to—Oh, I'm *sorry!*"

Master Michio raised his head and forced a smile. "No, Lady Badger; you have no need to apologize. You did nothing wrong. It's my own fault. I'm like a little boy who meets an *oni* on the road and thinks he can hide from that horrible mountain ogre just by covering his eyes. He tells himself, *If I can't see it, it can't see me, and when I open my eyes again, it will be gone.*" He shook his head. "But the *oni* is still here, and I must face it."

My hands were still resting on his shoulders. He shifted sideways, away from me, and turned so that we faced each other. "There is much to tell you," he said. "If I only knew where to begin . . ."

"Start by telling me one thing," I replied. "Was it my fault that we were conquered?"

Master Michio blinked rapidly, confused. "Was it

your—? By the gods, child, what makes you ask such a thing?"

I clasped my hands in my lap. "When I decided I couldn't stay here any longer, I joined a group of boys and girls who were going into the forest to gather nuts and mushrooms for the winter. As soon as I saw my chance, I slipped away from them. I'd spent a lot of time before that asking many questions about the Todomatsu clan, the seacoast people with whom you used to live. I did it to leave a false trail, so that when Father realized I was gone, he'd send a search party down the wrong road to find me and I'd be able to get away. Tell me truly now, Master Michio, did Father send men after me, men who should have been here to help fight the Ookami?" My voice rose shrilly. "Did my trickery cost our clan its freedom?"

"Ah! No, no, put such thoughts out of your head at once!" he exclaimed. "Your plan might have worked, but when your father ordered your eldest brother to lead the men, Aki argued with him. He insisted you hadn't gone to the Todomatsu and begged your father to let him track you down on his own. You can imagine how well your father liked being contradicted. The whole village heard him yelling at Aki, commanding him to do as he was told. Your mother, poor lady, begged him to let your second-eldest brother, Shoichi, lead the search party. All she wanted was to have you back, but the argument had become a contest of wills between father and son. When the Ookami struck, no one had left the village. Every fighting man of our clan was here."

He looked at the ground. "For all the good it did. We

fought fiercely, but there were too many of them. They threw torches over our walls, set fire to our gates, and when our men rushed out to meet them in battle, they over-whelmed us."

"Are they still here?" Kaya asked.

Master Michio shook his head. "They didn't linger. Why would they? Could you sleep securely in the midst of your enemies, even if you had defeated them? Once they were victorious, their chieftain ordered his men to pull down Grandfather Pine and made every one of us watch while they burned him to ashes."

Their chieftain . . . , I thought. *Ryu.* The name called up angry memories. Many seasons ago, before the Ookami had brought war to our gates, they had come to offer the chance to unite our peoples. Ryu's father was their ruler then, and while he and his men met with our nobles, I was told to entertain the Ookami chieftain's son. As we walked, I quickly learned that his handsome face hid a callous and arrogant heart. He saw other people as his playthings, his tools, his slaves, their lives worth only what they could do to serve his desires. I was able to save myself from him with the spirits' help, but the memory of his ruthless words still lingered.

And now this ruthless man had led the conquerors of my clan. I shivered.

"When the Ookami had done their work, they left, taking whatever they liked from us," Master Michio went on. "Who was left to stop them? We'll have a hungry win-ter, but it won't be the last one. When we harvest the rice we plant next spring, they'll send warriors back to claim as great a share as they please." He sighed. "We serve the Ookami now."

I clenched my hands so tightly that the nails bit into my palms. "It isn't true," I said. "It can't be. They defeated us, but we will not let them rule us. We will recover from this and cast them out of our lives. My kin are no one's servants. Father, Aki, and Shoichi will rally our fighters and—"

"No, Himiko." Master Michio's voice broke with sorrow. "No more. No . . . no more."

I could scarcely breathe. When I spoke, it was a hoarse whisper. "They are . . . gone?"

My teacher said nothing, made no sign. He let silence confirm the horrible truth. Bitter cold seeped through me from my skin to the marrow of my bones. I felt Kaya's arm encircle my shoulders, though I hadn't seen her move. I saw nothing. I was alone in a dark place, a land of awful shadows and taunting laughter.